**Married. She was married,
but in name only,
and Dinah hated to think
where her husband might be,
and with whom. . . .**

The stairs creaked, and she held her breath. It was Tristan. He passed her room, stopping briefly. She waited, expelling pent-up air when he walked on by. His door opened, then closed, and Dinah sighed, pulling her covers to her chin. She turned toward the window.

The door adjoining their rooms opened. She squeezed her eyes shut, pretending to sleep, hoping her erratic breathing wouldn't give her away.

She tried valiantly to appear asleep, but it wasn't possible to lie quietly. Opening her eyes, she was startled by the intensity of his glare.

"Out whoring, were you?" Lord, she hadn't been married a full day and she sounded like a shrew.

One corner of his mouth lifted. "Miss me?"

(more . . .)

PRAISE FOR JANE BONANDER'S PREVIOUS ROMANCES

WILD HEART

"*Wild Heart* is passionate and suspenseful! Ms. Bonander captures all the untamed wildness of the west. . . . Fans of western romances will be thrilled. . . . A memorable tale!"

—Kristina Wright, *The Literary Times*

"*Wild Heart* was perfect. Jane Bonander spun a tale of beauty and love that should keep anyone glued to the chair until reading the last page. The love scenes were sizzling hot. . . . I loved *Wild Heart.*"

—Donita Lawrence, Bell, Book and Candle

"*Wild Heart* is a wonderful story. . . . I enjoyed every page. . . . Everybody is excited about *Wild Heart.*"

—Adene Beal, The House of Books

"[The] subplots are so skillfully woven together, you will be moved by this romantic tale and the truth of the heartbreaking past. . . . These delightful characters will enchant you as they did me. An enjoyable treat."

—*Rendezvous*

DANCING ON SNOWFLAKES

"Stirring adventure. . . . A touching romance, a talented writer, and heart-stopping action. . . . Most enjoyable!"

—Anne Cleary, *The Paperback Forum*

"Jane Bonander gives her readers a lovely romance that will make your heart sing. . . . Ms. Bonander is a talented author, and *Dancing on Snowflakes* is fast-paced and unforgettable. Enjoy!"

—Mary Jayne Farpella, *Affaire de Coeur*

"Moving and delightful. . . . The characters are marvelous and amazingly true to life. . . . *Dancing on Snowflakes* [is] an exceptionally well-constructed, believable 'keeper.'"

—Gail Collins, *Romantic Times*

"*Dancing on Snowflakes* [is] a definite one-sitting read."

—Melissa Bradley, *Rendezvous*

"With a masterful and fearless touch, Jane Bonander created 'keepers' for . . . those who believe in the triumph of the spirit and the strength of the human heart."

—Ann Wassall, *Ann's World*

Books by Jane Bonander

Dancing on Snowflakes
Wild Heart
Winter Heart

Published by POCKET BOOKS

JANE BONANDER

Winter Heart

POCKET **STAR** BOOKS
New York London Toronto Sydney Tokyo Singapore

This book is a work of fiction. Names, characters, places and incidents are either products of the author's imagination or are used fictitiously. Any resemblance to actual events or locales or persons, living or dead, is entirely coincidental.

An *Original* Publication of POCKET BOOKS

A Pocket Star Book published by
POCKET BOOKS, a division of Simon & Schuster Inc.
1230 Avenue of the Americas, New York, NY 10020

ISBN: 0-671-52982-X

First Pocket Book printing May 1996

10 9 8 7 6 5 4 3 2 1

POCKET STAR BOOKS and colophon are registered trademarks of Simon & Schuster Inc.

Printed in the U.S.A.

For my sister Dr. Suellen M. Rundquist,
Professor of English linguistics—she knows why.

Could the dark secrets of those insane asylums be brought to light . . . we would be shocked to know the countless number of rebellious wives, sisters and daughters that are thus annually sacrificed to false customs and conventionalisms, and barbarous laws made by men for women.

—Susan B. Anthony
and Elizabeth Cady Stanton, 1861

It is a very fashionable and easy thing now to make a person out to be insane. If a man tires of his wife, and is befooled after some other woman, it is not a very difficult matter to get her in an institution of this kind. Belladonna and chloroform will give her the appearance of being crazy enough, and after the asylum doors have closed upon her, adieu to the beautiful world and all home associations.

—Lydia A. Smith, 1864–1871,
institutionalized in New York and Michigan

Winter Heart

Prologue

California, 1846

WHAT KIND OF SICK MIND WOULD GIVE AN INFANT AWAY TO A stranger?

Even in his wildest, most dismal nightmares, Cecil couldn't imagine it. His throat worked with emotion when he realized the infant the older woman held was staring at him. He knew he was a fool, but he felt the babe was scrutinizing him, sizing him up. His eyes were a startling shade of blue, circled with a rim of brown. Intelligent eyes. Probing eyes.

Certainly he was giving the babe far more credit than he deserved, he thought with a cynical lift of his brow. After all, the tad was only weeks old.

Beyond the platform, the whipster whistled as he watered his team. Soon the stage would be ready to leave again. There wasn't time to dicker or to be rational.

"I'll pay any price," he told the woman.

Standing beside him, his wife expelled a disgusted

sigh. "You'll do no such thing! Why, the idea of taking in a breed . . ."

The rest of her tirade fell upon deaf ears. Cecil wanted a son with such intensity, it would have been impossible to explain it to anyone, especially his nagging wife. "Zelda, you and I will never have another child of our own. I want a son."

"You want a son," she mimicked, her voice derisive. "I don't care what you want, Cecil Fletcher, I'm not taking in a breed and caring for him as if he were my own." She sniffed, a sound that ended in an unladylike snort. "What will people think if we show up with someone else's half-breed bastard?"

Cecil ignored her, accustomed to her harping. He usually gave in to her, and she expected it. He would surprise her this time. "If we take him in, he won't be a bastard. He'll be our son."

"May the Lord forgive you, Cecil. *Think!* Think what this will do to Emily."

All he had to hear was his three-year-old daughter's name, and he went soft and vulnerable inside. Even so, Zelda's threat did nothing, for he'd been waiting for her to mention Emily. It often brought him around to his wife's way of thinking, but not now.

His beautiful Emily. A crushing pain squeezed his chest, and he wondered if it was his bad heart or his love for his daughter. God had played a cruel trick on all of them, for she was perfect in every way, except for her mind. Even when she was a baby, months old, her eyes hadn't had the quick intelligence of the boy before him. She wasn't an idiot by any means, but she'd been slow to develop. Slow to walk, slow to talk, slow to train. Sometimes painfully so. His heart squeezed again.

Cecil had been willing to try once more, but Zelda had kept him from her bed for years, reluctant to chance having another child, fearing the flaw would be repeated. Praying he would be forgiven the blasphemy, Cecil decided God was capricious.

"Despite her shortcomings, Zelda, Emily will be overjoyed at having a baby in the house. We both know that." There was no deterring him. "We will take this child and raise him as our own, and you'd best get used to it."

She gasped. "How dare you speak to me that way, Cecil. How *dare* you!"

He didn't have to look at her to know that her narrow lips would be pursed so tightly they would nearly disappear. And there would be a mutinous look in her eyes as well. He would pay dearly for this, but it was worth the risk.

Digging into the pocket of his waistcoat, he retrieved a double eagle, then turned his attention to the woman who had offered him the baby.

"How much?" He had three double eagles on him. Sixty dollars was a small price to pay for a child; an embarrassment.

The woman's black eyes snapped. "Children should not be bought and sold like cattle. They're priceless."

Cecil frowned at her incongruous behavior. "Why do you want to get rid of him, then?"

The anger in her eyes was replaced by pain. "Because it's better than leaving him somewhere to die."

Her accent was thick; he could barely understand her. "But I want to give you—"

"No money." She thrust the baby at him. "Just take him and go away from here."

Cecil took the child and held him close. Though wrapped in heavy blankets, he felt solid. Strong. They exchanged glances again, and Cecil gave the boy a grim smile as Zelda muttered her dissent beside him. *You will need your strength, Son, but I promise I will love you enough for both of us.*

Fletcher Ranch, Sierra Nevada Mountains
California, 1858

"Tristan Fletcher!"

From his perch in the oak tree, Tristan cringed at the keening sound of his mother's voice. He stopped carving his initials in the trunk and sheathed his knife. If she found him with it, she'd take it away from him, as she had most of his treasures.

Closing his eyes, he leaned against the tree and tried valiantly to shut her out. Ever since Pa's death she'd been especially mean. She'd boxed Tristan's ears, pinched his arms, and spewed enough words of hate at him to break the strongest servant. But he wasn't a servant. At least he hadn't been one until Pa died.

It wasn't that he didn't want to work. When he worked she appeared satisfied and didn't bother him. Now, with Emily gone to a special school, his mother was more demanding of his time.

Tristan missed his sister very much. One of his earliest memories was of Emily rocking him to sleep in a big rocking chair by the fire. She had adored him from the day they'd brought him home. They had been close companions since the time he'd been old enough to feed himself. They'd done everything together. Played the same games. Enjoyed the same things.

It wasn't until his best friend Lucas, the foreman's son, had brought it to his attention that Emily was so much older than he and should enjoy completely different activities that Tristan had imagined she might be different.

She was a great artist; that's what Tristan thought, anyway. She could draw anything he asked her to, and it would miraculously appear on the page. Even when Zelda had raged at Emily, she could be calmed by taking pen in hand and moving it across a sheet of paper. But even then they couldn't let Zelda find Emily sketching.

Emily's pictures were, well, on the dark side, and Zelda hated them. She didn't understand that drawing made Emily feel better.

Zelda. If she ever imagined that he referred to her by her given name, he'd see the inside of hell long before he died. He couldn't help it. She was no more his mother than the mare out in the pasture.

Today he avoided her because he'd wanted to go fishing with Lucas and she'd refused to let him. He'd learned that he rarely, if ever, got to do what he wanted, but there was a place inside him that refused to back down gracefully. He'd felt that way a lot lately: angry, moody, itching to disobey, despite her threats. He thought it was because she'd sent Emily away. No other reason came to mind.

He would pay for his ornery attitude, and it would hurt, but for now, he reveled in her frustration and her fury.

Something jabbed his calf.

"There you are, you worthless half-breed. You've tried my patience one time too many. God will punish you for sneaking away and hiding from me, just you wait and see."

Tristan often wondered about this threatening God of hers. It wasn't the same one his father had worshiped, for Pa had spoken of him kindly, even though his eyes were sad when he did so.

Zelda poked him again with the broom handle, hard enough to leave a bruise but not hard enough to break anything. He'd learned long ago not to react, even though it hurt like the devil. Gooseflesh rose on his skin as the pain radiated through his body. He clamped his jaw shut, swallowing any sound of discomfort.

"Get down from there before I make you sorry you ever came to live with us."

He was already sorry. He ached to rub his sore calf, but resisted the urge. Why did Pa have to die? Tristan had never said it aloud, but he wondered why death couldn't have taken her, instead.

"Why can't I go fishing?"

"Fishing? You lazy slug. You don't want to work, that's what's wrong with you. Besides, all your kind are alike, lazy, good for nothing. Now, get down from there before I take a belt to your backside."

Tristan stiffened. He wouldn't ask again. He would never allow her to find his weaknesses, for he instinctively knew she'd feed on them. A militant anger spread through him. He had six more years before he could leave this place and go to college, then he'd be three thousand miles from her harping tongue.

"Did you hear me?"

How could he not? Her strident voice penetrated the air like a freshly honed blade. He continued to ignore her, climbing higher into the tree.

"Get down here this instant! There's work aplenty around here, and your share is collecting dust."

Tristan wanted to run away. Escape. Before Pa died, they had talked about it. Pa had brought the subject up, knowing Tristan would be tempted once he was gone. He'd made Tristan promise not to leave home until it was time, no matter how much he wanted to.

It hadn't been easy, but for Pa, Tristan would have walked through fire. He only wished Pa were alive. He missed him very much, and with Emily gone off to school, he felt completely alone.

1

Trenway Asylum, Upstate New York
February 1875

DAISY COUGHED INTO HER HANDKERCHIEF, KNOWING WITHout looking that what was there would be blood streaked. In a few moments, she would meet Dinah Odell, and the plan Daisy had devised would be put into motion. She would not follow orders and place Dinah in the punishment box. With the matron leaving on holiday, who would know? Daisy had other plans for Dinah.

Her lungs ached, had for weeks. She was weak and frail, barely able to carry out her duties. For her, life was at a close. For Dinah, it was just beginning. She had to convince the child. Child. A smile cracked her dry lips. Though they were only six years apart in age, Daisy felt ancient. It was the consumption, of course. It had ravaged her body almost beyond recognition.

The night before, she'd stood in front of the mirror and wept. Her small breasts sagged; her hipbones were so sharp she was surprised they hadn't penetrated her skin. The hair that had once been her pride and joy was no longer red but a lackluster carrot color, and it hung in lank strands around her face. She had lost most of the curls that had once grown thick and red low on her belly. What was left was dull, almost gray. She would never know a man's love, a man's passion. She would die dried up like a withered spinster because of the damned disease. She'd even cursed God, for who else was to blame if not He?

Reaching into her apron pocket, she pulled out the letter from the employer who had been going to release her from this hellish job. His proposition was generous, and a stunning surprise. She couldn't fathom why someone would offer so much. She reread the last page, still filled with awe.

> . . . and because our mutual acquaintance, David Richards, has recommended you so highly for the job of caring for my dear sister, I offer you something as well: marriage—in name only, of course, you have my word as a gentleman—in exchange for five years of faithful and compassionate service. At the end of that period of time, to guarantee your comfort for the remainder of your life, I will present to you a generous monetary settlement in the amount of . . .

Daisy read the amount again, knowing it was a fortune. A bounteous sum. Had she been healthy, she would have taken it. Had she been healthy, she would have married the devil to get out of this place. When Dr. Richards had approached her with the opportunity, he had assured her that Tristan Fletcher was an honorable man. Marrying a stranger was daunting, but it was done all the time. She had a cousin who had married a rancher in Wyoming, sight unseen. She was happy enough.

But Daisy knew she was dying; nothing would change that. Dinah was not. She was young and vibrant and full of life. She shouldn't languish in this godforsaken place.

It had been at that moment that Daisy had quietly put together her plan. But knowing the spirited Dinah as she did, she knew an arranged marriage would not sit well, even though it was temporary and worth a great deal of money.

Daisy held the sheet of paper by the corner over the candle flame, watching it turn to ashes. Whatever kind of life awaited Dinah Odell beyond these grim asylum walls was immeasurably better than the one she faced inside them.

A clock somewhere in the cavernous building sounded eleven bells, the echo reverberating dismally, reminding Daisy that the sooner she got Dinah out of this place, the better.

She found the other letter, the one she'd written exonerating Dinah of all guilt, and tucked it into the hidden pocket in her travel bag, the one she would give Dinah. Daisy had many things to tell Dinah, so many things to say. Her mind wasn't working as it once had. She hoped she would remember everything.

With difficulty because of her weakness, she closed her travel bag and went to meet Dinah in the remote storage room.

"It's the only way, dear."

Dinah stared in horror at the black metal discipline box, tearing her gaze from the shackles at the bottom. She remembered the times she'd felt the cold, cruel metal bite into the tender flesh at her wrists and ankles. Even now, they throbbed at the visual reminder.

Nurse Jenkins leaned against the wall, her face pale and drawn, her eyes swimming with feverish tears. She was thin and frail and appeared far older than her twenty-six years. She coughed and doubled over, clutching her stomach.

Dinah pressed her fingers to her mouth, as if doing so would banish her sympathetic pain. It wasn't possible. Fear, gratitude, and compassion clogged her throat. "But to willingly take my place, Daisy. Why?"

Daisy Jenkins coughed again, the sound deep and painful. What she brought up was pink and frothy, and she folded it into a handkerchief. "It means your survival, Dinah. I have little time left." She took a deep breath, one that rattled from her lungs. "You've seen how weak I am. I can barely carry out my duties here. I couldn't fool the matron another hour let alone another day." Coughing again, she scanned the room with her fever-laden eyes.

"I detest this place and everything it stands for. I would rather die saving you than live another moment having to serve the matron's whims."

The flickering candlelight hollowed out her already sunken cheeks, making her appear cadaverous. "You don't belong here. I know it and Matron Doppling knows it. You've been punished for being a free spirit. I've seen how you hide your pain behind your tough facade."

She laughed, but it turned into another fit of coughing. When she recovered, she gripped Dinah's arm until she caught her breath. "Had you not been so gently born and raised, you'd have had a successful run on the stage."

Dinah was unable to watch Daisy's swift deterioration. "I didn't know I was that transparent."

"To no one but me, perhaps. You're a chameleon."

It was true. Dinah had held on to her sanity in large part because of her ability to become whomever her jailers thought she was. If she could make them laugh, so much the better for her. Unfortunately, most of them thought she was merely cheeky. In part, they were right. But she also kept her spirit alive because to lose it meant to die. Death was a constant. It visited the inmates daily.

"You're here because Martin Odell wanted to get rid of you. Don't forget that."

At the sound of her uncle's name, thoughts of freedom became elusive, shuddering through Dinah like flickering aspen leaves in the wind. She kept her face turned away so Daisy wouldn't sense her feelings. "Yes, I know. But if Martin discovers I'm gone, he'll just find me and drag me back."

Since the untimely death of her parents, Martin had changed. No longer the doting uncle, he had first put her dear sister, Charlotte, away, claiming her fits required treatment she couldn't get at home.

That in itself should have been a warning to Dinah, but how would she have known? Since childhood, Charlotte had been sickly, and grieving for Mama and Papa had weakened her more. Even the doctor who came to call agreed that Charlotte would get better care in a sanitarium. Dinah had no way of knowing then that the sanitarium was actually an asylum for the insane, the very one from which she was now planning to escape.

It wasn't until Charlotte's death that Dinah discovered what kind of place Trenway actually was. Even so, it was hard for her to believe her sister had intentionally taken her own life. It was no wonder that Martin wanted Dinah out of the way. Her caustic tongue and fearless need to discover the truth about Charlotte's death had prompted her uncle to pack her off to the asylum, too. How effortlessly he'd done it! No one had questioned his motives or her state of mind. Not even the doctors.

"Yes," Dinah repeated, her heart heavy, "he'll just find me and bring me back."

"Not if he doesn't know."

She swung around. "How can he not discover I'm gone?"

"Oh, he may. Eventually." Daisy dug into her apron pocket and pulled out an envelope. She handed it to Dinah. "In the meantime, you'll be long gone, safely away from here."

Dinah took out the letter, read it, sifted through the other items in the envelope, then dropped into the chair by the old, battered desk. "Your train ticket is in here. And money. You want me to take your new position?" A fresh flood of fears surged through her. "I couldn't get away with it. They know your name, don't they?"

"Of course. But things change, dear. I've been meaning to write them and explain why someone else is coming in my place, but I've just not had the strength. Anyway, you'll think of something. You're a clever girl."

Dinah stared at the letter in her lap, running her fingers over the page. "I couldn't get away with it," she repeated.

"You can and you will. Would you rather stay here? Think about it. You have no future here. None."

Frowning, Dinah bit down on her lip, knowing she couldn't bear to stay behind asylum walls if there was any chance at all she could escape. Every day she felt as though she were suffocating. "I know, but—"

"You have a wonderful sense of humor, Dinah, and your instinct to survive is the only thing that has kept you sane. After I'm gone, there will be no one here to act as a buffer between you and the matron."

Dinah blinked, hoping to stem her tears. "But if I leave, you'll die." She was suddenly struck with an idea. "Why don't we both leave? Oh, Daisy, let's both go!"

With the effort of one scaling a rocky cliff, Daisy hiked a bony hip onto the edge of the desk. "I've already thought of that. I would only slow you down. Whether you want to believe me or not, I'm going to die. The efforts required to travel would be too much for me. Trust me, Dinah, I'm not trying to be a martyr. I have very little time left, and I think it's important that at some point, a body be found they can assume is yours." She pressed her handkerchief over her mouth. "We're of similar height. Though your hair is a more vibrant red than mine, it's comparable."

"But you're not going to die this minute, you'll—" Her argument was broken off by another fit of Daisy's coughing. This time, she actually slumped to the floor.

"Daisy!" Hurrying to her side, Dinah lifted her head into her lap.

Daisy's eyes were bright. "I don't have much strength left, Dinah Odell. Or time." Her voice was but a whisper, her breathing labored and bubbly. "Do this for me. Do this for *all* women."

"But, how can I possibly pass myself off as a nurse?" Dinah had a sense of panic. Her dreams of freedom dwindled further amidst the harsh reality of what Daisy wanted her to do.

"It's not so difficult. All most patients need is a lot of understanding. And love."

"But what if she's truly insane? What if . . . what if she's violent and mad and I'm not able to control her?" Suddenly the whole idea of escape seemed ludicrous. Farfetched. Fanciful.

"You've seen what goes on here, Dinah. Just remember that physical punishment never makes things better. It only compounds the problem." Daisy coughed again and her eyes rolled back, exposing the jaundiced whites.

"Oh, Daisy. Dear, dear Daisy." A breath-robbing tightness seized Dinah's chest as she stroked Daisy's hair.

Daisy's coughing became worse. "I won't last until morning. If you don't do as I say, they will somehow find a way to blame you for my death. And your uncle will gladly join the throng. At least leaving will give you a good head start."

Each word was spoken with great difficulty. Dinah had to bend close to hear. "Count on that, Dinah. In spite of my efforts to be deceptive about our relationship, the matron has seen how familiar we've become. Were I to leave you here, she would exact her most heinous punishment on you.

"She's gone for a few days to visit her no-account son, Edward. Now is the time to do this. Freedom is yours." Although her words were halting and barely audible, the message was clear.

Dinah said nothing. She sat on the floor and rocked Daisy in her arms long into the night, as a mother holds a dying child, grateful that no one disturbed them.

Freedom is yours. She couldn't count the number of times she'd prayed for release from the hell hole in which she now found herself. Thoughts of her sometime suitor, Charles Avery, flicked through her mind for the first time in weeks.

How childish she'd been all those months ago, when she thought he might intercede on her behalf with her uncle. She'd been just a girl then. A little girl who thought of parties and dresses and sweet kisses stolen on balconies. She'd clung to those sappy notions, wanting the sort of life her mother once had because she knew of nothing else.

That had been over a year ago. Such things no longer found a place in her mind; she had all she could do to think about survival. But to escape . . .

Daisy had been scheduled to leave the asylum for her new position in California, and at first, Dinah had thought she was meeting her to say good-bye. But when Daisy told her she meant Dinah to escape, Dinah could not have imagined the extent of her plan.

Dinah closed her eyes. California. The entire charade was worthwhile if it got her to California. Unfastening the top of her prison gown, she reached inside and pulled out Charlotte's diary, which she carried close to her body for safekeeping.

With Daisy's feverish head in her lap, Dinah opened the journal. Charlotte's spidery scrawl leaped out at her, causing her heart to lurch in her chest again, as it did each time she saw the writing. *He was here again today, my Teddy was, promising to take me away. To California.*

Dinah flipped to the last entry. *He has abandoned me and our unborn child. I have no reason to go on living.*

Tears blurred Dinah's vision, so she closed the book, returning it to the pocket Daisy had stitched inside her tattered camisole. Poor, darling Charlotte. Dinah hadn't had the chance to say good-bye. Yes, maybe it was worth the risk if it got her closer to finding out what had really happened to Charlotte. She might have been weaker than Dinah, but she wouldn't have killed herself. Even Daisy hadn't been able to find out exactly how Charlotte had died. *I have no reason to go on living* didn't automatically mean she'd taken her own life, did it?

Once again her gaze found the black metal box. She shuddered, for the box looked like a macabre black coffin. Even the lid came down and latched like a coffin lid. But instead of a silk lining and a fine pillow for one's head, there were noisy shackles for the limbs. Cold, heavy, iron shackles.

Because of her rebellious ways, she'd spent more time in the device than most of the other women. It was a harsh and cruel punishment, not fit for criminals, much less helpless, hapless women. If the matron had thought to drive her mad by putting her in the box, she'd made a mistake, however, for each new form of punishment made Dinah stronger. But she knew of women who went into the box and were never seen again.

Once the box was shoved into the bowels of the dark, dank room and out of sight, the person being punished could go undiscovered for weeks. Months. It had happened before. An easy way to dispose of a troublesome patient whose family didn't want her free. And with the matron on holiday herself, she would not be around to make sure Daisy had done her job.

It was nearly dawn, and everything was quiet when Daisy drew her last breath. Dinah expelled a sad, tired sigh and hugged her one last time. She put Daisy on the floor and undressed her, replacing the nurse's clothing with her own. Then, with difficulty, she lifted Daisy into her arms, struggling to put her body into the box. She cringed and almost cried out when Daisy's lolling head banged against the side.

Dinah placed the shackles around Daisy's ankles and wrists, shoving away her anguish at having to treat the body so. She said a prayer for Daisy's perfect soul, then crossed herself before closing the lid on the box and locking it.

She searched through Daisy's travel bag, which was now hers, and gasped in surprise. "My bear," she whispered, memories swamping her as she lifted the bear from the bag. She pressed her nose to the fur, its scent still familiar. She'd slept with the bear long before she'd come to Trenway, long after the time when a young woman should sleep with dolls or stuffed animals. The toy had been confiscated, along with everything else she owned, when she'd arrived here.

A week after that, Dinah saw one of the matron's fat daughters wearing her own velvet cloak. The matron's favorite nurse, a scrawny bitch with a pocked, red complexion, wore Dinah's pink and lavender gown as she left the building one day. Even her new slippers were gone, and her newly stitched unmentionables. She had nothing but the rags on her back, which were forced upon her the day she'd arrived. Tears, memories, and emotion tangled in her throat. But Daisy had saved her bear. She gave it a squeeze, returned it to the travel bag and snapped the bag shut.

The squeaking wheels of the death cart as it rounded the corner en route to the basement brought her up short, forcing her heart into her throat. She searched the room, frantic for a place to hide in case the attendants glanced inside. Spying a pile of dirty laundry, she dove under it, burrowing deep. She pinched her eyes shut and held her breath.

The death cart stopped.

"Is this lamp supposed to be lit?"

"I don't know. Looks like Jenkins's travel bag, though."

"Oh, yeah. She's leavin' tonight. Lucky whore. Wish it was me," said one attendant.

"Yeah," the other responded. "I wouldn't spit in the face of an opportunity like that."

Dinah heard the women shuffling about the room.

"Christ. Do you suppose someone's in the box?"

Dinah's heart nearly stopped.

The other attendant snickered. "Wanna find out?"

"Me? Hell, no. It ain't my responsibility."

Dinah heard one of them kick at the metal box. "Hey! Anyone in there?"

Both women cackled. "If someone was, they'd sure as hell be screamin' to get out, don't you think?"

"Yeah, they always do. I wonder where Jenkins went off to."

"Who knows."

"Should we grab this laundry while we're here?"

Dinah clutched herself to keep from shaking. The smell from the linens began to claw at her throat, and she swallowed repeatedly to keep from retching, both from the odor and from her own fear.

The other woman snorted. "It ain't our job."

"You're right. Well, Jenkins can't go any place without her clothes. She'll finish up in here. Let's get this body to the basement." The woman made a disgusted sound. "I ain't fond of this job."

"Yeah, but sometimes I'd rather take care of the dead. They ain't nearly so much trouble as the loonies upstairs."

Dinah waited until she was certain they were gone, then crawled out from under the laundry. She took a deep, purging breath. Her thoughts were scattered with fear of discovery, and she had to force herself to stay calm.

She quickly pushed the discipline chest into an obscure corner, hiding it behind chairs, chests, and mouse-eaten blankets, willing back feelings of guilt and tears of remorse.

After dressing in Daisy's traveling clothes and extinguishing the lamp, Dinah crept from the building, Daisy's travel bag clutched to her chest. Once outside, her pulse quivered in the crisp February air.

The train's beckoning whistle blew in the distance. Pulling the hood of Daisy's cape over her hair, Dinah hurried, head bent low, toward the sounds of freedom.

Fletcher Ranch, Sierra Nevada Mountains

Lucas held the last board in place while Tristan hammered it. After they were done, they stood back and examined the long, low building, their warm breath forming clouds before their faces. Erecting a bunkhouse in February was no easy task.

"How many of the children do you figure will be able to sleep in here?"

"No more than ten. There are eight of them now; that gives us two beds to spare in case we find others." Tristan pointed to a thick grove of oaks. "I want to build a stable over there, but I don't want to start it until the children return from the reservation school. They can help with it."

Lucas stroked his chin and shook his head. "It'll take longer if the children help."

Tristan dropped the hammer into the tool chest and wiped his forehead with the sleeve of his shirt. Despite the cool air, they had each worked up a sweat.

"Doesn't matter. I would have had them help with this building if there had been time, but they need a place to sleep when they get here. I hated like hell to have them sleeping in the stable last summer, but there wasn't time to do anything else. I want to start on the addition to the house as soon as possible, too. By next winter, they'll have rooms there."

"It sounds as if you'd like to arrange to have them schooled closer to home."

"I'm working on it."

Tristan shaded his eyes against the harsh February sun and squinted at the temporary bungalow they'd finished. "I don't imagine they'll mind sleeping out here, but damn it, Lucas, it makes it look like I'm running an orphanage, and I'm not. They'll all be Fletchers soon enough, and they will all live like Fletchers, not like orphans being given a handout."

"Each has a hell of a lot more now than he did when we found them," Lucas offered, "thanks to you. They consider you their hero, you know. Especially Little Hawk. Do you ever think you'll break him of his nasty habit of picking pockets?"

"He can always become a politician."

They both laughed, and Tristan's smile lingered as he remembered his first meeting with the boy with the crippled foot. He'd watched him work the streets of Sacramento, picking shoppers clean. When Tristan had grabbed the little guttersnipe by the ear and hauled him into an alley, the lad pretended Tristan was hurting him and screamed loud enough to bring the law.

"Is that what you want to do? Bring the police?" Tristan had asked, close to the boy's ear. "How will you explain the bounty bulging your pockets?"

Little Hawk's black eyes had snapped with intelligence. He had a quick tongue and a foul vocabulary. In the end, though, he'd come with Tristan willingly. Not that day, certainly, but over the next week, Tristan continued to witness his behavior until the day another gentleman, not nearly so generous as Tristan, had hauled Little Hawk off to the sheriff. After allowing the boy to fidget uncomfortably for a satisfactory period of time, Tristan intervened, claiming responsibility for the boy's actions. Little Hawk had been the first child to come and live on the ranch.

"I've had a good life, Lucas. I want to give a little back."

"You had a good life in spite of Zelda Fletcher?"

To this day, Zelda's name filled Tristan with immeasurable anger, and not only because of what she'd done to him. She hadn't seemed happy unless she made everyone around her miserable. Including his father. Especially his sister. "I despise her more for what she did to

Emily than for anything she did to me. Or even my father."

Lucas sputtered a sound of disbelief. "Combing the countryside for homeless half bloods wouldn't have anything to do with learning about your real mother, now, would it?"

They hadn't discussed his lineage openly. Tristan had wondered when Lucas would bring it up. Discovering that the woman who had given him birth had disposed of him and his twin brother like garbage had breathed new life into Tristan's complacent one. Learning that his brother had been left to die and was miraculously found by a kindly trapper made Tristan realize how lucky he'd been, in spite of the woman who had raised him.

"Knowing Wolf and I could have been two orphaned half bloods bordering on delinquency was reason enough for me to do something, Lucas. What I see in the eyes of those children I could easily have found in myself."

Lucas emitted a sigh. "Aw, and you refuse to call yourself a hero."

In spite of himself, Tristan allowed a reluctant grin. "Kiss my ass."

Lucas feigned an adoring look. "Ooooh, with pleasure, my lord." Sobering, he added, "Having eight extra children around all spring and summer will put a burden on Alice. She says she won't mind the cooking, but Leeta senses Alice doesn't feel up to it." He muttered an oath. "She's nearly sixty, Tristan. She's got problems she'd never complain to you about. Like her gout. Did you know she suffers from gout?"

Tristan felt a squiggle of discomfort. Alice Linberg had been old and a part of the family since he could remember. He didn't like to think about his life without her. She'd had the warmth and compassion Zelda hadn't.

"She's never complained to me about anything."

"And why would she? She'll be making your breakfast the day she keels over and dies."

Tristan vowed to lighten her load. The problem would be getting Alice to agree to it.

"Anyway, Leeta's already offered to help as much as possible with the children and in the house."

"Leeta deserves better than you. Why she puts up with you I'll never know." Tristan lifted the extra boards off the ground as if they were twigs, and swung them onto his shoulder.

Lucas picked up the tool box and followed him to the smithy. "Jealous?"

Tristan couldn't stop his smile. They'd been over this dozens of times before. "Not of the noose she has around your neck."

Lucas uttered a laugh. "I've told you before, you pitiful bachelor, it's only a noose if you're miserable, and I'm a happy man."

Coralee's defection so close to their wedding date still burned in Tristan's gut. He'd done a complete turnaround since. "Marriage isn't a natural state for a man."

"Didn't you say you've offered the new nurse marriage?"

"But that's different," Tristan explained, ignoring Lucas's expression of disbelief. "It's only an incentive. David has assured me that this woman I've hired is obedient, even-tempered, and reliable."

Lucas's shoulders shook with quiet laughter. "You've described your hounds."

Tristan hid his frown. So he had. "What difference does it make? Apparently she's also comely, compassionate, and badly in need of funds. Hell, I'll even destroy the agreement if she works out and promises to stay. She can have the money in any case, as long as Emily gets a few years of good, constant care."

"But why marriage, Tris? Just offer her the same agreement without the wedlock."

"Women need to feel safe. Secure. Hell, I don't expect to bed her. I've assured her of that much."

Lucas muttered an oath. "That's the craziest logic I've ever heard. Do you know what's wrong with you?"

"I'm sure you're going to tell me."

"You're a good man, Tris. You're generous, you have a good sense of humor when you allow it to show, you're kind to children and animals, but you have one major flaw."

Tristan eyed Lucas. "I keep you around?"

"No, you always think you're right."

Tristan shrugged. "I am."

"Let me get this straight. You're going to have a wife, but you aren't going to sleep with her?"

"Happens all the time. You've been living on the frontier too long, Lucas. Mistresses are the most natural possession a man has."

Lucas snapped his fingers in front of Tristan's eyes.

Tristan batted his hand away. "What are you doing?"

"Just wanted to make sure your brain hadn't gone numb," Lucas answered, shaking his head.

"I know what you're thinking, but I've got it all worked out. She understands the arrangement and has agreed to it. No one's going to get hurt."

Lucas's chuckle was gleeful. "I'd love to see you eat those words."

Lucas's young son, Miguel, waved and ran toward them. One of his arms was in a sling because he had sprained it falling from a tree.

"Seeing Miguel reminds me of something, Tris. Having those eight extra children around, plus my three, will probably mean lots of accidents, especially if they're going to be working with hammer and nails. Who's going to tend to those, and what happens if there's an outbreak of something?"

Tristan entered the smithy and dropped the wood beside an old battered table. "You worry like an old woman."

"Something I picked up from you, no doubt."

Tristan shook his head. "The nurse can surely handle a

few scrapes and bruises. I expect she'll be a great deal of help."

"Ah, Tristan, Tristan." Lucas ambled toward the big, square door. "When have things ever worked out the way you'd planned?"

At that, Tristan had to laugh. "The gods are bound to take pity on me and turn things in my favor one of these days."

"I wouldn't place a bet on that," Lucas countered.

"You should. You'd make money. I think this new nurse will be the answer to all our prayers. With Emily, with Alice, and with the children. She'll be a calming influence on all of us. I can feel it in my bones."

Lucas gave another snort of disbelief as they exited the smithy. "Your bones have been wrong before."

2

Early spring, 1875
Sierra Nevada Mountains

WET, MASSY CLOUDS TUMBLED DOWN THE SIDES OF THE mountains, gray as asylum laundry. Lightning flashed in the distance, followed by rumbling thunder, ominously heralding a storm.

Cold, damp wind slithered beneath Dinah's cape and gown, lifting the hem of her petticoat and wriggling over her legs like a snake. She shivered, clutching her valise closer to her chest as she trudged over the rutted road.

The wind bore down on her, requiring her to squint. In the distance a gloomy stone house stood silhouetted against the angry sky. She shivered. It belonged on a craggy cliff in a morose Gothic novel, not on a snow-spattered hillside in California.

She crossed her fingers, praying it was her destination, for she felt weak, both from hunger and from the uphill climb. The closer she got, the more unsure she became. Her imagination caught the threads of her unraveling resolve and she envisioned a gruesome scenario: a mad sister chained to a wall in the attic or the cellar, her screams piercing the silence and a brooding, tortured brother who would rage into a howling storm, cursing God for his plight.

Dinah laughed, nervous. It was the storm, that's all, and her first impression of the house.

Suddenly, from out of nowhere and over the sound of the impending storm, she heard the dogs.

Might as well be bears, she thought, for she had equal fear of both.

The wind was strong. Her eyes watered, and though she couldn't see the hounds, she could tell where they were coming from: the bloody haunted house. How fitting! With her heart slamming her ribs like a fist on a door, she dropped her travel bag, using it as a step to climb into the nearest tree.

She was perched on the lowest limb when they reached her, but when she saw their size, her eyes grew big and she scudded higher. They looked like horses! Their legs were long and gangly and their shaggy coats unkempt and dirty. They barked and howled, leaping higher and higher onto the trunk in their efforts to attack. Their jaws were strong enough to rip off an arm or a leg. She shuddered at the thought. Unfortunately for the dogs, she'd become quite attached to her limbs.

She tried to smirk at her play on words, but her fear stopped her. Sucking in huge gulps of air, she forced herself to climb to a loftier branch, although her knees quaked and her hands shook and the branch itself flapped wildly in the wind. Dogs. Damned dogs. She couldn't remember a time when she hadn't been afraid of them.

One of the hounds seized the hem of her cape between its teeth.

"Sweet Mary!" The force of the wind tossed her words back into her face. With her heart bounding in her ears, she grabbed at the bough above her, intent on climbing even higher. It snapped loose. Gripping the limb, she swung at the dog, clinging to the tree trunk with her other arm until she smacked the dog on the nose. It released her hem, yelping in pain.

"Help! Someone help me!" Again, the wind tossed her plea about, and she feared no one heard her. She squinted out through the leafy twigs that bowed before the gale. No movement came from the gloomy stone house, but someone exited one of the outbuildings and walked toward her. Her heart gave a lurch of desperation.

"It's about bloody time," she shouted, relief making her angry. "Call off your butt-ugly hounds!"

Her would-be savior ambled toward the tree as if he had all the time in the world. He was tall, his long legs encased in snug buckskin trousers. As he got closer, she noticed he wore a buckskin vest with no shirt beneath it. His coppery brown arms were admirably chiseled and gleamed with health. Anything but asylum pallor caught her attention.

Her pique increased as he strolled toward her; surely he could move faster than that. "You there! Hurry up!"

Her panic mounted as the dogs continued to bark. Didn't he care if his beasts ripped her to shreds?

Apparently sensing him, the dogs stopped barking and left the trunk. They loped toward him, long, brushy tails wagging. Deceptive, she thought. She wasn't fooled. They were vicious animals. One swish of a tail that size, and she'd be flat on her rump. She wasn't leaving the tree. Not until he called off his hounds. Period.

"Wolf. Amy. Heel." His command was barely audible, but the animals fell in beside him as he crossed to the tree. His eyes were dark and angry as he glared up through the branches. "Did you strike one of my dogs?"

She stared, dumbfounded. Most men would have been concerned about *her.* She'd been lucky to outdistance the beasts, had felt their hot, vile, stinky, mongrel breath on the back of her neck, and he was concerned about the *dogs?*

She shook the branch at him, barely missing his head. "I smacked one on the nose with this, and I'd do it again." What sort of man would care more for his dogs than he would for another human being? "The ugly creature was trying to kill me."

He raised one thickly muscled arm and jabbed a finger at her. "Never, ever strike my dogs."

"What was I supposed to do, let them drag me from this tree and devour me?" When he continued to stare at her, Dinah experienced the need to fling the branch at him. Instead she tossed it to the ground, and her anger turned to disbelief.

She smacked her palm against her forehead. "Well, what could I have been thinking? How silly of me to want to protect myself."

His gaze slipped over her so casually it was insulting. She suddenly became very aware of where she was. It was not a dignified position for a lady to find herself in. There was undoubtedly plenty to see from his angle. She shifted on the branch, trying to tug her cape lower to cover her legs. He refused to look away; she stiffened, indignant. There she was, trapped in a tree with the demon dogs still drooling over her as though she were lunch, and to add to her discomfort, the idiot of a man stared at her in a way that made her wish that one of them would disappear. Preferably he. Maybe the dogs. Or both.

Just then, her stomach growled. Lord, what else? She raised her eyes heavenward. Why didn't God strike the tree with a bolt of lightning? Her stomach rumbled again, reminding her that she hadn't eaten all day. Oh, what wouldn't she give for a hot cup of tea and a warm scone. She swallowed the saliva that pooled around her tongue.

"Who the hell are you?"

She bristled. "Who the hell are you?"

His angry gaze impaled her. "What are you doing on my property?"

Amidst her indignation, her heart sank. "Your property?" Her eyes went to the gloomy house again and she suddenly hoped it wasn't her destination. Crossing her fingers, she asked, "This isn't the Fletcher ranch, is it?"

One of his black, satanic eyebrows quirked up. "And if it is?"

Her stomach dropped. "You can't be Tristan Fletcher." Even as she said his name, there was a change in his angry eyes. Somehow it would be fitting if he were, she thought, for he, the dogs, and the house were a perfect trio. Foreboding, frightening, and gloomy. The consequences of trying to be something she wasn't struck her. She couldn't pull this off. There was no way she could fool a man like this one. Lord, he was angry because she'd smacked his dog on the nose. How mad would he get if he actually let her stay, then discovered she wasn't the women he'd hired? She wasn't qualified to care for anyone but herself, and right now even that was in question.

"I am." He crossed his burly arms over his wide chest, giving himself the stance of an executioner. All he needed was a black mask with holes cut out for his eyes and a great big hatchet. She shivered.

No longer hungry, she felt her stomach twist into nervous knots. If only she could slither down the tree and escape. She gnawed on her thumbnail. No chance of that. The beasts had positioned themselves between her new employer and the tree, as if somehow she were the threat.

She studied Tristan Fletcher, noting his hard, dark eyes and his ink-black hair. Standing before her, with nut-brown muscles so taut they appeared etched in granite, his maleness struck a chord of fear and disappointment inside her. The Tristan Fletcher of her thoughts and daydreams had been nothing like this. He'd been like Charles Avery, suave, charming, and highly amusing. Unthreatening. Sweet. Quick to laugh with her and admire her lively wit.

He wasn't this hard, stern, bitter man whose maleness was threatening, and who so blatantly flaunted himself in front of her. Why, he was as frightening as Satan. How fitting it was that he should have devil dogs.

How much easier it would have been to simply tell him she was lost. To make up the name of a family she was searching for, then hurry away, her tail between her legs. It was too late for that. Her mouth was forever getting her into trouble.

"I'm here to care for your sister." She inched her chin up, hoping for an imperious veneer. In spite of her false bravado, there was a sick feeling in her chest, for now there would be no turning back. The sensation that spread through her was similar to what she imagined it would feel like if she stepped off a circus high wire, knowing there was no safety net below.

He scowled. "You?" He sputtered a curse. "I asked David for a nurse, not some skinny, whiny urchin who can't even find her way to my door without disrupting my dogs."

Her eyes went wide with disbelief and her stomach started to rebel. Sweet Mary, he didn't want her no matter who she was. But it would be far worse for her if and when he discovered she was an escapee from a loony bin instead of a nurse employed in one.

She swallowed hard, his anger coming as a surprise. She hadn't given much thought to how he would feel about her. Most of her energy had been centered on how she felt herself.

"How was I to get to the door without disturbing them?"

"They wouldn't have hurt you, but don't be deluded. If they'd wanted to catch you, you'd never have made it to the tree."

She eyed the beasts, believing his words.

"Running was the worst thing you could have done."

"Now you tell me." Her perch was getting uncomfortable and her rump was numb. She adjusted her position.

"It wouldn't hurt to post a warning," she muttered. "You know, Beware of big, ugly, hairy spawns of the devil."

Unfortunately, he didn't find her amusing. His face was stony, his cold eyes dark and dangerous, but he didn't respond. Instead, he picked up her travel bag and started toward the house.

She stared after him, astounded at his rude behavior. "Excuse me?" When he turned, she said, her voice laced with sarcasm, "I could use some help getting down."

"You got up there by yourself, why do you suddenly need help coming down?"

Lord, chivalry was dead west of the Mississippi, just as that woman on the train had warned her. This man was an insufferable clod. Clamping her jaws in anger, she started down, losing her footing on the craggy trunk. She fell to the ground, gasping in pain at the abrupt contact.

Both dogs loomed over her. Her heart nearly sprang free from her chest. "Call them off! Get them away from me!" She scooted backwards so fast, her head slammed into the trunk of the tree, and she momentarily saw a profusion of stars.

The cold, arrogant clod whistled, and the dogs returned to his side.

With caution, she got to her feet, her eyes never leaving the huge, furry beasts. For a brief second, black spots danced in her vision and her head throbbed. "Keep them away from me."

"Listen." His voice was harsh as he turned to her. "I'm not too sure I even want you here. But if I were you," he threatened, "I wouldn't start giving orders."

She swallowed the dead lump of apprehension in her throat. What in the name of heaven was she doing here? She'd only arrived, and already she wanted to leave. Taking in a deep breath, she willed away her fears. She hadn't come this far to be turned out into the cold. If she were to leave, it would be her choice, not his. She grimaced. Brave talk, considering her current position. She'd never warm up to the dogs. To this day, she had the scars of teeth on her rump from when she'd been bitten by a dog as a child. After she'd tumbled from a tree and broken her arm. Even now, it ached, as if reminding her that she had absolutely no rapport with animals.

"Are you coming, or have your feet grown roots?"

She shook herself and inched toward him, her gaze going over the cold, stone house. There was movement in a second-story window, a slight fluttering of the curtains. A chill shuddered over Dinah's spine, raising the hairs on the back of her neck, but when she glanced upward, she saw nothing.

Training her gaze on the dogs, she swallowed a sigh. She was giving her imagination free rein, but considering the ominous appearance of the house, she wasn't surprised. None of this would be easy. At least at Trenway she'd had an ally in Daisy. As she followed Tristan Fletcher into the gloomy house, she doubted she would have one ally here.

The foyer was predictably somber. Obscure shadows flickered in the corners, and again, Dinah fought her imagination.

"Wait here," he ordered, dropping her travel bag. "My housekeeper will show you to your room. I'll want to see you immediately after that."

He disappeared down a long, dark hallway. Dinah allowed her gaze to travel over the entry. An enormous bear's head was mounted on the wall, glaring down at her with flat black eyes. She grimaced, despising anyone who would kill for pleasure.

Over the thumping of her heart, she heard noises in the far recesses of the house. Squeaks and moans. Distant voices. The slow, methodical ticking of a grandfather clock. Something hard struck the floor above her and she jumped, her heart in her throat.

She picked up her travel bag, clutching it to her chest as she closed her eyes. What in the devil was she doing here? She was crazy to stay. She wouldn't. She couldn't. She crept to the door, opening it carefully so it wouldn't make any noise, only to find the hounds from hell guarding the stoop.

Tristan's mood had worsened, if that were possible. After taking a quick bath, he dressed in fresh buckskins and went to his study to await the nurse.

Nurse. Now, seated at his desk, he glowered. She'd be as helpful as tits on a bull. God, what had David been thinking? Because Tristan had been as close to David at school in Boston as he was to his childhood friend Lucas, he'd left the decision to find the right person in David's capable hands. After all, he was a doctor, studying the insane, writing an extensive paper on the subject. He was highly qualified to find a sensible, compassionate, mature woman, who would speak only when spoken to. Who would be obedient and even-tempered. One who would blend into the background, quietly assuming her role as wife-in-name-only while she cared for Emily, allowing Tristan to go about his business as usual.

This nurse defied every quality he'd requested. *Obedient* was obviously a foreign term to her. Her flame-colored hair challenged any notion of a bland temperament, and she had the vocabulary of a guttersnipe.

He opened the top drawer of his desk and rummaged through it, searching for David's letter. The door opened, and his housekeeper poked her head in.

"Are you ready to see her?"

"As ready as I'll ever be, Alice," he muttered under his breath. He rested his elbows on the desk and waited. The urchin entered his study, head bowed and hands clasped in front of her as though she were going to the gallows. Tristan didn't soften. He motioned to a chair in front of his desk. She sat, gazing at the high wall of book-lined shelves behind him.

"Miss—"

"Odell. Dinah Odell."

She was the size of a bird; her mop of unruly red curls

gave her the appearance of an exotic parrot. In spite of that, her porcelain skin was pale and perfect and her heart-shaped mouth pink and inviting. Her gown was putrid, however, as if its maker couldn't decide whether to dye it brown or green, so had opted for both.

"What qualifies you to care for my sister?"

"I . . . I." She met his glare, then lowered her eyes.

He tried to ignore her titian-red hair, which was so vibrant it made every other color in the room pale by comparison. "Certainly the question wasn't too difficult for you."

She studied him briefly. "No, I—"

"Well, perhaps this will be easier for you to answer. How long were you employed at Trenway?"

She lifted a delicate, yet, he was certain, stubborn chin. "I was at Trenway for a year."

"What makes you qualified to care for my sister?" he repeated.

This time her gaze didn't waver. "I've been among women with many problems, Mr. Fletcher. Women who huddled in corners all day and cried at night. Women who banged their heads against a wall all day and howled at night. Women who tried to kill me. Women who soiled themselves, first out of fear, then out of apathy. I'm certain some of these women didn't come in that way. It's more than likely the asylum itself aided in their insanity." A fetching blush stole into her cheeks as her indignation mounted.

He stood, shoving his chair back, and went to the window, her words touching some private place inside him. He'd been in college when he discovered that the "school" Emily had been sent to was an asylum. She'd been there for years, until Zelda died. Then Tristan moved heaven and earth to bring Emily home, where she'd had good care, at last. Alice's sister, Crystal, had moved in and cared for her until the day Crystal died from a stroke. That had been two years before. Since then, he'd had a succession of nurses whose bedside manners were atrocious and whose sense of compassion was nonexistent.

After learning where Emily had been all those years, Tristan visited a number of east-coast asylums in his quest to learn something more about her illness. Though her body had developed, her mind had not. Not completely. She wasn't simple. He often saw flashes of brilliance. But she had mercurial mood changes, some with such violence that her previous nurses had tied her to her bed. Tristan wouldn't tolerate such treatment. There had to be another answer.

He'd visited Trenway on occasion, but hadn't seen anything that had shocked him, even though it was all disturbing. Of course, it was possible he wasn't allowed to see the most severe cases, even with David's introduction.

"What else can you tell me?"

"Places like Trenway are places of punishment, Mr. Fletcher, not help. Though I've never been inside a prison, I'd venture to say that convicts are treated far better than any patient at Trenway Insane Asylum."

He turned, pinning her with a hard stare. "I've visited a few asylums, Trenway included, and I can't say I found them pleasant, but—" He shook his head. "Surely they can't be as bad as that." He didn't want them to be. After all, that would be admitting that Emily had suffered.

Dinah Odell sat calmly before him, no longer fidgeting with her clothing. "I wouldn't expect you to understand. You are, after all, a man."

His eyebrows shot up. "My gender has something to do with my ability to understand?"

"In this case, yes." Her answer was quick and decisive.

He returned to his chair and rested his elbows on the padded arms. "Tell me about some of the *good* things that went on at Trenway."

She uttered a harsh laugh, then turned away. He caught a slight trembling of her mouth before she pressed her lips together, and her throat worked repeatedly, as though she were having trouble swallowing.

"Trenway Asylum has no goodness about it, sir. It was created by the devil, and the devil, as we both know, is a man."

Tristan digested her words and almost groaned. Oh, God, she was one of those. While in the east, he'd learned of the Seneca Falls hens and old maids who complained that men could do as they pleased, while women had no rights. It had sounded preposterous, especially since Zelda Fletcher had ruled the roost with an iron hand, and his father, bless his gallant soul, had never had a moment's peace because of it.

He pressed the heels of his hands to his eyes, blocking out the vision of this frail, porcelain-skinned, titian-haired harpy.

"Did you know, sir, that fifteen years ago, Susan B. Anthony helped a mother and her child escape from the woman's husband? He had previously committed her to an insane asylum, merely because he wanted to get rid of her. Miss Anthony likened the plight of some hospitalized women to that of fugitive slaves."

This time, Tristan's groan was audible. He had heard a few rumblings now and then on his visits of sane women claiming to have been put into asylums by their husbands. But that notion was insane in itself. Surely no one believed such ridiculous ravings. Now, however, wasn't the time to argue with her.

"Don't attack me, Miss Odell. I'm not your enemy." She wouldn't work out. She was too young, too cheeky. She had a fiery temper, and was about as obedient as a nest of hornets. She'd be too much trouble.

Making his decision, he leaned into his chair. "I'll see that your fare is paid back to New York."

She sat bolt upright. "What?"

He was exhausted. Emily had kept him up most of the night, weeping against his shoulder. He couldn't get her to tell him what was wrong. She'd been in the low phase of her moods for weeks. God, the frustration he felt at not being able to help her weighed on him like a ton of mud.

"Just what part of the sentence wasn't clear to you?" He pinched the bridge of his nose, his weariness making him lose patience.

Across from him, she uttered a shaky sigh. "Mr. Fletcher, I'll be perfectly honest with you. I've already thought about fleeing. I'd be long gone by now, but your hounds were guarding the door, and I was afraid to leave. I'd almost gotten my nerve to try when your housekeeper fetched me."

Tristan raised one eyebrow. "I'm sorry to hear that. It would have saved both of us this painful interlude."

"You didn't let me finish." Her voice was firm, brooking no nonsense. "I'm not what you think I am. I mean," she amended, "I'm not a wild-eyed man-hater, but I met many women in the asylum who appeared to be as sane as you and I."

Her eyes filled with pain. "They had been put there by their brothers, fathers, or guardians who wanted to get rid of them, and by their husbands for purposes I can't even imagine. These men didn't appear to need a reason to incarcerate them, Mr. Fletcher. Trust me, I know first hand that these poor women could do nothing about it." There was a catch in her voice, and she bit down on her lower lip.

"I . . . I just thought it was important for you to know that I'm grateful to be away from there. I'd like a chance to prove that I'm qualified to do this job."

Tristan studied the color that stained her cheeks and the silent appeal in her eyes. Even if he let her stay, he was certain she couldn't handle Emily. Women with far more experience hadn't accomplished it, how could this little bird?

"I don't believe in punishing patients no matter what they've done or what they do while they are in my care.

I'm really very indulgent, Mr. Fletcher. I'd like a chance."

Her professed indulgence would be sorely tested with Emily. Swearing under his breath, he dragged his fingers through his hair. Something about her bothered him. True, she was an intrepid thing, appearing to know her business and willing to work at it, but there was something else. Of course, she had none of the qualities he wanted. That was probably it. She would blend into the background about as well as a camel cutting cake at a wedding reception.

A sudden emotion, one akin to pity, found its way into his chest, but he stopped it before it reached his heart. Women and their theatrics. Why in the hell were they so good at chipping away at a man's armor?

His thoughts automatically went to his ex-fiancée, and his stomach boiled like acid. Coralee had played the sympathetic heroine, the woman who would live with him and share the burden of Emily. Until she realized it would mean leaving Boston and moving to the mountains of California. What good would it do if none of her society friends were around to watch her courageous performance?

"And . . . and I've come all this way."

Rubbing his face with his hands, Tristan shrugged off thoughts of the devious Coralee. "I'll give you a trial month. If, after that, I see no progress in Emily's behavior, we'll work out the details of your departure."

She closed her eyes and nodded, appearing to relax.

"Have you any questions for me?"

"Just one. What is your sister suffering from?"

His eyebrows went up. "You weren't told?"

A deeper flush crept into her cheeks and she twisted the ribbon at her waist. "Only that she needed care."

He found it odd that David wouldn't have told her, but he guessed it could happen. "My sister is thirty-two years of age, Miss Odell. More times than not, she has the mannerisms of a child. Her moods are mercurial. I will admit that she has occasional fits of temper. Sometimes she appears reasonably happy, but most often she does not. She cries for no reason. If we don't watch her, she will go days without eating. It seems, Miss Odell, that my sister has the same emotions other people do, except that they are extreme."

"Has she ever been evaluated by a doctor?"

The sheafs of papers from analyzing doctors filled two boxes in the attic. "Of course." He gave her an ominous smile. "Which is precisely why she's here, and no longer in an institution. She was in one for a number of years. Upon her mother's death, I saw to it that Emily was returned home. I may find it hard to believe the things you've told me about Trenway, but under the best of circumstances, I still wouldn't want my sister locked up there."

The little bird's eyes filled with apprehension. Perhaps he'd be rid of her sooner than he'd thought.

"Now, please find Mrs. Linberg and send her in here. Dinner is at seven."

Anxious for her to leave, Tristan reached for his reading glasses and turned to his papers. She dredged up in him a vulnerability he'd thought was long gone. Surely that was all it was. How else could a man feel toward a woman who was no more than a girl and had as many curves as a fence post?

She was different, he'd give her that. After Crystal's death, and before he'd thought to ask for David's help, he'd always hired older nurses. Nurses with years of experience. In theory, that was wise. In reality, it wasn't, for those women had been tired. Worn out. Lacking in patience and compassion. Most of them had wanted a soft job, one that would let them ease into retirement.

Mrs. Linberg popped her head around the door. "Ya, Tristan? What do you want?"

He held up an empty file. "Have you seen the letter

from Dr. Richards? The one explaining about the new nurse?"

Frowning, she crossed to the desk, adjusting the front of her dress over her generous bosom. "Ya, sure. I put it in a safe place."

Tristan gave her a wry smile. *Ya, sure* always came out sounding like ya*sure*. She'd been with the family for as long as he could remember, yet he'd never gotten used to her thick Swedish accent. "Which would be where, Alice?"

Alice Linberg pursed her lips and touched the empty file with her gnarled finger. "It ain't in the folder?"

He shook his head. "It's not here, and it's not anywhere in my desk. I've checked." From the time he was young, he remembered Zelda railing at the housekeeper for her forgetfulness. She'd always been a bit scatterbrained, and it had driven Zelda crazy. Not to be in control of every facet of one's life was a sin, according to Zelda Fletcher. Thoughts of her automatically made him tight jawed.

"Uff dah." Alice Linberg tucked a wayward strand of white hair into the braid at the back of her neck, then straightened the apron at her waist. "Now, let me see." She tapped her finger against her lips, then shrugged. "I'll think of it. It's important, ya?"

"Yes, but not crucial, Alice. Life as we know it doesn't hang in the balance." He knew the woman well. She'd wake up out of a dead sleep and know exactly where she put it, although it might take her a while.

In the meantime, he'd keep an eye on Dinah Odell. He massaged his neck. He wanted some peace around here. Were it up to him, he'd care for Emily himself, but there were too many other things that required his attention. Time didn't allow him to give her everything she needed.

He should have mentioned the orphans to Miss Odell, but he had a feeling he'd heaped enough on her plate, for the time being, at any rate. Although, it might have been exactly the news she needed to send her back to civilization.

He also hadn't made mention of the marriage arrangement. Surprisingly, neither had she. Once again, he reviewed the qualities she possessed that he hadn't asked for. If the situation weren't so serious, he'd have thought Dr. David Richards, old friend and college roommate, had played an elaborate trick on him.

3

Dinah closed the door to her room and slumped into a chair. He'd been willing to let her go! And, she thought, wrinkling her nose, she'd convinced him to let her stay. She was a bigger fool than she'd ever imagined and she hadn't even had to work at it.

Too late, she realized he'd innocently used an old ploy on her that had always worked for her father. Insist that little Dinah couldn't do something because she wasn't big enough, strong enough, smart enough, or fast enough, and Little Dinah nearly fell all over herself to prove she could. Even if she hadn't wanted to. Now, she wanted to leave, and Tristan Fletcher would have let her had it not been for her big mouth and stiff pride.

She let out a whoosh of air and studied the room. Gloomy, like the rest of the house. Faded bird-and-flower wallpaper clung precariously to the panels, pulling away at the corners near the ceiling. The walls were covered with interesting frippery, however, like needlepoint flowers, the intricate colors and shadows so alive, they nearly leaped from the oval frames. A funereal painting hung above the desk, the dead colors hauntingly appealing.

Another ominous painting was suspended on a wire over the brass headboard of the bed. Though the canvas was filled with trees and flowers, the center held a demon tree, large, purple, and grotesque, that appeared to devour everything around it. It was an ugly thing, certainly not something she wanted over her head while she slept.

If she was staying, that painting wasn't. She removed it and shoved it under the bed. Shivering, she reached for the knitted stole that had been at the bottom of Daisy's valise and wrapped it around her shoulders.

A light hung on a sconce between the windows, the glass thick with dust. A colorful parlor lamp sat beside a Bible on a table near the bed. A dry smile touched the corners of Dinah's mouth. No doubt previous nurses had found it necessary to sink to their knees in prayer and pour over Scripture in order to survive Tristan Fletcher's arrogant orders. Or maybe, she thought, her stomach pitching downward, to survive his sister's precarious moods. The earlier fluttering of a curtain reminded Dinah that whoever this Emily was, she was aware of her arrival. At least she presumed it was Emily.

Dinah rose and crossed to the window, folding back the shutters. It had begun to rain. Thick, wet droplets pelted the windows. The trees swayed in the wind, and the thick boughs of the evergreens bowed low, heavy with water. A sick feeling coated her stomach.

Sweet Mary, what was she doing here? She hadn't even met Emily Fletcher yet, and she wanted to flee like a rat from a sinking ship. Her vivid imagination had run away with her, creating problems that hadn't even surfaced. But, with her luck, they probably would. Her lips curved into a self-deprecating smile.

Resting her forehead on the glass, she closed her eyes.

She should be ashamed of herself. She must never forget what Daisy had done for her. Anything was better than the asylum. *Thank you, Daisy. Thank you for my life. I won't disappoint you, I promise.* Thoughts of her last moments with Daisy both saddened and sickened her, and she felt tears of remorse.

"I'm sorry, Daisy, I'm so sorry."

"Having second thoughts already?"

She swung around, unaware that he'd been at the door. With quick fingers she swiped at the moisture beneath her eyes. "Don't you believe in knocking?"

He tilted his head, as if bowing, yet not. He held a cloth-covered tray. "I did. You didn't answer." His gaze wandered over the room, stopping on her. He appeared to study her. It did odd things to her insides, things she'd never experienced before, but knew existed. Her pulse fluttered. Her breath quickened. She looked at the floor, unwilling to analyze her feelings.

She had blessed Daisy every day for creating new ways to make her unappealing during her incarceration. Her favorite had been when she'd convinced the lascivious guards that Dinah's red hair meant she was a witch, and if they molested her, their doodles would shrivel up between their legs and fall off. Daisy had assured her that no man would risk losing his doodle.

Dinah's mouth quirked into a smile. Until her stay in the asylum, she had never imagined a man's private parts, much less thought of them by name. If nothing else, the past year had been an education.

"Something amuses you?" He crossed the room and placed the tray on the desk.

She liked the way he walked, all fluid and graceful, like a panther or some such wild thing. The scene in the tree played in her mind, the beauty of his sculpted chest and arms swimming in her brain.

"Not really." The tray was inviting, no matter what lay beneath the white napkin.

He caught her perusal. "Alice—Mrs. Linberg—

thought you might like something to eat." A shadow crossed his face. "Dinner will be late."

In spite of her certainty that she could not eat, Dinah's mouth watered and her stomach grumbled loudly.

"Will I meet Emily soon?" She walked to the desk. Her stomach continued to growl, anticipating what was beneath the cloth. She lifted the corner, exposing a plate of rolls with shiny crusts and a dish each of butter and jam. She swallowed the rush of saliva in her mouth.

"Perhaps she'll join us for dinner."

Dinah dropped the corner of the cloth and turned toward him, anxious to have him gone so she could eat. "I look forward to meeting her."

His face was without expression. "I'll leave you to rest, then."

When he'd gone, Dinah sat at the desk, whipped off the cloth and gazed at the food. It wasn't as if she hadn't eaten since she'd left Trenway. The food on the train was a treat to her. She had squirreled away what she couldn't eat, savoring it at odd times, relishing the fact that it wasn't moldy or maggot ridden. And no one rifled through her things looking for her stash as they had at Trenway.

She split a roll with her thumbs, slathered it with butter and jam, and bit into it, closing her eyes with pleasure. But as delicious as it was, she couldn't finish it. Her stomach wouldn't let her. She wrapped what was left on the tray in a napkin and slid it into a desk drawer. It would give her something to nibble on before she went to bed.

She wandered around the room feeling nervous and short of breath, when it occurred to her that she wasn't a prisoner. She strode to the door, flung it open, and stared out into the dark hallway. Her nose twitched at the musty air; it didn't bother her. After a year of the worst odors any human should have to smell, a musty house was like a garden of flowers. She listened, hearing only muted sounds coming from downstairs. Dimly lit sconces flickered macabre shadows on the walls, tossing feeble light over the staircase.

Dinah counted three other doors besides hers. In the farthest recesses of the landing, another stairway disappeared into the darkness that was presumably the attic. Again, as before, a shiver stole up her spine, and she rubbed her arms with her hands.

The hairs on the back of her neck stood on end as a gust of air rustled her skirt from behind, pressing it briefly against her legs. She turned in time to see the door across from her own close with a quiet click. What passed for a cynical smile touched her lips, then was gone. Emily Fletcher, no doubt. Her mind filled with questions about the woman, and she was both eager and afraid to meet her. Eager, because in her heart she knew she could help the woman, and afraid, because she was in over her head. She smirked again. What else was new?

Turning to the banister, she ran her fingers along the wood and pressed her knee between the elegantly carved balusters. The stairway itself was much like the one in her home in New York: dark cherrywood with a cluster of balusters forming the newel post. She'd slid down the highly polished banister a time or two, much to her dear, sweet mother's mortification. And Charlotte's. Charlotte had always acted like a lady, even when they'd been children.

Memories brought a sudden rush of homesickness upon her, a feeling that surprised her. During her year at Trenway, thoughts of home had only angered her, for Uncle Martin had blatantly taken up residence there.

A current of air ruffled her hem again, and she forced herself not to turn. Something small and sharp struck her shoulder, and she inhaled in surprise as a stinging sensation penetrated her skin. The door closed as before, with a quiet click behind her.

Bewildered, Dinah squatted and moved her hand over

the carpet. She pricked her finger and gasped again, drawing it back and putting it in her mouth. With her thumb and forefinger she gingerly picked up the missile and brought it under the dim light of the wall sconce.

Frowning, she studied it. Only a piece of paper, wadded up hard, yet . . . Another shiver shuddered through her, for in the center, held in place by the paper, was a nail with a sharp point.

Dinah stared at the door behind which the infamous Emily lurked. So, she liked playing games. Dinah could play games, too. Why, during the past year she'd become a master at it. She wondered if this was how Emily initiated all new nurses. If so, the job would be interesting, she'd give her that. It would be anything but routine. Suddenly, for no sane reason, Dinah felt up to the task.

The fireplace in the great room was open on both sides. Stones framed the fire, going all the way to the ceiling. There was no mantle on which to display pretty vases, clocks, or plates. No ornately carved woodwork to give it a civilized air. Only cold, hard stone. Dinah huddled deeper into the wing chair.

The storm still raged; wind buffeted the windows with sheets of rain. Shuddering, she curled her feet under her, her gaze darting to the shadowy corners of the room. The place had the charm of a mausoleum. More wild animal heads adorned the walls, all appearing to watch her no matter which way she moved her head. The moose was particularly unappealing, for he had nostrils the size of gopher holes.

But the doe . . . She was certain the doe was sad, for her big, black eyes were beseeching. And why not? She'd probably had a fawn, hidden away to keep it safe. Dinah wondered if it had survived when the mother was killed. Thoughts of her own mother's death brought a band of sharp pains cinching her heart. No one should have to live without a mother.

The doe's plaintive eyes continued to study her. "I

know how you're feeling, you pretty thing, but I'm not to blame for your demise."

The grandfather clock struck, and Dinah jumped, for the room had been unnaturally quiet. Except, of course, for the haunting sounds that she was certain only she heard. The creaks, the moans, the howling of the wind as it searched for entrance. As she'd rested before dinner, staring at the ceiling, she swore she could hear someone in the attic, moving about. It was probably her imagination, or perhaps even a mouse, but had she not already encountered Emily on the stairs, she wouldn't have been surprised if the sister actually were up there, chained to the wall.

The clock struck eight times and Dinah clucked impatiently. Tristan Fletcher had excused himself after dinner, but had asked that she wait for him.

Dinner had been another uncomfortable event. Her year at Trenway had erased the breeding, deportment, and fine manners that her mother had instilled within her. As a patient, she'd had to protect her plate. She'd found herself doing that tonight, wrapping her arms on either side of it to keep it safe. She'd also tentatively taken a biscuit, half expecting Tristan Fletcher to snatch it from her, the way her fellow patients so often had stolen her food at mealtime at the asylum.

With a sense of relief, she touched the bulge in the deep pocket of Daisy's brown dress. If she forced herself to eat a little more at each meal, she hoped to stretch her stomach. She would need her strength for this job, of that she was certain.

She'd enjoyed watching Tristan Fletcher eat. Though he had a healthy appetite, he hadn't bolted his food. She snorted a laugh. Lord, this obsession with food simply had to stop.

She thought, instead, about his firm, square jaw and his sharp cheekbones, his thick, black hair and his wide shoulders. As compelling as he was, he had sad eyes. She hadn't seen him really smile.

Spying a picture on the far wall, she stood and crossed the room, studying it as she got closer. It was of a young woman. Again, her neck hairs prickled. Instinctively she knew this was Emily, even though she was very different from her brother. He was dark, she was pale. His hair was almost blue-black; hers was golden. And Tristan Fletcher was tall, broad shouldered, and muscular; his sister was dainty and fine boned. And hauntingly beautiful.

Dinah heard a soft sound behind her, and before she could turn, she was smacked on the head. She'd barely gotten her equilibrium when someone landed on her back, causing her to lose her balance. She clawed at the arm that pressed against her throat. Sharp fingernails dug into the thin flesh on top of her hand, drawing blood. Her heart hammered and her pulse raced, but she couldn't scream, for the arm pressed harder, preventing her from making any sound.

She stumbled forward, stepping on the hem of her gown. The searing noise of tearing fabric filled her ears as she tottered toward the hearth, swinging from side to side, in hopes of ridding herself of the weight on her back. She reached behind her, grabbed a thick braid, and tugged, eliciting a keening scream from her aggressor. A free hand seized Dinah's short curls, yanking hard enough to cause tears of pain.

Black spots danced before her eyes as she continued to claw at her neck. Suddenly she was free. Dragging in gulps of air, she turned, clutching her hand to her throat.

Emily Fletcher stood across from her, her tiny bosom heaving as heavily as Dinah's own. They squared off, neither speaking. The woman's eyes were huge, and her fists were balled at her sides, as if she were waiting for Dinah to retaliate. Whatever Dinah had expected, it wasn't this. It wasn't a woman no bigger than a child with the strength of a burly asylum matron.

"Did you know," Emily began, fighting for breath,

"that an aardvark and an aardwolf are two completely unrelated animals?"

For one stunned minute, Dinah simply stared. Then she nearly laughed, for she understood. And that understanding frightened her more than anything. Whatever Emily Fletcher was, she wasn't stupid. She could very well be insane, but insanity took many forms. And insanity didn't mean stupidity. In fact, she would be wise to remember that some of the most brilliant people in history were labeled insane.

Refusing to react the way Emily undoubtedly expected her to, Dinah answered with ridiculous calm, "Why, yes. One eats ants and the other carrion."

A flicker of surprise crossed Emily's face before she swung away. "How did you know that?"

Dinah massaged her neck, tempted to tell the woman she had a mind like flypaper, attracting all sorts of useless information. Instead, she asked, "How did you?"

Emily toyed with her long, golden braid. "I don't want you here." Her voice had a deceptively childlike quality to it.

I'm beginning to think that makes two of us. Dinah moved away, her heart pumping hard as she kept near the door in case she had to make a quick escape. "And, why don't you want me here?"

Emily made a petulant moue that became a frown. "Because you'll hurt me." She rubbed her wrist with her thumb, as if soothing an old injury.

"As you hurt me?" The memory of being dragged by her hair around the halls at Trenway made her scalp tingle. It hadn't taken her long to discover that was why most of the women kept their hair cropped short. Hers was just now beginning to grow out.

With her fists on her slim hips, Emily took a threatening step toward her. "I dare you to tell Tristan. I *dare* you. Because it won't matter if you do. I'll tell him you hurt me first. It worked with the others."

Conniving witch, Dinah thought. Clever, though. "I don't see why we can't—"

"Be careful what you eat," Emily warned behind a sly smile. "It could be poisoned."

Scare tactics. Dinah had seen them work before. In fact, circumstances had forced her to master a few herself. "Why would I—"

"Emily!"

They both turned as Tristan strode into the room. Water dripped from his hair and his shirt was plastered to his skin. His expression was a cross between dread and surprise.

"Tristan!" The woman ran to him and whimpered into his chest.

Absently stroking his sister's shoulder, he looked at Dinah, as if waiting for an explanation.

"We were getting acquainted." Dinah gave him a small smile, hoping none of her turbulent feelings showed.

He spoke to his sister, yet his gaze was on Dinah. "I thought we'd decided you would wait until morning to meet the nurse, Emily."

"I'm hungry, Tristan." She drew away and gave her brother a look of pure, innocent adoration.

Dinah raised her eyebrows. It was no wonder. After their scuffle, Dinah was hungry, too, in spite of Emily's threats of poison. She touched the biscuit in her pocket, hiding her disappointment when she discovered that during her tussle with Emily it had become a wad of crumbs.

"I'm sure Mrs. Linberg has prepared something for you." He touched the delicate line of Emily's chin. "What have you two been discussing?"

Emily tossed Dinah a blatant I-dare-you look.

Dinah ran her fingers through her short curls, biting back a groan when she skimmed the bruises on her skull. She had no intention of telling him anything, although she had a suspicion that's just what the woman wanted. Obviously other nurses had been foolish and gabbled about Emily's private tiffs. It was no wonder they hadn't lasted. Dinah felt she had a surprising handle on Emily Fletcher already. Of course, she'd always been a foolish optimist.

"Oh, we were talking about aardvarks and aardwolves, cabbages and kings." After tossing him an innocent smile, Dinah gave her skirt a tug. She cringed when the seam ripped further.

Tristan Fletcher raised his satanic brows in question but said nothing. Instead, he led his sister toward the kitchen. "I imagine you're exhausted, Miss Odell. Get a good night's rest and I'll see you in the morning."

Having been so soundly dismissed, Dinah made a face at his retreating back. As she took the stairs to her room, she wondered if there was a lock on her door. For a year she and Daisy had to dream up clever ways to keep her virtue intact. Now, her virtue wasn't the issue. It was her future and her job. Emily Fletcher wanted her gone. Dinah wondered to what lengths the woman would go to get her way.

Expelling a gruff sigh, Tristan left Emily asleep in her room. As he stepped into the dim hall, he stood and studied Dinah Odell's door and dove his fingers through his rumpled hair. Emily had pleaded for him to send the new nurse away. As she had before, she created a scenario in which the nurse was the attacker and poor, sweet Emily the victim.

Although others might have been fooled by such devices, firing nurse after nurse at Emily's request, Tristan was not. Unfortunately, the last nurse left of her own accord, as did the one before and the one before that. He had little hope for this one either, for their voices had reached him before he interrupted them in the great room, and he'd heard Emily threaten to poison the girl.

Because the girl hadn't said anything, Tristan felt there might be hope, but he wasn't sure how he felt about it.

Now, however, would be the real test. Alone, with no one to interfere, she might tell him what Emily had done to her. The others had, assuming that with Tristan on their side, it would be two of them against the patient. At that point, Tristan knew they wouldn't be long on the job.

Squaring his shoulders, he crossed the hall and rapped on her door. Now might be the time to clear the air about many things, the marriage, included. He heard hurried movements on the other side of the door before she opened it.

The muted light from the lamps in the room created a halo around her vibrant hair. She wore a voluminous white robe that hung on her slim frame, and her bare toes peeked out from beneath the hem. Her eyes, wide with caution, were the dark blue of a night sky.

"May I speak with you?" For some insane reason, he didn't want to bring up the marriage agreement. He wanted her to.

She tossed a nervous glance over her shoulder. "I—"

"If you'd be more comfortable, meet me in the library."

She looked down at her nightclothes, a pinkness blooming on her cheeks. "Should I—"

"Don't worry. I seldom accost children." He wasn't able to curb his disdain as he started for the stairs. Why did women always assume that a man was driven wild by the sight of them in their nightclothes? Especially nightclothes that covered far more than the clothes they wore during the day?

It wasn't that he didn't find women who were ready for bed provocative. Ever since his first foray into the pleasures of the flesh, he'd loved moving a searching hand beneath the soft fabric over their willing bodies, touching warm, dark, wet places that were kept secret from him during the day. But the women he hungered for always tantalized him, undressing slowly before him before slipping into something so deliciously filmy he could see their treasures beneath.

Even though Dinah Odell was oddly appealing in her white gown and robe, that attire was made for either virgins or gray-haired old maids, neither of which whetted Tristan's robust appetite. Usually.

He cursed as blood thickened in his groin. Being sequestered on the ranch had forced him into celibacy, and now, even the thought of a slim, boyish, man-hating harpy in a crisp, no-nonsense nightgown got him hard. It was time to go hunting for companionship, preferably a wild, lusty Spaniard whose screams of delight would make his ears ring.

He opened the door to his study, allowing her to go in before him. Her head barely reached his chin as she brushed passed him, smelling delicately of the lilac soap Alice had placed on her dry sink. He shifted, allowing for more comfort inside his snug trousers.

Before he'd come for her, he'd changed into dry clothes and built a fire in the fireplace. She took a chair near it, curling her feet under her, waiting for him to proceed.

He poured himself a brandy, settled in the chair across from her, and studied her languidly before he spoke. Her full lips were parted slightly, making her appear as though she were waiting to be kissed. He took a healthy swig of liquor and scowled into the fire.

"Why did you want to see me?"

Shivering, Dinah moved deeper into the chair, relishing the warmth of the fire. Her employer's brooding visage frightened her, but she pretended nonchalance.

"What's your impression of my sister?"

Wondering if it was a trick question, she toyed with the buttons of her robe. "I haven't formed an opinion yet, Mr. Fletcher. First impressions aren't always reliable."

He nodded, his expression remote. His long legs were spread wide, his soft buckskin shirt open nearly to his navel, his thick, brown chest visible to her gaze. And gaze she did, intrigued by his complexity.

He was both wild and restrained; he had the body of a woodsman and the mind of a scholar. He was massively built, but obviously could be gentle when it suited. Her gaze was drawn to the black hair that grew on the back of his hands. His long, strong fingers with the flat nails stroked the sides of the snifter, causing a different kind of shiver to steal over Dinah's skin.

"She can be physically violent when she chooses to be."

Don't I know it. Dinah sat forward, feigning surprise. "Violent? That slip of a woman?"

One side of Tristan Fletcher's mouth moved into a smile, but he said nothing. Instead, he nodded toward the wound on her hand, which she'd forgotten to dress with salve. "How did you hurt your hand?"

She gave it an indifferent glance. "Oh, that's hard to say. It probably happened when I fell out of the tree this afternoon." She waited a moment, then added, "When you refused to help me down."

His eyes accepted the volley, but he didn't return it. "I don't remember seeing the wound at dinner."

Dinah gave him a careless shrug. "I can't remember how it happened. It isn't important. Now, what did you want to talk to me about?"

He appeared surprised. "You have nothing to say to me?"

Again, she shrugged. She had the sense that he was waiting for her to unload, unburden herself regarding his troublesome sister. Perhaps this was a ritual he went through with each nurse he hired, and undoubtedly, if each nurse went through what she had, he got an earful.

"As I said before, I can't elaborate on her condition until I've spent some time with her."

He stood and moved to refill his snifter. "I'll be honest with you. Emily is a clever woman, Miss Odell. She'll probably drive you away, but I think you will leave here soon, anyway." He took a pull on his brandy, then came to stand near her.

He was a potent man, exuding both power and control. Dinah wondered if he ever just tossed his head back and laughed. She doubted it.

"And, why is that?"

He left her again, crossing to the bookcase. "We're in the middle of nowhere, Miss Odell. I'm surprised David sent someone so young. A person your age needs a social life, and you're certainly not going to get one here."

In spite of wanting to tell him that being here, as gloomy and forbidding as it was, was a vast improvement over where she'd been, she merely answered, "I'll get used to it. Remember, you promised me a trial month, no matter how you feel about me."

He slanted her a look that moved over her like searching fingers, stopping in places no gentleman would. "I did, didn't I?"

Beneath her layers of nightwear, her loose breasts tingled and there was a fluttering in the pit of her stomach that had nothing to do with fear. At least, not the kind of fear she'd felt up until now.

This awareness of him as a man was new to her. Now, instead of having to wrestle with her doubts about her ability to do this job, she had to fight the new-found attraction to her employer. She had no idea which would be more difficult, but starting tomorrow, she would find out.

4

KITCHEN SMELLS HAD ALWAYS BEEN DINAH'S FAVORITES. This morning, venison stew bubbled on the stove and bread was rising in a big bowl on a chair in the sunshine.

Inhaling deeply, Dinah stood at the kitchen window and studied the sun-splashed hills. Mourning doves wailed softly outside, the melancholy sound threatening her fragile mood. She'd endured Emily's petulance for a full week; three more to go to prove she was worthy of the task. There had been countless times when she'd have been grateful to pack up her meager belongings and hit the road. She'd thought the matron at Trenway had been clever, pinching her in places that didn't show. She smirked. The matron could have taken lessons from Emily Fletcher. Even now, the soft inner surface of her arm hurt from where Emily had grabbed it and twisted it the day before.

But she refused to capitulate and tell Tristan what was happening. She sensed he'd already gone through this, although no doubt other nurses told him what was going on. He'd been elusive this past week, seeming to skulk around, appearing out of nowhere when she least expected him. That, too, was probably part of his plan. To catch her doing something with his sister that he didn't approve of.

It was odd, though, that each time she saw him, her heart pounded hard and she felt a rush of blood to her face. He was quite a magnificent looking man, except that he rarely smiled and he never laughed.

Behind her, Mrs. Linberg stirred the stew, her metal spoon clanking against the sides of the pot. Emily sat at the table. There was tension between the two of them this morning. Dinah noticed it often. As for herself, she tried not to squirm, but she could almost feel the dagger in her back. The one she knew Emily wanted desperately to throw. Dinah touched her stomach, the tiny bit of breakfast she'd eaten weighing inside her like a stone.

"What a lovely day! Has either of you ever noticed how no two trees are the same shade of green? And the flowers!" She clasped her hands to her chest and sighed, forcing herself to sound enthusiastic. "I've never seen such colors."

Even though she was making small talk, it was the truth. Since leaving Trenway, she'd been stunned at how beautiful everything was, especially here. She didn't think she'd ever seen such a blue sky as that which framed the mountain tops.

Behind her, Emily snorted. "I've always known that."

Ignoring her, Dinah asked, "Mrs. Linberg, would it be possible to have a picnic in the gazebo today?"

The housekeeper's expression softened. "Why, that sounds like a wonderful idea. Better today than tomorrow."

"Oh? Why is that?"

"Tomorrow is the day you will be taking Emily to the hot springs. You do drive a rig, don't you?"

Dinah paused. Her? Drive a rig? Well, she'd ridden in

one often enough, she wondered if that counted. It would have to. "Oh, yes," she answered expansively, then crossed her fingers behind her back.

"Good. It should be a nice outing for both of you."

Alone with Emily? In a rig that Dinah couldn't handle over roads she wasn't familiar with? Youch, she thought with a sarcastic lift of her brow. A charming outing? It might well be her last.

"I don't want her to come," Emily groused.

"Well, she's going with you, young lady, and you'd better shut up about it. You've caused your brother enough trouble since the poor girl arrived." She shook her spoon in Emily's direction, catching the drips with her apron. "Mark my words, if you don't behave, he'll send you back to that place where no one will put up with your silly tantrums."

Dinah had noticed that in spite of Mrs. Linberg's obvious love for Emily, she had little patience with her. She harassed her often, but even Dinah knew her threats were empty.

Emily's eyes darkened and she clenched her fists on the table. "Tristan wouldn't do that to me. He loves me."

The housekeeper moved to the dishpan and rinsed the dishes, clanking them noisily. "Ya, sure, he loves you all right, maybe too much, I think."

"You can't love a person too much."

"I know it won't do any good to argue with you. It never does. But I don't happen to agree with you."

Emily stiffened.

"Before you go having another temper tantrum, little missy, remember that I can take you over my knee." Mrs. Linberg gave the pot another quick stir, then put a lid on it.

Emily tossed both women a veiled look through narrowed lids, then moved her spoon slowly through her cereal. But her knuckles were white.

Dinah dreaded the following day already. Surely they

wouldn't send her off alone with Emily. The dead lump of apprehension clogged her throat again, though she was beginning to get used to the feeling.

Mrs. Linberg dumped her bread dough onto the counter and sliced off a hunk, forming it into a round loaf. The process fascinated Dinah. Although she'd never learned how to cook, as a young girl, Dinah had often watched her mother's chef and wished she could dabble in the kitchen. Maybe she would have a chance here. That is, if she wasn't out on her scrawny rump at the end of the month.

Mrs. Linberg continued to form dough into loaves. "That poor brother of yours gets nothing done around here, and it's because of you and your childish behavior. Don't think you've fooled him, girl, because you haven't. He knows what you're up to. It wouldn't hurt him to threaten you once in a while."

Dinah usually enjoyed confrontation, or at least was able to tolerate it. This morning she wanted to slink from the room. She started for the door.

"What do you think, Dinah?"

Dinah stopped and ran her fingertips over the tabletop. "I think that he should be commended for not returning Emily to that kind of place, Mrs. Linberg. Remember," she offered, "I've been there, too. It's no place for anyone, no matter what's wrong with them."

Emily watched her with renewed interest. "I don't remember much about it."

Dinah wasn't surprised. Daisy had told her there were people who chose to forget their unpleasant experiences, and were able to do so. Surely part of Emily's hostility was based on what she'd been through during those years. But she was fragile, too. Not only physically, but mentally as well. Stress brought about Emily's unusual behavior, and Dinah had no doubt that her own arrival had exacerbated it. Emily's moods swung from one end of the pendulum to the other without provocation.

"Be grateful your brother hasn't considered sending you there again, Emily. Be grateful."

Fragrant honeysuckle grew up the slatted walls of the gazebo. Emily sat on a cushioned seat inside, in the shade, while Dinah lolled on a blanket in the sun, her eyes closed and her face soaking in the warmth.

"You should be wearing a capote," Emily suggested.

Dinah smiled. "A capote, huh?"

"I'll bet you don't know what a capote is."

Opening her eyes, Dinah saw Emily's smug smile as she sketched quickly on a pad.

"You don't think so?"

"None of my other nurses did."

Dinah stretched, feeling like a cat in the sunshine. Though Emily had a good vocabulary, she didn't use it often. Most of the time her sentences were short and simple.

"My mother used to wear a lavender one to match her purple cape. I could never see her head for the wide brim of the bonnet around her face."

Emily screwed up her tiny nose. "I thought I'd get you with that one." She studied Dinah. "Mama always told me a lady never sits in the sun without a wide-brimmed hat and gloves."

"My mother told me that, too. But believe me, after a year inside those dismal gray walls, etiquette is thrown to the wind."

"Sometimes I wish I remembered," Emily mused.

"I'd be grateful I didn't, if I were you. I, on the other hand, remember everything so vividly, it is as if it were yesterday." It almost was.

They sat together, sharing a quiet peace. Emily continued to sketch quickly on a pad she held in her lap.

Dinah scrambled to her feet. "What are you drawing?"

A guilty shadow crossed Emily's face, and she hid the tablet in the folds of her gown. "Nothing." She clutched her hands in her lap.

Dinah slowed her steps as she entered the shaded gazebo. "I'd like to see what you've done, Emily."

Emily's expression was defiant. "I won't show you. If you make me, I'll pinch you."

Dinah raised her hands in defeat. "Fine. It's probably a lot of scribbling, anyway." Daisy had used this ploy on a patient at the hospital. It had worked.

"I don't scribble."

Dinah gave her a careless shrug and turned away. "Whatever you say."

"Well, I don't. But, I . . . I can't show you."

Continuing to feign a lack of interest, Dinah examined the wildflowers that grew beside the blanket. She recognized some of them after finding them in a small book on California wildlife and wildflowers written by a California naturalist by the name of Ian MacDowell, who had lived for years in the Yosemite Valley.

She plucked a stalk holding a profusion of California buttercups and brought it to her nose, inhaling the fragile scent. "Fine. Then don't."

"If I show it to you, you'll take it from me."

Dinah stopped but didn't turn around. "Why would I take it from you?"

"Because Mama didn't want me to draw. Before I went away, she took all of my supplies and hid them. I don't remember much about being gone, but I do remember that the nurses there wouldn't let me draw. Mama must have told them not to."

Dinah sat on the gazebo steps. "Why would she have done that?"

"Because . . . because she didn't like what I painted."

"Has Tristan told you not to paint?"

Emily's brow wrinkled and she started breathing hard. "No, but he doesn't remember that I like to."

"Your mother is in heaven, Emily." Actually, she wasn't so sure the old hag wasn't burning in hell. Although she'd been taught it wasn't up to her to judge someone, she couldn't help hoping the woman was suffering for some of the things she'd obviously done to her own daughter. "She can't stop you from painting anymore."

"Yes, yes she can." Emily's agitation was real. "She told me she'd look down and watch me. And that bad things would happen to me if I did. I thought if I did it here, she couldn't see through the roof and discover what I was doing."

Dinah swallowed a disgusted sigh. What kind of mother would make threats that would reach out from the grave? "I'd like to see what you're doing, Emily. Won't you show me?"

Emily drew the tablet out from between the folds of her skirt and handed it to Dinah.

"Why, Emily," she said with a sigh. "It's beautiful." The rustic garden scene was alive with trees and flowers. Despite the fact that they were drawn in black pen, color seemed to leap from the page. That's how perfect they were.

All of a sudden, Emily's face was pinched with discomfort. "Tristan's coming. Please," she pleaded, grabbing for her pad, "he mustn't see it."

She stood, hiding the tablet as she hurried down the gazebo steps. "I'm going inside."

She stopped briefly, and Dinah heard her tell her brother she was going in to lie down.

Tristan continued to stroll toward Dinah, his worn buckskins clinging to his muscular legs. He wore the vest, as he had the day she'd arrived. His outdoor clothes transcended fashion, however she had the feeling that he could wear a loincloth and not be out of place anywhere. The sight of him made her tingle. He was without a doubt the most handsome man she'd ever seen.

The devil dogs appeared out of nowhere, loping beside him.

"They truly are ugly dogs," she remarked as the three of them approached her.

He appeared offended. "I'll have you know they're championship Irish wolfhounds."

"Irish?" She snorted a laugh. "Leave it to them to breed the most unsightly animals in the world."

"I would have thought that with a name like Odell, you were Irish as well."

"Me? No. Lord, no. Odell is a Norwegian name. There's no, you know," she explained, making a twist with her index finger, "no apostrophe after the O."

He actually laughed. Or made a sound that passed for a laugh. "Better not let Mrs. Linberg know that. According to her, every evil done to man was perpetrated by a Norwegian."

"Then she'd better not meet any of my uncles. They swear the Swedes haven't bathed since the fourteenth century, and even then they all used the same bucket of water."

This time, Tristan actually did laugh. A hearty, virile sound that sent shivers of delight over her skin. She was so surprised, she turned her gaze, lest he see the yearning in her eyes. Until now, he hadn't been the perfect man. Oh, he was handsome, strong, smart, and compassionate. But he'd been so sullen. Knowing she could make him laugh made him perfect, and that made him completely unreachable.

One of the dogs drew close and sniffed Dinah's shoe. She froze.

"She's a gentle creature, Miss Odell, but she can also smell your fear."

Dinah grimaced. "How can anything that size be gentle?"

"If she weren't, I'd have to put her down."

"Put her down? You mean you'd have to do away with her?" In spite of her fear, she was disturbed by the thought of having to kill a pet.

"If she weren't gentle, she'd be too dangerous to have around. Imagine a dog this size with an unstable temperament." Tristan scratched the dog's muzzle and she leaned into him, nearly knocking him over.

Dinah watched the love play between dog and master and was intrigued.

"I remember their names. You called them Wolf and Amy. I can understand Wolf, but Amy?"

The other dog, the big one, meandered over to her and rested its head on her lap, gazing up at her with limpid eyes. Something softened inside her, and she felt a tugging at her heart.

"Their names are Wolfgang and Amadeus."

She smiled. "You named your dogs after Mozart?"

"No, I named them after my brother."

She gingerly stroked the dog's head, eliciting a groan of pleasure from the animal. "Your brother? What an unusual name for a man these days."

"My brother is an unusual man."

Dinah studied Tristan but said nothing. His profile was regal, his cheekbones majestic. His haunted, dark-rimmed, stormy blue eyes gave him a vulnerability that made him human. Otherwise, he had the bearing of a god. The brother could be no more unusual than he was.

"How are things with Emily this afternoon?"

Dinah blinked, grateful he had interrupted her. "She was quite calm." She thought a moment, then made her decision. "Did you know she enjoys sketching?"

He frowned. "Of course. Until I saw that funereal piece of art over the desk in your room, I'd forgotten her passion for it."

"Ah, yes. There was another one hanging over my bed, but I've taken it down." She sighed. "I thought it was truly ugly, but I'm beginning to think I should put it back up. After all, it's the way Emily expresses herself, and I don't have to like it."

His face was hard, closed in. "Zelda didn't like any of Emily's paintings. I'm surprised she didn't have those two pieces destroyed as well."

"Destroyed?" What a terrible thought.

His smile was grim. "They made incredible fireplace fodder."

Dinah gasped at the waste. "They may not be pretty and superficial, but they're part of Emily, of who she is. It seems to me that to destroy them would be to destroy a part of her."

"Emily's view of the world wasn't what Zelda wanted it to be."

"But that doesn't make it wrong," Dinah countered. "Even now, your mother has a hold over Emily. She threatened to punish her from the grave."

He expelled a sound of disbelief. "What?"

"According to Emily, her pictures disturbed your mother, therefore she didn't want Emily drawing them. I think she reasoned that if they bothered *her,* they must have bothered Emily, too. But for Emily, they were a form of therapy." My, didn't she sound profound?

He seemed to think so, too. "I can believe that."

Dinah let out a quiet, relieved breath of air. "Drawing calms her down. It's better than any form of therapy or treatment I've ever seen. At Trenway, there was a woman who had the most beautiful singing voice. We discovered that if we let her sing, she was peaceful. If we asked her to stop, she became violent. Shrieked like a bloody banshee." She shrugged. "It probably wasn't the most professional form of treatment, but it worked."

His searching gaze made Dinah uncomfortable. One thing she would do, she knew for certain, was return that unsightly picture to its place on the wall. It was possible that Emily had put it there in the first place, just to get a rise out of her. And if she sneaked into Dinah's room and found it gone, she would know her ploy had worked.

Dinah inhaled the fresh mountain air and studied the distant, snow-capped hills. The trees that grew at the highest elevations appeared black and purple. "It's so beautiful here. I would never have believed any place on earth could be as perfect as this."

The view from her wing at the asylum had offered

plump, Trenway cattle grazing on thick, succulent grass. She'd often wondered who benefited from them. Probably that cow of a matron and her fat daughters, none whom ever missed a well cooked meal. It certainly wasn't the inmates. The memory of gray, spoiled meat floating in greasy swill nearly made her gag.

She crossed to a patch of elegant blue flowers resembling forget-me-nots and knelt in the grass to examine them. "Look at these," she said, tossing the words over her shoulder. "Did you know these are called hound's tongue?"

From a distance, she studied his hounds and made a face. "Not likely named after them, though. These flowers are as beautiful as your hounds are ugly."

She fell forward, moving her hands over the soft flowers and cold grass. The smell was intoxicating. In spite of everything, Dinah had felt revitalized the instant she saw the mountains from the train.

She rose and inhaled again, closing her eyes as the crisp, clean air filled her lungs. She spun in circles on the grass, flinging her arms wide, feeling alive and free. *Thank you, Daisy, thank you, thank you, thank you!*

"Oh, if I could sing, I'd belt out a song that would knock the antlers off an elephant."

He chuckled, not the sound he'd made before, but it was filled with humor, nonetheless. Her stomach did a little dip.

"I don't believe elephants have antlers, Miss Odell. They have tusks." This odd girl-woman was beginning to grow on him. What an unusual creature she was.

She laughed, a tinkling sound that rivaled birdsong. "Oh, of course. Well, you know what I mean."

"I've been here so long, I don't see the beauty of it anymore. I rather take it for granted, I'm afraid."

She stopped dancing on the grass, her face serious and filled with emotion. "Oh, you shouldn't let that happen." She inhaled again, raising her delicate shoulders. "Smell that." When he merely looked at her, she put her fists on her hips. "I mean it. Come on, smell that air."

To humor her, Tristan took a deep breath.

"What do you smell?"

He shrugged. "Air. It has no particular odor of its own."

"Nonsense." She inhaled, closing her eyes. "I smell . . . flowers. So many different kinds, I can't identify a single one. And I smell the grass and the dirt. And," she added, inhaling again, "pine." She made a sound of pleasure, not unlike a woman beginning to feel the stirrings of passion. Tristan was intrigued.

"What else do you smell, Miss Odell?"

"Oh, let me see." She sniffed again, then smiled, her eyes still closed. "Manure."

He laughed. "Now, don't tell me that's a pleasant odor."

"But it is. It's earthy and warm." She pulled in another noisy breath. "I like it."

He shook his head, unable to keep from smiling. "You've been behind asylum walls too long if you find manure a pleasant smell."

A change came over her so brief, he wasn't sure he'd seen anything at all.

"Yes," she answered, her voice soft, "I guess I have." She recovered quickly. "Now, come." She danced off toward the barn. "Show me the rest of the ranch. I want to see everything."

Tristan followed her as she skipped toward the outbuildings, her drab skirt flying up to expose her petticoats. She was refreshing, almost exhilarating. She breathed life into everything that had become stale around him. Even so, she was merely a wide-eyed child.

Something about her continued to bother him. He couldn't put his finger on it, but by God, he would. He was accompanying her and Emily to the hot springs in the morning, although he hadn't done it with any of the other nurses. He'd made himself too scarce, primarily because he preferred the numb armor that protected his heart from the feelings Dinah dredged up within him.

After dinner, Tristan pored over his ledgers. There was a rap on the door, and Alice stepped into his study. He glanced up briefly, then went back to the column of numbers.

"Yes, Alice? What is it?"

She clucked her tongue and stepped closer to the desk. "I've discovered the oddest thing."

He ran his finger down the column, stopping at the total. "What's that?"

A barrage of hard rolls and slices of bread tumbled onto his desk, the crumbs spilling over his books.

He cursed. "What in the hell?" He brushed the dried bread away with an impatient hand.

"You'll never guess where I found these."

Annoyed now, he murmured, "No, I never will. Why don't you tell me?"

"I was cleaning Miss Odell's room."

The finality of her statement was supposed to be clear. It wasn't. "And?"

Alice leaned over his desk, her face red, her pale eyes intense. "The hard rolls were in the desk drawer, rolled up in a napkin. Tristan," she scolded, "those are the rolls I sent up to her the day she arrived, over a week ago." She looked about, as if someone might be listening. "The bread was in her bedside table, hidden inside a napkin." She picked it up and crumbled it, the crumbs adding to the mess on his desk. "Not fit for anyone but the birds."

Tristan studied the bird food. "I'll admit it's unusual."

"And this," she said, drawing a partly eaten apple from her apron pocket, "was under her pillow. Can you imagine? *Under her pillow.*" She dug into the other pocket and, with two fingers, pulled out another napkin. She opened it and showed him what was inside, then dropped it with the other debris. "This was a piece of cake." She shook her head at the mess of frosting that clung to the cloth, then tugged at her bodice. *"Uff dah.* I baked it three days ago, and I found it on the windowsill."

Tristan sat back in his chair and crossed his arms over his chest. "It's odd, I'll grant you that."

"It isn't as if I don't feed her. I mean, after all, Tristan, I'm a good cook and I see that we have plenty to eat."

"That you do, Alice."

"Well, what do you make of it?"

He shook his head, completely baffled. "I haven't a clue, but if it's important to you, I'll find out."

"Ya, well it's important, for sure," she answered with a huff. "The way she's stashing food, a person would think she's afraid she'll go hungry." She leaned across the desk, shook a finger at him and blew a strand of gray hair from her face. "And nobody goes hungry when Alice Linberg cooks!"

5

She had stripped to her camisole and drawers as quickly and eagerly as a bawdy-house tart. Now, she bobbed in the heated water with Emily by her side, her face cloaked in rapture.

Of course, she'd thought he was gone. Indeed, he'd intended to go off, leaving them with the matron of the spa, but had chosen to stay.

There were many things gnawing at him. For instance, why she hadn't brought up the marriage agreement. For most women, it would have been the first thing they would mention, to be certain he hadn't changed his mind. A union in name only was perhaps the most desirable for a woman. In many ways, it was ideal for a man. Especially a man who had a mistress hidden away somewhere.

He had absolutely no desire for a wife, yet he had no mistress, either. He'd missed his calling; perhaps he should have become a monk. Brother Fletcher had a nice, safe ring to it.

As long as she didn't bring up the subject of marriage, he wouldn't. It gave him more time to decide what to do about her.

Through the glass partition, he studied the two women, neither of whom appeared older than sixteen, at best, although Emily was twice that. His gaze swung to the woman, Dinah.

He snorted a laugh. Woman, indeed. It was hard for him to call her that, for even in her camisole, she was, well, not very shapely. How he could feel anything toward her was a puzzle, for he'd never been drawn to a woman like this one. Though her hair was vibrant, redheads had never interested him. Their skin was usually red and blotchy, and they rarely had eyelashes. Dinah Odell's skin was pink and clear, and her eyes were rimmed with thick, russet lashes. But damn it, he liked a woman with curves, not one that was built like a jockey or a stable boy.

She floated to the surface of the water. Through the gauzy fabric of her drawers he could see the dark triangle at the juncture of her thighs. His groin tightened. A girl she was not, even if she didn't have the full breasts he usually liked in his women.

They'd arrived at the spa before he thought to ask her about her habit of hoarding food. It was a curious thing, although he was willing to let it go. However, Alice would not, so he'd better get an answer of some kind before they returned home.

Dinah stepped from the pool and briefly watched Emily work with the matron of the spa. With a look of confusion, Tristan studied her. She had curves, all right, and long, shapely legs. His mouth quirked into a sly smile as he remembered his brother's proclivity for derrieres. The few times they'd been together, they'd gotten to know one another's likes and dislikes well. His brother would like Nurse Odell's derriere. It was sweetly rounded, visible beneath the wet fabric that clung to her flesh. With a flash of surprising insight, he realized he didn't want to share this with anyone, not even his brother.

Reluctant to leave the warm, soothing water, Dinah sighed and glanced at the spa. Someone stood behind the glass partition and she instinctively knew it was Tristan. The air was cool, but a heat spread through her, sinking into her scalp. She wondered how long he'd been there, how long he'd been watching.

She'd been pleased to find him ready with the rig earlier in the morning, relieved that she didn't have to tackle the job herself. Not that she wouldn't have tried. Sweet Mary, she'd try anything once. Everything she'd done to this point was proof of that.

She didn't have clothing to swim in, but she couldn't ignore the warm spa water. During her incarceration, chilling ice-water baths had been weekly punishment. She'd taken sponge baths since she'd arrived at the ranch; a tub brought raw memories of things best forgotten.

When she saw the steam hovering over the warm spa, wild horses couldn't have kept her from it. Even without soap, the water was heavenly. And not to be held under until she lost consciousness was a sweet pleasure. These simple treats had become paramount to her.

Catching a glimpse of Tristan staring at her, she picked up her clothes, which she'd quickly dropped on the floor beside the spa earlier, and retreated to the safety of the dressing room. Once inside, she peeled off her wet drawers and camisole, studying herself in the small mirror that hung on the wall. Carefully undoing her breast wrap, she unwound it, uttering a sigh of relief when her breasts sprang free.

She supposed it was time to do away with the binder, but from the day Daisy had noticed her, she'd insisted Dinah wear it. One more thing to make her less attractive and less appealing to the guards. One more thing to keep them from harassing her. It had worked, but it was uncomfortable and oftentimes painful, especially at the time of her menses. Without it, however, she felt, well, vulnerable.

Wrinkling her nose, she picked up the soggy strip of fabric off the floor, deciding to dispense with it, at least until she could dry it out. She kicked at her other unmentionables, which were wet, too, of course.

She stepped into her dry petticoat, tied it at her waist, then pulled her dress on over her head. It felt different without the binder; she actually filled it out. Her nipples tightened, as if approving of the change. But it was odd, too, to have them loosely grazing the front of her bodice. And to be without her drawers was positively scandalous. A wicked, adventurous smile touched her lips.

After fluffing her curls to help them dry, she stuffed her wet things into the valise she'd brought for Emily, then waited for her in the changing room.

Tristan had become so distracted by the change in Dinah's bodice, he'd forgotten to grill her about the hoarding until they were nearly home. While Emily napped in the seat behind them, Tristan's gaze kept going to the front of Dinah's dress. He swallowed repeatedly when her nipples pebbled against the cloth. And her breasts moved when she did, affording him a view that warmed his already heated member.

He cursed his celibate state, sensing she would have no effect on him if he weren't living like a monk. No, the abstinent life was not for him, but breasts or not, she wasn't his type. Best get on with the business at hand and hope she'd forgotten about the marriage arrangement. He realized she'd be an unusual kind of woman if she had.

"Mrs. Linberg fears you don't enjoy her cooking."

Appearing surprised, Dinah swung toward him, as did her breasts. "But I do."

He cleared his throat, trying without success to keep his gaze above her neck. "She's found food in your room."

Dinah flushed. "Oh. Well, it's . . . it's just that I can't eat very much at one time. You see, um, that is, I was quite ill before I left the asylum, and my appetite was nearly gone." She gave him a tiny, apologetic smile. "I'm afraid my stomach sort of, well, shrunk."

He raised a doubting eyebrow, but said nothing. It was possible, he supposed. "Any time you're hungry, feel free to go to the kitchen and help yourself to whatever Mrs. Linberg has there. I'm sorry if that wasn't made clear to you."

She studied her hands, which were clasped in her lap. "Th . . . thank you. That's very kind."

He frowned again. Kind? "If you're hungry for something, Mrs. Linberg will fix it for you. That's one of her jobs, and she does it well. She's easily offended when someone appears unable to eat her cooking."

There was a strange plea in her eyes. He had to glance away.

"That's very nice of her. I'll remember that. Truly, she's a wonderful cook. I'm just not able to eat much at once. I'll explain that to her. I certainly wouldn't want to hurt her feelings."

They rode the rest of the way in silence, Tristan's mind whirling with the incongruities she presented, not the least of which was how she entered the changing room flat as a board, and emerged with a pair of perky, tantalizing breasts.

Trenway Asylum, Upstate New York

Martin Odell could feel the veins in his neck pop out. When he was angry, they strained at his skin, and at this moment, he was so angry his head was ready to explode.

When the matron from Trenway had sent word that they'd found a body locked in a metal box and that they feared it was his niece, he saw everything that he'd worked for threaten to go up in a plume of smoke.

One of the girls was already dead; he couldn't do a damned thing about that. Charlotte had been the weak one. Obviously, placing her in the asylum had been the wrong choice, but at the time, it had made sense. After all, she'd had those crazy fits. He shuddered, remembering how her eyes would roll back into her head and the spittle would collect in the corners of her mouth.

But the other one. He sneered. Now, that one deserved to be put away, if for no other reason than that she was too damned curious and she had a smart mouth. He couldn't afford to have her dead, though. Both girls dead would mean that his brother's money would go to the university. What a stupid-ass thing to do, bequeath one's entire wealth to furthering higher education if your children die. If something happened to his nieces, the money should go to him. It *should.* He deserved it. But, no. His brother was a fool, bestowing such wealth on pompous professors. What a waste! When word got out that the body at Trenway might be Dinah's, the board of regents contacted him, so eager to get their hands on the money that they nearly frothed at the mouth. Damned, lofty, high-brow frauds.

As he turned the corner en route to the morgue to identify the body, he was accosted by a thin, bespecktacled man with a bad complexion. A lawyer. A mealymouthed lawyer. Bastards. They were lying, stinking bastards, every last one of them. He could smell them a mile away, and they all smelled like a week-old weasel carcass on a hot, humid day.

"Mr. Odell?"

Martin sneered. Even the sound of the bastard's voice was shifty, dishonest.

"What do you want?" He kept on walking.

"I'm here about the will."

"What about it?" Martin was at the morgue entrance, but the weasel stepped in front of him, barring his way.

Martin had all he could do to keep himself from shoving the slimy piece of shit aside.

Not flustered by Martin's gruff behavior, the lawyer announced, "I understand that if the body is, indeed, your niece, Dinah Odell, the money from the trust automatically goes to the board of regents at the university. They are my clients, you know."

Martin saw his dreams of the good life dissipating before his eyes. As long as one of them was alive and without issue, he had control of the money until she reached twenty-two years of age. Keeping both girls locked away in the asylum assured him that neither would ever marry or live a normal life. Then he would have control of the money forever. "A stupid-ass stipulation, if you ask me."

"Stupid-ass though it might be," the attorney said, the vulgarism sounding ludicrous on his carefully cultured tongue, "I'm here to make sure of the outcome."

"Vultures." The word was spat with scorn. "You're vultures, every last one of you."

The lawyer refused to move. "I'm coming in with you, Mr. Odell, and we'll view the remains together."

Martin could feel the veins in his neck tighten. He had to relax. How in the hell could he enjoy his brother's money if he had a stroke?

He pushed past the vulture and entered the morgue. "Suit yourself."

The doctor in attendance greeted them with a toothy smile, one that indicated how much he enjoyed his work. The chief of police was also there; Martin had met him before. His name was Evans.

"Mr. Odell?" The doctor glanced at both men.

"Yes," Martin answered, trying to ignore the vulturine lawyer beside him. He nodded at Evans, who ambled toward them.

"You understand the seriousness of the situation, Mr. Odell."

Martin feigned despair. "I understand that beneath that sheet is a body that could very well be my dear, sweet niece."

"Ah, yes. You have my sympathy, of course."

Martin nodded and hung his head to show his grief.

"Come," the doctor said, rubbing his hands in anticipation. "The body is over here."

Martin held his breath between large gulps of foul-smelling air and followed the doctor to the table. A body lay on it, a shock of reddish hair protruding from beneath the sheet. Martin's stomach clenched with dread.

"Now, you must understand," the doctor began, his voice filled with excitement, "there has been a fair amount of decomposition."

"Get on with it." Martin's voice was abrupt. Impatient. Frustrated. Anxious. He was afraid of what he might find.

The lawyer inched toward the table, then took two steps back and leaned against a post, a handkerchief over his mouth.

The doctor whipped off the sheet.

Over and over again, Martin swallowed. Despite his nausea, he studied the victim. It was in vile condition.

"I'm afraid there was a small opening in the box. Barely big enough for a rodent or two to squeeze inside. That accounts for the condition of the face. Too bad, really," the doctor continued conversationally. "With the face gone, it'll be that much harder to make an identification."

In spite of the decay, Martin was sure the body wasn't Dinah's. He knew that wouldn't be enough, but a squiggle of hope, like a germ of wheat, sprouted in his chest.

"It's not my niece."

"How can you be so certain?" Evans and the doctor studied the body, and the lawyer inched toward them again, interested.

"The hair isn't the right color, and Dinah's is curly."

"Ah, but those things can change in death," the doctor stated.

Though the bones were not exposed, Martin's arm drifted toward the body, and he pointed to the forearm. "She broke that arm when she was a girl. Fell from a tree or something."

The doctor took an instrument and prodded the arm. "I'll check that."

Evans stepped away from the table, motioning Martin to follow. The lawyer took it as an invitation for himself as well. "Let's talk outside."

Martin breathed a sigh of relief. "Gladly."

They stepped into the corridor; Martin and the lawyer followed Evans upstairs to the office. Once he was seated, Martin discovered his hands and knees were shaking.

"Always a bad experience, Mr. Odell. I hope for your sake the body isn't your niece's, but if it isn't, then another question arises."

"What would that be?" The lawyer took out some papers and rifled through them.

"Who the hell are you?"

"I represent the university, Mr. Evans. If the body is Mr. Odell's niece, my clients, the regents, get the trust."

Ignoring him, Martin leaned forward and asked, "What question, Mr. Evans?" His facade was one of deep concern.

"The question of who, then, is on that table in the morgue, and why."

The doctor stepped into the room. Martin's pulse raced with anticipation.

"I checked the arm, radius and ulna, on both sides. No visible fractures."

Evans studied Martin, whose relief was real, if not for the right reason.

The vulturine lawyer cleared his throat. "You have

exactly six months to find your niece, Mr. Odell. If you can't locate her within that period of time, the trust automatically transfers to the university."

"There's another question, Mr. Odell."

Martin waited for the police chief to explain.

"If it isn't your niece on that table, where is she? And is she in any way responsible for the death of the woman we can't identify?"

"Are you insinuating that my niece might have murdered someone?" Murder. That would be perfect! He could have the chit put away forever. He squelched a nervous giggle.

"I found it!" Mrs. Linberg bustled into Tristan's study, holding the letter over her head. "Ya, I woke up last night and knew right where it was. Do you know where I'd put it?"

Hiding a smile, Tristan took the letter from her. "I can't imagine, Alice, but I knew it would come to you sooner or later."

She smacked the letter on the desktop. "It was in the bookshelf in the great room." She gave him an astounded look. "Can you imagine?" She turned and left the room, shaking her head.

Still smiling, he opened David's letter and scanned the contents, not at all surprised by what he found. Daisy Jenkins. The nurse David had hired for him was someone named Daisy Jenkins.

Tristan tapped the letter against his chin. How in the hell had Dinah Odell turned up on his doorstep instead?

He stood, shoving his chair back with such force it hit the wall. "Alice!"

He was at the door when the housekeeper appeared, her face a mask of worry.

"I'm going into Hatter's Horn to send a wire."

Tristan paced, hoping David had been home and was able to answer immediately. He pulled out his pocket watch. Two hours. It had been two hours since he'd returned to the ranch.

He was pouring himself a brandy when Alice knocked and opened the door.

"It's here," she announced, handing him the telegram.

He tossed down a gulp of brandy, ignoring the sting, and grabbed the paper. David wrote:

> Item in the *Times* says body found at Trenway Asylum not patient Dinah Odell STOP Guardian Martin Odell searching for escaped niece STOP Jenkins terminal with consumption maybe pressured patient to escape STOP Odell posted reward for niece's apprehension STOP Letter to follow STOP

Tristan sank into his chair by the fire. So the minx wasn't a nurse at all, but a patient. An escapee, at that. It was a frightening thought. Why wasn't he appalled?

Because she wasn't insane. Perhaps what she'd told him the day she arrived, about women being incarcerated for no reason at all, had more than a little truth to it.

He stared into the fire, frustrated because it would be weeks before David's letter of explanation would arrive.

Charlotte's beautiful strawberry blond hair floated around a face that had no features. But Dinah knew it was her sister. She cradled a baby in one arm, the other reached for Dinah, pleading for help, her beseeching voice coming from the obliterated face.

All at once, a man appeared, yanking the baby from Charlotte's arms. A mouth materialized on the faceless mask amidst her hair, screaming Dinah's name.

The man rushed at Dinah, shoving both her and the baby off a cliff. Dinah felt herself falling, frantic with fear because she couldn't reach the baby. They both tumbled into oblivion.

The sound of her own voice woke her with a start. She sat bolt upright and waited for her heart to stop pounding. She'd taken to sleeping with her light on; she hadn't gotten used to the dark yet, not since Trenway. Charlotte's diary lay on the bedside table.

Dinah sank into her pillows, unable to hold back her tears. Poor, darling Charlotte. Not a day went by that she didn't wonder what had really happened to her sweet, innocent sister. She carried around a load of guilt about that, too, because unlike their parents, Charlotte hadn't had a proper funeral. In fact, Dinah didn't know what had happened to her sister's remains.

She reached for the journal, knowing it was what had brought about the nightmare in the first place. Opening to the page that haunted her, she read it again. *He was here again today, my Teddy was, promising to take me away. To California.*

With a shaky sigh, she carefully closed the book and returned it to the table. What had she been thinking? Escaping to California to find the man responsible for Charlotte's death had been foolish. Futile. All it had done was get her away from Uncle Martin, which, of course, wasn't a bad thing. But how did one begin to look for a needle in a haystack?

Overhead, the ceiling creaked; she swore she heard footsteps. A shiver jolted her, and she huddled under her covers, clutching her furry bear to her chest.

She hid her bear safely away during the day, where no one would discover it, for she was ashamed that she needed its comfort. But when darkness came, and it was time for bed, Dinah dug it out from its hiding place and held it to her chest while she slept.

In the daytime, she called herself a childish numskull. The daylight made her brave. At night, all the names in the world didn't phase her, because night brought out Trenway's ghosts and goblins, and Dinah felt lucky if she could sleep at all.

6

DINAH SAW HER COMING BUT HAD NO TIME TO PREPARE. Emily pushed her, sending her sprawling to the floor, emitting a screeching sound that penetrated Dinah's eardrums as sharply as if it had been a needle.

Dinah lay there, trying to catch her breath. What in the devil had set her off? This sort of behavior hadn't happened since the day she'd arrived, three weeks before.

She struggled to sit, still fighting for breath. Her head pounded where it had hit the floor. Before she could get to her feet, Emily screamed again. Dinah looked up in time to see her coming toward her with something gripped in her fist.

"Emily!"

Tristan strode into the room, dragging his sister to him and wresting the object from her.

Dinah got to her feet, her head reeling.

"What in the hell happened here?"

Emily threw herself against Tristan's chest and sobbed.

"I'd tell you if I knew," Dinah answered, rubbing her rump.

He had one arm around his sister and the other stretched toward Dinah. "How did she get this?"

Dinah studied the weapon, a mother-of-pearl-handled letter opener. "I have no idea, but I'm grateful you came by when you did."

His gaze was piercing. "What sort of punishment do you intend to use?"

Dinah frowned. "Punishment?"

"Surely you won't let this go unpunished."

Dinah chewed her lower lip. "I can't punish her, Tristan. For all I know, I could have said or done something to set her off."

"How would they punish this kind of behavior at Trenway?"

One of Dinah's hands automatically went to her other wrist, and she massaged the skin, her memory vivid and chilling. "They would have . . . tied her to her bed and left her there for days, or . . . shackled her in a tub filled with ice water, then dunked her until she fainted."

Both forms of punishment Dinah had experienced first hand. Once when she'd admitted to another inmate's transgressions because she knew the woman wouldn't have survived the torture, and once when she'd tossed her plate of spoiled food against the wall.

Tristan's curse was like an angry hiss and although he embraced Emily, rocking rhythmically with her in his arms, his intense gaze was on Dinah, and she had the oddest feeling that he knew more about her than he let on. It was probably only her guilt, knocking hard at the door to her conscience.

Dinah's fourth week was almost over. Her month was nearly up. She'd worked hard at becoming indispensable, not only to Emily, but to Alice, too. It would be more difficult for Tristan to send her home if both women had come to rely on her, even in some small way.

Take today, for instance. Alice was in bed with a severe case of the gout. Her big toe had swollen to the size of a lemon and her foot couldn't bear weight. Dinah had insisted she stay in bed.

"But it's bread day," Alice had lamented.

Dinah had fluffed the pillow and straightened the bedding. "Leave the bread making to me."

The housekeeper had been incredulous. "You? You can bake bread?"

"Certainly. I've done it dozens of times before," Dinah had answered with a flourish. Well, she'd watched it being done that many times and more. Surely that accounted for something.

Now, enveloped in one of Alice's enormous aprons, she looked at the lumps of browned dough she'd removed from the oven, and her heart sank like a stone. They were the same size coming out as they'd been going in. They hadn't risen. Not even a smidgen.

With a knife, she sawed through the hard crust, only to discover that the insides were doughy. She glared at the four weighty blobs. Maybe they could use them as doorstops, she thought with a wry smile. Who would have thought it would be so difficult to make a simple loaf of bread?

Sighing, she tapped her lips with her finger. She had to do something. Get rid of the evidence, first of all, then somehow replace the bread.

Scooping the failed loaves into her apron, she crept from the house, looking carefully to make sure no one was around. Then she hurried across the yard. She stepped into the chicken coop. Chickens ate anything, didn't they? Her flypaper mind held on to that bit of information from somewhere. Even if they didn't, it was worth a try.

The pungent smell of chicken manure wafted through the air. A rooster swaggered about, stopping now and then to peck at the ground. Dinah dumped the doughy loaves onto the dirt-packed floor, one loaf tumbling into the recesses of the shed, then left.

On her return to the house, she lifted her nose and sniffed the air. Bread. Honest to goodness bread, certainly not lumps of baked stone. Following the smell, she discovered six loaves cooling near an open window of the foreman's cabin. His wife, a pretty Mexican woman—Dinah thought her name was Leeta or something like that—was weeding the vegetable garden.

Dinah turned in that direction. It was about time the two of them got better acquainted.

After graciously accepting two loaves of delicious bread and putting them in the kitchen, Dinah hauled the laundry out to the line and began hanging it. At least this was a chore she could handle without looking like an inept boob. She rather enjoyed it, too. With the wind on her face and in her hair, it was quite pleasant. The more she could be outside, the better she felt. Small, tight places, sometimes even big rooms, continued to distress her.

Glancing toward the road, she saw Lucas, the foreman, talking with a peddler. They both watched her work, so she smiled and waved. Lucas returned the greeting. With a sense of worth, she finished her chore and returned to the house, anxious to prepare dinner.

David's letter finally arrived. Tristan finished reading it and stuffed it into his pocket, then mounted his Arab and headed for home.

The letter had explained a lot. Having influence at the asylum because of the paper he was writing on his work with the insane, David gave Tristan information about Dinah's sister, Charlotte, Martin Odell, the trust fund and the death of Daisy Jenkins, which had yet to be fully explained.

From the letter, Tristan decided that Martin Odell was a dirty bastard. What decent man could incarcerate a perfectly sane woman, merely because he wanted control of her money? It was reprehensible. Criminal. Not only had Odell offered a reward for Dinah's return, but he was assisting the police in their search so they could talk with her about Daisy's death. At this point Dinah wasn't suspected of murder, but there were numerous unanswered questions, one of which was how Daisy Jenkins ended up in the punishment box in the first place.

The police, he discovered through David's missive, didn't feel Martin Odell had committed a crime. Incarceration was a family's prerogative. And doctors could be bribed to diagnose insanity where none existed.

David's fury was palpable on the pages of the letter, and Tristan knew that if anyone could help bring mental health out of the dark ages, it was David Richards.

The day Dinah had arrived, when she hadn't known he was behind her in her room, she'd mumbled the name Daisy. She'd said it with a certain amount of despair. He didn't believe for a minute that Dinah had killed Daisy Jenkins, but he was very curious to know what exactly had happened.

Intrepid little Dinah. Since discovering who she was, he'd taken to watching her more carefully. For someone who had been incarcerated for a year, she was surprisingly strong and confident. She was quick to laugh and prompt to help. Now and then he caught a sadness in her eyes, and he wondered what she was thinking, but it was quickly gone, replaced by a laugh or a smile or a humorous story about her Norwegian relatives.

But he'd been inside Trenway. Could she have escaped unscathed? Even if he hadn't been allowed to see the worst of the place, what he had seen was bad enough. Although Dinah hadn't been there when he'd visited, for his visits had been two years before, he wondered how a sane woman could stay that way once inside asylum walls. She would have to be remarkably strong. He wondered if Dinah's strength went deep, or if it was only a facade.

Over the past few weeks, he'd discovered what she was doing. She was trying valiantly to become so helpful that if and when he found out the truth, he'd be hard-pressed to send her packing. She'd had it planned from the beginning, he was certain. The deception should have bothered him; it didn't.

He dismounted and led his horse to the barn. Lucas was there, shoveling out the stalls. He grinned as Tristan entered.

"Saw your little nurse out talking to Leeta earlier. Seems they're finally getting to know one another."

Tristan was about to tend to his horse when Miguel took the reins and led him into a clean stall.

"How's that arm, Miguel?"

The boy grinned and wiggled his wrist. "I gotta work it to make it as strong as it was before."

Tristan returned the smile. "Smart boy."

Leaning on the shovel, Lucas watched Miguel disappear. "He's already talking about playing kick ball when the children arrive. Leeta's afraid he'll hurt his arm again. I told her we can't wrap the boy in cotton. Maybe Dinah has some suggestions. Have you told her about the children yet?"

Tristan kept Dinah's true identity to himself. "She'll find out about them soon enough. They'll be here from school tomorrow." He wondered what sort of sound advice she'd give Lucas regarding Miguel's mending arm. He had an odd feeling that she'd probably come up with a satisfactory solution. She hadn't dug herself a hole too big to get out of, yet.

Lucas continued his chore, but began to chortle like an idiot.

"What's so damned funny?" Tristan pushed a dipper into a pail of water, pulled it out, and drank.

"Is Alice sick today?" Lucas asked around a laugh.

Tristan nodded. "She's in bed with a bad case of the gout."

"Well, I'm not saying your nurse had ulterior motives

for getting to know my wife, but Leeta did give her a couple of loaves of bread."

"What's wrong with that? Next to Alice, Leeta makes the best bread this side of the Canadian border."

Lucas continued to chuckle. "I'd take a gander in the chicken coop, if I were you."

Curious, Tristan left the barn and crossed to the coop. Stepping inside, his gaze went to the ground, on which lay three brown lumps. With a puzzled frown, he squatted and brought one to his nose. Bread? Or, at least something that passed for bread. A smile tugged at the corners of his mouth.

His smile lingered as he got to his feet, but a strange squawking noise drew him deeper into the coop. From a dimly lit corner, his rooster peered up at him, clucking frantically. One of his feet was stuck in bread dough all the way up to his spur.

After reading over David's letter for the third time, Tristan knew he had to mention the part of the bargain to which neither he nor Dinah had referred. The contractual marriage. Now he wondered if Dinah was even aware of it.

Lucas had been right. It had been an insane offer in the first place. He'd been willing to sacrifice his freedom for a few years to find a pleasant, compassionate companion for Emily. David had assured him that Daisy Jenkins was such a person. All right, so he hadn't put much emotional thought into the plan, but marriages were contracted all the time for a multitude of reasons. He didn't think his was any crazier than most.

He felt a twist of guilt, however. In his perfect plan, the woman with whom he had envisioned this agreement bore no resemblance to Dinah Odell. The woman he'd imagined would have found the marriage a benign, agreeable interlude until it was over. He'd imagined this woman floating soundlessly through his house, disrupting nothing and no one, especially him. She would take care of Emily's needs, rock beside the fire, knitting blankets or stockings or sweaters, until it was time for bed. Then she would flutter up the stairs to her room and leave him to his own devices, happy to do so. That was as much of her as he'd wanted to see.

She would not have wanted to share a bed, and he would have happily found his pleasures elsewhere. No one expected a man to be celibate for five years.

Surely there were women in the world who were amiable and would have agreed to such an offer. Not that Dinah Odell would want him in her bed. Hell, she might well be traumatized by the idea of it. But she had no demure qualities. She couldn't pass through a room without drawing attention to herself, for even if she didn't speak, and she usually did, she was too pretty and vivacious to ignore. Sometimes she literally vibrated with energy.

He couldn't imagine her being still long enough to knit anything, although there had been times when he feared that if she'd had a set of knitting needles in her possession, she would use them as a weapon against him. He'd seen only traces of her temper, but he sensed it would be formidable if she were provoked.

Time was of the essence. For all Tristan knew, Martin Odell could be close on her heels. This union would be temporary. He could get it annulled, for he had no intention of sleeping with her. He could ignore the fact that he was drawn to her and had been since the first night she had been here. He wasn't an animal, he was a gentleman, and although she was not the recipient of his initial offer, he would not go back on his word.

If she balked at marrying him, he would use Emily to blackmail her. Hell, she could do far worse. There wasn't a single woman around who wouldn't jump at the chance to become his wife, and most of them would gladly share his bed.

For the first time since he'd drawn up the plan, he became uncertain of its merits or its sanity. The one thing that kept him from chucking it was that he knew that by having his name, Dinah Odell would be spared immediate action by her uncle.

And why not marry her? She was by far the most interesting and intriguing woman he'd met in years. Maybe his life.

There was another thought that rattled around in his brain. It had to do with ownership and possession. He refused to allow it to take root, but he couldn't get rid of it, either.

From everything he'd read about Martin Odell in David's letter, Tristan knew he was a threat to Dinah. He didn't know the precise contents of her father's will, but it was obvious that Odell wanted the trust at any cost. Clearly, having Dinah carefully put away somewhere under lock and key enabled him to do that. David had indicated that Martin Odell couldn't afford to have her free to make choices.

Now, as Tristan sat in front of the fire in the great room, the dogs curled up beside his chair, he decided it was time to approach the subject they had both avoided. With any other woman, he could have thought it out reasonably. Mentioned the subject with ease. With Dinah, however, nothing was ever reasonable. Or easy.

She entered, wiping her hands on Alice's apron. Her cheeks were flushed and her eyes were bright with lingering enthusiasm. At the moment, she looked like a girl playing dress-up in her mother's kitchen clothes. Even so, he found himself disarmed.

"I'm glad you're here." He gestured toward the opposite chair. "Have a seat. I want to talk to you."

Dinah frowned, not liking his tone. It was so authoritative. Inhaling sharply, she brought her fingers to her mouth. Sweet Mary, he'd discovered the bread! She shouldn't have dumped it in the chicken coop. She should have buried it. Oh, why hadn't she taken the time to bury the disaster?

Or maybe, she thought, her stomach making a fist, it was something else. Maybe he was throwing her out.

"It hasn't been a month, Tristan. You . . . you can't make your final decision yet."

He smiled. Faintly. "I realize that. In fact, I'm wondering if you're ready to fulfill the rest of your contract."

Amy, the female wolfhound, had risen when Dinah entered and had sauntered to her chair. Dinah had been scratching the dog's ears, but the minute she heard Tristan's words, her fingers stopped. Calm yourself.

"The rest of the contract?"

At his terse nod, she bit down on her lower lip and frowned again. She hadn't been aware of anything else. And she'd read the letter over so many times, she knew every word by heart. Daisy hadn't mentioned any further responsibilities on her part, either. Of course, Daisy had been so ill, it might have slipped her mind.

Dinah desperately wanted to stay. In spite of the problems Emily occasionally caused her, she could cope with them. The woman was no longer pinching her, and it had been a while since she'd attacked her. The situation was better than any alternative she could think of.

Also, much to her dismay, she'd grown very fond of Tristan. Oh, he was a brooding sort of man for the most part, but when she was able to make him smile, even laugh, something touched her heart, and she knew she could easily fall in love with him. The fact that he was so devoted to his sister that he wouldn't consider putting her into an asylum was reason enough. But there were a whole passle of other reasons, all physical, all of which took her breath away.

And last, but certainly not least, Dinah was afraid to return to New York. Not only because Uncle Martin would toss her into Trenway again, but because she was worried about whether anyone had ever found the body in the punishment box. If they had, and knew it was

Daisy, would they then come after her? For all she knew, she could be hunted down for murder. She hadn't allowed herself to think about the consequences of her actions, but if someone came and hauled her away, she'd go kicking and screaming.

There wasn't a soul who knew about her and Daisy's switch but the two of them, and Daisy was dead. Who would believe her? No, she wouldn't return to New York. She'd book passage to China, first. If she had any money.

Tristan's look was quizzical. "You don't remember the contingency?"

"What? Oh," she answered nodding expansively. "The contingency. Of course. Yes, of course. The contingency. I was . . . um . . . waiting for you to bring it up."

He slapped his knee. "All right. It's settled then. We'll get the paperwork done and the vows will be exchanged a week from Sunday."

Attempting to conceal her astonishment, she merely sat and stared at him, blinking erratically. "Vows?"

"Why, yes."

"You . . . you mean in order to stay, I . . . I have to become a nun?"

He threw his head back and laughed, startling the dogs, who obviously had rarely heard such sounds from their master. Tristan's laughter tunneled deep into Dinah's fragile heart.

He wiped his eyes with a handkerchief. "No, Dinah Odell, in order to stay, you have to become my wife."

Dinah's heart thumped so hard she feared it would ooze out her ears. "Your wife?"

He raised an eyebrow. "It was part of the agreement. Surely you remember."

"Well, I . . ." She swallowed. "Refresh my memory." Oh, that made her sound terribly bright, didn't it?

"You don't remember?"

She didn't like the sly look in his eyes. "Of course I do. I just want to make certain *you* do. How do I know you won't make up something outrageous?"

A smile hovered on his lips. "Do you want me to repeat it, word for word?"

She primly straightened her gown, hoping he didn't notice that her pounding heart caused her entire body to vibrate. "I most certainly do."

He recited the agreement, including the part about the marriage, and the money.

She attempted to hide her feelings but her brain spun with questions. He'd been willing to marry any woman, sight unseen, and because of Dr. Richards's high praise, Daisy had been the chosen one.

She pinched the bridge of her nose. How in the bloody hell would she get out of this one? If what he told her was true, she knew why Daisy hadn't mentioned it to her. She was stubborn enough to rebel, even if it had meant giving up her chance for freedom.

He rose, as did the dogs. He ordered them to stay. "Now that your memory is refreshened, I can assume the matter is settled."

Settled? *Settled?* Everything was about as settled as a Swedish housewife's fat rump atop a galloping horse. But to act surprised would seal her doom. Surely there was time to think about this.

After he'd gone, she stared into the fire. One of the dogs rested its head in her lap, and she stroked it automatically. Marriage. To Tristan Fletcher. Her first instinct had been to tell him she'd marry whom she pleased when she pleased.

This deception was getting her in deeper and deeper. One day, if she wasn't careful, it would bury her. She ran a nervous finger between the neck of her gown and her throat, feeling a frantic sense of suffocation. Maybe it was the rope of her own deceit tightening around her neck.

The shock she'd first felt at his news had slowly turned to guilt. If she went through with it, she would be marrying him under false pretenses. How could she do that and still look him in the eye?

She sighed. Amy, who had become her constant companion, nuzzled closer, a gentle paw scratching at her gown. Dinah resumed her ministrations on the hound's ears. Amy's big, limpid eyes were trained on her.

"But, how can I tell him the truth? I can't," she answered herself. "I can't."

Each of Amy's eyebrows wiggled in turn, as if she were mulling over an answer.

If Dinah told him the truth, he'd send her away. Book her return passage to New York. He wasn't a man to trifle with. She remembered his moody anger the day she'd arrived. Even then, she'd wondered what he would do if he ever discovered she'd lied to him. In all honesty, she didn't want to find out.

But if he did find out, he'd want a real nurse, and who could blame him? He'd want one qualified to care for Emily. She grimaced. Not someone who'd bumbled her way through a month, somehow not making things worse in spite of her ignorance.

But that wasn't her only problem. Thoughts of good old Uncle Martin always popped out of a box like some big, ugly, hairy-faced opossum when she felt threatened.

She rested her head on the hound's neck, finding odd comfort in the contact. In spite of the many reasons there were not to go through with the foolish sham of a marriage, she knew she would. She knew it would give her a bit of leverage against Uncle Martin, even if it was in name only. Perhaps she was thinking of herself, but if she didn't, who would?

But she would tell Tristan the truth. Eventually. When the time was right. When people flew to the moon. She massaged the knot in her neck and gave herself a disparaging smile. No, she'd have to tell him before that.

That settled, she assumed the twisting ropes in her stomach would disappear. They didn't, for new thoughts bombarded her, making her frantic with worry and anticipation. Thoughts of marriage. Of weddings.

She trudged up the stairs to her room, her feelings at

war inside her. In the days before Trenway, she would have found relaxation in a warm tub of water. Now, she couldn't bear the thought of sitting in one. It could have been filled with fragrant toilet water and bubbles, but Dinah knew her only thoughts would be of shackles and drowning.

After her first week here, Alice had filled the tub for her, insisting she use it. Dinah knew Alice meant to be kind, and before Trenway, she would have wallowed in it. Before Trenway, she would have fallen asleep in it, reluctant to get out even when the water got cold. But of course, before Trenway, she wouldn't have had nightmares about someone holding her head under water until she gasped for breath, inhaling the water as if it were air.

She coughed, an automatic gesture whenever she was forced to think about her losing battle with the bathtub. After she undressed, she poured water from the teakettle Alice had left for her into the basin and sponged herself off.

She rescued her bear from its hiding place in the folds of one of Daisy's old petticoats, turned the lamp down slightly, then slid into bed. Once there, she raised her eyes to the ceiling and pondered her fate. It wasn't long before she no longer thought about herself, but concentrated on the noise above her.

She caught her breath, pressing her bear to her chest to still her heart. Something or someone was in the attic; she was certain of it. She'd been hearing the same noises for weeks.

Her heart continued to clatter as she listened. Rarely did she hear the sounds during the day, for if she had, she might have gotten up the nerve to go up there and find out for herself. Maybe. Then again, maybe not.

At Trenway, there were dark, dank corners in abundance. Cruel guards threatened to lock the women in rooms without windows. And they weren't always threats. Once, before Daisy intervened, Dinah had found herself in such a room. Black as a witch's heart. Moist as the devil's handshake. The only sounds had been her pulse pounding in her head, her breathing, and something scurrying across the floor.

To this day she shuddered and the hair on her arms and legs prickled when she saw a mouse. That the scurrying in that darkened room had not been a furry little mouse but its larger, more evil cousin, was something she refused to think about.

That was why now, though the scuffing noise from the attic continued, Dinah listened but did nothing to allay her fears. It was best not to wake the snakes. Better the devil you know than the devil you don't.

7

STANDING IN HER UNMENTIONABLES, DINAH WATCHED ALICE study the meager contents of her wardrobe. "This is it? These are the only gowns you brought with you?"

Yes, Dinah thought, and even at that, none of them were hers. She often wondered if Uncle Martin had gotten rid of all of her beautiful dresses. She would have sold her soul for even one of them at this moment. She had nothing to get married in that wasn't dark, dull, and dingy.

"I'm afraid that's what I could manage, Alice."

The housekeeper clucked her tongue. *"Uff dah.* If you knew there was a chance you would be married, why didn't you bring an appropriate gown?"

Dinah couldn't lie. She'd stretched the truth so many times she was certain her nose was growing. "I'm afraid I was so eager to leave that dreadful asylum, I didn't think about my clothing."

Alice looked her up and down. "You and Emily are

about the same size. I'm sure she has something more appropriate. I'll go check." She turned to leave.

"Alice?" Emily was in the midst of a terrible depression. She was mildly depressed much of the time, but on occasion she was too distraught to reason with. Tristan had told Dinah that these deep depressions occurred almost monthly and lasted for days, sometimes a week. During that time, she refused to dress and ate only when forced to. Dinah wondered if this bout of depression had been initiated by her pending marriage to Tristan.

"Yes, dear?"

"Alice, ask her first, please."

"Ask her? Ask her what?"

Dinah sighed. "Don't go in and take whatever you think I might be able to wear. Please. Ask Emily if she has a gown I can borrow for the day."

Alice paused. "Well, then maybe you should ask her yourself."

"You're right. It should be up to me." Dinah slipped into her long white robe and went across the hall to Emily's room. She knocked on the door, not expecting an answer and not getting one. Bracing herself, she turned the knob, opened the door, and stepped inside. Emily was in her nightclothes, staring outside.

The room was lovely. A perfect pink and white coverlet lay across the bed, one that matched the ruffle that edged the canopy above it. Youthful touches were everywhere. That's what struck Dinah as strange. Emily was not a teenager, although her room had the appearance of belonging to one.

"Emily?" When she got no response, she went to her, going down on her knees. Emily appeared so ageless. It was obvious that she wasn't a girl, but she had none of the harsh, cruel qualities that often followed a woman as she aged, even if the woman had been gently raised.

Tears tracked Emily's cheeks, sending a rush of pity into Dinah's chest.

"Emily, I need your help."

The woman didn't respond.

"Emily, are you upset that your brother is getting married?" Still no response. "It doesn't mean anything will change, you understand that, don't you?"

Tears dripped from Emily's chin onto her bed jacket.

Taking a shuddering breath, Dinah swiped at her own tears of sympathy. "Alice thinks my dresses are too ugly to get married in. The problem is," she added, sitting on the floor cross-legged, "I didn't bring any others with me. She thought that maybe you had a dress I might borrow for the day."

Emily's bottom lip quivered, but she didn't answer.

Dinah opted for a different tactic. "Did I ever tell you about my Uncle Engvald?"

Emily sighed.

Undaunted, Dinah went on. "Uncle Engvald liked liquor and he fancied himself a sort of ladies' man. He dressed in his Sunday best and took strolls in the park, hoping to meet a companion for the evening." She wiggled her eyebrows, eliciting the briefest of smiles from Emily's tear-dampened lips.

"He was married three times. The problem was, he never divorced any of the women, so by law he was a bigamist, but he didn't give a diddly about that. That doesn't have anything to do with the story. I thought you might find it interesting." She got comfortable on the floor.

"As I said, he loved his whiskey. I swear to you he smelled like an Irish distillery most of the time. I think the stuff oozed out from his pores."

She got onto her knees and wiped Emily's chin with her handkerchief. "One night, as usual, he was drunk as a one-eyed sailor with a wooden leg, and he heard a noise outside by his barn." Her eyes shifted dramatically around the room.

"He peered out the window, and Lord love a bloody

duck, he saw a bear by the barn, ready to attack his horses!"

Dinah's hand went to her chest. "He took his rifle and stumbled outside, sneaked up on the beast, and shot him. Dead as a tree stump. In spite of his drunken condition, he was an amazingly good shot," she added. "He congratulated himself, staggered into the house and poured himself another glass of whiskey."

She shook her head and sighed. "It wasn't until the next morning that he realized he'd mistaken one of his own cows for a bear and had shot the poor beast right between the eyes."

Emily looked at her and actually smiled. "That can't be a true story."

Dinah made a cross over her heart. "I swear it's true." And it was. All of her stories were true, they just weren't her stories. They were usually Daisy's. Except for Uncle Martin, Dinah had no one left. Daisy had kept her sane for countless hours, entertaining her with tales of her bizarre kinfolk.

Dinah put her hand on Emily's. "I'd really like you to do me a favor."

Emily's gaze went to her wardrobe, which literally bulged with gowns.

"No, it's not that. If you don't want me to wear one of your gowns, that's fine. It was Alice's idea, anyway."

Emily appeared ready to speak, but Dinah shook her head. "Listen to me, first. What I'd like more than anything in this world is for you to paint me a picture of Tristan."

"Tristan?"

Smiling, Dinah nodded. She really did want one. It would be something she could take with her when he discovered she'd lied to him. "Would you mind?"

Emily's face relaxed, and she returned Dinah's smile. "I'd like that."

"But we'd have to keep it a secret. I want it to be a

surprise. Do you think you can paint him from memory?"

Emily leaned into her chair, her tension appearing to subside. "I could paint a picture of Tristan with my eyes closed."

"Well, fortunately that won't be necessary," Dinah answered with a wry smile. "Do you need anything? Any supplies?"

"No." Emily rose from the chair and crossed to her wardrobe. "I have everything I need, including a canvas." She yanked on the doors, opening them to reveal her gowns. "Please, Dinah, take one of my dresses."

Truly touched by Emily's generosity, Dinah could only gasp. Even her own closet at home in New York hadn't contained so many clothes. "I wouldn't know where to begin," she murmured. "You choose one for me."

Emily rifled through the gowns, pulling out three, then laying them across her bed. "I think one of these would be fine."

Alice stuck her head around the door. "Oh, good. Emily, honey, I have fresh cinnamon bread. It's still warm. Why don't you come down and have a bite to eat?"

Dinah and Alice exchanged glances, for Emily had eaten very little the past few days. Dinah held her breath.

Emily faltered, her face going through many expressions. "I guess I am a bit hungry."

Alice nodded, sagging with relief. "Good." She took Emily's arm and led her from the room.

Dinah turned to the gowns on the bed. They were all lovely frothy things. She shrugged out of her robe, standing before the long cheval glass in her camisole and drawers. And, she thought, twisting uncomfortably, her breast binder. She realized she no longer needed it, but it was a hard habit to break. It made her feel safe, from what, she couldn't say.

But, she didn't want to get married in one. She

removed her camisole and studied her flattened chest. The binder covered her completely except for two small swells above the device where her breasts refused to be squashed.

She wiggled around, trying to make it more comfortable, then gave up.

"Sweet mother of God!"

Dinah turned at the sound of Tristan's voice and crossed her arms over her chest. She stared at him, speechless.

He strode into the room. "What in the hell is that contraption?"

She continued to stare, her eyes wide, her throat dry. She still couldn't speak.

He studied her, mouthing a curse. "What is it?"

She swallowed. "It's . . . it's a binder."

"Why in the devil are you wearing it?"

His anger was so palpable she moved toward the chair where she'd dropped her robe.

"Well?"

She wondered why he thought he had a right to know, then realized that perhaps he did. After all, she'd foolishly agreed to become his wife, whether it was in name only didn't matter. She would become his property. That thought rankled, too. She wondered why men always made the rules.

"I . . . got used to wearing it at Trenway. A lot of the nurses did," she added hastily.

"Why?" The word came out a snarl.

Her mouth worked wildly before she spoke. "Because we didn't want the guards to notice us."

Some emotion in his face changed. He stood before her, long legs wide and fists on hips. "Remove it."

Relief made her sigh. "I will. Truly, I will." She shrugged into her robe.

"Now."

Her movements stopped mid air. "Excuse me?"

"Remove it now."

Her eyes widened further. "Now? With . . . with you standing there?"

He moved closer. "I think I have the right to watch, don't you?"

"Maybe after tomorrow, after we're married, but . . . but certainly not today." Her heart was stammering, seeming to lurch and stop at will.

He moved closer. "Remove it now, or I'll remove it for you."

She balked. Oh, but she hated being threatened. She'd had enough of it to last her a lifetime. "Then go right ahead, you bloody barbarian. But hear this. If you put one hand on me you'll be no better than the Huns who strutted the halls of Trenway." She thrust her stubborn chin in his direction, daring him to do it, knowing he wouldn't because he was too much of a gentleman.

One satanic brow lifted and he reached for her.

Shocked, she gasped and stepped away. "You wouldn't!"

"I would and I will. I have a right to see what I'm getting." His voice was deadly calm, assuring her that he meant business.

She felt a burst of panic and grasped for the first threat that came to her mind. "If you so much as touch me, your doodle will fall off."

He stopped, snorting an involuntary laugh. "My *what?*"

She had her fist clenched, ready to punch him. "You know what I mean."

"I don't." He didn't move. "Explain it to me." His voice was smooth as a duck's wake.

She wanted to warn him that if he touched her she'd hit him, but what good did it do to take a swing at someone if he knew it was coming?

She stared into his eyes, noting a tenderness she'd never seen before. "If . . . if I have to explain it to you, then you're a bigger dolt than I thought."

His grin was wide, not quite intimate but not sarcastic,

either. It should have pleased her that she was able to make him smile. It had been one of her goals. Amidst all of her other worries, it now seemed trivial.

He pulled her to him, holding her waist with one hand while he removed her binder with the other. Her fist opened, her arm falling to her side as her breasts tingled. Her nipples were hard before the wrapper hit the floor.

Her breeding and good sense told her what he was doing was indecent. Her pounding heart reminded her that, fool though she was, she wanted to please him.

He slipped her robe down her arms. Letting it slide to the floor behind her, Dinah stood proudly, although she was completely unaccustomed to baring herself, wantonly or otherwise. Her nerves jangled like a jailer's keys.

Tristan's fingers moved to the pulse that fluttered at her throat. Her entire body tingled at his touch, even in places that had never tingled before.

"To allow you to keep yourself bound up like a trussed turkey would make me a bigger dolt, Dinah." He bent and pressed a light kiss at her neck. For some reason, her knees went weak and she shivered.

He raised his head, his eyes dark and languid, then he lowered his mouth to hers.

On a sharp intake of breath, Dinah felt the touch. With open lips, he rubbed back and forth across hers, his breath warm. He nibbled. He nipped. Until Dinah opened for him.

He dove inside, searching for her tongue, his kisses wet and insistent. She was faint with exquisite new feelings. Flinging her arms around his neck, she pressed closer, but his hands spanned her ribcage, drawing her away just far enough so he could nudge her nipples with his thumbs.

Sensation skittered through her like water droplets on a hot skillet.

His hands cupped her breasts and he fondled them. He lifted his mouth from hers, bent, and ran his tongue first over one nipple then the other. Gasping in surprise, she felt a burning pressure low in her pelvis.

Then he released her.

Although she was breathing hard, he appeared calm. In control.

"You will never wear that damned contrivance again. Is that understood?"

Fighting through her sensual haze, she bristled. "No one, not even my future husband, or whatever the bloody hell you're supposed to be, orders me to do anything. I'll wear it if I please."

"If I find you wearing it, I'll strip you and remove it."

She thrust her chin at him. "If you do, I'll put it on again. And . . . and I'll punch you in the stomach."

One side of his mouth lifted into a smile. "Thank you for the warning, but if you put it on again, I'll just have to remove it. Again."

Dinah realized this was like a game, and much to her surprise, she was a willing participant. "Then I'll—"

"Be careful, Dinah." He shook his finger at her. "Rousing verbal exchanges between husband and wife can lead to delightful tussles in the bedchamber."

Thoughts of beds and bedchambers and dark, intimate nights sent wild sensations scampering over her skin. Dredging up her anger, she threw him a deadly glance and bent to retrieve her robe.

"They are exquisite."

She stood hastily, her breasts jiggling from the movement.

"It's criminal to flatten them with anything but your lover's hands," he remarked lazily.

Heat flooded her face as she scrambled into her robe. "I hope you've had a good, hard look, Tristan Fletcher, because it's the last one you'll get."

"Don't be childish, Dinah." His liquid, arrogant stare heated her blood. "Not only will I see them whenever I want, I'll touch them"—He took a step toward her, reached beneath her robe and cupped one—" whenever and wherever I want."

She swallowed hard, attempting without success to ignore what he was doing to her. "Are you changing the rules?"

His hands rested on her hips. "Rules?"

"In the agreement, you promised to be a gentleman and not touch me." She was amazed that she could sound so rational when acrobats did tumbles in her stomach.

He dropped his arms to his sides. A dry smile touched his lips, his eyes were cold. "My apologies. I'll remember that I'm to find my pleasure elsewhere from now on."

He strode from the room, leaving her angry and confused and aching with desire. She slumped onto the bed and scowled, biting back a frustrated scream. If he would leave her alone, she could get through this. If he didn't, well, she didn't know what she'd do. All she knew for certain was that his touch did something to her that she'd never felt before. The worst part was, she'd enjoyed it.

Tristan bolted for the brandy the moment he got to his study. What had gotten into him? He poured himself a drink, noting that his hands shook.

Hell, he knew. He'd been so shocked to see what she'd done to herself, he'd nearly gone crazy. Breast binder. He swore again. He didn't care if this marriage was a sham, no wife of his would wear such a stupid, inane device.

He flung himself into his chair and took a healthy swig of liquor, holding it in his mouth until the insides of his cheeks stung.

Trenway. She'd worn the binder to keep the guards at the asylum from noticing her. Accosting her. A physical anger twisted at his guts, and he sucked in a painful breath of air. Thoughts of anyone touching her made him ill. Images of what some lust-filled guards could have done to her tore at him, leaving him in agony about things he could only imagine. His shame deepened when he realized he was no better than they.

Scowling into his drink, he swore. When he had first seen her breasts, he had wanted to change the rules. He'd silently vowed to take her on their wedding night, make her his wife in every way. His body had ruled. He'd lived like a monk for long enough, damn it, and a wife was the perfect receptacle for his lust.

He finished his brandy, then ground the balls of his thumbs into his eyes. He couldn't do that. If she'd had to fight off the unwanted advances of asylum guards, she was probably traumatized. What was wrong with him? He'd promised not to touch her, and he had to keep his word. His father had told him it was the most important thing a man had.

Once Martin Odell was no longer a threat to Dinah, Tristan vowed again that he would have the marriage annulled so she would be free to make her own choices.

He dropped his arm, allowing the snifter to dangle from his fingers. He swung it rhythmically. Why did he care what happened to Dinah Odell, anyway? He barely knew her.

With a heavy sigh, he closed his eyes. Yes, he barely knew her, but he couldn't tolerate men who preyed on women, and Martin Odell was preying on Dinah like a vulture on carrion.

He enjoyed thwarting men like Odell. Maybe that was the reason he was willing to go through with this. Perhaps it had nothing at all to do with Dinah and everything to do with her uncle.

Real marriage was a foolish trap, anyway. He hadn't known one union that was happy. Well, he amended, Lucas appeared to be. And, of course, Wolf and Julia were happy. But they were the exception, not the rule. It was far better to arrange a marriage that he could control than to have one that would control him.

The vision of Dinah, bare to the waist, floated before

him and he growled. On paper, everything had seemed perfect. Had Daisy Jenkins showed up instead of Dinah, Tristan was certain everything would have gone according to plan.

But this could work. He had to get control of his hunger, that's all. He'd deserved her angry words. He was horny. It was time to find a good, loud mistress.

The idea made perfect sense. He was angry and surprised that it left him cold.

8

THE DAY OF THE WEDDING DAWNED SUNNY AND WARM, AS usual. Not since the day Dinah arrived had there been another storm. Hardly a cloud had marred the perfect clarity of the blue sky. At any other time, she would have imagined it was an omen of good things to come.

At any other time.

The good thing was that Emily's mood had begun to lift again, slowly. Her depression seemed to come and go in cycles. She was on the upswing again.

The bad thing was Tristan. Since stripping her of her binder, and doing all of those other things to her, he'd made himself scarce. For that she was relieved, wasn't she? In the quiet recesses of her mind, she wondered what she wanted from him. What to expect from him.

Before she got too involved, conjuring up daydreams that wouldn't happen, she'd do well to remember that he had offered marriage to a woman he didn't even know.

He was only marrying her because he thought she was that woman.

She could never be like Daisy Jenkins. Daisy had been a saint. Tristan would have been lucky if Daisy had become his wife. Daisy was sweet, and honest, and good. Dinah was not. She was a liar and a coward, unable to tell him the truth about who and what she was.

"There you are. *Uff dah,* but there's work to do today." Alice bustled into the room, set the teakettle on the dry sink, then started straightening Dinah's bedding. Dinah joined her.

"Don't you find it odd that Tristan would offer to marry a total stranger, Alice? Even if it would benefit Emily?"

Alice squared the corners of the bedding. "Not so odd. Tristan's given up on marrying for love, I think."

An unpleasant feeling attacked Dinah's stomach. "What happened to make him feel that way?"

"He was engaged to be married once before." She tested the water in the pitcher on the dry sink, then poured it into the basin, adding hot water from the kettle. She stood back and frowned. "I don't see why you won't let me fill the tub for you. There's plenty of time for a bath, dear."

Panic at the mere thought of sitting in a tub was enough to remind Dinah that she wasn't ready to try it. She had enough to cope with today without adding that. "No, don't bother, Alice. This will be fine. Really."

She couldn't get Tristan and his other love out of her head. "Who was he engaged to?"

Alice returned to the bed and fluffed Dinah's pillows. "Some rich girl from Boston. He came home one summer, all excited and in love. Poor boy, after his papa died, he didn't get much loving from his mother. I don't want to stir up Zelda Fletcher's ghost, but she never did like Tristan."

Dinah was astonished. "But, she was his mother."

Alice made a grumbling sound. "In name only."

"What do you mean?"

Alice stopped working and sighed. "I think that's something you should ask him about."

She would. She wasn't sure she'd get an answer, though. "What happened to his fiancée?" She envisioned him losing her in some horrible accident, suffering the anguish of a lost love for the rest of his life. She couldn't compete with that sort of thing.

She frowned. What had made her think that? She was in competition with no one. This wasn't a marriage, it was a mockery of one.

Alice used the edge of her apron to wipe off the top of Dinah's desk. "Once she found out that Tristan didn't live in San Francisco, but on some lonesome ranch in the mountains, she called it off. No Boston city girl wants to live on the wild frontier."

Dinah went to the dressing table, sat, and began brushing her hair. "How sad. But I still don't understand why he would offer to marry a woman sight unseen, even if it was to stabilize Emily's care. Any other kind of agreement would have made more sense than this."

"Tristan's a man of contradictions, dear. If you want answers, you'll have to ask him. But don't expect to get them. Getting him to talk about his feelings is a little like predicting Emily's moods."

Dinah had to try. She needed answers. Too many things had gone wrong in her life because she hadn't questioned them. Never again.

"Come now," Alice said, running her fingers through Dinah's short curls, "take your bath, then I'll help you dress. You don't want to keep the groom waiting, do you?"

Not only did she want to keep him waiting, but she suddenly wanted to call the whole thing off. She at least wanted some answers. The situation was ridiculous. Grabbing her robe, she shrugged into it. "Where is he?"

"What? You mean Tristan? You can't see him now, dear, it's bad luck."

"Horse manure. If this is a business arrangement, then none of those stupid rules apply." Dinah sailed from her room and went in search of her husband-to-be-in-name-only. Or whatever he was.

She found him in the barn, preparing food for the dogs. He appeared startled to see her.

"Explain to me again why we must get married, Tristan." Even to her own ears she sounded more confident than she felt.

He paused, then put two enormous bowls of victuals on the ground. The hounds approached their food with regal reticence. "Do you always run around outside in your nightclothes?"

She realized she had little on under her robe, but she was covered up well enough. She shook a finger at him. "Don't change the subject. The letter I received said nothing about a wedding. I read it over so many times before I left Trenway, I have it memorized. Down to the dotted *i*'s, the crossed *t*'s, and the periods."

She followed him out of the barn and into the smithy. An array of tongs skirted the forge. The fire was low. Even so, the warmth felt good.

"I don't know what happened to the rest of the letter, Dinah. I would have no reason to lie to you about it. I may be a lot of things, but trust me," he said, giving her a firm glance, "I'm not a liar."

No, she thought, frowning to hide her guilt, but she was. It was certainly possible that Daisy had purposely not given her that portion of the letter.

"It's only a business arrangement, Dinah. I don't understand why you're getting your knickers in a knot over it."

"But why is a marriage necessary?" she probed.

"Because I want a binding commitment."

"Then, why not just write a binding commitment? Why a marriage?"

He appeared to be losing patience. "Because women

take marriage seriously, especially if there's a comfortable sum of money involved."

A quiet burning crackled through her. "So you thought if you dangled money in front of me, like a worm on a hook, I'd be a more willing worker."

"Something like that."

She studied the hard line of his jaw, noting the knotted muscles below his ears. "What if I hadn't worked out?"

"Then I would have paid your fare back to New York, as I thought I'd have to do, and as I still can do, if you don't stop asking so many questions."

She bristled, a feeling she was becoming accustomed to when talking with him. "Don't you dare treat me like a child."

His face was hard and his eyes filled with danger. "You want answers?"

She had the urge to step away, but didn't. "Yes."

He took a deep breath, then expelled it and straightened the wood stacked near the fire. "Marriage is for fools. You're putting way too much emphasis on it, because to me, it means nothing. It's a word. Only a word. My parents were married. I'll never understand why, because if I'd been wed to a crow like Zelda Fletcher, I'd have eventually gone mad, divorced her, or died young. I might even have considered murder. My father's greatest flaw was his honor, and it brought him nothing but misery.

"So you see, marriage means nothing to me. I could as easily have used the words business arrangement, but I know women. Marriage has a magical meaning for them. It means security. Count yourself lucky, Dinah Odell. You can tell the world you're married, but you won't have to suffer any of the messy trappings."

The calculated way in which he informed her of the details sent cold chills up her spine. "What if I refuse to go through with it?"

He moved a bucket of horseshoes with the toe of his

boot, the pail leaving tracks on the dirt floor. "Then you're free to leave."

She muttered a mild oath. How did she get herself into such stupid situations, anyway? "Before I can leave, you'll have to pay me my wages for the month."

"No, I don't think so."

"But that's not fair!"

He turned and slanted her a dangerous look. "Fair? Let's talk about fair, Dinah. If you leave now, you'll be letting Emily down. As hard as it might be for me to admit it, you've done some very good things with her. Your absence would undoubtedly cause her to regress. Is that what you want to do?"

Dinah swallowed hard. "No. Of course not, but—"

"I'm offering you an arrangement no sane woman on earth would turn aside. The safety of marriage without the marital trappings. How much fairer can I be than that?"

She stared at him, her mouth open.

"I vowed I wouldn't touch you, and I won't. Are you happy now?"

"I don't know. Should I be?"

"Most women would be delighted to have the protection of marriage and none of the obligations." He was almost sneering.

"But, why would you want that?"

He spat a curse. "Don't be cheeky, Dinah."

"I'm not. I mean, I don't mean to be."

He gave her a cold, humorless smile. "Then you're the most naïve girl on the face of the earth."

She knew she should quit while she was ahead, but she couldn't. "I probably am. But if you had no intention of making this marriage real, why did you insist on removing my binder, not only from my person, but from my room, as well? Why would you care one way or the other what I look like?"

"Because you're not at Trenway now, Dinah. There are no gawking guards from whom you need protection."

"No," she quipped under her breath, "only you, you big, ogling dolt."

He moved to the forge. "Don't flatter yourself. You might be an exquisite creature, but you are not my type."

She raised her eyebrows, feeling both flattered and disappointed. "What's your type?" She heard him curse under his breath, then he rubbed his neck as if trying to relax his muscles. "Well?"

He spun to face her, his eyes glittering like shards of blue ice. "I like my women to come with a bit of experience, Dinah. Experience in the bedroom, if you know what I mean. I like them to wear filmy, provocative clothing. Things I can see through, not virginal white nightrails that cut off their blood supply at the neck and wrists."

She swallowed and brought her hand to her neck, remembering the snugness of her own chaste nightgown. "I . . . could do that." Had she actually said that?

He gave her a dry smile. "I wonder. Could you howl your passion so loud that the windows rattled?"

She suddenly realized he was purposely trying to rile her. "I guess that would depend on you, wouldn't it?"

A smile lurked at the corners of his mouth, but he swung away from her again. "Touché. But don't offer me something I won't ask for, Dinah. Surely you understand that many men find their pleasures outside the marriage bed."

His words hit her like the snap of a wet towel. Of course. He had a mistress tucked away. She should have thought of that. Now who was the dolt? She felt a foolish emptiness.

All of her youthful daydreams about marriage had included a husband who would love her so much he wouldn't dream of seeking his pleasure anywhere else. It had been fanciful thinking, but she'd been a child of whimsy all of her life. She didn't know what she wanted, but she definitely didn't want this, even if it wasn't real.

"Why bother to marry me, then? I won't do it." She

put her fists on her hips and glared at him. "I'll stay, Tristan Fletcher, because I owe Emily that much, and I'd miss her if I left, but don't do me any grand favors."

His eyes were still icy. "You'll marry me, Dinah Odell, or you'll be on the first train out of here bound for New York."

She tried to swallow the cloying nausea that pushed into her throat and lingered there. "What makes you think I wouldn't rather leave than live under these conditions?"

He lifted an anvil off a stump as easily as if it were made of paper, the muscles in his forearms tightening beneath his brown skin. "I don't like idle threats, Dinah."

"You don't like. It comes down to that, doesn't it?"

"This is my house and you are my employee. It's fitting for me to have the last word, don't you think?"

"No. I think people have been letting you have the last word your whole life. Well, those tactics won't work with me. This is my life, Tristan, the only one I have. You have no idea what kinds of hell I've been through, and maybe I should be grateful for any bone you throw me, but I'm afraid that's not the kind of person I am. In many ways, I've already experienced what it's like to be a prisoner. I didn't like it."

She stepped close to him, finding it necessary to tilt her head in order to look up at him.

"I won't become a hostage in a hellish marriage of convenience, knowing that every night you're probably out whoring with your mistress while I sit home knitting wool stockings and caps with silly tassels."

He almost smiled again. "Somehow I can't imagine you sitting passively by if you discovered your husband had a mistress."

"You've said as much, Tristan," she reminded him.

He took her arm and led her outside. "But this won't be a real marriage. Believe me, if at any time during the course of our contract you find a man who loves you the way you deserve, I will set you free. Hell, I'll give you away, and with a dowry besides. This is temporary. Damn it, Dinah, don't think of it as a marriage. Think of it as . . . as an investment in your future."

She stared at him, unable to believe anyone could be so overbearing. "You are bloody incredible."

"What's wrong with what I'm doing?"

"You really don't know, do you?"

He spread his arms wide. "Crucify me for trying to make your pitiful life easier."

She clutched her stomach, unwilling to believe he was so impossibly arrogant. If he knew how pitiful her life really was, he wouldn't be so callous.

"My life may be pitiful, but it is my life." She shrugged a sigh and dug at the dirt with her slipper. "The only thing that's keeping me from packing my things and leaving is Emily. Even at that, I'm tempted."

"Where would you go without money?"

She shrugged. "Into that town down the road. Surely I could find a job there."

He stiffened. "Hatter's Horn is no place for a young lady."

"I'm beginning to think this," she said, swinging her arms to indicate the ranch, "is no place for me."

Spitting out a curse, he pulled her around to face him. "What in the hell is wrong with my offer? Any woman within a hundred miles would jump at the chance to become my wife."

She stared at him, incredulous. "Well, pin a rose on your nose, you cocky bastard. Go find one, then."

He lifted a brow. "Name calling isn't very ladylike, Dinah. Now go get ready. We leave for the chapel in two hours." He released her and returned to the smithy.

She planted her fists on her hips again. "Haven't you heard a word I've said?" Receiving no answer, she stormed off.

She was calling him every vile name she'd ever learned when she heard laughter. Curious, she followed the sound, which took her down a path past the barn. There, in a shady grove, sat Leeta, surrounded by a group of children.

She was telling them a story, one that had them in stitches.

Leeta saw her and waved.

Dinah returned the greeting and tried to smile as Leeta rose and came toward her. "Good morning."

Leeta beamed at her. *"Buenos días."*

Dinah nodded toward the children, who were watching them. "Whose children are these?"

A softness stole over Leeta's pretty features. "Three of them are mine. The others are . . . well, they have no families. They will soon, though."

Dinah frowned. "But, where do they live? I haven't seen any of them before."

"Oh, they live here. For now, over there." She pointed to a long, low bungalow that was nearly hidden in a thicket of trees. "But they have just returned from school."

"School?"

"Si. Tristan, he sends them to the reservation school. They stay there and learn to read the English, and when it is time to plant, they come home."

"They work here? Like field hands?"

"Si, but Tristan does not work them hard. It is only to make them learn the value of the money he pays them."

Dinah looked past her at the ring of children. Most were in their early teens, some younger. The smallest one she knew was Leeta's own child, who was perhaps no older than six or seven years. "Why does he do this, Leeta?"

"It is because of something he learned after discovering he had a twin brother." She gave Dinah a delicate shrug. "I do not know exactly what it is, but it is a fine thing to do, *si?"*

Though she was curious and puzzled, Dinah nodded.

"So, are you excited about your wedding?"

She gave Leeta a wry smile. "About as thrilled as being led to the hanging tree."

Leeta frowned. "You are not excited?"

"It's only a marriage of convenience, Leeta. It's a business deal. I don't see how I can possibly go through with it." Merely speaking of it made her angry.

"I see," Leeta murmured. "Why, then, are you so upset?"

"What do you mean?"

"I mean," she explained, "if you know it's only business, why does it bother you?"

"Well, because . . ."

"Because you don't want it to be business?"

Dinah expelled a whoosh of air. "I don't know. It goes against everything I'm feeling. He's so blasted arrogant, assuming all he has to do is offer marriage and I'll fall to the floor and gratefully kiss his feet. Why do men think they're God's gift to the world?"

Leeta's smile was shy. "Tristan is a fine man. I know many girls who would marry him under any circumstances, hoping that they could make him fall in love with them. Why, think about it. No matter what kind of marriage it is in the beginning, it is a marriage in the eyes of God. What you make of it depends on you."

Dinah nibbled at her bottom lip. That part was true. The question was, did she want the marriage under any circumstances?

"I was thinking about going into Hatter's Horn and finding a position there rather than go through with this sham."

"There is nothing in Hatter's Horn for a nice lady like you."

"Surely someone could use my help. I could care for children, be a companion."

"You have someone to care for here. I have not seen

Emily so content. It would be a shame to leave her. Whatever bad feelings you have for Tristan should not spill over onto Emily."

Dinah massaged her temples, hoping to ward off a headache. "I don't feel right about this. He makes a mockery of marriage."

"He is just a man. You must make allowances for him. And have patience. Let him think he is winning. A man like Tristan Fletcher is worth fighting for, don't you think?"

Dinah wasn't sure. As far as she could tell, he was an insensitive clod. Oh, he was good to his sister and he was kind to animals and, obviously, to orphans, but that alone wasn't enough to convince her he was anything special. Was it?

When she first arrived, she thought that once she'd gotten him to laugh he would be the perfect man. She knew now, that he was far from it.

As she gazed at the orphaned children, she began to feel there might be a compassionate man beneath his veneer. But it was one thing to provide for their physical care; it was quite another to become personally involved in their lives. She would have to learn more.

"I guess I'll stay. For now, anyway."

Leeta's pretty face split into a wide smile. "Good. Then we will see you at the chapel."

Leaving Leeta standing near the children, Dinah shoved her fists into the pockets of her robe and walked to the house. Her holier-than-thou attitude toward Tristan was ludicrous. At least he had been honest with her. He flat out told her what their life together would be like. For the duration of the contract, anyway. He'd been honest. Painfully so. That was more than she could say about herself.

Even dressed in a gown of pale ivory, her hair adorned with sprigs of white wildflowers, Dinah didn't feel like a bride. The nervous knot in her stomach was something brides probably felt, but no doubt it was a knot of excited anticipation, not dread. And brides probably didn't feel as if they were going to throw up.

She'd never imagined her wedding day to be anything less than a gala affair. Of course, that was before Mama and Papa died. Once at Trenway, she'd given up the idea of marriage completely. Too many painful thoughts crowded her mind. Even trying to imagine marriage to Charles wasn't enough to replace the hurt. Stir together the anguish of Mama and Papa's untimely death, add Charlotte's, presumably by her own hand, which she didn't believe for an instant, toss in Uncle Martin's betrayal, and Dinah had been stripped of her innocence. Her youth. Her joy and reason for living.

But here she was, marrying a man she didn't know, who had about as much common sense about life as a vacuous Boston debutante. He actually believed the incredible blather he spewed.

Before she saw the children, she'd been ready to leave the ranch. The sight of those children had stopped her. Leeta's words had made an impression, too, although she wasn't certain what to make of them yet.

She peered into the tiny chapel. It was surprisingly full. Alice was there, and Emily. Lucas and Leeta and their three children sat to one side, behind them sat the eight other children she'd seen earlier in the morning. Oh yes, she thought with a wicked twist of her mouth, and of course King Winterheart, himself.

Even now, knowing that it was a mockery, she felt a foolish, nervous excitement. But Tristan's cold stare changed that, intensifying her nausea. She was going to throw up. She knew it. She swallowed and grimaced at the bitter taste in her mouth.

She'd had plenty of experience with insanity, and this whole idea was definitely insane. Taking a couple of deep breaths, she began the short walk to the front of the chapel. Not because she was eager for the marriage, but because at this point she felt she owed it to Emily to stay.

Even under these circumstances. A fluttery part of her brain suggested that maybe everything would work out eventually. But work out to what end?

She stopped beside him. His gaze was on her.

"For God's sake," he muttered, "try to smile. In spite of how you feel, this isn't a damned execution."

"Don't curse in church," she scolded, staring straight ahead.

Tristan stood on the great stone steps and listened to the sounds of the night. Crickets chirruped in the grass. Years ago he'd built a bird bath down the hill next to the Jeffrey pines. Tonight he heard frogs croaking in the darkness and he knew the males and females had commandeered the bath until morning. Couples. Doing what all couples did. Except him and his new bride.

He felt a modicum of guilt as he'd watched Dinah walk down the aisle. Though her head had been high and her chin at a stubborn angle, he'd known she was putting on an act. Her hand had trembled beneath his own as they stood before the minister.

He hadn't meant to call her life pitiful. She'd had no control over what had happened to her; he had been unfair. And he'd probably hurt her feelings, too. It wasn't like him to treat a woman this way.

When the short ceremony was over, he had bent to kiss her. Her translucent lids with their russet lashes had fluttered closed, and her perfect mouth had been soft, pliant. He'd intended to kiss her cheek. At least he thought he had.

Afterward, Alice had insisted they open one of the bottles of champagne he'd bought in San Francisco on his last visit. The children got cider. A cake and cookies miraculously appeared, and they had a small celebration, in spite of his insistence that they not. Of course, he hadn't argued very hard. He wasn't a slave master; each of his workers needed time to let down his hair.

Besides, he'd enjoyed snagging gazes with Dinah. She had blushed like a real bride. He'd felt a warm, swimming sensation as he watched her. It was the damnedest thing.

He should attach a clothespin to the end of his randy root to remind himself to behave.

As they'd stood together before the minister, he thought he would experience panic. He had experienced something, but it wasn't panic. It was . . . pain. And pleasure. He cursed, then cursed again. This wasn't going as smoothly as he'd expected.

His marriage vows were mere hours old, and his only companions were his hounds. He was the pitiful one. The sky was rife with stars, the air crisp and clean. He caught a hint of honeysuckle that grew up the trellis near the gazebo. The wind was from the west.

With a dry smirk, he wondered what Dinah would smell. No doubt she'd be able to detect rabbits copulating at one hundred feet. And, he thought, his smile softening, she'd tell him about it, too.

He shook himself. How in the bloody hell would he get through another day or week without kissing her again? But kissing would lead to other things, and if he was nothing else, he was honorable.

There was a flickering light in the smithy. Tristan stepped off the porch and crossed the grass, the dogs at his side. He found Lucas bent over the blade of a hand plow.

His forearm swore and shook his head. "What are you doing roaming around? I'd sure as hell think you had better things to do tonight."

"What I do with my time is my business."

Tristan watched Lucas work. He was the most talented blacksmith in the area, having learned the craft from his father.

"So, what are you doing out at this hour?"

"You're not going to leave it alone, are you?"

Lucas grinned. "Not even if you take a swing at me."

Tristan returned the smile. "Keep an eye on who comes and goes, will you?"

Lucas stopped working and took a drink of water. "I always do."

"I mean, keep a real sharp eye."

At the mysterious tone, Lucas focused his attention. "What's wrong?"

"So far, nothing. Let me know if anyone comes around asking about Dinah."

Lucas dropped the dipper into the pail and wiped his mouth with his sleeve. "Come to think of it, someone already has. Well, they didn't exactly ask about her."

Dread shot through Tristan like a dart. "Who? When?"

"Must have been a week ago." He gave Tristan an apologetic glance. "I didn't think much of it at the time. I mean, he didn't actually call her by name or anything."

Tristan reined in his alarm. "Tell me exactly what happened."

Lucas bent to the plow blade. "I was near the road. Dinah was hanging clothes on the line. It was the day we discovered the bread in the chicken coop," he added, his eyes briefly flashing humor.

Tristan made an impatient movement with his hand. "Go on."

"A peddler came by. Had all the trappings. It didn't dawn on me that he could be anything else, and I'm not sure he *wasn't* a peddler, Tris. We talked for a few minutes, then stopped and watched her. He wasn't offensive in any way, he was very mannerly. All he said was, and I remember it well because I was thinking the same thing, 'Her hair sure catches the light, don't it?'

"I made some comment about it being bright as a new penny or some such nonsense."

"Then what did he say?" Tristan's jaw was tight.

"He asked if she was my wife."

"And?" Tristan held his breath.

"And, nothing. Hell, Tristan, I didn't have a reason to keep anything a secret."

Tristan nearly grabbed Lucas by the collar, but stopped himself. "What was your answer?" He repeated the words with emphasis.

Lucas swore again and rubbed his neck. "I told him that Dinah wasn't my wife but that she soon might be yours."

Tristan groaned, smacking a post with his fist. "You used her name?"

"Tristan, I apologize. Leeta and I had thought she'd be good for both you and Emily. How in the hell was I to know someone was looking for her?"

Tristan took long, steady breaths. "It was my fault. I should have told you sooner."

"Told me what?"

"I'm going to tell you what I know. When I'm done, we'll be the only two who know about this. Besides Dinah. But right now, she doesn't even suspect that *I* know the truth."

After he'd finished the story, he watched the anguish on Lucas's face as he cleaned up his work area. "A hell of a life for a young, pretty girl, her own uncle doing this to her."

When he finished, he nodded toward the back of the smithy. "Come on. I think we both need a drink."

9

DINAH KICKED AT THE COVERS, SAT UP, AND STARED AT THE door. Not the door that went into the hall, but the one, now exposed, that had been hidden behind the wardrobe. The door that joined her room with Tristan's.

As usual, she'd left the lamp lit to keep the goblins that devoured her mind at bay. The noises in the attic were silent, but even so, she jumped at every sound. Though she tried to convince herself that nothing in her life would change, hope and dread were twisted together inside her, one like a ribbon and one like a rope.

She could have run. Perhaps she should have, but that would have meant leaving Emily, and she didn't feel right about that. She had also made a silent promise to Daisy, and she couldn't go back on her word, not even to a dead person.

She would stay because of Emily, not because of any marriage contract, although she believed in honoring the vows, once taken. Tristan had said that it wouldn't change anything. Maybe it didn't change anything for him, but it did for her. She was married now, for better or for worse. Worse, probably.

As for him? She didn't care whether he kept his vows or not. He'd already made it clear that he wouldn't. Right now he was probably off in some other woman's bed. Some painted harlot with breasts the size of circus balloons.

Even though Tristan had ordered Alice not to do anything special after the ceremony, they'd had a small celebration anyway, and she'd met the children. She'd been nervous and now couldn't remember their names.

The stairs creaked, and she held her breath. It was he. He passed her room, stopping briefly. She waited, expelling pent-up air when he walked on by. His door opened, then closed, and Dinah sighed, pulling her covers over her and clutching her bear. She turned toward the window.

The door adjoining their rooms opened. She shoved the bear further beneath the bedding and squeezed her eyes shut, pretending to sleep, hoping her erratic breathing wouldn't give her away. She knew he was near her bed when she caught a whiff of whiskey.

She tried valiantly to appear to be asleep, but it wasn't possible to lie quietly. She knew he watched her because the sensation on her face was palpable. Opening her eyes, she was startled by the intensity of his glare.

"Out whoring, were you?" Lord, she hadn't been married a full day and she sounded like a shrew.

One corner of his mouth lifted. "Miss me?" There was a slight slurring to his words.

She drew the covers to her chin. "How can I miss something I've never had?"

He continued to smile. It confused her.

"Dinah, Dinah. You already regret this, don't you?"

She turned to her other side and studied the door, blinking back tears. "I regretted it before I did it."

Why did she feel like bawling? She'd been through

worse things in her life. Drat, she thought, sniffing, the entire past year had been a living hell, and even then she hadn't felt what she was feeling now.

"I can smell the whiskey on your breath. What's the matter? Is your whore so ugly you have to get liquored up before you crawl into her bed?"

"Is that what you've been doing? Lying here imagining me with my mistress?" He continued to sound amused.

She felt his weight on the bed, then his hand caressed her hip. Even through the bedding she felt his touch. It radiated through her like a pebble being dropped into a pond and she squeezed her eyes shut, hoping to block the sensation.

His hand snaked beneath the covers, and Dinah hurried to shove the bear toward her feet. She could imagine his reaction if he discovered how pathetic she was, having to sleep with a stuffed animal, like a child. He'd really think her life was pitiful.

"Will you be all right?"

His concern surprising her, she rolled over. He removed his hand from under the covers. "Do you care?"

"Of course I care. In spite of what you think, I'm not a brute."

Again, she felt an inane squirt of tears, and she hiccoughed as she swallowed.

"My God," he murmured, "what have I done to you?"

Attempting to control herself, she shook her head. "It's not your fault." She uttered a watery laugh. "You didn't t-twist my arm, not really. And . . . and for the life of me, I can't imagine why I'm carrying on so. This certainly isn't the worst th-thing that's happened in my life."

"What have I done?" he repeated, caressing her hair.

That tiny bit of affection did it. That speck of hope cracked her heavy facade, and she cried, anxious to stop pretending she was tough. Eager to be close to anyone, even him, and even if he didn't like her very much. She needed to be loved, and if not that, then at least she wanted someone who could learn to care.

He took her in his arms, unable to believe what a gigantic mistake he'd made. How had he convinced himself this was right? What damned lofty perch had he sat upon, deciding her fate? It had started out as a way to keep her safe from Martin Odell. Now he wondered who would keep her safe from him.

Lucas was right. Tristan's greatest flaw was that he refused to believe he was ever wrong. He wouldn't listen when accused of making bad decisions. He saw with clarity that this was one of the most stupid, insensitive decisions he'd ever made in his life.

She wept onto his shoulder, and he brushed her hair from her face with his fingers, disgusted that he could have done this to her. He kissed her temple, more to repair the damage he'd done than to arouse, but her mouth found his, and suddenly he was kissing her. She returned kiss for kiss, making sweet, artless sounds of pleasure in her throat.

She kicked at her covers.

He tried to pull them up.

"Please, Tristan. I hate to beg, but . . . but all I want is for you to hold me. Just hold me, please." She kicked off her covers again and hugged him.

He swallowed a groan, for she smelled like fresh bed linens and she was soft, nubile, receptive. He stroked her shoulders, his mind twirling like a runaway top. She drew one leg over his, as if needing to be closer.

Despite his good intentions, his arousal began.

She raised her face to his, her breath on his mouth. He kissed her again, slanting his mouth over hers. She offered her tongue; he accepted it.

His hand roamed her hip, and she pressed closer still. When he lifted the hem of her nightgown, she stopped moving. His fingers grazed her upper thigh. It was soft, so damned soft.

He hardened behind his fly and his fingertips moved across her stomach, causing her to gasp, but she didn't pull away.

Stop this, you damned fool.

When she shuddered against his mouth, he could no longer hear the scolding voice in his head. He took her bottom lip between his and caressed it with his tongue while he grazed the hair at the top of her thighs.

She made another sweet, ingenuous noise, and he dipped lower. She began to shake; she was frightened.

He removed his hand.

"No," she murmured on a gasp, drawing it back.

He gazed down at her; her eyes were closed and her mouth was open slightly as she breathed. He continued to watch her as he stroked her, saw the surprise and heard the swift intake of breath when he found the place that was already firm, and the size of a cranberry.

She spread one leg, bending her knee, and he fondled her, driving back his own hunger as he watched her amazement at discovering her own.

She stiffened beneath his touch, her gasps becoming whimpering moans of pleasure as she rose to meet fulfillment. He cupped her mound and bent to kiss her, swallowing her cries. She clutched at him, tugging his hair, pushing his shoulder, drawing him near, until she collapsed on the bed.

She hadn't opened her eyes. God, when was the last time he had seen innocent pleasure like this? He couldn't remember. The last time he'd been with a woman had been mundane compared to this, and this time, he hadn't even been satisfied. There was satisfaction in watching her. Damn.

He was stiff behind his fly. And he couldn't have more.

Finally, she opened his eyes. They were dark, innocently inviting, and filled with hazy surprise. He had to get out *now*.

His sigh was gruff as he pressed her toward her pillow.

"Go to sleep." He flung himself off the bed and bolted toward the dressing room, slamming the door behind him, leaving her alone.

She raised herself up on her elbows and stared after him, her heart pounding, but shame oozing through her stomach. What had she done? She didn't know what had gotten into her. One small gesture from him and she was all over him like moss on a log. She *was* pitiful, wasn't she?

Sweet Mary, how would she face him? She'd spread her legs like a whore, allowing him—no, inviting him—to touch her. She wouldn't be able to look him in the eye. Not ever.

She flopped onto her pillows. One way or the other, she would not yield to this feeling again. She refused to pant after him like a puppy. If this was supposed to be a business arrangement, then she'd make sure it was one.

She recovered her bear, and huddled beneath the covers, praying for sleep that wouldn't come.

Tristan sat on the edge of his bed and held his head, keeping it down to avoid the intrusive morning light. He hadn't been hungover in years; now he remembered why. A tiny gnome was inside his head, hammering against his skull.

He stood and paced, hoping to work out some of the kinks in his body, cursing Dinah, and himself. But his curses were far less abusive than he would have thought.

How in the hell he was going to get through this foolish farce without touching her again? If he wasn't careful, she would become an obsession. Hell, she'd merely wanted comfort from him and he hadn't been able to keep his hands off her.

It had been less than a full day since his wedding, and already he knew he was insane to think a benign marriage to Dinah Odell would work.

Swearing again, he crossed to the dressing room,

anxious to dunk his head into a basin of cold water. He flung the door open and stopped short. Dinah stood there, naked to the waist, her perfect breasts quivering with surprise.

He tried to speak, but nothing could get past the lump in his throat.

He wanted to caress her, take each breast into his mouth and feel the nipples harden against his tongue. He wanted to bury his face between them, lavish himself in her bounty.

He longed for the freedom to touch her whenever he chose, to come up behind her and feel her melt with desire when he cuddled her breasts in his palms or drew his hand under her gown to feel the moistness between her legs. He itched to have her naked against his chest and feel her pink nipples drag across his flesh.

Instead, he cursed and spun away. "Perhaps we should work out an arrangement for this room."

"I was here first."

She appeared to possess none of the fantasies he did, for she picked up a long strip of linen and, starting at her waist, began wrapping it around her stomach. She moved slowly, an inch at a time, toward her breasts.

He felt a physical pain when she bound them. She finished by sticking the flap like the end of a towel into the top, beneath the swell of her straining bosom. She had not glanced away.

The mutiny in her eyes was the catalyst that made him reach for her camisole before she had a chance to don it.

She searched for another, but he quickly moved and pulled out the flap of her binder.

Her eyes filled with rebellion. No remnants of her arousal from the night before remained. "Are we always going to go through this charade?"

Unable to help himself, he bent and pressed a kiss to the pulse that fluttered at the base of her throat. She tasted so damned sweet. He wanted more. Much, much more.

"It's up to you. If you continue to defy me, I'll take it as an invitation."

"Why can't you leave me alone?" Her voice was a mere whisper, but the words were said with strength.

He didn't answer. Instead, he unwrapped her binder, experiencing a sense of relief when her breasts were free once again.

"I told you." He traced the delectable globes with his hands, noting that they shook. "I'll leave you alone when you stop challenging me."

His touch made her tremble; he felt it through the tips of his fingers. Again, he questioned his sanity.

"This may not be a marriage, but it is not a case of master and slave. I will do as I please."

He forced himself to drop his hand to his side. "Defiance becomes you."

"Lechery doesn't become you."

Her perfect mouth drew him, and he dragged her to him and kissed her, knowing he would burn in eternal damnation. She stood lifeless in his arms.

"Tristan? Yoo hoo! You in there?"

He threw Dinah one of his shirts in case Alice poked her nosy head inside. Dinah scrambled into it, her eyes shimmering with anger as she drew it tightly around her.

"I'll be right there, Alice." He pinned Dinah with a hard glare, then said under his breath, "I don't want to find that binder crushing your breasts ever again."

Without waiting for her response, he went to face the housekeeper.

Dinah sagged to the floor, biting back the urge to bawl. He was right. She'd been defying him. At least she'd been trying to. Had Alice not interrupted, she would have buckled, she was sure.

In her need to have love, she'd turned to him, and now and forever, he would remember it. Not until the day she'd escaped from Trenway had she thought she would ever have a normal life again, for she didn't think she'd ever have the chance. Now, all she wanted was someone who would take the time to learn to know her, the person she was inside, the one that was fragile and sad.

Her deep loneliness erupted, and she bent her head, pressing her face into her knees. Something was definitely wrong with her. She'd let him touch her in the most intimate way, and drat it all, she'd enjoyed it. She should burn in hell for that.

The binder lay beside her and she automatically reached for it. Her hand stopped mid air. Expelling a sigh, she picked the linen wrap off the floor and dropped it into her lap. Since she'd been in the spa with Emily she had worn the binder every day. Part of her refusal to go without it was Tristan's insistence that she do so, but part of her felt safer wearing it. It had become as essential as her unmentionables.

But this game they played regarding it could make her weary. Now that she understood that it aroused him to remove the cloth, she should quit wearing it altogether.

She hunched her shoulders, sensing the physical vulnerability she would experience if she went without the binder.

She wouldn't be caught in this situation again. She would dress and undress in her room, in the dark if she had to, but she wasn't ready to give up the security the binder gave her. She stood, removed his shirt, bound herself tightly, and dressed.

His shirt lay in a heap. She brought it to her face, breathing deeply. It smelled of him; it made her tremble. Before leaving her room, she tucked the shirt under her pillow.

After breakfast she discovered Leeta had come for Emily, and they were with the children.

Curious, she hurried outside to join them. Her steps slowed as she neared them, for they were urging Tristan to tell them a story.

"But Leeta is the storyteller."

"Please, Tristan," Leeta urged. "I'll be happy to have

you take my place. They are getting weary of Indian stories. Perhaps you have something different for them to hear. In the meantime, I'll go help Alice prepare some lemonade."

"Yes, Tristan," Emily encouraged. "Tell the one about the sausage."

Dinah watched as he glanced at each child, his expression and his stance relaxed. He looked different when he was with other people. He smiled. He was open. With her, he was guarded and often angry.

He shook his finger playfully at Emily, who blushed, lowering her head to her sketch pad.

"My big sister wants me to tell you the one about the sausage. Mrs. Linberg used to tell us many old Swedish folktales when we were unhappy, or when it was raining and we couldn't be outside. Is anyone here unhappy?"

The children shook their heads.

One of the handsome young boys rested his elbows on his knees. "I'll be unhappy if you don't tell us a story, Tristan."

"Little Hawk speaks for all of us," another child added.

Dinah sat on the grass apart from the rest and hugged her knees, waiting for the story. This was a different Tristan from the one she'd come to know.

Tristan hunkered before them. "Once there was an old woman who was minding her business in her cottage one evening, when a stranger came by, asking to borrow her brewing pan because her daughter was getting married.

"The old woman was terribly impressed with this stranger, for she was dressed like a grand lady and appeared very important. She loaned the woman her brewing pan without even asking her name, and the grand lady told her she would pay her when she returned it.

"Two days later, the grand lady returned the pan and told the old woman she now had three wishes. Then the grand lady was gone. The old woman could hardly wait until her husband returned, for she didn't know what to wish for. They needed a big barn and could use a box full of money. Oh, wouldn't the neighbors be envious then?

"In the meantime, the supper she was preparing for her husband was made up of watered-down milk and dried bread. She remembered seeing a juicy sausage at her neighbor's, and she said, 'Ah, deary me, I wish I had that sausage here!' The next moment, a big sausage lay on the table right in front of her.

"When her husband came home, she shouted, 'Father! Father! all our troubles are over! I lent my brewing pan to a fine lady, and in return she gave us three wishes. See? The sausage is proof, for all I did was ask, and it appeared on the table.'

" 'What do you mean, you silly old woman?' The husband was angry. 'Why do you wish for such stupid things as sausage when you could wish for anything in the world? I wish the sausage was sticking to your nose, since you haven't any better sense.' "

The children laughed, their eyes bright, their faces sweet and innocent. Dinah bit her bottom lip and smiled.

"What do you think happened?"

"The sausage stuck to his wife's nose," one of the children offered, still laughing.

Tristan nodded. "Absolutely. All at once the poor old woman gave a cry, for sure enough, there was the sausage, sticking to her nose. She tried to remove it, but the more she tugged and pulled, the firmer it stuck.

"The old woman cried and cried, and the old man tried to get rid of the sausage, but it wouldn't budge.

"But they had one wish left. Ah, what to wish for. They could wish for something grand, but what good would it do them if the mistress of the house had a long sausage sticking to the end of her nose?

"It was a hard choice for the old man," Tristan said, shaking his head sadly. "To be so close to having everything, yet not being able to enjoy anything because of the sausage hanging from his wife's nose. What do you think he did?"

"If I were the old man, I'd wish for lots of money, then I'd buy a good knife and I'd cut the sausage from her nose. I'd still have the rest of the money to do what I pleased with," the one called Little Hawk announced.

His arrogance added to his good looks. Dinah thought that one day he would be very handsome. He reminded her of Tristan, and she wondered how much like this boy Tristan had been as a child.

Tristan threw back his head and laughed. Dinah stared at him as longing washed through her. She remembered that he'd laughed with her like that, once.

"Good thinking, Little Hawk, but that would ruin the moral of the story."

"What did they do, then?" asked another child.

"They wished to be rid of the sausage, of course. When it was gone, they danced around the room with glee, for a sausage might be a tasty thing to have in your mouth, but it's quite different to have one sticking to your nose all of your life."

The children applauded. All but Little Hawk. He shook his head. "I'd have wished for the money to buy a knife. It makes no sense to think they couldn't have cut it off."

Tristan reached over and rumpled the boy's thick, black hair. "You have a practical mind, Little Hawk. I think one day when you're older I'll put you in charge of my stock."

The boy's cocky facade slid away and his eyes grew big. "You mean it? The horses, too?"

Tristan gave him a playful punch to the shoulder. "Of course, the horses, too."

Tristan turned, and Dinah knew by his expression that he hadn't known she'd been there, listening. "Come, Little Hawk, say good morning to Dinah."

Dinah's heart pounded as they drew near, but she forgot her own discomfort when she saw that the boy limped. How had she missed that yesterday? One of his legs appeared shorter than the other, and his foot was like a club, turned inward so that he walked on the outside of it. She felt a quick rush of sympathy.

They stopped in front of her, and Tristan rested his hand on the boy's shoulder, his gaze on Dinah.

"What do you think, Dinah? Does Little Hawk make sense, or does it ruin the moral of the story?"

"He has a point, of course." She offered Little Hawk a smile. It was met with intense scrutiny.

"You're very pretty for a White."

She didn't know why, but she blushed at the back-handed compliment. "Thank you. I think."

The boy appeared puzzled. "You're Miss Emily's nurse, too?"

She nodded.

"I won't have a wife when I grow up. They are nothing but a nuisance and a bother," he proclaimed.

Intrigued, Dinah asked, "Who told you that?"

He gave her a guileless shrug. "Tristan, of course."

She tossed Tristan a skeptical look. "Of course."

Tristan cleared his throat. "Isn't it time to do your chores, Little Hawk?"

"But, Tristan . . ."

"The young man who will one day be in charge of my stock doesn't ask so many questions or make such comments in front of a woman."

The boy studied Dinah. "One more question, Tristan."

Though Tristan appeared impatient, Dinah knew he was not.

"One more, then."

"When you have children, will they be half blood or White?"

Dinah's cheeks flamed and Tristan coughed again as he turned the boy in the direction of the barn and gave him a gentle shove. "Get going or I'll take a stick to you," he threatened.

With a sharp laugh, Little Hawk limped toward the barn. "You wouldn't, and we both know it."

Tristan's nearness was stifling Dinah. They exchanged glances.

"Irreverent urchin, isn't he?"

She watched the boy disappear into the barn. "You encourage it."

"Is that disapproval I hear in your voice?"

What Dinah had learned about Tristan in this brief interlude confused her; he had exhibited a side of himself she hadn't known existed.

"Not really. I can tell that for some reason I don't fully understand," she began, tilting her head toward him, "the children find you quite fascinating."

He merely grinned.

Dinah couldn't help returning the smile. "You didn't tell me about the children when I first arrived, Tristan. Was there some reason to keep it a secret? Are they, perhaps, products of your many indiscretions?"

"And, if they were, would that make me a bigger heel in your eyes, or a bigger hero, because I'm taking care of them?"

Leave it to him to twist her words. She hadn't yet learned that he was a master at it.

Emily appeared at her side. "I should have asked that you tell them the story about the orphaned boy, Teddy. It reminds me of Little Hawk."

He displayed a warm smile for his sister. "I'll leave that for another day. Now, what have you been drawing while I've been telling tales?"

She showed him the sketch. Dinah craned her neck to see it. "Why, Emily, that's beautiful." It was of Little Hawk astride a horse, and he wore a grand feathered headdress.

"He's on a horse because it pains me to watch him walk," she explained, a sad catch in her voice.

Tristan said nothing, his tortured expression speaking volumes.

"Is there no way his leg can be fixed, Tristan?"

This was the first time Dinah had heard Emily express concern about anyone but herself.

"What do you think, Dinah?"

Surprised, she simply stared at him. "You're asking me?"

His eyes were hooded. "You're the nurse. Tell us what you think."

She'd almost forgotten how she came to be there. Leave it to Tristan to remind her. "I . . . I really don't know. Maybe you should ask your friend, Dr. Richards."

He took Emily's arm and started toward the house. "I already have."

Dinah hurried to catch up. "What did he say? Can it be fixed?"

"It's possible. I'm not sure I want to put Little Hawk through it, though. It's very expensive, but that isn't the problem. It's a new procedure. I wouldn't want the boy butchered." He squeezed Emily's arm, and they shared a private look, one that made Dinah feel more like an outsider than she already did.

Emily didn't need Dinah for the rest of the day. All of the children were busy with chores, and Alice had chosen today to travel to Hatter's Horn to get supplies, and she had taken one of the older boys with her.

As darkness fell upon the house, Dinah felt nervous and restless. On paper, she was mistress of this big, gloomy, dismal manse. In reality, she was an appendage. A useless one, at that. Today, the first full day of her marriage, had been the most depressing yet.

After dinner, she climbed the stairs to her room, the subtle noises around her growing more pronounced. She closed the door and stood in the darkness. Alice usually lit her lamp at dusk, but Dinah realized she shouldn't expect such treatment. She was capable of lighting her own lamp, it was just that coming into a dark bedroom brought back too many ugly thoughts. Hugging herself, her gaze darted to the gloomy corners, where the ghosts of her imagination lurked.

Moonlight suddenly flooded the room, filtering through the leaves of the oaks and the boughs of the firs. It danced on the rug, a sad, funereal ballet that moved across the floor, up the sides of the bed to the painting that hung over the desk, making Emily's work appear even more macabre.

Attempting to shake off her mood, Dinah lit her lamp and undressed. She freed her bear from its hiding place and slipped quickly beneath the covers. But as she lay there, attempting to sleep, the noises in the attic began again, causing her heart to stir with alarm.

The black room at the asylum loomed in her imagination. She could almost smell the stink of fear of the hundreds of women who had been locked in the room before she had.

She turned onto her stomach and pressed her face to her pillow. When would images of Trenway leave her? How long did she have to be away from the place before she could begin to forget?

A thud from the attic gave her a jolt. She slid to the edge of the bed and stared at the ceiling. Another thud, then a cry echoed into her room, sending her heart further into her throat.

She could stand it no longer. Whatever was happening up there would drive her mad if she didn't find out what it was. As eager as she was to discover the source, she had to work up her nerve to do it. She listened until she heard no more noise, hoping whatever it was would be gone before she investigated.

She tucked her bear under the covers, making certain his head was on the pillow, then left her room. She picked up the peg lamp off the table in the hallway before she started up the dark staircase. The light flickered before her, sending ghastly shadows over the old, flower-patterned wallpaper that lined the stairwell. As she approached the dark landing, a dusty, musty odor, one that reminded her of Trenway, penetrated the air. She attempted to swallow her fear; she wasn't entirely successful.

She paused, trying to listen for the noises that had brought her there in the first place, but she heard nothing. Only the hammering of her heart against her ribs. *Oh, be brave, you foolish coward.* She took a deep breath, leaned against the wall, and closed her eyes. How she hated the dark! But as tempted as she was to scurry back to her room and hide under the covers, she didn't. She had to grow up sooner or later. Later would have been nice.

Taking another healthy breath, she stepped into the shadowy, windowless room and swung the lamp from side to side. Her hand shook, causing the light to flicker erratically.

She didn't know what she had expected to find. Her imagination had dredged up aberrations, perhaps even the ghost of Zelda Fletcher. That thought was only fleeting, of course, because she wasn't a child and she didn't believe in ghosts. Not really.

What she found was a storage trunk, thick with dust, crouched beneath the eaves. A rocking chair with a missing arm sat beside it. Closer examination revealed a porcelain doll with a cracked face sitting on the cushion.

She moved the lamp over the doll. Its haunting blue eyes stared at her. She picked it up and blew on the dusty ruffle that circled its neck, sneezing when the dust tickled her nose. The sound was deafening in the quiet room.

With the doll resting in the crook of her arm, she turned the lamp on the opposite wall and gasped in surprise. She stepped closer, shifting the lamp over the artwork. There were dozens of paintings of all shapes and sizes.

She put the doll on the floor and as she studied the first painting, her heart nearly broke. The background was made up of a series of wavy lines, and in the center was a young girl, one looking suspiciously like Emily, with her eyes wide, her mouth open, and her hands over her ears. Her clothes were torn away and there was an ugly incision painted on her stomach.

Dinah touched the canvas, pulling away in surprise when she discovered it was wet.

Others were wet, too, as if they'd all been recently worked on. Each was as disturbing as the first.

Dinah covered her mouth, so distressed by her discovery that she felt a ridge of panic. Emily. The noises had to have been Emily, sneaking into the attic to paint. But why? Everyone had encouraged her to paint openly. Why would she find it necessary to paint up here?

Out of the corner of her eye, she caught a glimpse of a canvas lying apart from the others. She moved the lamp to it and found long slashes torn through the figure of a woman with a long, sallow face and yellow eyes. Her lips were mere slits on the canvas, and her neck was scrawny and bony.

Distressed, Dinah spun to leave, wondering what had prompted Emily to begin painting such pictures now. Her mood had been less depressed. Perhaps these particular paintings were a catharsis for her, a purging of the feelings she was unable to express any other way.

Dinah vowed to find out.

Tristan knocked at the adjoining bedroom door. He'd forgotten to remind Dinah that they were due at the dressmaker's in the morning.

When she didn't answer, he opened the door, expecting to find her asleep. Frowning, he stepped into the room. It was empty. He turned to leave, but something caught his eye.

"What the—" He crossed to the bed and flipped the covers, exposing a stuffed bear. A tattered, stuffed bear. Mumbling a curse, he sank to the bed, his stomach hollow. The image of Dinah huddled in a dirty asylum corner, her big eyes wide with frightened tears, alone in the world save for a ragged toy bear, was like a fist to his gut.

How many times would he forget who she was and where she'd come from? He was to blame for everything, of course, even for what had happened last night. He might have remembered the reason she'd turned to him in the first place, but once he'd touched her soft, warm flesh, he was lost.

Her peppery, lively, enthusiastic behavior was an act. Until last night, she'd given the impression of being defiant and independent. There had been nothing about her that reminded him of weakness. The first day, when she was obviously talking about herself, she appeared to be grieving for other women who had other struggles, different from her own.

He'd been too busy playing games with her. Not just with her body, but with her mind. He'd treated her like any normal woman who attracted him. No, that wasn't true. He'd never treated a woman like this before. Always before, he'd thought he was quite genteel. In Boston, he'd never had trouble getting a woman. He'd been a curiosity, a half blood attending one of the finest colleges in the east, and he'd had his pick of women. Married ones found him intriguing. He'd bedded a few, not thinking about the fact that he was participating in cuckoldry, or caring, for that matter.

As he studied the ratty bear, he wondered how hard Dinah had had to work to keep him from seeing her pain. He hadn't remembered that no matter how spirited she was on the outside, she was damaged on the inside.

From the beginning, he hadn't let himself think about it. To think about what she'd been through would have meant he'd begun to care, and God forbid he should do that, he thought with a disparaging lift of his brow.

If he'd been the gentleman he professed to be, he would have announced his discovery to her after Alice found the letter or after he'd uncovered who she was and where she'd been and why she was trying to hide. He'd have found a nice safe place for her to stay, far away from him, obviously, for even now, she wasn't safe anywhere near him. Maybe with his brother's family. Some place where there were children to love and women to laugh with.

She had all that here, but he'd used emotional blackmail to talk her out of leaving him, knowing that she wouldn't walk away from Emily, not if he made it clear how much Emily needed her.

He should have acted like a responsible adult, not like the damned fool he was. He thought he could protect her from her past by marrying her, when even as he was doing it, he'd known, deep inside, that it was neither fair nor reasonable.

His thumbs moved over the stuffed bear's face. The animal no longer had eyes or a nose, and the stitching that formed its mouth was ragged and torn.

He tucked the bear under the covers the way he'd found it, wondering if Dinah was as tattered on the inside as the bear was on the outside. As he went to his own room, Tristan felt another chink in his armor.

10

Dinah hadn't slept. Her mind had been filled with thoughts of Emily. At dawn, she finally gave up and dressed, turning her attention to the doll.

The crack on its face was disturbing, she didn't know why. It wasn't so unusual. Some of her own dolls had been damaged merely because she'd played with them.

The doll wore a long satin dress that had once been a brilliant blue, the color now preserved only in the creases of the fabric. The rest of the dress was crusted with dust and dirt. Dinah shook it out, brushed it off, and put the doll on her bed.

She sighed, feeling a strangled rush of memories. She and Charlotte had had so many things as children. Their room had been filled with expensive toys, frills, and luxuries. Dinah's most cherished possession had been a doll house Papa had built them. He had made miniature furniture to go into every room. Dinah smiled sadly at the warm memory.

Her favorite room had been the kitchen, with its wee stove, butter churn, standing cupboards, and table with the most exquisite chairs. The floor even had a cellar lid, with a tiny rug to cover it. Charlotte's favorite had been the salon with its little grand piano and minuscule bench. The windows in the house opened out, onto what Dinah had pretended was a vivid flower garden.

Once she and Charlotte had Papa's valet carry the dollhouse out to the garden, but Mama scolded them, explaining that to have it outside would ruin it. Dinah had never tried to take it outside again. She'd wanted it to stay beautiful forever. Now, with Uncle Martin at the helm, it had probably become fireplace kindling.

There had been a crystal mobile that hung near the window by her bed, where it caught the light and exploded into color.

How frivolous she'd been in those days, she thought. A twist of nostalgia threatened to make her cry, but she stopped herself. All she did was bawl lately. It did no good to think about the past. The past was gone and no amount of wishing or crying would bring it back.

She was blowing her nose when Alice stepped into the room.

"Aren't you ready?"

Dinah stuffed her handkerchief into her pocket. "Ready? For what?"

Alice sniffed and thumped her hips with her fists. "He was supposed to tell you to be ready to go into Hatter's Horn to the dressmaker this morning."

"Dressmaker? Whatever for?"

Alice frowned at Dinah's dull gown. "We'll be having a party to build the addition onto the house for the children. You can't be the hostess of this ranch in a getup like that. *Uff dah.* It's uglier than a Norwegian's lumpy behind."

Dinah swallowed a smile. "He didn't mention anything to me yesterday."

"He don't treat you near like he should."

Dinah dreaded having the neighbors over, especially if she had to paste on a smile. She didn't know how long she could act as if everything were fine when it wasn't.

"Alice, did you know that Emily has been painting in the attic?"

Alice pinched her pale eyebrows together and frowned. "She has? Why?"

Dinah shook her head. "I don't know. I've been hearing strange noises from there since I arrived. Truthfully, I was a bit cowardly about going up there, but last night I couldn't sleep and thought I heard someone cry out. When I arrived, there was no one there, but some of the canvases were wet. The paintings that are up there are quite disturbing."

"Well, she don't talk much about the time she spent in the hospital. In fact, I don't think she's ever talked about it. Maybe those paintings are her way of—"

Tristan stepped into the room through the dressing-room door, his presence stopping Alice mid sentence. He glared at Dinah. "Are you ready to go, or are you going to stand there all day gossiping about my sister?"

"I wasn't gossiping," she said defensively, "and you neglected to tell me we were going anywhere."

"Alice, don't you have work to do?" It sounded like a threat, not a question.

Despite the color that crept into Alice's plump cheeks, she scolded him. "You might try a little sweet cream for that sour temper of yours, Tristan Fletcher."

After Alice had gone, Dinah turned to her husband. "Don't scold her, Tristan. She didn't offer me any information I didn't ask for."

His face was hard. "Emily's youth is best left alone." He lifted Dinah's shawl from the chair by the desk, stopped, then picked up the doll off the bed. "Where did you find this?"

He didn't sound angry anymore, but she couldn't determine what was going through his head.

"In the attic."

His fingers moved over the doll but he didn't turn toward her. "What were you doing in the attic?"

"I wasn't snooping, if that's what you're implying."

He made a soundless laugh. "What would take you to the attic unless you were snooping?"

Her face burned. She wasn't about to tell him she'd been frightened by the noises for weeks. "I heard a noise up there last night and went to investigate."

She noticed he hadn't returned the doll to the bed. "Was that Emily's?"

He flung it away. "Well, it wasn't mine."

"Tristan, I found some disturbing paintings upstairs."

"The attic should have been gutted years ago."

"These are freshly painted."

He turned slowly and she caught his concerned expression. "That's not possible."

"The proof is upstairs. If I'm going to help Emily, I have to know why she painted these specific paintings and why she felt she had to do it in secret."

He rolled his shoulders, then massaged his neck. "I have no idea what's up there."

Dinah lit the peg lamp and went to the door. "Then it's about time you did." She held out her hand, half hoping he'd take it. He didn't. "What time are we expected at the dressmaker's?"

"Not until ten."

"Then we have time to look at the paintings. Perhaps you can explain them to me."

He sighed and dove his fingers through his hair. "It's against my better judgment."

Her smile was wry. "Naturally."

He lifted a black eyebrow. "You're getting cheeky again, Dinah."

She started for the door with the lamp. "I'd apologize, but it's not in my nature."

"As if I had to be reminded," he grumbled, following her.

They stepped into the attic, Tristan holding the lamp.

Dinah went to the paintings that leaned against the wall. "This one particularly disturbs me."

She watched Tristan's features nearly crumble as he gazed at the painful pictures. "Mother of God." The words were mere choking sounds in his throat.

His expression was so tortured she ached for him. "I'm sorry, so very sorry, if they disturb you, Tristan, but can you explain why Emily would have painted them?"

"This one," he offered with a shuddering sigh, indicating the one of Emily screaming, with the gash painted on her abdomen, "this one is probably about something that happened when she was hospitalized."

Hospitalized. Such a civilized term for something so completely and utterly uncivilized, Dinah thought.

"Mother told them to perform surgery on her."

Alarmed, Dinah clutched at her throat. "Why?"

"So she wouldn't have children."

Dinah's stomach churned and her hand went to her mouth. Tristan's jaw was so tight she saw the knots in his muscles. No further explanation was necessary; having been in the same surroundings herself, she understood. She'd known of women who had gone through similar traumas at their family's request, but only after they'd been impregnated by one of the vile guards.

"If my father had lived, none of this would have happened. He wouldn't have sent her away. He hadn't been ashamed of what she was. As Emily grew into a young woman, she became an embarrassment to Zelda. The other ranch wives talked and bragged about their children. Their grandchildren. Zelda couldn't. Her only daughter wasn't right in the head, and her son, well, he was a dirty little savage.

"Sending Emily off to 'school' to get rid of her made Zelda's life easier. Much less painful. She wasn't constantly reminded of her failure to produce a normal child. I wasn't as easy to dismiss. I think at times she was tempted to drop me down a well, but Father made certain he wrote me into his will in such a way that she couldn't get rid of me if he died first. Unfortunately, he did."

Dinah had yet to learn all of Tristan's history, but she detected the hidden anguish in his voice. She was certain it was in her own, too, when she spoke of those she'd loved and lost. It was also telling that Tristan would use his mother's given name. To her it said the woman hadn't filled her role with much affection or satisfaction.

"She exposed Emily to butchery." His voice was tight with emotion. "For that, I'll never forgive her. Never."

He was silent for a long time. "When you first told me about normal women who had been put into asylums for no reason at all, I didn't want to believe it. You see, Zelda was a domineering woman, not likely to have been forced to do anything she didn't want to do. I didn't stop to think that all women weren't like her.

"When she finally died and I brought Emily home from that contemptible place, I didn't want to know anything about her past. Not until you talked of your hatred for Trenway did I begin to even think about what Emily might have gone through. Until then, all I knew was that she was home where she belonged and was getting good care. Now I can see that although Emily has never spoken of her years in the hospital, she hasn't been able to resolve them, either. I know she isn't normal, Dinah. What concerns me is that she's unable to express what happened to her."

Dinah gazed at the paintings, nibbling on the end of her thumb. "I think she's expressing her feelings right here. It isn't pretty, but I think it's healthy."

He nodded. "It's a start."

A man she hadn't believed existed was emerging from within the body of Tristan Fletcher. A compassionate man. A caring man. A man worthy of her love.

The ride to the dressmaker's was endless, for neither she nor Tristan spoke. Her thoughts were wrapped around the picture of a mutilated Emily. From the angry expression on Tristan's face, Dinah guessed his thoughts were focused on the woman responsible.

"Tristan, are you certain you want to do this today?" Dinah wasn't. She had the urge to go home, find Emily, and cradle her in her arms. Knowing Emily, though, it wouldn't be an easy task.

Oddly enough, he turned to her and smiled. "What's done is done, Dinah. I allow the past to eat at me often enough, but I don't want you to let it eat at you. Emily needs your help, not your pity. We have to go forward now. I've been letting myself stagnate where she's concerned.

"At any rate, Belle is expecting us." His searching gaze moved over her. "She's anxious to work with a woman who doesn't require camouflage."

Dinah warmed at the compliment. And truth to tell, she was anxious to have some nice things of her own to wear.

Belle Harvey was an attractive woman who looked as if she should be running a fancy New York dress salon, creating gowns for the rich. Instead, she ran an out-of-the-way shop in bucolic Hatter's Horn, making gowns for ranchers' dowdy wives. Dinah figured there was a story there, but couldn't imagine what it might be.

The minute they came through the door, Belle took Dinah by the hand, pulled her toward a dressing cubicle and stripped her. Dinah wasn't surprised that the first thing to go into the trash bin was her binder. Belle uttered a colorful string of cuss words at the idea that any woman with Dinah's beauty would wear such a thing at all. Dinah didn't argue; it was easy enough to make herself another if she chose to.

Now, she studied herself in the mirror. Belle, who stood behind her, had pinned in the waist of a linen camisole with a scooped neckline. It was quite revealing, for her breasts plumped out over the top.

"Lord, a strong wind would blow you off your feet."

Dinah glanced at Belle in the glass. She had a figure any woman would envy: a full, round bosom, a small waist, and rounded hips. She was very beautiful, too, with rich mahogany hair swept up and caught with a comb. Women with her class and sophistication didn't spend the best years of their lives in Hatter's Horn. Not without a darned good reason.

"I'm not as small as you might think." Dinah turned sideways, automatically hunching her shoulders when she saw her curves.

Belle snorted. "With that binder strangling your chest, it was hard to tell. Why in the devil would you wear such a thing? I thought binders were for women who wanted to dry up their milk supply."

Dinah felt herself color. "I had a . . . position that required that I be around rather unsavory men. I thought it best to cover myself."

"But your hair, alone, would draw an appreciative male crowd."

Dinah released a sly smile, recalling Daisy's doodle threat. "I found ways to discourage them."

"You know that every single woman within a twenty-mile radius envies you. Even some married ones. Tristan Fletcher has eluded them since he turned fifteen."

Dinah tugged at the camisole's neckline, trying to hitch it higher to hide her cleavage and her feelings. Despite the circumstances of her marriage, she felt foolishly possessive of her husband.

Guilt ate at her, too. She should have told Tristan who she was weeks ago. Considering the hell both he and Emily had been through because of Zelda, they deserved someone who could actually help them. Not an inept runaway who was such a coward that she found it easier to assume someone else's identity and hide than to face her uncle. She had to tell Tristan the truth soon. Very soon.

"So I've been told." She attempted a smile. "Tristan

himself never neglects to tell me how much in demand he is." She glanced at the mirror and caught Belle staring at her. "Do you envy me?"

It dawned on her that Belle would be the perfect mistress for Tristan. She felt sick about it too, because Belle wasn't a painted harlot, but a beautiful, pleasant, and undoubtedly warm woman.

Belle laughed, rich and deep, the sound lusty and uninhibited. "Damned right I do. I'd be a fool not to. You're a lucky woman."

The chime over the door sounded, and Belle excused herself, leaving Dinah alone to mull over her answer.

She didn't feel lucky. The marriage was ridiculous. She had deceived him from the beginning, but hadn't cared enough to enlighten him because he didn't seem to deserve to know the truth. Of course, the fact that she was a coward had nothing to do with it. She gave herself a disparaging smile.

The frustrating thing was that each day something happened that showed him in a better light. His love and compassion for his sister. His fondness for the children. His patience with everyone he employed. It would be her luck if she started to fall in love with him about the time he discovered she was a phony. When that happened, no amount of effort on her part would make her marriage work, because it would be over and she'd be out on her rump.

Her feelings for him had already changed. She didn't think she'd ever feel this way about another man. Only Tristan. For the first time in weeks, she thought of Charles. Sweet, baby-faced Charles. He might just as well have been her brother, for she felt nothing stronger toward him and never had.

She twisted and gasped, emitting an *ouch* as a pin poked her in the breast. She tried to reach the menacing object, but it was too awkward.

"Dinah? What's wrong?"

Tristan's voice sent shivers through her, especially

when she wasn't expecting it. "I thought you'd be over at the saloon, drinking with your cronies."

She had no idea where she thought he'd be, but she surely hadn't expected him to hang around the dressmaker's. Unless, of course, he'd come to see Belle.

She pushed a noisy sputter of air out through her lips, pretending she didn't care. The nausea in her stomach told her otherwise.

On the other side of the curtain, he laughed, a lazy sound that sent her pulse pounding. "Don't get your hopes up. I had to stay and make sure you didn't hoodwink Belle into letting you keep that damned binder. Makes you look like a stable boy, you know."

She made a face at the curtain. "How nice of you to notice."

"What happened in there? Did you hurt yourself?"

"I've pricked myself with a pin." She gasped again as it dug further into her flesh. "Can you find Belle? Every time I breathe it sticks me."

He pulled the curtain aside and entered, filling the small room so completely Dinah could hardly breathe.

"What are you doing? You shouldn't be in here." She crossed her arms over her breasts.

Cursing quietly, he went behind her. "Don't be foolish. Belle's busy. I can help you."

Memories of the morning before in their shared dressing room made her wonder what kind of help he planned to offer.

"Where's the pin?" Brow furrowed, he unfastened the camisole.

She watched him work in the mirror. He obviously knew his way around a woman's unmentionables. The thought made her jealous, and that surprised her. "My, you're quite skilled at undoing a lady's clothing, aren't you?"

He concentrated on her snaps. "Why wouldn't I be? With the number of tarts you seem to think are begging for my affections, I'd be hard pressed not to learn to undress a woman as quickly as possible." A smile lurked at the corners of his mouth. He pulled the camisole toward him.

"Ouch!"

"What! Damn it, where's the pin?"

"In . . . in front," she explained with a vague movement of her hand.

His fingers went still. "Don't move." He carefully pulled the edges of the camisole apart, then put his hand inside, slowly reaching around to the front. His fingers sent gooseflesh galloping over her skin.

Sweet Mary, how much of this was she expected to take? She tried to remove his hand, but in doing so, pressed the pin into her breast, causing another sharp intake of breath.

"Please," she pleaded, breathless. "Let me get it."

Ignoring her, he pulled the camisole over her arms, freeing her breasts. Her gaze went to the mirror, where the picture of him standing behind her, cradling her bosom, made her heart sprint like a runaway horse.

Blinking furiously, she looked down and saw the pin jutting out on the inner surface of the fabric. "Oh, here it is." She plucked it out and jabbed it into a pincushion that sat nearby.

"It stuck you. You're bleeding."

A tiny drop of blood had soaked into the camisole, and another was on the surface of her breast.

"Oh, that's nothing, I'll—" She gasped as he bent and pressed his lips to the tiny wound.

Desire swamped her. She put her arm around his neck, more to keep her balance than anything else. Her fingers gripped his shoulder as his mouth moved restlessly over her breast. He found her nipple, kissed it, then washed it with his tongue.

Through a fog of desire, she detected a bite of anger that his touch could affect her so. She'd promised herself she'd be stronger than this. Gathering her strength, she cursed and yanked at his hair.

"Tristan! Why in the name of God are you doing this to me?" Her emotions were atumble, and she wanted to scream and cry and beat at his chest.

He raised his head, his eyes dark. She saw them change, and he swore, turning from her to face the curtain. "You're right." He jerked the curtain aside. "Thank you for reminding me."

Closing her eyes, she slumped to the bench and rested her head on the wall. How would she stand it? She'd been married less than two full days, and she wanted to escape. Not because of anything he'd done, although he hadn't kept his word about not touching her, but because, in the deepest recesses of her soul, she wanted his touch—and more.

She knew the only way to stop him was to tell him the truth. She faced a dilemma: whether she told him the truth or not, she would lose.

11

Upstate New York

MARTIN PACED IN THE LIBRARY, FROM THE BOOKSHELVES BY the window, around the expensive rosewood desk with the rich, leather-upholstered chair, across the thick carpet of floral medallions, past the table with the expensive mosaic boxes that stood beneath the carved mirror, to the cabinet that held the liquor, then back to the bookshelves.

He dug out his pocket watch and checked the time. Damn. The fool was late.

Hearing a conveyance pull up outside, Martin stepped to the window and scowled at the man who exited the buggy. "It's about blasted time," he muttered under his breath.

Moments later, his guest entered the study, carrying a travel bag.

"What took you so long? Your train leaves in less than two hours."

The man appeared surprised by Martin's impatience.

He dropped his travel bag onto the floor. "I had to pack, didn't I?"

Martin's answer was a growl as he crossed to his desk and yanked open a drawer. He pulled out an envelope. "In here are your instructions and money to cover your trip."

The man grabbed the envelope and peered inside, thumbing through the contents. His eyes filled with anger and disbelief. "You don't expect me to live on this, do you?"

Martin stood firm. "McCafferty has done all the work. He's already posed as a peddler and combed the countryside searching for her. Found her, too. He's willing to keep up the charade until you get there and get her ready for me." He pulled out a cigar, stuck it between his teeth, but didn't light it.

"We were damned lucky to discover that that nurse was scheduled to leave for California and that my niece did, indeed, use the ticket." He chewed on the cigar, softening it the way he liked it.

"Aren't the police looking for her, too?"

Martin gave him an impatient nod. "That's why I want you on that train immediately. I must find her before they do. Now, go," he commanded. "The only thing you have to do is confirm that she's actually there, and find a way to keep her there. That's your only duty. Anything else and you'll scare her. If she runs, I'll know why."

"When are you coming?"

"Soon enough. I'll get a message through to you." He smirked, the cigar still tight between his teeth. "Then we'll have some real fun."

The man's eyes narrowed and he frowned. "You're an evil man, Odell."

"Not so evil," Martin amended. "Just greedy. Haven't you heard that old expression, what's mine is mine and what's yours is mine? That's the way I've always felt about my brother's money."

"When will I get my final payment?"

"When I can see for myself that she's taken care of. Permanently."

"You mean, after she's been returned to Trenway and under yours and the doctor's thumbs, again? What if they charge her with murdering the nurse? If she's hanged, you get nothing."

Martin couldn't stop a knowing smile. "There are many forms of punishment for a crime. Life in prison without parole comes to mind."

The man tucked the envelope into his breast pocket, grabbed his travel bag, and went to the door. "I know we're not friends, Odell, but I sure as hell wouldn't want to be your enemy."

"That's nice to know," Martin answered with a smirk. "Just don't forget it."

When his spy had gone, Martin poured himself a snifter of his brother's expensive brandy and settled into a velvet wing chair that stood by the fireplace. He sighed, a rich, contented sound. How lucky for him that there were cases of it in the wine cellar.

As he sipped his cognac, relishing the sting, he knew that life was good. The only dark spot was that damned independent niece of his. He scowled into his drink. Leave it to her to find a way out of a veritable prison and spoil all of his plans.

It had been over a week since they'd been to the dressmaker. Tristan and Lucas were busy building the new stable, allowing all of the boys to help. The girls had been asked, but they chose to help in the house.

Dinah was relieved that Tristan was busy, because she was more in control of herself when he wasn't around.

After Tristan had told her about Emily's surgery that morning in the attic, Dinah had been anxious to speak with her. As difficult as it was, she knew it would help them both if she could get Emily to talk about her incarceration. She didn't have to be a nurse to know that it wasn't healthy for Emily to keep her feelings bottled up inside her.

Now, although it was barely dawn, she found Emily in the attic.

"Emily?"

Emily didn't turn. "What are you doing up here?"

Dinah sat on the floor beside her. "That's what I wanted to ask you. You don't have to hide your paintings. I . . . I had no idea you were in so much pain. These paintings tell me you're hurting from the time your mother had you put away."

Emily shuddered, clutching the brush in her fist. "When Mama first came to visit after sending me away, I tried to tell her what they were doing to me, but she ignored me." Her voice was filled with tears, like a child's when no one stops to listen or understand.

Dinah swallowed a knot of emotion. "If anyone understands what you went through, Emily, it's I. I wish you'd tell me about it."

Emily used the end of the brush as a pointer and directed it at the painting that showed her screaming. "They cut me there."

Dinah winced. "Did your mother tell you why?"

Emily shook her head. "They told Mother it was some kind of new treatment. I heard her talking to the doctors, but they didn't talk to me. No one told me anything. I wanted Tristan so badly. Tristan would have told me, but Tristan never came to see me."

Dinah had heard bits and pieces of conversation about a new experiment that involved removing a woman's uterus, which was considered the place where her insanity originated. Daisy had told her that the newest wrinkle in psychiatry was that the very processes of menses, giving birth, and lactation were identified as primary causes of insanity in women.

"Leave it to a man to put that crazy puzzle together," Daisy had criticized. She'd assured Dinah it wasn't so. Dinah chose to believe her.

"Tristan didn't know you were there, Emily."

"I know that, now." She uttered a watery sigh. "Papa wouldn't have let them do that. Papa wouldn't have sent me away. I was Papa's princess."

Dinah pressed her forehead to her knee. "Do you want to talk about the hospital, Emily?"

"I was sad there."

Dinah stroked Emily's shoulders. "I was sad there, too."

"But you worked there. Did it make you sad to see the unhappy girls?"

"Someday I'll tell you my story, Emily, but yes, it made me very sad."

"I cried."

Emily's reactions appeared superficial, but Dinah wondered if that wasn't all she was capable of expressing. In words, anyway.

"You don't have to paint your pictures in the attic, Emily."

She became agitated. "Mama will punish me if she catches me."

Dinah continued to massage Emily's shoulders. "I thought we'd straightened that out. Your mother is dead. She can't punish you. Your brother and I want to make things better for you, and if it helps for you to paint these pictures, then feel free to do them in your room. Or in the great room."

She had a brilliant idea. "Maybe Tristan and Lucas could build you a room to paint in, like the studios of famous artists in Europe."

Emily brightened. "How about the room off the kitchen?"

"You don't mean Alice's room, do you?"

"No, the other room. The porch. It has windows and I could see outside, watch the birds and the animals." Her face was lit up like a child's.

"Why don't we ask Tristan about it?"

"All right." Emily briefly rested her head on Dinah's

hand. "I'm working on that picture of Tristan. It will be ready soon. I'd . . . I'd let you see it, but I want it to be a surprise."

Dinah patted her shoulder. Obviously she had nothing more to share. If there was anything else inside Emily's head, Dinah knew of no way to get at it.

"Will you at least promise me you won't sneak up here and paint anymore?"

"You don't care what I paint?"

"No," Dinah answered with a smile. "Not if it makes you feel better." She crossed to the stairs and was ready to descend when Emily called her.

"Yes, Emily?"

"I like you."

Dinah felt the sting of tears. "I like you too, Emily, very much."

Suddenly remembering the doll, Dinah asked, "Emily, I found a doll up here wearing a blue gown. What happened to her face?"

Emily stopped painting and looked at her lap. "Mama hit it with a wooden spoon."

Dinah cringed. "Why would she do such a thing?"

In a rush of breathy words, Emily answered, "Because I was playing with the doll instead of listening to Mama."

Dinah shook her head and left. She didn't think she'd heard one nice thing about Zelda Fletcher since the day she arrived.

She returned to her room to straighten it before going down to breakfast. As she made her bed, she thought about Tristan and how he'd invaded her dreams. He was there, doing things to her that would awaken her from a dead sleep. She wondered what it would be like to have him beside her. There were times that, miserable as she was, she would have traded her poor stuffed bear for Tristan's warmth.

Once her bed was made, she crossed to the window. It

was another bright, cloudless day. Golden poppies and white daisies swayed to and fro on the hilly slopes. Birds twittered and sang. There was movement in the garden, and Dinah knew it was a rabbit. She pitied the poor thing if Alice caught it.

She hugged herself. It was too glorious a day to be stuck inside. She and Emily would have to go out.

Though none of her new gowns had arrived yet, the outfit she'd ordered specially from Belle, one she'd asked her to keep silent about, had come the day before. She wondered if she'd ever get a chance to wear it.

With a reluctant sigh, she pulled herself from the window, threw on her wrapper over her nightgown, and hurried downstairs. She'd grown accustomed to taking a cup of tea with Alice before Emily awakened, and before they started their day together. She'd had no idea that Emily had probably been awake and in the attic painting long before the rest of the family had stirred.

She bounced into the kitchen. "Good morning, Alice." The room smelled wonderful. The scent of spices, robust ham, and fried potatoes lingered in the air.

The housekeeper was taking a sheet of molasses cookies from the oven. "Morning, dear. Tea's ready."

Dinah inhaled, exhaling a noisy sigh. "It smells good in here." As a girl, she'd been shooed from the kitchen when her mother caught her there, and told some ridiculous story about how it was no place for a gently bred young lady.

She poured herself some tea, then swiped a fresh cookie off the counter.

Alice clucked her tongue. "Now, is that the sort of breakfast a person should have?"

She bit into the cookie; it melted in her mouth. "It's the sort of breakfast I'm going to have." What a luxury to eat what she pleased. She nibbled the cookie, and Alice placed a bowl of porridge, swimming in cream and melting butter, in front of her.

"You expect me to eat that, too?"

"Cookies are fine after breakfast. You need something that sticks to your ribs."

Dinah felt a twinge of guilt knowing that her friends at Trenway were eating gray swill with mysterious chunks floating in it, while she groused about eating Alice's delicious cooked cereal. Of course, that shame was merely perched on top of the heavy burden of guilt she carried with her constantly because she couldn't bear to tell Tristan who she really was.

There were footsteps on the stoop. Even before the door opened, she knew who it was. Her body betrayed her. She hadn't recovered from her dreams, in which he'd been her seductive lover.

Tristan stepped into the kitchen, stopped, and gave her a casual glance. A shiver stole over her.

"You're awake early." He crossed the to the stove and poured himself a cup of coffee.

"I'm here at this time every morning." She studied his wide shoulders, snugly encased in the buckskin shirt he wore when he worked outside. He was so beautiful he took her breath away. The thought seemed corny to her, but she knew of no other way to describe him.

Alice put a plate of breakfast on the table and ordered him to sit. He unfolded the linen napkin and dropped it onto his lap, then caught Dinah watching him. He gave her a lazy smile, sending her stupid, lovesick heart into her throat.

"I'm cooking a batch of beans for lunch today," Alice announced. "Also have a ham and some cornbread for those youngsters. My," she said with a sigh, "it does my old heart good to have someone eat and enjoy my cooking." She tossed Dinah a knowing glance.

"Alice, I love your cooking. I wish I could convince you of that." Dinah was slowly experiencing the return of her appetite. Ever since Tristan had told her of Alice's pique regarding her inability to eat, she'd made a bigger effort to do so. She'd also quit storing food in her room, which was probably a good thing, because one night she was certain she'd heard a mouse. In the morning, half of the piece of sugar cake she'd saved was gone. The idea that she'd had a furry visitor while she slept made her skin crawl. Many a night at Trenway, she'd awakened after a creature had scurried across her body.

"You are getting better, I will admit that." Alice plunked another slab of fried ham onto Tristan's plate. "When do the children start working?"

Dinah shoved Trenway from her mind and perked up. "The children? You're working with the children today? Oh, I'd love to come with you."

Tristan's expression was closed. "It's time to plant the corn. Besides, Emily is plenty for you to deal with."

Dinah sniffed at him. "Despot."

The merest hint of a smile touched the corners of his mouth. "Hooligan."

Glaring at him, she ate a spoonful of porridge. "Tyrant."

His eyes flashed as his gaze moved over her hair. "Witch."

She gave him a menacing look. "Devil."

He studied her chest, his gaze roaming over it as palpably as if he'd touched it.

Her nipples pebbled against her nightgown.

"Stable boy," he murmured, slicing through the thick hunk of meat.

She felt the blush steal over her chest and into her neck. "Despicable Hun," she responded in kind, heat climbing to her face.

His gaze told her he remembered well their exchange in Belle's dressing room. "You won't wear it today."

She took another casual spoonful of cereal, swallowed, and daintily wiped her mouth. "Wear what?" She tried for innocence.

"You know damned well what."

She continued her naiveté. "Is that an order, master?"

"It is," he ruled.

She gave him an obsequious nod. "Then, by all means, I will honor it."

He seemed surprised. No, she thought, he was shocked. She hid her smile.

"You won't wear the damned thing?"

"No," she said with an exaggerated sigh, "not today, anyway." She wondered how long his request would last once she donned her new outfit.

She watched him eat, mesmerized by every move he made. To make certain he didn't catch her staring at him, she gave him a quick grin each time he glanced at her.

"Do you mind if Emily and I watch you work with the children today?"

He raised a brow. "Might be tedious."

She hid her smile. "Oh, I don't think it will be tedious at all. Emily can sketch and I can . . . fetch."

"Like a puppy?" His smile was indolent.

"No, like a well trained wife," she assured him. She crossed her fingers beneath the table.

He laughed, the sound so genuine it sent Dinah's heart into her throat again.

"That will be the day." He shoved his chair from the table and stood. "That will indeed be the day," he repeated as he strode toward the door.

"Oh, Tristan?" When he turned, she asked, "Would it be possible for you and Lucas and maybe a few of the boys to fix up the porch off the kitchen here as a room where Emily could paint? Would you have time?"

"What a good idea," Alice acknowledged.

Tristan opened the door to the porch. "She can use it now."

"Nothing has to be done to it?"

"Not until fall. Then we can insulate it, make it ready for winter. We'll be starting the bedroom additions for the children very soon. We'll finish off this room then, too."

Dinah couldn't hide her surprise. "You're building bedrooms for the children?"

He scowled. "Of course. What did you think I'd do, keep my own children in a separate building, like orphans?"

"Your own children?"

"Yes," he answered with a growl. "As long as no one else wants them, they're mine."

Ignoring his frown, she smiled, her heart expanding with this new feeling she had for him. "Of course."

Obviously puzzled by her demeanor, he returned to the other door and left.

She went to the window and watched him take long, easy strides to his devil-black mount and ride toward the fields.

"Allowing Emily to have a studio of her own should have been done years ago." Alice removed another batch of cookies, sliding them onto the counter.

"No one knew she was in such pain."

"Interesting conversation, before you started talking about the porch and the new addition," Alice observed.

"We rarely have any other kind."

"So, if you've promised not to wear the cursed binder today, I imagine you have something else up your sleeve."

Dinah felt a rush of surprise. "You know about the binder?"

"Dear girl, I've straightened that dressing room often enough. I've also been around for some time, and I know there aren't too many uses for a lengthy strip of linen. Wore one myself when my Rory was born. I had so much milk I could have fed three infants. Unfortunately," she said, her voice sad, "Rory didn't live long enough to enjoy my bounty."

Dinah felt a crushing ache in her chest. "He died?"

Alice nodded. "More'n twenty-five years ago."

"Oh, Alice, I'm sorry."

"It still hurts, sometimes." Alice slanted Dinah a

curious glance. "I can't for the life of me imagine why you'd want to wear a breast binder."

Dinah returned to the table and toyed with her cereal. "It's a long story, and it doesn't bear repeating. He doesn't want me to wear it, but to be honest, I've worn it for so long, I feel lost without it."

There was a knock on the door, and one of the girls, Dinah thought it was Sarafina, stepped into the kitchen. She gave Dinah a quick smile, then turned to Alice. "Miss Leeta says to tell you she'll take care of lunch and dinner, Mrs. Linberg."

"Well, young lady, you tell Miss Leeta that I have lunch cooking, but she can feed you tonight, with my blessings."

The girl smiled and turned to go.

"Sarafina?"

"Yes, ma'am?"

"This is your house as well as mine. You don't have to knock to come inside."

The child's smile widened, and she ran out the door.

"She has such a pretty name," Dinah observed.

Alice nodded. "Ya sure, it's nice she has something pretty. She's twelve, and has already lived a hard life."

"Are her parents dead, too?"

"Poor little thing," Alice murmured, "I'm not sure she ever knew who they were."

"How can that happen?"

"Oh, Indians get killed all the time. Don't seem to be a reason for it. But as for Sarafina, as best as I can recall, she's one who lived with a small tribe further up into the mountains. Renegades came through and killed everyone. Least, they probably thought they had. Sarafina and her older brother, Henry, were off picking berries or something, and when they returned, everyone was dead." She clucked. "Terrible thing for children to see. Terrible. *Uff dah.*"

Dinah couldn't imagine such a thing. Her own horrors had been hard enough to deal with. She couldn't imagine what those children had gone through. "How did Tristan find them?"

"He and Lucas were returning from Nevada and found them asleep by the side of the road. They brought them here. *Uff dah,* they were dirty little stragglers. They was surprisingly well mannered, though."

Suddenly, Dinah was more than eager to get to know them better. "I'm anxious to watch Tristan with the children."

"He's very gentle with them, but stern when they need it. He'll make a good father."

An image of Tristan cradling a child of their own sent longing through Dinah. The feeling surprised her. And frightened her.

"Thank the Lord Tristan's papa didn't pass on any sooner," Alice was saying. "Without his influence on Tristan's life, the boy might have turned out to be a real scoundrel."

"Leeta has told me the children are orphans. How did Tristan find the others?"

"Oh, they're not hard to find, dear. There are too many of them out there, unwanted and unloved, making nuisances of themselves."

"They have no families?"

"Most of them are breeds. Some are children whose parents have been killed. Maybe the whole tribe is dead, like Sarafina's and Henry's, and they have no place to go."

"I listened to Tristan tell them a story the other day. They seem bright."

Alice mixed up a batch of cornbread. "Some are too bright for their britches. Like that rapscallion, Little Hawk."

Dinah remembered. "The boy with the deformed foot. I felt sorry for him."

"Don't pity him, dear. He's the brightest of the lot. Limp or no, he'll be a handful. He'll either become the biggest scoundrel of the bunch or the most successful." She snorted a laugh. "Maybe both."

"Then, Tristan will keep the children until they're grown?"

"Oh, of course. He's already seen a lawyer in San Francisco about adopting them."

Dinah almost groaned. So that's what he meant. Slowly she was learning that Tristan Fletcher was a warm, generous, kind human being. If she learned he had any more good qualities, she'd have to nominate him for sainthood. She forced herself to finish her porridge, then stood.

"When Emily comes down, tell her we're going to watch Tristan work with the children today and I think she should bring her sketch pad."

"Are you going to wear one of your new outfits?" Alice tossed the question over her shoulder.

"Oh, by all means. I can't wait." Dinah skipped toward the door.

"I'm glad. Tristan will be pleased."

Dinah scurried up the stairs and into her room. Pleased? She went to her wardrobe and pulled out the two pieces. No, she thought with a tiny bite of apprehension, she didn't think pleased was the word.

Miguel stopped the buggy on the edge of the field. The children were working, some sowing seeds by hand, others using the horse-drawn plows. Dinah noticed as they rode up that the children changed chores so they all could get a chance to work with the horses.

With Miguel's assistance, Emily stepped from the buggy. He offered to help Dinah, but she waved him off. Shouting a greeting, he raced toward the others.

Dinah lifted the blanket from the buggy and spread it under a fruit tree. Emily sat immediately and opened her pad.

A light breeze ruffled the leaves. Dinah smelled grass

and the tang of horse flesh. Shading her eyes, she watched a hawk glide overhead. He emitted a high pitched *kee-argh.* She touched Emily's arm. "Look at him. Isn't he beautiful?"

Emily lifted her gaze. "It's a redtail."

"How can you tell?"

"By the color," she responded, making a quick sketch on the pad. "See?"

Dinah moved closer and studied the drawing. It depicted the brown hawk in mid flight, wings wide, nose down as if hunting for prey. "You did that just now?"

Emily shrugged, as if it were nothing unusual.

A thought began to form in Dinah's brain. They could do something for Emily and her art if Tristan would agree. She would have to ask him when he was taking another trip to San Francisco.

She leaned toward Emily again. "What else are you going to draw today?"

From beneath her big straw hat, Emily squinted at the working children. "Them," she answered simply.

Dinah felt, rather than heard, Tristan stomping up behind her. The earth shook.

"What in the bloody hell are you wearing?!"

Pasting on a pleasant expression, she turned. "Don't use that kind of language in front of the children."

He had the appearance of a volcano ready to blow. His eyes were dark, threatening; the veins in his neck bulged, reminding her of plump earthworms.

"Where did you get those . . . those trousers and that . . ." He sputtered. "Shirt?"

She'd never seen him speechless before. "Belle made them for me." Though her heart slammed against her ribcage, she tried not to be affected by his anger.

His Adam's apple worked frantically. "What are you trying to prove?"

"Prove? Why, nothing." She began to wish she hadn't worn them. She tried to brush some lint from her shirt front but stopped when her breasts shook beneath the clingy fabric.

"Stop that." The request was barely audible, but it was filled with fury.

She felt herself flush. "You ordered me not to wear the binder, and I'm not wearing it. How much more can I do for you?"

He grabbed her arm, his thumb moving over her palm as he dragged her from Emily. The mere touch of him sent shivers over her skin, and from the thunderous expression on his face, she knew she was flirting with danger.

He yanked her to him. "Have you any idea what that outfit will do to those adolescent boys?"

Both boys and girls had watched her and Emily arrive, but they had since ignored them. Dinah tried to stifle a laugh, but it snorted through her nose. "Tristan, they aren't even paying attention. If they do, it will be because of the scene you're making."

The telltale knot developed in his jaw. "Why are you doing this?"

"Because all of my life I've wanted a pair of trousers." She smoothed her palms over her hips.

"For the love of God, why did you wait until now to try them?"

His gaze was focused on her chest, and her nipples tightened. She was beginning to wonder about that herself. "I didn't think you'd mind," she lied, crossing her fingers behind her back. There she was, fibbing again. Perhaps one day her nose really would grow.

He swung away, his hands balled into fists.

"Teddy?" Emily's voice was filled with concern.

"What is it, Emmy?"

"Are you angry?"

"Not with you, pretty one."

At the endearment, Emily smiled and went back to her sketch pad.

Once Tristan had returned to the field, Dinah collapsed on the blanket. Strangely, his reaction didn't make her feel as good as she had thought it would.

Red spots of fury wriggled before Tristan's vision. The sneak deserved a spanking, that's what she deserved. Maybe she'd even get it. He couldn't understand why she'd be so blatantly outrageous. She knew how she affected him. She knew, yet she brazenly wore pants that suggestively cupped her butt and hips and a shirt that hid none of her charms.

He closed his eyes, hoping to eradicate the memory of fabric clinging to firm, round breasts and pert nipples thrusting toward him, but it was burned inside his eyelids.

Boyish pants and a loose, full-cut shirt. How any woman born could be seductive in that outfit was beyond his reasoning. Yet she was. Damned seductive. If he had any sense at all, he wouldn't think about how it would feel to dip his fingers beneath her waistband and touch her soft, pliant flesh. There hadn't been room for drawers, he was certain of that.

So what was she wearing under them? Nothing at all? He cursed. Think of it. Behind the buttons of that mannish fly were rusty red curls. Soft, wet lips that would swell at his touch. He groaned a curse.

He couldn't go on like this. If he wasn't careful, he'd take her. He would ruin her, simply because he wanted her. It wasn't fair. But try as he might to remember the stuffed bear and the thoughts it dredged up, he was aroused, and nothing short of a cold swim in the river would help him. Even that wouldn't drench the fire.

Mouthing another curse, he knew what he had to do. He had to undo the mistake he'd made by marrying her, yet somehow keep her safe from Martin Odell.

12

Dinah stood before the painting in progress of Tristan. Emily had painted him as an adult, with a smaller image of him as a child sketched into the background.

"It's wonderful, Emily. You've captured him perfectly," she complimented. The hard, square line of his jaw. The mysterious depth of his expressive eyes. His high, sharp cheekbones. How often had she wanted to touch his face? Run her fingers over the skin, feel the swells and hollows? More times than she could count.

"He's very handsome," she mused, admiring the work.

"He's a half-breed, you know."

Dinah wasn't entirely surprised. "But you're not."

Emily's smile was warm. "No. Mama and Papa brought him home one day after they'd been visiting near Sacramento."

She picked up her needlepoint and began working on

the outline of a flower. "Mama never liked him much. She wasn't happy that I did. He was like a doll to me at first. And having him around, even when he was cross, always made me feel better."

She shook her head. "Mama didn't understand that. I don't think she wanted to, because"—She stopped working, her hands resting in her lap—"because Mama never wanted Tristan in the first place, and she didn't care who knew it. Including poor Tristan."

Dinah was beginning to understand the fierce bond between brother and sister. She could only imagine how Tristan must have felt when he learned Emily had been institutionalized.

"I think it's wonderful that you two care so much for each other."

Emily looked up, surprised. "Do you really?"

"Yes. Why wouldn't I?"

Emily shook her head. "Before Mama died, she warned me that if Tristan ever became interested in another woman, he'd stop caring for me."

Dinah disliked Zelda Fletcher more with each passing day. "That's a terrible seed to plant in a young girl's mind, Emily." To say nothing of the fact that Tristan wasn't interested in her. No matter how one looked at it, Dinah was no threat to Emily.

Emily's fingers flew over her needlepoint, yet each stitch was impeccably clean. "Tristan almost got married once before."

"Yes, I heard that."

"I didn't want her to come. I would have been mean to her if she had." Emily paused. "Like I was when you first came."

"You might have liked her," Dinah answered generously.

Emily shook her head but didn't look up from her needlework. "I would have hated her."

Each time Dinah thought about the tantrums Emily

had shown since she'd arrived, she remembered her hospitalization and subsequent surgery. Probably no one would ever know what horrible memories she had locked away in her mind. Dinah could guess, and she would probably be right.

There were a few women like Emily at Trenway, whose minds were not fully developed and who didn't understand why they were there or what was being done to them. Dinah remembered the puzzled expressions on those women's faces when they were treated badly, for they didn't know why. Chances were that there was no reason. They were easy targets for overzealous matrons and licentious guards.

She bent and kissed Emily's smooth cheek. "I love the picture of Tristan, Emily. You're very talented. Other people should be able to enjoy your art. Would you like that?"

Emily's shrug was noncommittal. "How would they do that?"

"Oh," Dinah answered, her plan forming in her head, "we'll find a way. Is there anything I can get for you before bed?"

Emily kept her gaze down and shook her head. "Alice will be here soon with some warm milk."

Dinah offered a smile. "Good night, then."

"Night."

Dinah strutted to her room, still wearing her trousers and shirt. She could get used to dressing like this. The clothes allowed so much more freedom than skirts and petticoats, which she often tripped over.

Of course, over dinner, Tristan had refused to acknowledge her. That wasn't a good thing. With a half-troubled sigh, she flopped onto the edge of the bed, raised her ankle over her knee and removed one of her new boots.

She wasn't sure what she'd thought to prove by wearing the outfit. She'd gotten his attention, but it wasn't the kind of attention she'd expected. Or wanted. Oh, hell's bells, she didn't know what she wanted. She hadn't supposed that he would ignore her.

She rolled her eyes and frowned, tossing her boot across the room. It hit the wall, falling to the floor with a thud, and she followed it quickly with the other.

She stood and studied herself in the mirror. The outfit wasn't feminine. Maybe that was it. He probably liked his women dressed in fussy, ladylike gowns. That was why he was so adamant about being at Belle's, so he could monitor her choices.

"Live and learn," she muttered with a dejected sigh. She began unbuttoning her shirt, and suddenly felt the hair on the back of her neck bristle. She turned, her fingers poised on the buttons. Tristan leaned against the dressing room door.

"Don't worry, master," she said with mock servility, "I'm taking them off."

"Don't touch those buttons."

She raised her eyes heavenward. "If you don't want to watch, then leave the room."

"Have you any idea what I've gone through today because of you?"

She gaped at him. "What you've gone through?"

He ignored her pique. "Do you have any idea what it's like to try to concentrate on a menial task like planting corn, when all I can think of is planting a damned seed in you?"

Her jaw worked frantically. "Don't be crude."

She retreated as he strode toward her. He stopped an arm's length from her when the curved surface behind her knees hit the bed. She could smell the brandy on his breath.

"I want to scold you, damn it. I even thought about taking you over my knee and spanking you, but knowing you," he added, his eyes dark and hot and his voice slurring slightly, "you'd probably enjoy it."

She gave her head a violent shake. "No, I—"

"And if you enjoyed it, you can be damned sure I would." His heated gaze moved over her, stopping at the buttoned fly of her trousers. "What are you wearing under those things?"

"N-n-nothing. I—" His sharp intake of breath stopped her from continuing.

"It's as I suspected."

"I . . . I meant to, but they were snug and there wasn't room." The words dwindled to a whisper when she noticed his expression.

He pulled her shirt from her trousers, tucked his hand inside the waistband and tugged her close. She had no choice but to follow. His fingers on the flesh of her lower belly made her knees weak. He dipped lower, one finger nudging her. The overwhelming sensation stunned her, and she grabbed his arms as her knees buckled.

He followed her onto the bed, kissing her hard. His tongue was in her mouth, moving in and out, just as his fingers stroked between her legs. His strength frightened her, as did her own desire.

He stopped kissing her and growled into her neck. "I want to touch you. I only want to touch you."

She was no longer afraid. Innocent and naïve perhaps, but not afraid. She rubbed her cheek over his hair, threading her fingers through the inky mass as hunger heated her flesh.

He kissed her again, slowly this time, his mouth opening over hers. He drew away, his breath warm on her lips as he nudged them with his tongue. She met his tongue with her own, finding herself breathless with a yearning that went beyond desire. He seduced her, taught her how to arouse him with the merest touch of tongue tip to tongue tip.

As he unbuttoned her shirt, he bent to kiss her skin. With slow deliberation, he spread her shirt wide and gazed at her breasts, a palm cupping each, a thumb moving across each nipple.

Through her hazy hunger, she saw the pain in his eyes

and she reached for him, tugging him down beside her. But he stilled her hands, pulling her to a sitting position and coaxing her to remove her shirt.

His Adam's apple bobbed as he swallowed, and he bent and took first one nipple, then the other into his mouth, rolling over them with his tongue. She gripped his hair, pressing him closer as a hot, vital yearning tracked a path to her pelvis and lower.

He turned her around, drawing her to him while he continued caressing her. He kissed her neck, her ear, her bare shoulder. His hand moved over her ribcage to her abdomen, circling her navel beneath the waistband of her trousers.

She automatically inhaled when his fingers moved lower, innocently allowing him access. He stroked her again, and through her arousal she felt his behind her, thick and hard.

He slowly unbuttoned her fly. Her heart pounded, roaring in her ears as she waited. When he'd finished, he moved his hand inside, caressing her hip, moving to her buttocks where he dipped his fingers around to her front, titillating her.

She heard the sounds she made in her throat, although she'd never made them before. And, oh, sweet Mary, what his touch did to her! There was an ache of pleasure, an instinct that if she surrendered, she would know more satisfaction than she could ever have imagined.

"I want to see you there," he whispered, close to her ear. He tugged her trousers down over her knees. In her desire and her haste to please him, she kicked at them, sending them sprawling onto the floor.

She lay on her back, her heart pounding wildly as he gazed at her.

"So red." His fingers barely touched her, yet her breath quickened at the contact. "I knew it would be this color."

His words made her brave, and she moved one leg to the side, bending her knee.

He gently rested his head on her stomach. She felt the heat of his breath close to her private place and she experienced a sudden burst of emotion-laced desire. She emitted a shuddery moan before she bit her lip to stop herself.

He kissed her low on the stomach, and her yearning was so intense she couldn't protest, nor did she want to. His mouth rested on her mound, and she gripped the bedding in her fists and pressed her lips together, fearing if she uttered even the smallest of sounds he would stop.

He kissed her there, and she felt pleasure and pain as her arousal built. He moved between her thighs, kissing her flesh on either side, returning to the place that surged with hunger for him. His tongue moved over her, parting her, lunging inside, then flattening against the nub, and finally searching the length of her.

"Oh, oh, sweet heaven." The words were almost lost as she felt it coming, that exquisite, splintering burst of pleasure that brought her pelvis off the bed as her knees imprisoned him between her thighs.

He kissed her as he slowly moved up her body. He reached her mouth, his eyelids heavy, his eyes dark.

"I'm going to kiss you. I want you to taste how delicious you are."

His lips came down on hers, and she sampled the musky flavor. She was not aroused by her own scent, but she felt stimulated that he was.

She clung to him, hooking her bare legs over his and feeling him against her, hard and strong behind the fly of his trousers. The roughness of his clothing on her flesh excited her, and she ran her hands along his shoulders and moved with him, sensing the rekindling of desire.

A tortured sound tore from his throat and he flung himself off the bed. "No!"

Her emotions were tangled inside her. She wanted to make love with him, not have him make love to her.

His head bowed, he stood at the dressing room door, his fist on the doorjamb.

She left the bed and tentatively touched his shoulder. He flinched.

"Tristan, it's all right."

He spun around and grabbed her arms. "It's *not* all right. This wasn't supposed to happen." He cursed and crossed to the window. "What an ass I was. I thought I could live a celibate life with a woman. I thought if I offered her enough money, she would stay in the background, care for Emily, and keep out of my way. Maybe I could have done it. Maybe. Then *you* showed up."

She didn't know what to say. "I don't care about the money, Tristan."

He shuddered a sigh. "I know you don't." He stared into the night. "Why couldn't you have been the woman I'd imagined, Dinah? Why couldn't you have been merely pleasant looking? Quiet and prim and obedient?"

He'd described Daisy. He'd have been happy with her. Dinah knew that as certainly as she felt the sinking in her stomach. Daisy was everything she was not.

"You weren't exactly what I'd expected, either," she countered.

He uttered a humorless laugh. "I don't suppose I'm much of a prize, with a sister who needs constant attention, not to mention eight half bloods who will soon bear my name."

There was silence in the room. Dinah didn't know how to answer him. Those things he thought were offensive about himself were the very things that had made her fall in love with him. She shivered, hugging herself.

"I can't go through with this, Dinah. I can't do this to you."

"But, I'm—"

"I know what you're going to say. That you're my wife." He cursed again. "You shouldn't be. With anyone else, maybe I could have gone through with it. It wasn't a bad offer. Hell, it was a damned good one, as stupid, arrogant, asinine offers go," he added, trying to smile.

"But you don't deserve this. You're so young. You have your whole life ahead of you. You shouldn't have to waste five years of it in a loveless marriage."

She swallowed, then pressed her hand to her mouth, forcing anger through her pain. "Then why did you make me? I wanted to leave, Tristan, remember? All you had to do was pay me the wages I'd earned, and I would have been gone. Now, just—" She took a deep breath, annoyed that she'd begun to cry. Just as she was beginning to fall in love with him, he wanted to call the whole thing off.

But she wouldn't beg, not for him, not for anyone. "What are you going to do, then? Divorce me? You'll have to, Tristan, because I won't do it. I won't."

"Divorce won't be necessary. I haven't touched you. Not that way. We can have the marriage annulled."

Annulment? Making their marriage invalid? It shouldn't be allowed, because he had touched her. In so many ways. Again she recounted all of the things that had made her fall in love with him. The things that had touched her heart. But apparently those touches didn't count.

"If . . . if you had touched me, then what?"

"I don't know, Dinah. I honestly don't know."

Tristan's clever ploy to keep Dinah safe from her uncle had backfired on him. He couldn't keep her here for five more days without making her his, much less five years.

Closing his eyes, he pressed his knuckles against his lids. How stupid was he, anyway? What made him think he could do this with any woman? The initial agreement had been absurd. It had looked good on paper; in theory it was generous. In reality, it was unfair, and God, so damned stupid. Lucas had known this, but Tristan had been too arrogant to listen. Had he thought he could simply give a woman his name, then ignore her for five years? Had he imagined he could live like a monk for that length of time?

He knew he would not. But he'd fancied finding a lusty mistress to care for his needs. Did he once think about the woman? Had he imagined she would be so sexless that she would agree to be his wife in name only for five damned years and not want anything from him in return but the money? He cursed again, dredging up vile words that fitted his mood.

And to have that woman be Dinah, of all people. Dinah, who had already lived through one hell and was prepared to live through another with him. Dinah, who was so insecure she slept with a tattered teddy bear. Dinah, who had been so starved for decent food she'd hoarded it in her room, afraid she would go hungry. Dinah, who had only asked that someone care for her.

God, but he was a fool. His motives for marrying her might have been arrogantly noble, but the underlying truth was, he'd wanted to. He'd wanted her. His lust had ruled, and because of it, she would never have the life she deserved. The love she deserved. But he had the ability to change that, now, and he would.

What a cocky bastard he'd been to think he was the answer to any woman's prayers. How blinded he'd been by his own self-worth. His own, pompous, stupid self-worth.

Suddenly, he felt restless. He had to leave. The timing was bad, but Lucas could continue with the planting. There was not much left to do, and Lucas had excellent rapport with the children.

But what of the peddler? His imagination had run away with him, that's all. No one knew Dinah was here. David had assured him of that, and the peddler hadn't returned. If there was a threat, Tristan would have continued to feel it. Or David would have wired him to warn him.

As he finished dressing, he knew what he had to do. He dashed off a note to Alice, explaining where he was going. What he didn't add, was that he was also going to have his marriage annulled.

Dinah continued to feel empty long into the night. He was going to dissolve their marriage before it had even become one. At first light, she dressed, feeling listless. All of the things she'd done to provoke him seemed petty now. The binder, the trousers, they had been foolish tricks. She'd thought she was so clever, and all the while, she'd been childish. Look where it had gotten her. She'd worried needlessly that when he discovered who she truly was, he'd dump her like bad stew. Sweet Mary, he'd dumped her without even knowing the truth.

She gave herself a cursory glance in the mirror. A few of her new gowns had arrived the evening before. The two-piece ecru silk and cotton she wore now was pretty. It could have been sackcloth and it wouldn't have mattered. What mattered now was keeping busy so she wouldn't have to think about what he was going to do. She couldn't stop him, but she wouldn't make it easy. Once he freed her, he would undoubtedly expect her to leave.

Whether he believed it or not, she was needed here. Emily needed her, and Dinah saw a great need with the children. How had he expected them to be cared for? Surely he knew that Alice couldn't do the job, and Leeta had a family of her own.

Children weren't stick people that he could stack in a corner when he didn't have time for them.

She left her room, taking the stairs to the kitchen. "Good morning, Alice."

"What's good about it?" Alice removed a cloth and punched her bread, the dough making sucking sounds as it adhered to her fists.

"Oh-oh, someone got up on the wrong side of the bed this morning." Dinah went to the table and poured herself a cup of tea.

Alice nodded toward the counter. "I was fine until I read that note."

Dinah took her teacup and crossed to the counter. The note was from Tristan, and even before she read it, her stomach churned. After reading it, she tried to hide her disappointment. "He's gone? To his brother's?"

"Ya sure. Must have left before dawn, because I've been up since five."

"Did you know about this?"

Alice shook her head. "Probably a spur-of-the-moment decision. Can't understand it, though. He only goes off like this when he's upset, and it's been a while since the last time."

Dinah's stomach continued to churn. It was because of her. Telling Alice he was going to see his brother was an excuse to get away from her. Dinah had no doubt that he would visit his mistress. She was innocent and naïve, but she knew that men had their needs, and obviously, she thought, her chest hurting, he didn't want her to satisfy his. She also had no doubt that when he returned, they would no longer be married.

"How long was he gone the last time?"

"Oh, a couple of days. No more than a week." Alice heaped hot cereal into a bowl, sprinkled it with sugar, and doused it with cream. "You'd best eat something, girl. You'll need your strength. When Emily discovers he's gone, she's going to throw a royal fit."

Dinah slid into a chair and stirred her cereal with little enthusiasm. "What are the children supposed to do today?"

Alice gave her a tired sigh. "I don't know, but I have enough to do just keeping them fed. Entertaining them isn't my responsibility."

She sounded upset; Dinah knew the cause. "I'll find Leeta and see what she wants me to do. I'm sure I can be of some help."

"I don't know why Tristan would go off like this,

especially now that the children are here. It isn't like him to be so irresponsible."

When he returned, Dinah promised herself, she'd tell him the truth. Better late than never. She should have admitted it last night. After all, he'd bared his soul, she should have done the same.

In spite of everything, she should have insisted that he stay with her so she could talk with him, but he'd seemed angry and remote, and she'd been afraid to ask.

Now, it was probably too late. For all she knew, he could be out hiring a replacement for her at this minute—after he'd warmed himself between his balloon-breasted whore's thighs.

Her thoughts were petty, but as long as she kept them to herself, she didn't care.

13

McCloud Ranch, in the shadow of Devil Mountain

JULIA SNUGGLED DEEPER INTO THE BEDDING AND ROLLED toward her husband. He put his arm around her and drew her close.

"The clock just struck four, Mac."

Early in their marriage Julia began calling him Mac. Years ago, when he'd asked her why, she'd told him that Wolf had been wild and dangerous, but Mac was the man she'd grown to love. "I don't have to get up for an hour." He nuzzled her ear.

"I know, that's why I mentioned it." She smiled into his shoulder. "If we're quiet, the girls won't hear us."

He reached under her gown and touched her, making an appreciative sound. She moved her legs apart.

"I don't like it quiet. I like it noisy."

She chuckled, drawing in a breath as desire warmed her. She'd been ready for him before she woke.

"I'll never get tired of loving you." He hiked up her

gown and pulled her on top of him; he was ready, too. "I'd slay dragons for you."

Contentment oozed from her. "There you go, sounding like a savant, again."

His hands roamed beneath her nightgown, snaking to her nipples. He rubbed one and then the other. "Ah, another one of those words that gets me all hot."

She laughed softly, then made a purring sound in her throat as she straddled him.

"You sound like a cat in heat." One hand dipped low, stroking her where their bodies joined. "I like it."

"Lord, I'd better not be." She shuddered with desire and moved, allowing for deeper penetration. No longer able to speak, she concentrated on loving her man. When she felt herself coming, she tugged at him and he rolled over, entering her the old-fashioned way.

They rode the crest of their passion together.

Afterward, she clung to him, threading her fingers through his inky hair. "We'd be insane to have another child with Joanna and Joy barely a year old."

He breathed hard to catch his breath. "Not to mention Marymae and Bethany." He no longer thought of Marymae and Beth as being Julia's sister's children. He stroked her behind. "I love your ass, woman."

Her chuckle started deep in her throat. "You always have."

"I always will," he promised.

From far away, she heard one of the twins began to cry. "Joy's awake."

He cursed gently. "How in the devil can you tell?"

"I just can." Footsteps followed, passing above them. "She's gotten Mattie up."

"Thank the good Lord for your salty Aunt Mattie. If she hadn't decided to stay, we'd have had to search for a nurse. Or a nanny. Four children under the age of three is too much work for any woman, but especially for the woman whose ass I've admired since the first time I saw her."

"Hmmm. And, just who might that be?"

"Aw, some prickly farmer's daughter whose charms weren't discovered until I came along," he teased.

"How lucky for her that you did."

He kissed her, his tongue sweeping the inside of her mouth. "Damned lucky, I'd say."

He was ready for her again. With gentle fingers she fondled him. "Is there time?"

Just then, there was a pounding on the front door. Mac muttered a mild oath. "Who in the hell is up at this hour?" He lit the lamp beside the bed, rose, and jammed his feet into his jeans. "Keep the bed warm, darlin'."

"Mac?"

He turned, a questioning look on his face.

"I love your ass, too."

He gave her a hot, half grin, buttoned his fly and pattered from the room in his bare feet.

Tristan felt guilty rousing his brother so early in the morning, but he'd already napped in the barn for a couple of hours with his brother's dogs. They'd smelled Wolf and Amy on his clothing and had curled up next to him as if he were an old friend.

Halfway here, he'd felt a rush of guilt at leaving Dinah, slinking away like a coward without an explanation. But he knew that if he stayed, he'd be tempted to take her. Tristan realized that his brother might be an old married man, but surely he would agree with Tristan's decision to have his marriage annulled.

The door opened. Wolf leaned against it, clad only in half-buttoned jeans, a peculiar smile on his face. "Well, well. Now, don't tell me this is a social visit. Not at this time of the morning."

Tristan answered the smile. Though they'd been together less than a half dozen times, they were comfortable with each other. "Thought you might need a hand with all of your women."

Wolf's grin widened, and he jerked his thumb toward

the interior of the house. "Get in here. I'll rustle up some coffee."

Tristan followed his brother into the large kitchen. Wolf and his wife had moved from their small ranch to a larger one after the birth of their twins.

He took a seat at the table. "Four girls, Wolf? Four? How in the hell did you manage that?"

Wolf smirked at him over his shoulder while he prepared the coffee. "I'm just doing my job, Tris. Just doing my job."

Footsteps behind him announced Wolf's wife.

"By the sounds of it, my love," she murmured, standing on tiptoes to kiss him, "one would think you produced them all by yourself." She came to Tristan, took his hands and gave him a warm smile. "It's nice to see you again, Tristan. We don't see nearly enough of you."

Julia was a pretty woman. Not beautiful, by any means, but after meeting her the first time, Tristan understood what had attracted his twin to her. She had a wise, ageless soul, and he saw the love in her eyes every time she looked at Wolf.

He watched as she nudged her husband aside and finished making coffee. "I'm sorry I got here so early, but to tell the truth, I've been in the barn with the dogs since two A.M."

Wolf guffawed. "Something must be really gnawing at you to sink that low."

"Gnawing like a beaver on a branch." An image of Dinah's sweet face floated before his eyes.

Wolf caressed his wife's neck. "Must be bad if you're sinking to folksy expressions."

Julia cleared her throat. "I think I'll leave you two to mull over Tristan's problem. Anyway, I'm sure Mattie needs help with the babies." Before she turned to leave, she said, "There are cinnamon buns in the pie safe, darling. They should satisfy you until breakfast."

"I'd have been more satisfied if someone hadn't

knocked on the damned door a minute ago." Wolf gave his wife a leer.

"You're shameless." She blushed and left the room.

Both men watched her leave. Warmth stole into Wolf's harsh features and Tristan felt a hard knot of envy.

They exchanged glances.

"You're missing out on something pretty damned special, Tris."

Tristan expelled a heavy sigh. "It's only special if you're lucky enough to find the right person."

One side of Wolf's mouth lifted. "So it is. Now," he said, "what's on your mind? Let me see," he continued, stroking his chin. "Can't be the ranch, you're richer than God. I can't help you there. Can't be Emily. You wouldn't ride straight through to me for advice on her."

He pulled the plate of buns from the pie safe and put them on the table, then went to the stove and poured them each a cup of coffee. He set Tristan's in front of him. "Must be a woman."

Tristan stared into the steam that rose from the cup. "Emily has a new nurse."

Wolf straddled a chair and faced the table. "Don't tell me someone finally broke through to that wintry heart of yours."

Tristan toyed with the handle on his cup. "That's not the worst of it."

"Don't keep me in suspense." Wolf crossed his arms over the arching ladder of the chair.

"I married her."

Wolf tried to stifle his laughter, but he failed. He threw back his head and roared.

Tristan swore under his breath, but he understood his brother's amusement. From the first time they'd met nearly two years before, Tristan had vowed to remain single forever. "You're really enjoying this, aren't you?"

Wolf shook his head and wiped his eyes. "I'm sorry, but if you'd bet me your ranch that this would never happen to you, I'd be a rich man now."

"It's not as damned funny as all that," Tristan groused. "I shouldn't even be here. I married her to keep her safe from a conniving uncle."

Wolf sobered immediately. "If you really thought she was in danger, you wouldn't be here."

"After I married her, I began to realize what an arrogant, selfish gesture it was. It started out as a simple agreement, one that insured that Emily had continuous care by a capable, compassionate nurse. Hell, people have gotten married for flimsier reasons, haven't they?" Without waiting for an answer, he added, "She even tried to get out of it, but I wouldn't let her."

He swore again. "Why in the hell wouldn't I let her? My actions make no sense to me at all."

Wolf studied his brother. "Can I say something?"

"Can I stop you?"

Wolf's quick smile returned. "I'll tell you this much. I married Julia because without marriage, neither of us would have gotten what we wanted. And besides, her sly old pa made certain we'd tie the knot. But hell, Tris, I wouldn't have married just anyone. Whether I chose to admit it or not, I wanted her. I didn't know if I loved her, but I was damned sure I wanted her. What I didn't know then was that if the seeds of love hadn't already been there, I wouldn't have agreed to the marriage even if I'd been promised the moon."

Tristan muttered a curse of disbelief. "I'm not like you."

Wolf gave his brother a comforting smile. "Hell. You *are* me. I'm you. As Julia so aptly puts it, God was so pleased with the way I turned out, he made you."

In spite of himself, Tristan laughed. "Or, the other way around."

"Not according to Julia." Wolf's smile was warm. "Now, tell me everything."

When Tristan finished the whole story, he found Wolf still grinning at him. "Stop that," he ordered. "You look like a mindless idiot."

"Staying long?"

Tristan shrugged. "A couple of days, no more. I have things to think about before I go home."

"You really want to have the marriage annulled?"

Tristan dragged his hand through his hair. "It's the only thing that makes sense."

"To you?"

"Of course, to me."

"What about her?"

"Why would she want to be tied to me for the next five years? What if she fell in love?" The idea sent a bolt of possession through him.

Wolf studied him. "Maybe she already has."

"With me? Get serious."

Wolf bit into a cinnamon bun. "Do you want to know what I think?"

"Not really, but I'm sure you'll tell me." Tristan's stomach was in knots.

"I think you're afraid you won't be able to keep yourself from making love to her. And if you make love to her, it means she's yours, in every sense of the word. Then the marriage will be real, and you'll be forced to admit how you really feel about her. I think you could easily fall in love with her, and that's scaring the hell out of you."

Tristan stood, grabbing the chair before it struck the floor. "You're crazier than a bedbug."

"What's not to love, brother? She sounds perfect. She's smart, compassionate, and funny. She's spirited and pretty. She's a damsel in distress and you're her rescuing knight on a white horse."

Tristan shoved his fists into his pockets. "I don't love her."

"I don't believe you."

"I don't give a damn what you believe," Tristan snarled at him.

"How many times have you seen your mistress since Dinah has been with you?"

"I don't have a mistress."

Wolf had taken a slurp of coffee; it nearly snorted out his nose. "You mean to tell me you haven't been with a woman since Dinah showed up on your doorstep? Or, to be exact, in your tree? How long had it been before that?"

"Long enough," he shot back. "But it's been my choice. It has nothing to do with her."

Wolf pulled his shirt off a peg near the stove and shrugged into it. "Then go into town and find someone. Have a good, lusty screw, Tris, because if you don't, I'm afraid the top of your head will blow off."

Tristan was beginning to understand his feelings. "I can't do that."

"Why not?"

Wolf's expression of innocence was annoying. "I don't want anyone but her."

A sneaky smile spread across Wolf's face. "I rest my case." He slapped his brother on the back. "Come on. You can come and help me with the stock."

It was dawn when they trudged to the barn, and although Tristan was glad he'd told his brother everything, he wasn't any closer to making a decision.

He wanted Dinah, he freely admitted it. But wanting someone wasn't the same as loving them. And every woman you wanted wasn't going to be the one you loved. Wolf had been lucky. What he'd said had made sense for him. It wasn't the same for Tristan. Was it?

He stepped into the smoky, stale-smelling saloon. A gnarled, toothless barkeep was behind the bar, wiping glasses with a greasy rag.

"Good morning, good sir." He gave the barkeep a wide, innocent smile. He knew he did that look well; he'd been cursed with a baby face.

The old man looked up from his chore. "Mornin' yerself. What kin I gitcha?"

He plunked a shiny half eagle onto the bar.

The old man cackled. "I ain't got change, mister. And there's nothin' in here worth that, unless ya want a bottle."

"Just some information, friend."

The old timer gave him a steady look. "Information, huh?"

He glanced around the dimly lit room as if expecting someone to be listening. "I'm on the trail of a woman who killed her husband," he lied.

The old man's eyes grew big, but his jaw continued to work as he moved a plug of tobacco to the other side of his mouth. "Naw."

Nodding, the young man pulled out his press identification and flashed it quickly at the codger. "Police business."

The barkeep squirted tobacco out of the side of his mouth; it landed on the floor with a splat, near the young man's foot. "Naw. Really?"

He put his elbows on the bar and leaned in close, trying to ignore the unwashed smell of the bartender.

"Like I said, I'm looking for a woman. If you can help me, there's another one of these in it for you." He pushed the half eagle toward him.

The barkeep quickly pocketed the coin. "I'll try."

"Any strangers hereabouts? Women, I mean?"

The codger stroked his feedbag whiskers. "Not that I can recall. Not in town, leastwise."

He bit back his impatience. "How about in the surrounding area? The ranches, maybe?"

"Mebbe one."

His heart sped up, but he didn't want to tip his hand. "Is she blond, and sort of plump?" He carved an hourglass figure in the air with his hands, purposely creating a different picture from the one he wanted.

The old man shook his head. "Nope. 'Tain't her. This un's got curly red hair and she ain't built like no brick shithouse. Kinda skinny, if'n ya ask me."

Dinah Odell had red hair. She wasn't skinny, but a

year at Trenway could have taken its toll on her. The reporter gave the man a look of mock pity. "Damned shame. Oh, well. The woman I'm looking for might be passing herself off as a countess."

The old man snorted. "Hell, this un's a nurse. Carin' fer that crazy Fletcher woman."

He almost grinned, but kept his face passive. Now, all he had to do was find out where that crazy Fletcher woman lived, and half his job was done. McCafferty could help him with that.

"By the way," he said smoothly. "Anything to rent around here? I'm looking for a nice, secluded place. Preferably near a river. I love to fish, know what I mean?"

The old man stroked his whiskers. "The Adams shack ain't been used fer some time. Not since ol' man Adams got ate by that bear."

"Is it nice and private?"

The barkeep giggled. "If'n yer lookin' fer privacy, it's the perfect place."

As he listened to directions, he gave the old fool a benign smile. How simple it had been to get everything ready for Odell. Now, he had to find McCafferty. It would have been wiser to get his information directly from him, but he'd always enjoyed a bit of drama.

"Oh, one more thing, my good man. Where can I buy something special for a young woman?" He leaned close and winked. "Can't call on my lady without bringing a trinket, you know."

The geezer cackled. "There's a peddler man what stays down by the smithy. He can he'p ya."

He flipped another half eagle on the bar, touched the brim of his hat, and left.

"That ball was out of bounds!" Dinah stopped running and tried to catch her breath. The dogs darted back and forth among the children.

"It wasn't," shouted Little Hawk, who had kicked the ball into the middle of the field. "It was on the line."

The children had dared her to join them in a game of kick ball. She'd promptly changed into her trousers. It had been a game of the boys against the girls. All of the children, including the girls, played well. Little Hawk was surprisingly swift, despite his bad foot. He was also a bit of a cheat. No, Dinah amended, swallowing a smile, he stretched the rules.

"What's the score?" She hadn't caught her breath. She was doubled over, breathing hard, her palms resting on her thighs.

"Emily's keeping score," he shouted at her from across the field. "Emily, what's the score?"

Emily stood and cleared her throat. "Dinah, you, Sarafina, Rose, Dawn, and Flicker Feather have three points. Little Hawk, Swift Elk, Miguel, Jose, and Henry have four."

"We won!" Little Hawk leaped into the air, then hobbled toward Dinah.

Continuing to fight for breath, she smiled and shook her finger at him. "That last one was out of bounds, and we both know it."

His handsome face broke into an answering grin. "Honest, it wasn't. It was on the line."

Dinah realized that limp or no, when he grew to manhood, women would discover he was a heartbreak waiting to happen.

"I guess I'll have to take your word for it." She flopped to the ground beside Emily, who was busy putting the finishing touches on her sketch of the game.

The dogs loped to Dinah, and Amy knocked her over, licking her face. Dinah rolled on the ground, clutching Amy's furry neck. "What a good dog you are," she cooed.

Beside her, Emily made a scolding sound. "Do you think Tristan would want you playing ball with the children and rolling around on the grass with the dogs, Dinah? It isn't very ladylike."

Tristan. It had been five days since he'd gone. She refused to mope. Emily had sulked enough for both of them. Dinah hadn't told anyone that Tristan was going to have their marriage annulled. It meant she had somehow failed, and she hated failure. She almost dreaded his return. She'd lain awake nights wondering if he was in the arms of another woman.

She rolled to a sitting position and continued scratching Amy's neck. "I enjoy the exercise. Besides," she added, giving Emily's shoulder a squeeze, "you're doing so well, I don't have much to do anymore. I can't sit around twiddling my thumbs."

"I will admit the children like you. I like the stories you tell them. They laugh and it makes me happy inside, too."

Spying Leeta coming toward them with lunch, Dinah got to her feet. "Everyone wash up. Lunch is coming!"

After making sure the children were fed, she and Emily strolled to the house.

"I found an old painting," Emily told her. "I want you to see it."

They entered Emily's room. A large painting rested against the wall.

"That's Hatter's Horn."

Dinah stood next to her. "I should have recognized it."

With a smile, Emily answered, "You couldn't have. I painted it the way I wanted it to be, not the way it is."

"It almost looks like a fairy tale," Dinah mused.

"In my mind, it was a fairy-tale town. I used to go there."

Surprised, Dinah asked, "Really? Why?"

Emily ducked her head. "I wasn't supposed to. I used to sneak away from the house and walk there. It was far. I got tired, but it felt good to be away from Mama sometimes, even though she would punish me when she found me. I'd forgotten about my trips until I saw the painting." She gazed at it, her eyes soft. "Tristan loved it."

Dinah nudged Emily toward the chair she'd pulled out from the desk, then sat on the floor next to her. "Tell me about it."

Emily continued to smile. "From the time he was barely old enough to speak, he'd ask me questions about it. He used to sit in front of it for hours. He'd ask me the same questions over and over again. It became a game."

She pointed to the tiny house where she'd painted lamplight behind the windows. "See that? He'd ask, 'Emmy, who lives in that house?' I'd tell him a cobbler lived there who made shoes for elves.

"And there," she added, pointing to the grand house on top of the mountain. "He'd always have a question about who lived there. Although he knew the answer, he tried to fool me."

Her smile was so sad, it nearly broke Dinah's heart. "Who did you tell him lived in that house, Emily?"

"A handsome prince, I would tell him. His answer was, 'It'll be my house one day, Emmy, and I'll take care of you.' After a few years, I knew that he wanted to live in that painting, because his life here was so bad."

Tears snagged in Dinah's throat at the thought of a sad young Tristan.

"Why did Tristan leave this time?"

Dinah had kept her feelings well hidden. "I wish I knew. His note said he went to see his brother. Have you met his brother, Emily?"

"Yes," she answered with a nod. "The first time his brother came to the house, I met him."

"Did you like him?"

Emily's smile brightened. "Oh, yes. He was nice. It was a little spooky, though, because they are so much alike. I think it even scared the two of them." She giggled, sounding like a small child. "They even tried to trick me. One night Wolfie pretended to be Tristan, but I knew he wasn't." She laughed again. "He called me Marmalade instead of Emily, so I knew he wasn't my brother. I think he did it to make me laugh, and I did."

Dinah yearned for the warmth of a family, something to replace the cold, harsh years since her parents had died. And Charlotte . . . "Has Tristan gone to visit his brother before?"

Emily nodded, suddenly appearing anxious. "A couple of times."

"Please don't worry, Emily. I'm sure he'll be back soon." Then Dinah's marriage would be over.

Emily began breathing hard. "I know he will, but every time he goes away, something bad happens at home."

Dinah rose to her knees and hugged Emily's waist. "There, there. Lucas is here to protect us and all the children. And don't forget Wolf and Amy. They wouldn't let anything happen to us."

At the mention of the dogs, Emily uttered a rickety sigh. "He always said he'd have something of his very own."

Puzzled, Dinah asked, "What do you mean?"

"Mama scolded him for not appreciating everything they'd done for him. She told him that he should be happy with what they'd given him, because he was just a little brown savage and didn't deserve them."

She plucked at her gown. "He'd run to me after Mama shouted at him, and bury his head in my skirt, vowing to buy things of his own one day and not have to be grateful to anyone for anything. He wanted to live in that make-believe castle on the hill with dogs and a horse, just like the painting."

She stood and moved closer to the painting. "If you look closely, you can see the dogs." She pointed at the castle. "See? Dogs just like Amy and Wolf. I'd seen pictures of them in a book."

Dinah crossed to the painting and studied it. Indeed,

two wolfhounds stood guard on either side of the castle door.

"And here," Emily explained, indicating an ebony mount, "is the black stallion. He vowed to have one of those, too. And he did."

Although she'd been able to calm Emily, the agitation seemed to transfer to Dinah. For the rest of the day and into the night, she felt a caustic dread eating away at her stomach, and she couldn't imagine why.

14

Fletcher Ranch, Sierra Nevada Mountains

SIX DAYS. TRISTAN LEFT THE BARN AND TRUDGED TOWARD the house. He'd been gone six days, and for six days he'd wanted to make love to Dinah. Hell, it could have been six thousand, and the desire would be no dimmer. He was anxious to see her, but he was certain the feeling wasn't mutual.

Watching Wolf and Julia hadn't helped his condition. Although they hadn't been overtly demonstrative, from the way they looked at each other and Wolf's occasional caresses, Tristan knew without a doubt that they were deeply in love. It was as if Wolf couldn't keep his hands off his own wife. Imagine, he thought, being so much in love with your wife that you couldn't wait to take her to bed. Those were the looks they often exchanged in front of him, and he didn't think either was aware of it. If Tristan hadn't been so deep into his own misery, he might have found it amusing.

He had come to one conclusion, however. He couldn't let Dinah go. His brother's words haunted him. He knew deep in his soul that he wanted her to stay, but he wouldn't blame her if she left. He'd treated her badly. She hadn't deserved it. He wanted to make it up to her.

He searched the yard for the dogs; there wasn't a sign of them. He did hear the children, who were obviously playing a game of some sort, because there was periodic hooting and shouting. Drawn by the sound, he took the path to the grassy field. As he entered the clearing, he found his wife. Relieved, he also felt warmth spread through him at the sight of her.

Clad in her trousers, she raced across the field, kicking the ball ahead of her. Little Hawk was close at her heels. Her short coppery curls gleamed in the sunshine, she was laughing, and when she booted the ball over the goal line, she whooped with glee, leaping high into the air.

Tenderness spread through him, a warm compassion that was so powerful, it left him weak. Tristan would never have believed how much he'd missed her.

"That's a foul!" Little Hawk protested.

Dinah appeared to have trouble catching her breath. She bent over, her palms on her thighs, and continued to laugh. "You're a sore loser, that's all."

"The girls have never beat us before," he argued.

She threw the ball to him and he caught it. "Then I guess you boys will have to work a bit harder."

Amy and Wolf, who had been frolicking on the field with the players, caught Tristan's scent and bolted toward him. He bent and scratched their ears, his gaze on his wife.

"Tristan! You're back!" Little Hawk waved and ran toward him. Tristan admired how confident the boy was in his athletic skills despite his disability.

Dinah stood, inert as a statue, at the other end of the field. His gaze locked with hers and he could tell even from a distance that she was surprised to see him. And wary. At least she was here. At least she hadn't left him; that's what he deserved.

As Tristan crossed the field toward his wife, he turned his attention to Little Hawk. "Did I hear that the girls beat you in kick ball?"

Little Hawk frowned, disgusted. "It's the first time. I think it's because Dinah is playing. We beat 'em yesterday, but she's a good runner. And you know what? She organizes them so they all know what to do. That ain't fair."

The space between Tristan and his wife was narrowing. "Maybe it's time you men do some organizing. I know how tough it is to be bested by women. We might be stronger, but they're far more clever."

Tristan was getting close enough now so he could see the flush on Dinah's cheeks and the tiny beads of perspiration on her upper lip. She was breathing hard. He longed to kiss her, taste the salt on her skin.

"Maybe you can help us get organized, huh, Tristan?"

Dinah's eyes were shiny with victory, and there was the barest hint of a smile on her lips.

Little Hawk tugged at his jacket. "Huh, Tristan? You can help us beat them, can't you?"

Tristan's gaze locked with his wife's. "If you'll take my travel bag to the house, Little Hawk, I promise that the next time you want to play, I'll help you and the other boys get organized."

Little Hawk shouted happily, then limped off to do Tristan's bidding.

Dinah's tomboyish stance was appealing. Her hips were round and seductive, her legs long and slim beneath the trousers. Her exquisite breasts, which he'd kissed barely a week ago, were not obvious beneath her shirt, but he could tell they were not bound, either.

"So, you're finally home." Her face held more color than it had when he'd left. Sunshine agreed with her. He even detected a sprinkle of freckles.

"Emily was very upset that you left without telling her."

As always, the pulse at the base of her throat drew him. He touched her there, drawing from her a breathy gasp as he felt the pulse with his fingertips.

"I'll apologize to my sister." He studied her moist lips and her winsome nose, the nostrils flaring slightly as she breathed. Her chin came to a soft point, giving her face a somewhat heart-shaped appearance; he hadn't noticed that before.

"You're quite a skilled ball player. I enjoyed watching you run." His fingers moved to her upper lip, where he wiped the perspiration away with his thumb.

She continued to stare at him, the victory in her eyes fading to wariness. "I have no doubt what you enjoyed watching."

"Still a verbal sparring partner, aren't you?" He touched his thumb with the tip of his tongue, tasting her.

"It's the only kind of partner I can be certain I am," she countered. Her eyes were wide, and she concentrated on his mouth.

"Then, let me put your mind at rest."

He took her elbow and they walked across the grass toward the house.

She appeared surprised by his gallant touch. "Trying to let me down easy, are you?"

He decided to put her out of her misery. "I didn't get the annulment, Dinah. That should make you happy."

She yanked her arm from his. "If you didn't go through with it solely because of me, then . . . then you can go to the devil, Tristan Fletcher."

He hauled her into his arms. "I'm trying to woo you, dear wife. You're making it damned difficult."

Her angry visage changed gradually, and she bit back a reluctant smile. "If that's your idea of wooing, you have a lot to learn."

"I have no doubt of it. I'm relying on you to teach me."

They stood close and Dinah brought her hand to his cheek. Her mouth beckoned, and he bent to kiss her. She tasted sweet, salty, fresh. He remembered her flavor; he'd missed it. His thumbs grazed the sides of her breasts, and she gasped into his mouth. She stood on her tiptoes and flung her arms over his shoulders. He devoured her, changing positions so he could take more of her into his mouth. He trailed his lips over her cheek to her neck, to her ear, drawing a sound of pleasure from her. He discovered he couldn't get enough of her. He wanted to hear more of her throaty, whimpery noises. He was desperate to make love to her.

Reluctantly, he raised his head. It took her a moment to open her eyes, then she rested her forehead on his chest.

He pressed his face to the top of her head, nuzzling her curls. "I could kiss you for hours. I want to kiss you everywhere. Again."

He felt her shuddery intake of breath. "Well," she murmured, "I guess that's a start."

Tristan vowed to continue his seduction over dinner. In the meantime, he looked in on Emily and found her asleep. Just as well, he thought, for he had a lot of work to do.

He spent the major part of the afternoon with Lucas, going over the ledgers. Lucas had purchased a mare while Tristan was away and they had received word that the cattle Tristan had bought from England would arrive any day.

He also learned that Dinah and Emily spent much of each day with the children, and all of them, boys and girls alike, spoke glowingly of his wife. And why wouldn't they? How many white women would don trousers and engage in a rousing game of kick ball with a bunch of ragged half bloods?

When he finished his duties, he returned to his room. He bathed and changed and was descending the stairs in search of his sister when he heard Dinah's tinkling laughter followed by an amused male voice. He stopped and listened.

"But they're so ugly," the man was saying.

"I thought so too, at first. But now I adore them. You saw how they protected the property. Why, the day I arrived, I had to climb a tree to escape them."

"You? Climbed a tree like a hoyden?" He laughed. "That's not the picture of Dinah Odell I remember."

Tristan felt a brief sense of possession. Who was this man in *his* house, talking with such familiarity to *his* wife?

"And which picture do you remember, Charles? The one where I sedately brought you a cup of tea and tripped over the rug, dumping the tea into your lap, or the time you tried to kiss me and I shoved you into the mud?"

Kiss her? Their mingled laughter made Tristan frown. His sense of possession grew.

He stepped into the great room, fighting the urge to charge in shouting, *"Aha!"* like a suspicious husband. Dinah and the young man were on the settee beside the fireplace, the one that faced the other wall, their heads together as they gossiped like old women. An odd feeling, one Tristan had never experienced before, ate at him, and with stunned surprise he realized it was jealousy.

The dogs rose from their spot at Dinah's feet and moved toward him, their enormous tails wagging.

"Wolf? Amy? What's—" Both Dinah and the man she was entertaining turned. Dinah blushed when she saw Tristan standing there.

"Tristan! You're finally done with your chores." She rose and hurried toward him, her blush spreading.

"And not a moment too soon, it would seem." He studied the round-faced young man on the settee.

"Oh, Tristan, the strangest thing happened. While

Alice and I were in Hatter's Horn getting supplies this afternoon, we ran into Charles." She nodded toward her guest. "Charles is an old friend of mine. From New York."

"How convenient," Tristan murmured under his breath. He felt a knot of apprehension at the appearance of someone from Dinah's past.

The young man stood and offered Tristan his hand. "Charles Avery, sir."

Sir. The word made Tristan sound like Dinah's father instead of her husband. With reluctance, he gripped the pup's hand, finding it soft, like a woman's.

"What a stroke of luck to run into Dinah, way out here," Charles Avery announced with what Tristan assumed was supposed to be an engaging smile.

Tristan scrutinized him. "Yes. What a stroke of luck. Excuse me, I must attend to my mail."

He walked toward his study, knowing Dinah would follow. Once inside, he heard her close the door behind her. He turned, his expression bland.

She stepped from one foot to the other in front of him, wringing her hands, looking delectably fetching in one of her new gowns.

"Tristan, shame on you for not seeing Emily. She's been worried sick about you."

"When I found her, she was asleep. I didn't want to wake her."

Lifting a brow, he gave his wife a careful once-over. He thought again about how much he'd missed her. Sometimes he'd imagined her standing before him in her trousers and her loose shirt. Other times, she wore only the shirt. Occasionally, only the trousers. Often, she had worn nothing at all. He itched to see her that way. Ached for it.

"You should have. She worries so about you."

He thumbed through the mail on his desk, glancing at her periodically. The bite of jealousy made him petulant.

He'd planned to pursue her over dinner. Now, they would no doubt have a guest. One who would need a very clever explanation to keep Tristan from wondering what he was doing here.

"Leave it to you to twist things around to make me appear the guilty one."

She blushed further. "I didn't go off and leave you without so much as a good-bye."

"I apologize. It was inexcusable of me to go off like that."

Her expression changed; she appeared puzzled by his acquiescence. "Yes, it was."

Having an acquaintance of hers arrive so conveniently made him less than tolerant, however. He tossed her a vague glance, unwilling to show the depth of his concern. After all, she had yet to tell him the truth about herself. "You don't find it odd that an old suitor would show up here?"

Her expression turned fierce. "Charles is not my suitor."

His provocation continued. "How do I know you didn't invite him out, assuming you were going to be rid of me?"

She gasped, doubled her fist and punched him.

With a cough and a strangled groan, he forced himself to stay upright.

"In six days? Sweet Mary, but you're a boob. How would he have gotten here so quickly? Fly?"

He rubbed his stomach and drew in a deep breath. "Christ, woman, where did you learn to hit like that?"

"I've been working in an insane asylum, remember? I learned to do a lot of things that come in handy, you . . . you miserable cur." She cradled her fist with her other palm as if it hurt. He imagined it did.

"How dare you insinuate such a thing, Tristan Fletcher. This marriage might not mean that much to you, but I take it quite seriously."

"I'm beginning to realize that," he mumbled, continuing to rub his tender abdomen. He took her fist and ran his thumb over her knuckles. "Women's hands weren't made for fisticuffs, Dinah."

"Then don't say things that will make me angry." She pulled away. "Why is it we can't have a single conversation without arguing?"

"I've often wondered that myself."

The pulse at the base of her throat continued to vibrate, and he wanted to kiss her again, apologize for his boorish behavior.

Restraining himself, he returned to his mail. "Tell me. Who is this suitor and what's he doing in my home?"

"I told you he's not my suitor."

"Explain his presence in my home, Dinah." His impression of the youth he'd observed earlier was of a round-faced, balding young man who would one day turn to fat.

"He's an old friend."

"Never a suitor?" Why he kept harping on this, he couldn't understand.

"Well, no, not really. He was a friend before—" She brought her fingers to her mouth again and just stared back at him.

Tristan gave her a languid smile, knowing she'd caught herself before telling him the truth. "Before you took your position at Trenway?" he suggested smoothly.

She blinked and sighed, appearing relieved. "Exactly."

He lowered himself into his chair, rested his elbows on the desk, and steepled his fingers, peering at her over the tops. The surprise appearance of someone from her past didn't bode well for any of them.

"Don't you think it's time for the truth, dear wife?"

A look of horror crossed her features. It turned quickly to resignation.

"Th-there's nothing between us, Tristan, I promise."

"Go back and entertain the pup, Dinah. When you can tell me the truth, come and find me. Until then, I'm too busy to fuss with you." He was angry that she wouldn't tell him the truth, and jealous that she could laugh so gaily with another man. Both emotions made him miserable.

"Am I being dismissed?"

Nodding, he studied a voucher, not really seeing it.

She went to the door. "Yes. I'd better see if Charles is all right. We left him with the dogs. They could have had him for dinner by now."

"By all means, see to your suitor. But don't worry about the dogs. They've never acquired a taste for soft, balding young men."

She made a sound of annoyance, then slammed the door, leaving him alone.

He rose, shoving the chair away with his calves, and left the study in search of Emily. Tristan wanted the boy to stay long enough for him to discover what he was up to. He wasn't fool enough to believe Avery's appearance in their lives was as innocent as it seemed. First thing in the morning, he'd send a wire off to David asking him to dig into this pubescent pup's background. Tristan had learned long ago not to trust those who appeared too innocent.

He knocked on Emily's door, then entered. His sister turned from the canvas she was working on, her face lighting up at the sight of him.

She drew a cloth over the painting, rose, and went to him. "I hate it when you leave without telling me, Teddy."

"I apologize. I have no excuse." Stroking her silky hair, he gazed over her head toward the large painting that sat against the wall. He smiled. "I haven't seen that picture in years."

Emily turned in his arms. "I found it in the attic. Remember all the questions you used to ask me about it?"

They crossed to the painting together. The tiny house with the warm light behind the windows brought back memories. "Does the cobbler still live there, Emmy?"

She laughed, and a little gasp escaped with the sound. "Look at the dogs, Teddy. They're just like Amy and Wolf." She turned a beaming face to his. "You always said you'd have dogs like that, and a horse like that," she added, pointing to the black stallion who reared in the background.

She clasped his arm. "You will take care of me, as you promised, won't you? Marrying Dinah won't change anything, will it?"

"Nothing will ever change, Emmy." At least, not between the two of them. He wondered what changes would come out of his relationship with his wife.

There was a bubble of agitation in his stomach that threatened to explode. Things would have been so much simpler if he'd let Dinah go when she'd wanted to. But in retrospect, he hadn't wanted her to go even then. Perhaps there was no way to protect her. If this suitor could find her with such ease, how easy would it be for Martin Odell to do the same? For all he knew, the boy could be working with both Odell and the police.

As he held his sister, he wondered if his good intentions would put them all in danger. He also knew it was a chance he would have taken even if he'd known the dangers beforehand.

He wasn't yet willing to admit he loved Dinah. The smarting jealousy that had assaulted him with such force and surprise when he'd seen her with another man meant something. As he'd grown to manhood, he'd yearned for things of his own, not things that had been given to him by a reluctant parent. That's why he'd bought the dogs and the stallion. They were his choices. And whether he chose to believe it or not, Dinah Odell had been his choice for a wife.

Dinah escaped to her room to rest before dinner. Even though she hadn't expressed it, she was concerned about Charles's arrival. Until now, days could go by without her remembering she was a runaway. Seeing Charles brought all the bad memories back. Tristan's homecoming might have started out wonderfully, but it was becoming a dismal failure.

Oh, how she felt when she saw him standing there. At that moment, she knew that no matter what, she loved him. It was as if all of her blood had left her head, making her feel dizzy. Part of it might have been because she'd been running, but part of it was because of him. The sight of him had thrilled her. And frightened her. And infuriated her.

Even now, she simmered at how he could raise her hackles with a few well chosen words. She reached for her brush and yanked it through her hair, relishing the pain as the brush met with snarls.

His words continued to haunt her. Tell him the truth? The truth about what? Her nonexistent affair with Charles? How foolish Tristan was to accuse her of such a thing. She tossed the brush onto the dressing table, her scalp tingling from the harsh brushing. She had to speak with him before dinner. Alice had invited Charles to stay, and if Dinah didn't talk to Tristan first, he might order Charles to leave his private, personal, beloved property. He was good at giving imperious orders.

Actually, she was torn about Charles's appearance in her life. On one hand, she'd felt a certain nostalgia when they talked. On the other, she was afraid because her past had caught up with her.

Having decided to change before dinner, she crossed the room and threw open the dressing-room door. Tristan stood at the dry sink, wiping his chest with a towel. Her mouth turned to cotton fluff and her palms began to sweat.

"You want the bloody truth?" She focused on his face; his naked arms and chest would only distract her.

He tossed the towel aside and turned, causing her heart to skip. "That would be refreshing."

She attempted to study the clothes that hung on the rod behind him. "Charles Avery was a suitor of mine.

He . . . we didn't have a lengthy relationship, because . . . because—"

"You got a job at Trenway?" His voice was as smooth as a hustler's tongue.

She nodded. "Yes."

"Has he come to ask for your hand?"

She rolled her eyes at the ceiling. "Rather difficult, don't you think, since I'm already married?" She swallowed. "That is what you said, isn't it? That we are married?"

He shrugged into a clean shirt, drawing her gaze to his chest again. "If you were free, would you marry him?"

Her stomach caved in around her hurt. "Do you want to free me so I can?"

His jaw tightened as he buttoned his shirt. "When I left here, you were chaste. Can I assume that nothing has happened to change that?"

Anger bubbled up through her pain, oozing over it like swill. "I already told you I take my vows seriously, even if you don't, you miserable savage." She could not rid herself of the image of him, slaking his lust with another woman.

He raised an inky eyebrow. "Name calling isn't very ladylike, Dinah, even if the name is accurate."

That stopped her for a moment, then she stiffened. She would not be affected by those tactics. Not this time. She was too angry.

"You are so clever at turning my words around and using them against me. But I won't let you get away with it this time, you . . . you . . . horny whoremonger."

"Tsk, tsk. Your language leaves much to be desired, Dinah. Too much time spent in the gutters of Trenway, no doubt."

"Oh, you don't know the half of it, you pompous, randy billy goat."

He gave her a sly smile, taking in her curves, then glanced away. "No more name calling, Dinah."

She swallowed hard. "No?"

He moved closer and she smelled his soap. "Just one."

"Naturally you get the last word," she answered with a smirk.

He dragged her to him, his eyes no longer languid. He gave her a shake. "Liar."

She gaped at him. "I'm not—"

He flung her away. She stumbled but did not fall. "You are a liar, Dinah Odell. When were you going to tell me who you really are and how you came to be here?"

Her heart sank like a stone. "Oh, sweet Mary."

His eyes shimmered. "You're not a nurse, Dinah Odell, you're an escaped inmate."

She sank to a stool, clutched her knees, and rocked. She'd known this time would come. She'd hoped to have control over it, but she'd waited too long. "How did you find out?"

"That's not important. When were you going to tell me? When someone came around to get you? Like that soft-bellied suitor you've been entertaining in my great room?"

She opened her mouth to argue, then shut it. Surely he didn't suspect . . . "Charles?"

He turned on her. "Did it ever occur to you how convenient it is that he found you?"

She swallowed a morsel of fear. "He told me how he found me."

"Well, tell me."

"Um . . . he's with the *Times.* The newspaper. He saw the article about . . . about me and . . . and—"

"I know all about that, Dinah. I know about Daisy Jenkins, the nurse David hired for me, and how she was identified as the body found at the asylum."

Dinah lowered her face to her hands, feeling them shake against her cheeks. "What else do you know?"

"Everything."

She pressed one hand over her heart. "Everything? Even about Uncle Martin?"

"Everything. Your uncle. Your father's will. What

happens to the money if you marry and have children or die before that happens. As I said, Dinah, I know everything."

She caught her breath and frowned at the floor, biting down on her lower lip. He only thought he knew everything. If he did, he wouldn't be so angry with her. He'd have a little more compassion for what she'd been through. "How long have you known?"

"Long enough."

She had a flash of insight. "Since before we were married?"

He gave her a sharp nod.

"There was no marriage stipulation, was there?"

"Yes, there was. I was anxious to get a compassionate companion for Emily. Believe me, Dinah, there was an agreement." He stood before her, his arms across his chest.

"Why didn't you tell me you knew who I was?"

He glanced away. "I'm not sure I can."

Hope sprouted in her chest. "Try."

Some of his arrogance slipped away and he sighed. "At first I didn't because Emily was doing so well, thanks to you."

Getting him to commit his feelings was like bathing a cat. "And later?"

He drew in another labored breath, exhaling noisily. "Later it seemed the right time had passed. That's why I felt the only decent thing to do was have our marriage annulled to set you free. I'd deceived you and I couldn't forgive myself for that."

She gave him a humorless laugh. "Oh, but I'd deceived you as well. At least I thought I had." She gave him a wry look. "All the time I was feeling guilty about not admitting who I really was, *you* felt guilty because you knew, and didn't tell me."

One corner of his mouth lifted in a smile. "Perhaps we deserve each other after all."

She'd known it from the beginning, but she said

nothing. His wry admission had not included any great feelings for her. She drew her lip between her teeth once more. "If you knew I wasn't a nurse, why did you go through with the marriage? You could have simply kept me on as Emily's companion. Marrying me made no sense, Tristan, no sense at all."

"I was trying to protect you." The words sounded like a threat.

Incredulous, she asked, "Protect me from Uncle Martin? But, why?"

He cursed. "If I knew the answer to that, I'd be sleeping nights."

He cared for her. On some level, he actually cared. There was a flowering in her chest as their conversation whirled in her brain. "You honestly think Charles could have been sent by Uncle Martin? Oh, Tristan," she said, shaking her head. "I don't see how. Uncle Martin hated it when Charles came to call." She continued to shake her head. "No. Charles may not appear like much to you, but I believe he's honorable. Even if Uncle Martin had wanted him to do this, he wouldn't have. It's too sneaky. Anyway, I could tell when Charles was lying to me. He wore his emotions on his sleeve. He still does."

"You don't believe he'd do this for money?"

She frowned, remembering the times he'd talked about his ailing mother and how much it cost to care for her. "I'll be honest with you, Tristan. Charles always needed money. His mother was very ill. But unlike Uncle Martin, Charles chose to care for his mother in a fair, valorous way. Not toss her into an asylum because she'd become a burden to him. And he could have, Tristan. A lot of families did just that to unwanted women. I'm . . . I'm proof of it."

Tristan went to the door to his room, bracing himself against the doorjamb. "You sound fond of him."

She uttered a humorless laugh. "Not as fond as I would have been had he tried to get me released from Trenway."

Tristan appeared to study his boots. "If you were free, and he could promise to keep you safe from your uncle, would you go with him?"

Something in her chest seized up. "We've already been over this, remember?"

"Answer me, damn it."

"No. I wouldn't go with him under any circumstances. I don't love him, Tristan. I'm fond of him, and perhaps that's enough for some women, but it's not enough for me. If I . . . If you wanted me to leave," she answered, knowing it would break her heart to do so, "I'd find another position."

He gave her a wry smile. "You aren't a nurse, Dinah."

She stiffened. "I'm aware of that. But since you know where I was before I came here and what I've been able to do for Emily in spite of my inexperience, surely you'd agree that I could be of some use somewhere."

He studied her from the doorway. "You're of some use here."

In spite of the ache in her heart, she gave him a sassy look. "Even though I'm an escaped mental patient?"

"No more levity, Dinah. For now, I don't want you to tell your friend anything."

"He's harmless, Tristan, I'd stake my life on it." She could only hope she was right. After all, she'd told Charles nearly everything already.

"If we're not careful, it may come to that. Humor me. Please. I'm only thinking of your safety."

She sighed again. At least that was something. She turned to leave, then remembered what she had come into the room to tell him. "I'd appreciate it if you would be a good host tonight. To be honest, I'm not exactly sure how I feel about Charles. I never quite forgave him for not trying to get me out of Trenway, although he probably couldn't have done anything about it anyway. He's not a powerful man. Not like you."

A hint of a smile tugged at his mouth. "Are you buttering me up?"

She bit her lip and grinned. "No, but he's staying for dinner. Alice invited him."

"And the night, too, I suspect."

"Yes." She studied his handsome face. "I was happy to see him, Tristan." She gave him a smile and shrugged. "It was my first link with home since Uncle Martin put me away. In spite of your feelings, you will be a good host, won't you?"

"In spite of my feelings, I'll try."

She turned to her gowns and studied them.

"Dinah?" His gaze locked on to her chest again. "Change your dress. Wear the purple one."

"The purple one? You can't be serious. I look like a spinsterish schoolmarm in that gown. Lord, next you'll demand that I wear the binder."

"That was my next request." He gave her a quick smile before he disappeared.

She wrinkled her nose. He wasn't serious, not when he smiled like that. She turned and studied her gowns again, grimacing when she found the purple one. She hadn't liked it when she'd tried it on, but for some reason, Tristan had insisted they get it. Had it been silk or velvet, it might have been pretty. As it was, it looked no better than the gown she'd arrived in.

He wouldn't truly want her to wear it. He was probably just testing her to see if she'd become a dutiful wife. Unfortunately, she wasn't able to change overnight.

She searched through her new gowns, stopping at one with a shaped, jacket-like bodice and apron of coral faille. It had a scarf and train of ivory silk and fine wool and the chenille garland trimmings were of green foliage, caught at the waist and train by red poppies. The square neckline and shoulder-strap sleeves drew her. Steam would come out of Tristan's ears if she wore it tonight.

Uttering a menacing sigh of pleasure, she lifted the gown from the rod, draped it over her arm and went into her room to dress for dinner.

15

WITH NERVOUS FINGERS, DINAH TOUCHED THE GOLD PENdant that hung from the black velvet dog collar at her throat. As she descended the stairs, she heard Tristan's voice coming from the great room. Fortunately, he sounded civil. She pulled her new Chantilly shawl around her shoulders; the room might turn chilly, despite the fire, once he saw what she was wearing.

She crept to the door, intending to listen briefly to their conversation. It wasn't meant to be. Both men turned toward the doorway as if she'd sent each a signal.

When Tristan took in her attire, he appeared to want to throttle her. Charles, on the other hand, was properly impressed.

"Dinah! You look ravishing." He hurried to her side.

"Why, thank you, Charles." She took his arm and stepped into the room, her gaze returning to Tristan's. She almost winced, for she detected a black cloud hovering over his head. His eyebrows were shoved down over his eyes, and she noted the telltale knot of muscles in his jaw just below his ears.

She should learn to be obedient, if for no other reason than to save her husband's health. "I'll have a glass of sherry, Tristan."

His eyes were hooded behind his lids. "Oh, you will, will you?"

She smiled. She couldn't help it. He almost appeared jealous. "Please?" She lowered herself into a chair by the fire and Charles took a seat across from her.

Tristan poured her a drink and brought it to her, bending so close to her ear, she felt shivers the length of her body.

"I think you need a leash attached to that velvet collar that circles your lily-white throat, my dear wife." He spoke in a whisper, his tone mingling menace and banter.

She couldn't ignore the trembling of her pulse at his words. "And I suppose you want to be the one to yank it when I don't behave," she responded, giving him a sweet smile.

He returned the smile, but the devilish gleam in his eyes remained. "You're beginning to understand."

Charles cleared his throat and Dinah jumped. She'd almost forgotten he was in the room.

"I'm sorry your sister isn't feeling up to joining us, Mr. Fletcher."

When Tristan didn't respond, Dinah answered for him. "She finds evenings very tiring, Charles."

After another period of awkward silence, Charles nodded toward the ugly moose head mounted on the wall. "So, you're a hunter, sir. I've always found it a fascinating sport."

Tristan fixed himself another drink. "Those are my father's trophies. I've never found much pleasure in hunting game."

Another lengthy silence, although this time, Dinah

looked at Tristan in a new light. She was happy the animal heads weren't his souvenirs. At least they agreed on something.

Soon, Charles broke the silence again. "Before you came down, Dinah, I was telling your husband about the plunder of the buffalo. They say three million are killed every year, just for the hides."

She sipped the sherry; it was warm going down. "I remember that sight from the train, Charles. It was the worst thing I'd ever seen." Unlike every other passenger on the train, she found it so disturbing that after the initial display of carnage, she'd refused to look. She didn't need any more pain to store away in her head. She had plenty of painful memories of her own to cope with.

"The farmers on the Plains still haven't recovered from last year's grasshopper plague, either," Charles offered.

Dinah blushed under Tristan's constant scrutiny. His gaze lingered on her, but she attempted to focus on Charles and his small talk. "All that wheat gone. How long will it take to overcome a disaster like that?"

Charles's answer was long and drawn out. Dinah could hardly concentrate on what he said, for Tristan had stepped behind her and rested his fingers on her shoulder, as if claiming possession. He added little or nothing to their conversation, and Dinah drank her sherry a bit too quickly, accepting another glass as Charles continued to babble. She was so relieved when Alice called them in to dinner she nearly bolted for the door.

She was gratified as well when dinner was over and she could escape to her room. During the course of the meal, it had become imperative that she get away from Tristan. He had insisted that she sit next to him rather than across from him as she usually did. She knew it was no accident that his knee kept pressing her leg beneath the table and his arm touched hers. At one point, while he cut his meat, his elbow jostled the side of her breast, making both nipples stand at attention.

She had bid both men a hasty good-night, then escaped to her room and flung off her clothes, shrugging into one of Tristan's shirts rather than her cumbersome nightgown. She hugged herself, running her palms over the soft fabric of the shirtsleeves. She enjoyed the loose-fitting garment, savored the freedom of having her legs free and unencumbered by her heavy cotton gown.

She stood before the window, listening to the muted sounds of night that came through the glass. Crickets. An owl. A frog in the garden. She smiled. Two frogs. Playing a mating game, perhaps. She often wondered if that's what she and Tristan were doing.

There was a soft sound behind her.

"You left me to show your guest where to sleep."

She didn't turn, but continued to stare out the window, even though the sound of his voice sent shivers over her skin. "I would imagine, then, that he's bedded down in the barn."

Tristan chuckled quietly. "It crossed my mind."

She smiled as well. "I have no doubt that it did. You weren't an especially good host, Tristan." She felt, rather than heard, him come up behind her. Her body tensed.

"I've been gone for six damned days, and you expect me to entertain your house guest?"

His voice so close to her ear intensified the fluttering she already felt in the pit of her stomach. "I guess I couldn't hope for more than civility. You were civil, Tristan. For that I thank you."

His hands found her shoulders. She closed her eyes at his touch and leaned into him, enjoying the sensation of his breath against her cheek as he bent close.

"Entertaining choice of night apparel." He unbuttoned the shirt, his palms grazing her nipples. "Also an interesting gown you wore for dinner. Somehow I knew you would defy me. Women who appeal to me often do. Maybe that's why I'm drawn to them."

"Does your balloon-breasted mistress defy you?" She

couldn't leave it alone. She'd wanted to, but it wasn't possible. She had to know.

His fingers stopped and he spun her to face him. Even in the dim light from the lamp at her bedside, she could see the fury etched on his features.

"I'm going to tell you this one time, and one time only. I have no mistress. I haven't slept with a woman in nearly a year."

"But you said—"

"Damn what I said. Anything I might have told you about a mistress was said because I wanted you to know that at that time, this marriage was a pretense."

She swallowed. "At that time?"

He turned from her, presenting his handsome profile. She ached with love for him. Did she dare believe she would truly have a real marriage?

"I had every intention of keeping you pure, Dinah. I'm basically an honorable man, I think, but—"

"Keep me pure for what?"

He didn't answer her. Instead, he raised his arms, bracing them against either side of the window. "Once I learned who you were and that you'd been in the asylum, I wasn't even sure you hadn't already been violated."

"Daisy found ways to keep me safe." His concern softened her.

"She must have been a special woman, indeed. I don't imagine it was a small feat to keep men of all sorts away from you."

His flattery softened her more. "That sounds like a compliment. I think. I'm glad you find me comely."

"You're far more than comely, and I think you know it." He shook his head and sighed, a rumbling sound that started deep in his chest. "If you must know, I've been fighting a physical attraction to you for weeks. Hell, before that. Even before I learned about the binder. I wondered how I could be attracted to a woman who had no more curves than a fence post."

She reached for him, then drew her hand back. "I wouldn't have minded if you had taken me, Tristan."

He swung around, his fists clenched at his sides. "You should have." He combed his hair from his face with his fingers. "I suppose even now I could give you to someone else in good conscience, if I had a mind to."

She pulled in a sharp breath, her hackles rising. "You could *give* me to someone else?"

Unaware of her rising pique, he answered, "It was my hope that you would find a suitable husband one day. I just wanted to make certain you were safe from your uncle."

Anger swelled inside her like gas bubbles on a putrid pond. "Why, you arrogant son of a dog's mother. Despite what Martin Odell did to me, I've survived quite handily on my own until now, and I don't need your help finding a suitable husband," she mimicked. "Pardon my stupidity, but I thought I had one."

He grabbed her arm, securing it with his fingers so she couldn't pull away. "I came home to woo you, to try to change your opinion of me. I was ready to acknowledge my feelings for you, and what do I find in my great room? One of your old beaus."

Shocked at his stupidity, she shot back, "Acknowledge *this,* you lickspittle!" Doubling her fist, she shoved it into his diaphragm.

He let out an appreciable whoosh of air and doubled over.

"You . . . you *man,* you." She'd run out of choice words to call him. She winced as pain shot up her arm. "Your wooing skills are woefully lacking."

He uttered a surprisingly mild curse. "Somehow I've got to train you not to fight so dirty."

"I don't need training, Tristan. I'm not one of your dogs. All you had to do was show me some consideration as a person and I'd have been happy."

"I've been an arrogant bastard, haven't it?" His knuckles grazed her chin, her neck, the tops of her breasts. Moving his fingers inside the shirt, he discovered her erect nipples. He stroked them. Fondled them. His touch aroused her and softened her anger. It always did.

"I supposed you'd be offended if I considered you a possession."

She could smell him. His woodsy fragrance, the brandy on his breath, the special scent of him that would not leave her, even when he wasn't there. She locked her knees to keep from weaving toward him. She remembered Emily's words about his possessions. Even though she understood them, the very idea that he considered her no more important than his dogs or his horse annoyed her.

"You can't possess other people. Unlike animals, we can't be trained. At least I can't. If you find that an offensive quality, then go to the devil, Tristan Fletcher, because I won't ever kowtow to anyone, not even you."

His hand had been moving over her abdomen. It stopped. The whites of his eyes still glittered in the darkness. "Don't be a shrew. If you think so little of me, why do you want to remain my wife?" He folded her shirt over her breasts and walked away.

He was leaving? Good riddance, then! "I often wonder the same thing myself."

After he'd gone, she stared at the door, tears of frustration tangled in her throat.

They had resolved nothing. Now more than ever she realized that even though they talked, they never settled anything. They couldn't sit down like two civilized people and discuss their problems because they ended up fighting.

Dinah rolled to her side, hugging her stomach. She couldn't sleep knowing that he thought she was a shrew. She hadn't meant to sound that way. She hadn't even wanted to sound that way, but he often brought out the worst in her. How else could she feel, knowing he had planned to pawn her off on someone else as if she were no more important than an indentured servant?

When he'd told her his plan, she should have sat him down and quietly told him that no woman likes to be treated like chattel. Explain it to him. Patiently. But, no, she thought with a self-deprecating smirk. She had to fly off the handle and punch him in the stomach. Again. Hearing him calmly tell her he'd wanted to save her for some other man had made her temporarily insane. Not only because it was a stupid thing to think he could do, but because she loved him so much she didn't want to leave him at all.

And what a way to woo her. She made a face in the darkness. He had a lot to learn. She wondered if other women had simply thrown themselves at him, giving him nothing to do but enjoy their favors.

She flopped over and stared at the dressing-room door. She should apologize tonight. How many times had her mother told her that she and Papa had never gone to bed angry with each other, no matter how heated their arguments?

Sliding from the bed, she buttoned the shirt, then crossed to the dressing-room door. She stepped inside; his door was open and there was light flickering in his room. She went to the doorway.

He sat in bed, reading. His chest was bare, brown and hard. Manly and enticing. No hair covered the finely cut muscles or the dark, flat nipples. His chest looked warm. Seductive.

Her gaze moved languidly to his face. Reading glasses were perched on the end of his nose. She smiled to herself, amused at the picture. He looked at her over the lenses, snagging her gaze.

Her smile spread. "You look like a very threatening schoolmaster."

He didn't return her smile, but his eyes were warm. "Did your schoolmaster often teach without wearing any clothes?"

Her stomach jumped, and her gaze swept the rest of him that was hidden under the bedding. “I suppose he could have if he’d looked like you,” she countered.

He touched his glasses, as if to remove them.

“No, don’t take them off.”

One of his black eyebrows went up, but he said nothing.

She gave him an embarrassed smile. “They civilize you.”

“Make me less threatening?”

“Something like that.” She fiddled with the buttons on his shirt.

“What do you want, Dinah?”

She studied the floor. “I came to apologize for punching you and calling you so many awful names.”

He closed his book and laid it on the table by the bed, removing his spectacles as well. “I deserved it.”

With a shake of her head, she asked, “Why can’t we sit down and talk about our problems like two polite people?”

His gaze hadn’t left her. “I wish I could answer that.”

“Oh, Tristan.” She uttered a sigh. “You make me so angry sometimes, I can’t think straight.”

He gave her a boyish, lopsided smile. It sent her heart racing.

“It’s a gift.”

She choked on a laugh. “I just wanted to apologize. Mama and Papa never went to bed angry with each other. I . . . I know we’ve had our problems,” she added, hurrying on, “but I couldn’t sleep, thinking that I might have hurt you.”

He swept a hand over his body. “Do you want to take a peek and find out?”

Her gaze went to his chest again, but she blinked and glanced away, trying to ignore the warmth that spread through her. “I didn’t mean to punch you so hard.”

“I might have been able to protect myself if I’d known it was coming.”

She gave him a slight shrug. "That's the point of hitting someone. To catch them off guard."

"You learned to fight dirty at Trenway," he observed.

Memories swamped her. The matron shoving her face into the swill she'd refused to eat; one of the guards slamming her against the wall with such force, she'd nearly passed out; crazy old Marnie, yanking her hair so hard she'd almost felt her neck crack; the days she'd spent in the punishment box, lying in her own foul excrement. The memories not only brought the sting of tears, but anger that had recently begun to surface.

"It was the only way to survive."

He patted the spot beside him. "Come here."

She went, feeling like a child in need of affection from a parent. Once she was beside him, she curled into the crook of his arm and placed her hand on his chest.

"Tell me about Trenway, Dinah."

Expelling a tired, shaky sigh, she answered, "Must I?"

"I may never fully understand, but I'd like to try."

She suddenly felt vulnerable, alone, and incredibly sad. Tears tracked her cheeks, dripping onto his chest. "No one, not even someone who is insane should be forced to live that way. Animals are treated better than we were."

He stiffened, tightening his grip. "Tell me."

She began hesitantly at first. Then it was as if a dam broke somewhere in her soul, and she couldn't have stopped herself if she'd tried. She told him of the filth, the rats, the poisonous, repugnant food, the beatings, the casual and cruel raping of the most passive, stupefied women, the drowning ice baths, the straitjackets, the small, windowless rooms that allowed no sound to be heard from the other side, the merciless torture of the punishment box, the grief, the agony, the madness of those who became that way only after they'd been tossed inside.

"A lot of things bother me still," she finished. "I can't

stand to sleep without a light on and I haven't been able to take a tub bath since I got here. And . . . and I don't like small, dark places. When I'm in them, I feel as though I'm suffocating. It's . . . it's getting better, though," she hurried to inform him.

She couldn't look at him, afraid she would see the disgust on his face. In his eyes.

He hadn't moved during her entire discourse. He briefly shifted and extinguished the lamp, casting the room in darkness.

She moved to leave; he drew her to him.

"I wish there was something I could do or say to make you feel better. Words are damned inadequate. One night—the night before we went to the dressmaker's—I came in to tell you what time to be ready the following morning. You weren't there, but I found your teddy bear."

She groaned into his shoulder, feeling embarrassed.

"It was then that I finally realized what you'd been through. Until then, nothing you said or did sounded like a woman who had suffered as you had. You were strong, Dinah. You hid your pain so damned well, it made me treat you like any other woman. Hell, that's not true. I treated you worse than I've ever treated a woman in my life. I felt shame, but somehow I justified it. After all, I told myself, you continued to pretend you were someone you weren't. I'd given you plenty of opportunities to tell me, yet you didn't."

"I meant to, Tristan. Even earlier today I meant to tell you. I was so afraid. Afraid that you'd boot me out on my rump."

"I know. I could see you struggling with yourself. Even so, I should have been careful with you. Kind. Compassionate. Forgive me for being rude and boorish."

Without another word, he scooted down in the bed with her in his arms and stroked her hair. Her shoulders. Her arm. Her hip.

She drew in a wet, shaky breath and nestled against him, feeling a peace she hadn't known since before her parents died. "I love you, Tristan."

Giving her behind a gentle pat, he answered, "I was hoping you did."

She smiled into his chest, the scent of him the last thing she remembered as she drifted into sleep.

16

SOMETIME DURING THE NIGHT SHE AWAKENED, UNDER THE covers and in Tristan's arms. She moved to leave.

"No," he ordered softly. "Stay."

She nestled closer. Her hand was on his chest. She put it under the covers to warm it, stopping at his navel when she realized he wore nothing to bed.

He kissed her forehead, her eyelids, the tip of her nose. His lips touched hers. She longed for his kiss, had dreamed of it, afraid she would never experience it again. The kiss deepened, yet he was gentle with her, drawing from her a sound of pleasure and the need to be close. His mouth left hers, and he planted wet kisses on her neck, flicking his tongue into the shell of her ear.

She wrapped her arms around him, loving his hard, warm flesh against her palms. The tenderness made her want to cry, for it was the first she'd known in such a long time. She held back as long as she could, then quiet sobs shook her.

"Shhh," he murmured. "It's all right. I won't hurt you."

"Oh, Tristan. It isn't that." She sniffed, wiping her face with her hand. "It's . . . it's just that I n-need someone to love me. For so long I've been alone. You . . . you said you forgot what I went through because I didn't show it. I learned to be tough. I had to be. But even then, inside I was soft and all I wanted was to be loved."

He swore, and she knew it wasn't directed at her. "I love you, Dinah, but when I should have been treating you as you deserved, my emotions were at odds inside me, like two mountain goats butting heads."

Peace and joy stole over her, and she clung to him, never wanting to leave.

Their legs touched beneath the covers; his were firm, and the hair was rough and intriguing as he moved against her. She ran the bottom of her foot along his calf.

"Your legs are hard and hairy," she announced.

He snuffled a laugh into her curls. "That's not the only place that is."

Blushing, she smiled in the darkness, for there was another part of him that was hard; she was aware of it against her thigh.

"Could I . . . would you mind very much if I touched it?"

He took her hand, moving it under the covers to his navel. "It would be proud and honored."

Her smile widened; her blush deepened. For all of her salty talk and audacious pretense, she was still very innocent. "It would, would it?"

"Yes." He placed her hand on him. "Feel how he stands at attention for you? He's a lordly appendage. Hasn't had much to stand tall about lately, though."

Her laugh was caught up on a breath; her heart pattered wildly as she examined him. With a bold and inquisitive touch, she folded her hand around him, sliding the skin over the hard shaft.

His lips captured hers as she stroked, and his tongue plundered her mouth.

His hand moved along the inside of her knee to her thigh, where he crept higher until his fingers touched her. She spread her legs, expelling a sigh of pleasure when he fondled her there.

"Oh, I remember this," she murmured around a shuddery smile. She tried to concentrate on him, but her own ecstasy was fast approaching.

He groaned beside her, removing her hand but not letting it go. "Sorry, love, it's been too damned long. If I let you continue, I'll embarrass myself.

"Here," he instructed. "I want you to feel something." He drew her to her own flesh, where he brought her index finger to the top of her mound.

She gasped, surprised, for there was a nub there, hard and swollen. He used her finger to stroke her, and she moved her head from side to side, bucking occasionally on the bed.

"There's more, you know." He enticed her with his voice, his touch, his experience.

She continued to touch herself as long as his hand was guiding hers. It felt naughty, but she was too far gone to care. She felt it coming again, that powerful sense of pleasure that radiated through her body from the place at the top of her thighs. She arched her back, dug her heels into the bed, and allowed it to come.

When she could speak, she said, "Please, Tristan, I want more. I want . . . I want you to make love with me."

He moved between her thighs, gently nudging her with the tip of his shaft, rubbing it across her flesh. Though his arms were stiff on either side of her, he shook. She reached between them and guided him in.

"It will hurt only briefly, my love." With a grateful sigh, he plunged inside, stopping at her sharp intake of breath. When the sting had passed, she wrapped her legs around him and rose to meet his thrusts.

She felt it coming again, that urgent, erratic ecstasy that made her ears ring and her body seem to splinter into pieces. As she breathed, she moaned, the sound becoming louder as her rapture increased. At one vivid, shattering moment, she had no control, but as she was about to scream, Tristan's mouth came down on hers. He stiffened above her; she was certain she felt his seed spatter the inner surface of her womb.

They drifted down together, and Tristan rolled to his side, bringing her with him. She snuggled and rubbed her palm over his chest. He was the first to speak.

"Have you ever touched yourself there before?"

She knew what he referred to; she wouldn't be coy. "No."

"I didn't think so. You seemed surprised at what you felt."

"I was," she answered on a sigh. "I had no idea my body changed like that."

"There are many other changes, too. We'll explore every one of them together." He smiled into her hair. "I look forward to it."

Her heart swelled with love.

With indolent fingers, he stroked her hip. "That place down there has a name, you know."

In spite of the intimacy they'd just shared, she blushed again. "I know it does."

"Oh, there are other names for it. We'll talk about them, too. The first time I felt it, the night we were married, it reminded me of a cranberry."

She smiled, biting down on her bottom lip, embarrassed. "And you'll never be able to eat a cranberry again."

He shook with quiet laughter.

"What's so funny, you cur?"

"I may want to eat nothing but cranberries, yours included. Or should I say," he amended, his fingers slipping over her thigh to touch her again, "especially yours."

She parted her legs, knowing a sense of pride that she pleased him. She wanted it to continue. "Tristan?"

"Yes, love?"

Her heart expanded at the endearment. "I don't want to fight with you anymore."

"Hmmm. The fight makes the loving that much more intense, Dinah."

"I'll admit I enjoy those games we played, but I don't want us to go to bed angry with each other ever again. I was wondering, though . . ." Her voice trailed off.

"Talk to me, love, don't hold anything back."

She swallowed. "I was wondering if we would always have to create disagreements just so we can make up."

"I have a feeling that after this, we won't need much of anything to ignite a spark." There was a smile in his voice.

Dinah was intoxicated with sensations. Feeling a fierce sense of possession, she wrapped her arm around his torso and held him tightly. "If I thought there was another woman out there somewhere, waiting for you to come to her, I think I'd find her and . . . and—"

"Punch her in the stomach?"

She rubbed a soothing hand over his. "Something like that. I'll tell you again, Tristan Fletcher. I'm in love with you."

"I'm happy to hear it. The feeling is mutual."

She caught her lower lip between her teeth to keep it from trembling with emotion. "Tristan?"

He made a questioning sound in his throat.

"I'd like to see your—" She leaned close to his ear and whispered the word in his ear.

He choked, coughing hard beside her.

She raised herself on her elbow, concerned. "Are you all right?"

After he'd cursed and coughed and caught his breath, he answered, "Your request caught me off guard, that's all."

"Am I being too bold?"

He sat up and lit the lamp on his bedside table. "You're full of surprises, aren't you?" He rested against the bed frame, humor lurking in his eyes. "I don't think I've ever heard a woman actually use that word before."

She blushed. "I know it's not proper, just like it's not proper to say the word breast, but what should I call it, then, your—" She whispered a much less acceptable word.

He choked again, this time coughing so hard his eyes watered. "Where in blazes did you learn that term?"

Her eyes were wide. "At Trenway, of course."

He cursed again. "From whom, for God's sake?"

"Some of the women. Adventuresses. Strumpets. Women like that."

"You mean, whores."

She nodded. "There were many of them there. They talked boldly all the time. Sometimes outrageously so. I think they did it to shock people like me."

"It obviously didn't work, at least not for long."

"After a while, it didn't mean anything anymore. I'll never forget Mitts. Her real name was Maudie, but everyone, especially the guards, called her Mitts because it rhymed with . . . well," she hesitated, "you know. She had a large chest. Anyway, I remember the time she called to one of the most disgusting guards and told him that if he dropped his drawers, she'd blow his socks off."

Tristan made a choking sound again. This time she realized he was laughing. She shook her head. "You'll have to explain it to me, because I still don't know what she meant. Everyone else thought it was hilarious."

Tristan rubbed his hand over his face. "Let's keep this kind of conversation between the two of us, all right?"

She was indignant. "I wasn't going to write it down and mail it to the newspaper."

He just sighed and shook his head.

"Well, can I see it?"

"I'm not sure it's up to it, knowing how the poor thing is maligned by women everywhere."

She was fearful that she'd offended him. "Men are very proud of them, aren't they?"

"Believe me, we'd be lost without them, for many reasons." He stroked her mouth with his thumb; she captured it between her teeth. He flipped off the covers.

Then she stared. "Oh, my goodness," she said on a delighted breath. It thickened before her eyes and grew from the bush of black hair that surrounded it. She touched it, feeling the velvety skin again, discovering the sac below. When she'd finished her examination, it lay thick and hard against his hairy abdomen.

She gazed at him, amazed. "Did I do that?" At his nod, she murmured, "What does it look like when it's relaxed?"

He gave her a wry smile. "As long as you're around, I doubt that you'll ever find out."

Desire stirred in her again as she continued to look at him. "It's a shame to waste it."

He drew her to him, the erection pressing her belly. "I didn't intend to."

They made love again, not at a leisurely pace, even though they'd done it before. It was hard. Intense. Fulfilling. After they'd finished, she wondered if it would always be that way. She crossed her fingers. She could only hope.

Morning came quickly for Tristan, but he left the bed without disturbing his wife. His wife. She slept on, snoring softly. He studied her delicate features, an ache settling in his gut as he remembered what she'd told him the night before. Trenway. Scourge of God. Satan's brothel. He was only beginning to understand what she'd gone through. Although he suffered for it, he wanted to know everything. Any pain he experienced couldn't be measured against hers.

With reluctance, he went to the dressing room, washed up, and dressed. Giving her one last glance, he walked to the bed, bent and kissed her forehead. She smiled in her sleep, uttering a throaty sigh.

He stopped in the kitchen, where Alice was preparing porridge for the children, and told her where he was going. Without waking anyone else, he left the ranch and rode to Hatter's Horn to send David a telegram. He would be an impatient bag of nerves until he learned as much as he could about Charles Avery.

Charles crept to the window and watched Fletcher ride toward the village. No doubt on his way to send a message, he thought, a smile touching his lips. He couldn't blame the man for being suspicious. It had been an incredible coup to find Dinah before anyone else had. Odell would be pleased. But because of Fletcher's suspicions, Charles knew he would have to lie low.

He started to dress, remembering the possessive way Fletcher had silently told him Dinah belonged to him. He hadn't had a real chance with Dinah before and he didn't expect to have one with her now. That was all right. He had other things to concentrate on.

He was good at his job. His innocent, baby face often misled people. It had been a curse in his youth; now he found it a blessing.

He waited until he was sure Fletcher wasn't going to double back, then he dropped a note for Dinah on the dining-room buffet, crept to the front door to avoid alerting the housekeeper, and left the house and the ranch. They would think he was gone; he would be close enough to know what was happening.

Dinah woke in Tristan's bed, sensing before she opened her eyes that he was gone. As much as she longed to curl up and think about the night before, breathe in the smells around her, and hug his pillow to her chest, she knew it was later than she usually awakened and there was plenty of work to do.

Also, Alice was probably talking Charles's ear off,

although knowing how he'd enjoyed her cooking the night before, Dinah was sure he wouldn't mind, as long as it got him a good breakfast.

She sprang from the bed, wincing at the discomfort between her legs. It was brief and a sudden gush of happiness made her dizzy.

Falling onto the bed, she closed her eyes, remembering Tristan's gentleness, his concern, his lovemaking. Perhaps she was starry eyed, but she couldn't see a cloud on their horizon. Not one.

Charles wouldn't do anything to hurt her; she felt sure of that. She was also certain that if he tried, Tristan would protect her. They'd come a long way together. She was happy she was no longer alone. She had a family again. She had a husband, a sister-in-law, a crusty housekeeper, and eight children!

The only thing she would change would be to have Mama, Papa, and Charlotte know that she was happy and safe.

By the time Dinah came downstairs, Alice had Sarafina, Rose, and Flicker Feather making tortillas. Dawn stood on a stool at the stove, stirring what smelled like beans.

Dinah poured herself some tea. "What's going on in here?" she asked around a yawn.

"The girls asked if they could make dinner," Alice explained.

"That's a wonderful idea." Dinah was pleased the girls had become so helpful.

"By the way," Alice added, "Tristan was up bright and early, as usual, but I swear he'd changed, somehow. I'd ask if you know why, but it wouldn't be ladylike."

Dinah blushed, hurrying to change the subject. "What can I do to help?"

"Well, if it were up to me, which it isn't, I'd serve up platters of steak and potatoes tonight. The children took a vote, and we're having chicken, tortillas with beans and fried potatoes, along with fresh fruit pies. Here."

She handed Dinah a paring knife, then nodded toward the fruit bowl. "Best you start peeling them apples."

Dinah suddenly remembered Charles. "Where's Charles this morning, Alice?"

She shook her head. "I haven't seen him."

"Oh." Sarafina's smile was shy as she dug into the pocket of her homespun skirt. "I was coming through the dining room and saw this note. It's got your name on it, Miss Dinah."

Dinah took the note and read it with a sense of disappointment. "He's gone."

"Gone? Gone, where?"

"He has an appointment in San Francisco. Says he'll stop by on his way home."

"I'm almost ready to say good riddance."

"But, why? I didn't even get a chance to ask him about his mother."

"You obviously didn't see the way Tristan glowered at him. Jealousy was written all over his scowling face."

Dinah couldn't stop her smile. "Really? How nice."

Alice made a *tsk* sound with her tongue and returned to the stove.

Dinah floated through the morning chores. After peeling apples for the pies, she polished the silverware, shook the rugs, dusted the banister, and even learned how to churn butter. Flicker Feather was astonished that Dinah, a grown woman, had never learned such a necessary task.

When it was time to feed the children lunch, she and Leeta enlisted Emily's help, insisting Alice take a short rest. Later, when Dinah crept into Alice's room, she found the woman asleep.

With Leeta and Emily in the kitchen, Dinah took the outside entrance to the root cellar to get some potatoes, leaving the wide doors open. It was a dark, windowless room with a dirt floor. She waited for the panic to come and was surprised when it didn't. Not that she wanted to spend an afternoon down there, but at least her heart wasn't pounding.

A shadow crossed the opening. Startled, she turned.

"Hello." His voice was seductive.

Her heart was pounding now. "Hello," she answered, unable to keep from smiling.

He stepped into the cellar, his nearness making her quake. He stepped closer. "I'm glad I found you alone."

"Maybe I should scream." Each word was an effort. Her body vibrated like a tuning fork.

He wagged a playful finger at her. "Not before. Only during."

He dragged her into his arms and kissed her as though he hadn't seen her for days. It was a possessive embrace, yet tender. Dear. She melted against him. When he lifted his head, their faces were close, their breath mingling. His eyes were warm. "I've been waiting all day to do this," he admitted, close to her mouth.

She swallowed, reveling in the rasp of his beard on her skin. "You . . . you have?"

"Umhmm. Now, you're supposed to say you've been waiting for it, too."

"I have." Her answer was guileless. Unadorned. Even in the dim light of the cellar, she saw his eyes darken.

He brought her hand to his fly. She touched him, noting his size.

He made a groaning sound of pleasure. "All the way back from the village I've been thinking about you. You're on my mind constantly. I want to take you right here, on the cellar floor."

Her drawers felt damp, and she leaned into him to steady herself. "I saw a blanket by the potatoes," she offered.

He left her briefly, shook out the blanket, and put it on floor.

She went into his arms again and they sank to their knees. He hiked up her petticoat and gown, finding the slit in her drawers. She was so hungry for him, her knees quaked. He was hard against her stomach.

He groaned into her hair. "God, but I love a woman's unmentionables."

With greedy fingers, she unbuttoned his fly, releasing him.

"Come," he ordered softly, lifting her over him. "Ride."

She followed his lead, feeling anxious and unskilled, until she was poised over him. She lifted her skirt and guided him inside, shuddering with a sigh of pleasure as she sheathed herself around him.

She moved on his shaft, helping him undo her bodice to free her breasts. He caressed them as she rode, and when she felt the familiar bursting of pleasure inside her, she waited until he stiffened beneath her, then she slumped to his chest.

"Dinah? You down there?"

Dinah's heart leaped against her ribs.

"It's Alice," he whispered against her ear.

She struggled to sit and hurried to fix her bodice. "Yes, Alice, I'll be right up."

"What are you doing?"

Tristan muffled a laugh.

"Nothing, I'm . . . ah . . . just getting some potatoes."

Tristan's laughter exploded.

"Tristan?"

When he recovered, he answered, "Yes, Alice."

"What are *you* doing down there?"

"I'm helping Dinah."

Stifling a laugh of her own, Dinah swatted him.

When they were certain she was gone, they checked each other to make sure nothing was amiss, then left the cellar. As they strolled into the kitchen, Alice gave them a strange look.

"What's wrong?" Tristan demanded.

"I thought you were down there getting potatoes."

Dinah gasped and covered her mouth, hiding her embarrassment and her smile.

Tristan simply gave Alice a good-natured pat on the shoulder. Before he returned to the cellar to retrieve the vegetables, he announced, "We'd better get the guest room ready. I picked up a wire at the telegraph office earlier. David will be here sometime tomorrow."

17

THE FOLLOWING MORNING, DINAH ACCOMPANIED TRISTAN TO the outskirts of his property to search for a stray calf. They rode double on his mount, but once the ranch was no longer in sight, Tristan instructed her to turn and face him. Her thighs lay over his and she crossed her ankles behind him, resting her arms on his shoulders.

With one hand, he tugged her closer, nesting his groin to hers.

"I've never ridden double with someone in trousers," he murmured, dropping a kiss on her mouth.

A surge of weakening desire washed over her and she snuggled closer, her breasts flattening against his chest. She felt a bite of ownership, suddenly understanding his need to possess that which he loved. "Have you ridden double with someone in a dress?"

His hand roamed her rump. "Do you want the truth?"

"Absolutely." With bold fingers, she reached between

them and cupped him. "Just remember that I hold your life in my hands."

He made a sound of pleasure, and Dinah felt him swell behind his fly. "I haven't cared about anyone else enough to let them ride Rogue."

That he would admit she was special made her love for him that much stronger. She continued stroking him, her hunger rising. "That's his name? Rogue? All these weeks and I've never heard it."

"We haven't exactly had normal conversations, if you recall."

She smiled into his shoulder, remembering their peppery exchanges. "Well?"

"Well, what?"

"Do you like riding with a woman in trousers?"

"It's interesting," he answered, continuing to move his hand over her curves.

She pinched his side, eliciting from him a *youch* of pain. "Only interesting?"

"To be perfectly honest, I kind of like a long skirt, petticoats, and slitted drawers for a position like this." His fingers came to the juncture of her thighs, and he touched her. "Much easier to make a woman horny if everything on the surface appears normal. With skirts and petticoats hiding things, our activity could be more . . . engaging, if you know what I mean."

She drew a shuddering breath. "Any more engaging and we'd tumble from the horse."

Rogue stopped and Tristan turned Dinah sideways, lowering her to the ground. He dismounted, looped the reins around the low branches of a juniper and took Dinah's hand.

"Come on. I want to show you something."

She came willingly, but asked, "What about the calf?"

"What calf?"

"The one we came to find."

They jogged through the trees, up a slope, then down

to a trickling creek. "Oh, that. They're all present and accounted for."

She jerked on his arm. "You mean this was a ploy to get me out here?"

He turned, gracing her with a boyish grin that set her soul afire. "Dirty trick, huh?"

She couldn't resist an answering smile. "Very dirty trick. I think you need to be punished."

He stopped beside a rock formation that arched over the creek and gave her another heart-stopping grin. "Surprise me."

Standing on tiptoes, she removed his hat and threaded her fingers through his hair. How she loved it when his eyes twinkled with warmth. "I'm only a beginner. It's up to you to teach me the ways you like being disciplined."

He nodded toward the creek. "We can start here."

She peered around the rock at the water. "A mite cold, don't you think? How does one get in there without getting wet?"

His grin widened. "One doesn't. And it's not cold. There's a hot spring in there."

Her slow, sly smile told him she understood. "You mean you want me to take off my clothes? Right out here in broad daylight?"

He pulled his shirt from his buckskins and started unbuttoning it. "I plan to take mine off. It's far more fun if we're both naked."

She was mesmerized by his body. "I remember the first time I saw you." She ran her palms over his chest, across his sculpted shoulders, down to the black hair that swirled around his navel.

He stood, allowing her hands to roam. "What was your first thought?"

She couldn't stop her smile. "My first thought was that you were a barbarian."

His hands covered hers, and he drew them to his fly. "What did I do?"

"You told me no one ever strikes your dogs." She

rubbed her palm over his fly, shuddering at the thickness of his shaft. "I thought, how can any man care more for dogs than he cares about people?"

He began unbuttoning her shirt, then bent to kiss her. "I'm sorry I was such a ogre. What else?"

She uttered a groan of pleasure. "Your skin was so brown. I'd become accustomed to asylum pallor. I thought you were the most beautiful man I'd ever seen, even though you were rude. I thought to myself, He doesn't want me here. What will he do when he discovers I'm not even the woman he hired?"

He chuckled, the sound warm and thick as syrup. "From the day you arrived and I caught you in my tree, I was certain David had played a gigantic trick on me. I'd asked him for an obedient, sweet-tempered, pleasant-looking companion for Emily. Someone I could marry and forget about. And look what I got."

"Were you disappointed?" She leaned into him and pressed a kiss on one dark nipple.

"Of all the emotions I've had since the moment I first saw you, disappointment has not been among them."

He bent and kissed her forehead while she fondled his nipples. "You know, that works much better if I do it to you."

"Although I'd like that," she admitted, "I feel funny undressing out here in the open."

He pulled her shirt from her trousers. "There's not a soul around for miles. Think of it as an adventure."

By the time he'd removed her shirt, the adventure was well under way. She allowed her breasts to touch his chest, then dragged her nipples over his skin.

At his sharp intake of breath, she asked, "Why do you like that?"

He cupped her rump. "Because it makes me horny."

"Besides that." She nuzzled closer, wanting to take him between her thighs.

"I guess it does for me what this," he said, pushing her pelvis tightly to his, "does for you."

Desire tumbled through her. "Oh," she answered with a sigh. "I see."

He lifted her, hoisting her legs around his waist, then bent to kiss her breasts. She leaned away, allowing him access until she felt him shake. Then she slid her legs down his hips.

"Now your trousers," he whispered against her ear.

"Yours first," she ordered boldly. Anxiously.

He stepped away, his gaze on her while he unbuttoned his fly. He sprang free, long and thick and hard. As he removed his boots, then his buckskins, his shaft bobbed, as if it were greeting her.

"Oh, I do love the way you look. I had no idea all of that could be hidden behind a pair of trousers."

He stood naked. She touched the base of his shaft, then ran her fingers to the tip. Liquid oozed from it, wetting her fingertips. She brought them to her lips, tasting it with her tongue, remembering how he'd kissed her, asking her to taste herself.

"You taste different from me."

He made a strangled sound in his throat and brought her palm to his mouth and licked it. "If I let you continue your education, I'll be required to take you right here, right now."

The idea of making love outside seemed as naughty and exciting as touching herself. She swallowed hard. "I'm beginning to think it's not such a bad idea."

His gaze was hot. "Take off your trousers, Dinah. I want to see for myself how wet you are."

She sagged to a rock, desire making her dizzy. She yanked off her boots, then stood and began removing her trousers.

"Wait." With two fingers inside her waistband, he drew her close, then dipped his fingers lower. "I love this part." He found her. "Ah, you're wet, honey. Wet and swollen."

He teased her with his touch, then helped her remove her trousers. He was on his knees before her, then he drew her hand to her mound. "Touch it. Feel how wet you are."

She did, experiencing mounting hunger.

Suddenly his mouth was there, and her knees buckled.

"Tristan," she scolded, her breath coming fast as she gripped his hair. "Dear heavens, I'm ready to fly apart."

He stood and pulled her toward the water. "Then by all means, let's get to your lesson."

Initially the water was cold, but as they waded farther under the rocky bridge, Dinah felt the warmth swirling around her.

It was intoxicating, this sensation of warm water on her aroused body.

"Do you swim?"

"Oh, no. Dear me, no." She brought her hand to her chest, feigning alarm.

He drew her to him, wrapping one arm around her waist, then started swimming on his back.

"It's like floating." Finding his rhythm, she kicked her feet and they glided through the water.

"I could teach you to swim, if you'd like," he offered, appearing not the least bit winded by her weight.

"That would be fun. Teach me now."

"What? Now?"

She wriggled from his arms. "Yes. Please, Tristan, teach me to swim, now."

Frowning, he uttered a gruff sigh. She could tell he wasn't the least bit excited about the prospect. She hid her smile.

"All right. I'm going to hold you, but first I want to show you the movements. Your arms should move through the water like this," he instructed, making swimming motions. "And when you learn that, I'll teach you how to kick. Now, lie on my hands."

She swallowed a sigh of pleasure as she sank onto his hands, one of which was low on her belly and the other just below her breasts. "Now, what do I do?"

He cleared his throat. "It's damned hard for me to think with your sweet ass in my face."

She hid her face and grinned. "Come on, Tristan, tell me what to do next."

"Er . . . ah . . . move your arms the way I showed you."

She attempted a graceless movement.

"That's not too bad, I guess. Keep trying."

She thrashed at the water, artless as a beginner. "Oh, dear." She took a breath and gasped, gulping in a mouthful of water. She sputtered and coughed, flailing her arms. "Don't you dare drop me, Tristan Fletcher, don't you dare!"

"I won't drop you. Now, get your rhythm going again, Dinah. Come on, that's a girl," he encouraged.

"Oh! Oh! I think I've got it. Let me go, Tristan, let me try it."

He gave her a condescending laugh. "I hardly think you've learned to swim in two minutes."

"I'm going to try. Catch me if I sink, all right?" Before she heard his answer, she swam away, taking long, graceful strokes. "Why, this is easy." She arched her back and dove to the bottom of the pool, touching the rocks, bringing up a smooth stone. She broke through the surface and gave him a triumphant grin.

Though his expression was sardonic, he gave her an answering smile. "You swim like a fish. You're a witch, do you know that?"

She'd enjoyed the charade. "It was fun getting the lesson."

His expression became a mock threat. "I'll show you fun." He lunged for her and she bolted away, eluding him in the warm depths. He grabbed her ankle, but she wiggled out of his grasp. Each time he seized her, she found a way to escape.

Finally, he got a firm hold around her waist, then drew her close. His eyes twinkled. His teeth gleamed against his brown skin. His smile was exciting. Intoxicating.

"Marriage to you is going to be full of inventive surprises," he predicted.

"I want to try everything with you." She straddled him, sucking in a shaky gasp when he went deep. His thumbs caressed her nipples; she felt more tensing low in her abdomen.

He was motionless inside her. "Tease."

Discovering the muscles that circled him, she squeezed, drawing from him a throaty groan. "Brute."

He placed his hands on her waist and lunged. "Hooligan."

She fastened her legs around him, pressing close to get the most out of what she was feeling. Her head lolled as the sensation intensified. "Love—" She swallowed as the waves of desire began. "Love me."

His breath was ragged as his mouth covered hers. They rocked in the water, Dinah clamping her thighs around her husband's waist as he thrust inside her and finally spent.

Afterward, they bobbed and attempted to catch their breath.

Tristan lifted her and kissed her breasts. "You know I already do."

Afraid her heart would spring free, she threw her arms around him and hugged him, salty tears of joy mingling with the fresh mountain water.

They floated in the water, satisfied.

"Tristan?"

"Yes, love."

She kissed his forehead. "Tell me how you came to be here."

"You mean here with you?"

"No, you know what I mean."

"I imagine you've heard some of it."

"Yes, from Emily. Tell me everything." She continued to straddle him.

"All right." He kissed her.

"One day two years ago this spring, a man on horseback arrived at the ranch. Although he was dressed differently, he looked like me. Even had the same kind of mount."

"Your brother, Wolfgang Amadeus."

He nodded. "He told me how he'd searched for the woman who had given us birth. He hadn't known at the time that he was a twin, yet something inside him told him there was more to the story than just finding her."

"He found her?"

Tristan nodded. "He'd tracked her to a ranch. She was a wealthy widow with a son. Our half brother."

"Was she surprised to see him?"

"Devastated is more the word. She'd thought she was rid of him. Of us. She had ordered her mother to destroy us as infants. Apparently she'd been raped when her family passed through Indian country on their way to California."

Dinah's heart gave a twist. "How terrible."

"Don't pity her, Dinah. She has a wicked streak that makes her quite unsympathetic. From what Wolf says, she probably hadn't been raped at all, even though that's what she continued to profess. She and her son plotted to destroy Wolf."

Dinah gasped. "His own mother?"

"As I said, she doesn't deserve your pity or your sympathy."

Dinah took Tristan's face between her hands and kissed him. "The Fletchers took you. What about Wolf?"

He was buried—"

"Buried? Alive? Oh, Tristan."

"—beneath some brush. Fortunately he was found by an old Scottish trapper before a wild animal dragged him off."

Dinah caressed her husband's shoulders, letting her fingers roam over his hard flesh. "How could she do that?"

"The old woman, my grandmother, I guess, couldn't follow her daughter's orders and kill us. Last year she told Wolf she'd gone back to get him and had found him gone. She didn't know if he'd been rescued or dragged off."

"Poor Wolf. You had the better life, didn't you?"

He pressed a kiss to the hollow of her neck. "My life wasn't bad until my father died. Zelda never did care about me. It didn't matter as long as my father was alive. He was a good man. Too good for her, anyway. He deserved better. When he died, I became Zelda's personal servant."

"Was Alice here then?"

He nodded. "Alice has been here as long as I can remember. I guess she came to live with the Fletchers after her husband and son died."

"Rory," Dinah offered, feeling a bite of sadness.

"Yes. Alice was more of a mother to me than Zelda. I would often escape to the kitchen because it was warm and smelled good. Zelda would find me and beat me with a broom handle."

Dinah closed her eyes and pressed her face into his neck.

"So, as far as material things, I probably had the better life. I got an education, too. Wolf had two crusty old miners to look after him. He didn't have a pot to piss in, but those old men raised him with affection."

She had a flash of insight. "Is that why you decided to adopt Little Hawk and the others?"

"Yes." They continued to bob together in the warm water.

She suddenly remembered something. "I have an idea. Do you want to hear it?"

He hugged her. "I want to hear every idea you have."

"When are you going to San Francisco again?"

"When I can take you with me. We never had a honeymoon, you know."

There was a warm glow around her heart. "That sounds exciting." She licked the water off his shoulder. "I'd like to find a gallery that would display some of

Emily's paintings and drawings, especially those of the children."

He had been rubbing her hips; his hands stopped. "What would that achieve?"

"It would draw attention to her talent. She absolutely glows when she gets compliments, Tristan. Think how she would feel if someone wanted to buy something from her? It would give her a degree of independence. Give her something to work for besides pleasing you and me."

He kissed her and lifted her from his lap. "My dear wife, you are absolutely brilliant."

"Well, I guess it hasn't taken you too long to discover that for yourself," she teased.

They swam lazily, touching and stroking until they were both hungry again. Once they were satisfied, they left the grotto with reluctance.

When they'd dried off and had begun to dress, Dinah gasped with surprise. Through the trees, up from the creek, was a tiny building. "Tristan," she whispered loudly. "There's a cabin over there."

He followed her gaze. "Ah, yes. That's the old Adams place." His eyes narrowed and he stopped buttoning his shirt.

"What? What is it?"

His expression changed and he smiled at her. "It's nothing, love. There hasn't been anyone there for years."

She tried to calm her racing heart. "Oh, Tristan, if I had even the tiniest notion that someone had watched—"

He put his index finger to her lips. "Don't worry about it. It's empty."

As they rode to the ranch, Dinah clinging to Tristan's waist, she wondered at the change in his mood.

Charles stood motionless until they had gone. Fletcher had studied the cabin. Had he seen something?

He swung away, jamming his fists into his pockets. He wasn't a voyeur. He thought it was a sick thing to do, but he'd watched until they disappeared under the rocky bridge, and again when they had emerged.

So. That was what Dinah Odell looked like naked.

He experienced a stirring as he remembered, but ignored it. He felt a bigger fool when he thought about Fletcher's size. His own meager organ had nearly shriveled with despair. Normal men were not so generously endowed, and the world was full of normal men. Like himself.

He cursed for letting his mind wander. He had work to do. Martin Odell would arrive any day, and he would expect the cabin to be ready. He was in for a surprise, however. He didn't think Odell was aware of his niece's marital status.

Charles winced. He hated to be the one to tell him.

Dr. David Richards's arrival brought a jolt of reality to Tristan's life with Dinah. They had skirted the serious issue of what was happening in New York until after dinner. Then, with the three of them seated around the empty dining-room table, David shared the news.

"He's sent someone out here, I'm sure of it," David remarked.

"Have you any idea who it is?" Dinah twisted her handkerchief in her lap.

"I think I know." Tristan took in Dinah's look of disbelief and refusal to agree. "What are our choices, Dinah?"

She shook her head. "I can't believe Charles would be involved in this."

"Charles Avery?"

Dinah shot Tristan a look of fear.

"What do you know about him?" Tristan tried to appear calm, for Dinah's sake.

"He's with the *Times.* Came to see me a few months ago, but I wasn't available. He spoke to a colleague of mine."

"See? Charles shared all that with me. I told you he

was telling me the truth, Tristan." Dinah appeared a bit relieved.

"Yes, but to have him show up so conveniently." He shook his head. "Too coincidental."

David rested his elbows on the table and tapped his chin. "You are wanted for questioning regarding Daisy's death, Dinah."

Dinah put her face in her hands. "Poor, dear Daisy."

"Everyone's speculating as to how she got into that discipline box."

Closing her eyes, Dinah folded her hands, prayer-like, and rested her lips against them. "Daisy planned the entire thing. It sounds as if I'm merely shifting the guilt, but I'm not. Daisy died in my arms."

She took a deep breath. "It wasn't until the day she was to leave that she told me what she wanted to do. Neither of us thought this far ahead. At least, I didn't. When she finally convinced me it was the only thing to do, I didn't look back and wonder how others would perceive what I'd done. All I knew," she added, shaking her head, "was that I would be free from that . . . that despicable place."

Tristan took her hand, gripping it in his. "They can't seriously consider foul play, David."

"The physical evidence is pretty damning, but they're willing to listen to Dinah's story."

"I'm surprised Uncle Martin hasn't convinced them all I'm a homicidal lunatic."

"Oddly enough, your uncle was championing your cause. In a way."

Dinah looked doubtful. "I find that hard to believe."

"I think he wants a hand in whatever decision is made about you. On the surface, he appears to be working with the police. I would bet that he's doing his own investigating behind their backs. He doesn't want you hanged for Daisy's murder because then he'd lose the trust, so he's mouthing platitudes about your innocence. As long as you're alive and incarcerated one way or another, he controls your trust fund." David opened a flat leather case. "Don't ask me how I got this, but this is your father's will."

Dinah nodded. "I've seen it before."

David shoved it toward Tristan. "In essence, as long as Dinah's alive but not free, she's right where Odell wants her. However," he added, "when she married you, it became a problem for him. The last I heard, he didn't seem to know about it. I'm sure, though, that if he's given the possibility a thought, it's undoubtedly been his worst nightmare."

"I'd rather hoped it would be." Tristen winked at his wife, who tried to smile, but failed. Her fingers were cold beneath his.

Tristan scanned the contents of the will. At age twenty-two, Dinah would become a very wealthy woman in her own right. "What strikes me as odd about this is that the loophole Odell found is big enough to drive a rig through."

"Papa had no reason to believe Martin would do such a thing. While I was growing up, Martin appeared to be the perfect uncle, brother, and brother-in-law."

Tristan shoved the will across the table. "What do you suggest we do?"

"I wish I had the answer to that. Unfortunately, I must leave the day after tomorrow. I'm scheduled to deliver my paper on women behind asylum walls in San Francisco.

"Oh, that reminds me," he added. "Dinah, the laws are changing for women. The matron at Trenway was fired for cruelty. You must remember that it will take a long time to reverse things, but it's starting to happen. With more funding, I see real progress in the future."

After bidding David good night, Tristan circled Dinah's waist with his arm and they retired to his room. She was quiet. He knew nothing he said or promised would help her.

"I think tomorrow we should bring some of your

things into my room. Get that one cleaned up. We can always use another guest room, especially when Wolf and Julia come with their brood."

Dinah gave him a half smile. "Yes. I'll see to it."

He hauled her into his arms again and stroked her hair. "I know you can't stop worrying, sweetheart, but worrying won't help."

She sighed. "Just when I thought things were going to be wonderful, this happens."

They stood close. "Things will be wonderful, trust me. I'll be with you from now on. I have to make a quick trip into the high country tomorrow to check on some strays, but David will be here. So will Lucas. Martin Odell is walking a very thin line, Dinah. He's a thief. A crook. Possibly even a murderer. After all, your sister would have lived had he not locked her up."

She raised her head and gave him a puzzled look. "Did you know about Charlotte before you read the will?"

He frowned, trying to remember. "I'm sure it was in David's letter." He kissed her forehead. "I imagine you miss her very much. What was she like?"

Dinah shivered in his arms. "She was beautiful, Tristan. She had shiny blond hair and a perfect complexion. She was petite and dainty and had a sweet, gentle disposition." Her words were caught up in a sob. "I always wanted to be more like her. She was like Mama. She would have made a wonderful wife. And mother too." Her sobs deepened and she burrowed her face against the front of Tristan's shirt.

He held her and let her cry. God, what this woman had been through. He was surprised she had any spirit left.

After she composed herself, she asked, "What if Uncle Martin convinces the law to arrest me for Daisy's murder?"

"Let's take this one step at a time, love. First of all, I don't want you wandering off the ranch alone. Don't even go into Hatter's Horn until this is resolved. If you're tempted to accompany Alice in to buy supplies, send one of the boys, instead."

He drew away and looked into her fearful eyes. "Will you promise me that?"

She shuddered and went to the window. "I'll feel like a prisoner all over again."

"Promise me," he ordered. "Now that I've got you, I don't want to lose you."

She gave him a faint nod. It was something.

18

Cleaning her room helped take Dinah's mind off Uncle Martin. For all she knew, he could be in California right now, plotting to return her to Trenway. She refused to believe she'd gone through all that she had this past year only to find herself back where she started.

Tristan had held her long into the night. It had been comforting; he made her feel safe. She knew, however, that if Martin Odell had a plan for her, she wasn't safe anywhere.

She set the doll with the cracked face aside, determined to return it to the attic. It obviously held painful memories for Emily.

After depositing the last of her personal items in the room she now shared with Tristan, Dinah picked up Charlotte's diary and flipped through it, stopping briefly at the page that always filled her with such pain. Whoever Charlotte's Teddy was, he was responsible for her death. Inadvertently, perhaps, but responsible just the same. With a shake of her head, she closed the book and put it in a drawer. Would she ever learn the truth? It would haunt her forever if she didn't learn how Charlotte had died.

A bittersweet feeling clung to her. Everything would be fine if she didn't have to think about her uncle. Charlotte's painful, lonely death weighed heavily on her mind as well, but that thought would be etched there forever.

Dinah had a stack of old clothing and other things she wanted to discard, including Daisy's battered travel bag. As she descended the stairs, her arms full, she spied Little Hawk at the door to the kitchen.

"Little Hawk?" When he limped to the stairs she asked, "Would you mind putting all of these old clothes in Alice's rag bag?"

He took them in one arm, then gripped the broken handle of the bag. "What do you want me to do with this?"

"Throw it away, I guess. I don't need it, and it's torn. The handle is barely attached."

When he left, she glanced up the stairs. She should stop in to see Emily, but she was afraid her own agitation would spread to her. It didn't matter. She had to check on her.

She took the stairs again, then knocked on Emily's door. Emily called a muffled come in on the other side and Dinah entered.

Emily turned and gave her a triumphant smile. "It's finished." She moved away from the portrait.

Dinah brought her hands to her mouth. "It's incredible." She found Emily's gaze and smiled. "It's absolutely incredible."

"I've named it too. See?" She pointed to the lower part of the canvas.

Dinah bent and read: *Tristan/Teddy Portrait of man and boy.* She frowned, for the name Teddy clearly jumped out at her, causing a feeling of dread to hover near her stomach.

She looked at the window and chewed on her thumb, trying to calm the sick feeling in her stomach. She was being foolish, she knew. Teddy was a common nickname. She was merely jittery because of Uncle Martin. Still, she couldn't shake the odd sensation.

"Dinah? Is something wrong with the picture?"

She heard the rejected tone in Emily's voice, but her mind was busy with other words, other names. "No. It's . . . it's fine. It's wonderful." The contents of her stomach continued to pitch and toss. Emily said something else, but Dinah didn't hear.

"Dinah?"

"What?" For some reason, Emily looked crushed.

"Are you sure you like it?"

"I love it, why?"

Emily shrugged one shoulder. "I asked you where we should put it and you didn't answer. As if you didn't want to put it anywhere."

Forcing aside her feelings of discomfort, Dinah reassured Emily. "I've got something on my mind. I'm sorry, Emily. I think it should go in the great room. What do you think?"

Not convinced, Emily nodded. "That would be fine. Now . . . now I have something else to do."

"Yes, of course. So have I. I'll see you again before lunch, all right?"

Emily turned away before she nodded.

Dinah almost reassured her again. Instead, she hurried from the room. The names were a coincidence, that's all. Teddy was a common nickname. It was often short for Edward and Theodore. She'd heard Emily call him Teddy before and it hadn't struck her as unusual. Besides, Tristan wouldn't do anything to hurt a woman, and certainly not one who could be taken advantage of. She was edgy because of Uncle Martin and depressed because of Charlotte, therefore she saw the return of the goblins that had haunted her mind over the past year. Even so, she had to tell Tristan, to put her mind at rest. She went to look for him.

She found him preparing to leave for the high country with two of the older boys.

Her body reacted to the sight of him. She loved him so much. Why had the troublesome thought even entered her mind? It meant nothing. Today her mind was filled with new worries and fears. Even so, it wouldn't hurt to tell him. She wanted to be honest with him about everything from now on. "Tristan? Do you have a minute?"

The look on her face brought him quickly to her side. "What's wrong? Has something happened?"

Dinah swallowed the snag of apprehension. "This is probably a silly question, but when did you visit Trenway?"

He gave her a puzzled frown. "What?"

"When did you visit Trenway? What year?"

He stroked his chin. "Two years ago. Why?"

"That . . . that's when Charlotte was there."

He nodded, still perplexed. "If you say so."

"I know you would have told me if you'd met her there, but . . . You didn't, did you?"

He studied her, frowning. "Why would you ask me that now?"

"I . . . I'm sorry, I know it's an odd question, I just—" She shrugged. "Well, I know I'm being silly, but I'd like to clear something up. Did you meet Charlotte there?"

He turned and dug into his saddlebag, searching for something. "How the hell should I know?"

His tone took on a hostile edge, and she should have let it go but she couldn't. "But you mentioned her last night. You didn't even seem surprised that I had a sister."

"I told you I'd read about her in David's letter. It's in

my desk, Dinah. Go get it if you don't believe me." He turned and examined her, as if unable to understand this new mood. "I saw many pretty young women when I was there. I even spoke with a few. They reminded me of Emily. I felt sorry for them."

He was becoming defensive, impatient with her. And he had every right. He gripped her shoulders. "What's this about?"

With an embarrassed shrug, she shoved the diary at him, opening it to Charlotte's last entry, then watched his face. "This is just . . . I just . . ." She couldn't explain her reasons for doing this. They'd become dumber by the moment.

His gaze roamed the page, then it grilled Dinah. "You have some foolish misbegotten notion that this Teddy she refers to is *me?"* His anger was palpable.

"No, not really, I—"

"I can't believe you'd think such a thing. Do you know me so little? Haven't I proved I'm a better man than that?" He spat a curse, then tightened the cinch strap on his saddle. "I have no need to seduce mental patients, Dinah. Certainly some of them were pretty. Maybe I even saw your sister, I don't know. But for you to think that I could do that . . ."

He turned away from her, swung into the saddle and kicked Rogue into a gallop. Miguel and Henry, on mounts of their own, raced after him.

Dinah turned her fearful gaze on Lucas, who gave her a sympathetic smile, then went into the barn.

She returned to the house, unsure of how she got there, for her knees were weak and her heart heavy with remorse. Of course he couldn't have done that. She shouldn't have approached him at all.

David was sitting at the kitchen table drinking a cup of coffee. He was a fine looking man, but his beauty paled beside Tristan's.

"You look as if you just lost your best friend."

She sagged into the chair across from him. "I think I have." She opened the diary to the last entry and shoved it across the table. "Tristan thinks I've accused him of causing my sister's death. I had wanted to tell him that having the same nickname as the man Charlotte spoke of in her diary *had* caused me brief concern, but that I didn't believe for a minute that he had anything to do with it. I wanted to explain that with Uncle Charles practically breathing down my neck, I've been in a frazzled state of mind. But Tristan rode away angry before I had a chance to say any of this."

David swung the book around and thumbed through it. "I didn't know Charlotte kept a diary."

Dinah's heart leaped with anticipation. "You knew her? I mean, you didn't just know of her?"

He nodded. "She's one of my case studies. I talk about her in my paper."

Dinah put her arms on the table and leaned toward him. "Tell me what happened, David. I truly must know."

He studied her. "You may not like what you hear."

"I'll take my chances."

David looked at her for a long moment before he began. "Your sister didn't belong in Trenway any more than you did."

Dinah nodded. "I know that." Even so, she was relieved to hear someone else say it.

"Part of my paper deals with women like Charlotte. They have physical ailments that frighten their families, or—"

"My family was not afraid of Charlotte's fits."

"No, but I'm beginning to understand Martin Odell's plan. I don't believe he thought she would actually try to kill herself."

"If that's what you think, then you're wrong. Charlotte wouldn't have done that."

David sighed and stroked the end of his blond mustache. "She may not have been insane when she was committed, but trust me, Dinah, she was not completely sane when she died."

Dinah pressed her fingers over her eyes. "It was that place, wasn't it? That horrible, filthy place killed her."

"She escaped into a fantasy world. It was the only one in which she could survive. A lot of women do that." He continued to flip through the diary. "This is proof."

"The diary is proof that she wasn't sane?"

He leaned into his chair. "We're not talking about a nice, sweet sanitarium where the rich go to dry out, where one could maybe meet someone and fall in love. We're talking about Trenway. You should know that what she describes in these pages bears no resemblance to that place."

Dinah studied her hands. He was right, she knew that. "I didn't want to believe there was anything wrong with her," she murmured softly. She was almost afraid to ask her next question.

"What about her pregnancy, David? Was it real or imagined?"

Sighing, he closed the book and pinched the bridge of his nose. "I'm afraid that was real. I don't have to tell you how that might have come about."

An ache so physical it might have been a blow, made Dinah clutch her stomach. Her poor, darling, frail Charlotte. "And this Teddy that she calls her lover?"

"Edward Doppling. The matron's son. His nickname was Teddy, and I'm quite sure he wasn't her lover. Unfortunately, he was probably her rapist."

The word clawed at Dinah's ears. Of course. The matron's son. "He wasn't there when I was, but I do remember some of the talk."

"He left Trenway that spring after Charlotte died. Not necessarily because of that, but his mother thought it prudent to ship him off for someone else to worry about. He was the male equivalent of Matron Doppling, only worse because he was stronger and could do more physical harm.

"Oh, sweet Mary. If he raped poor Charlotte, her mind could have snapped from it. Was she insane, then?"

"Well, if it helps, I wouldn't consider her insane. Not really. I think she created a world unlike her surroundings in which she could be happy."

"Do you think she killed herself, David?"

He toyed with his coffee cup. "As you well know, patients aren't allowed to have anything that can be used as a weapon."

"Then she couldn't have killed herself." Dinah felt a surge of hope.

"Knowing Charlotte as I did, I don't think so. Even with her fragile hold on reality, she fought to keep fragments of her life together."

His admission softened the sharp edges of Dinah's pain. "Was nothing ever found to prove it one way or another?"

He stirred his lukewarm coffee. "No one cared, Dinah. I'm sorry if that's blunt, but to the hierarchy at Trenway, dead is dead. But I did discover something."

Again, Dinah swelled with hope. "What?"

"I believe she died trying to deliver her baby."

Dinah pinched her hands together in her lap. She closed her eyes against the image of Charlotte trying to deliver a child in Trenway's filthy conditions. "Was it a boy or a girl?"

There was a heavy pause. "I don't know."

"She aborted?"

He shook his head but didn't look at her. "Whatever she had was full term, but it was never found and there's no record of the delivery. At least none I could find."

Dinah's hands went to her mouth. "You mean there might be a child somewhere?"

"I didn't want to tell you this, because I didn't want

you to get your hopes up. I suppose it's possible she could have delivered a healthy child, Dinah, but I don't think you should dwell on it."

"Not dwell on it? How can I not?"

He put his hand over hers. "Because there's no way to trace it. If you try, you'll only be disappointed."

She jerked her hand from his. To ask her to simply ignore the possibility of Charlotte having had a living child was like asking her to ignore breathing. She wouldn't pursue it with him, but she definitely would tell Tristan. He would help her. He wouldn't give up on it.

With shaky fingers, she picked up the journal. "Thank you, David. I didn't necessarily want to hear the news, but I had to.

"I certainly hope there's a way to make Uncle Martin pay for all of this. I'd like to confront him myself and make him tell me to my face why he did what he did."

"Dinah, I know Tristan warned you to keep alert. Don't take any unnecessary chances. Martin Odell could be anywhere."

"Oh, I know. I'm not going to do anything foolish, David. I can finally put my fears to rest about Charlotte, anyway. And also let her poor memory rest in peace." Even so, Dinah felt guilty that she hadn't had a chance to say good bye.

"I'm sorry I didn't have better news."

She gave him an apologetic smile. "I'm not so fragile that I can't take the truth." For the first time, she felt some hope regarding Charlotte. Oh, she knew Charlotte was dead, but now there was a possibility that out there somewhere was her baby. With Tristan's help, Dinah would move heaven and earth to find the child.

She glanced at the bouquet of wildflowers one of the girls had picked that sat on the windowsill. She wished she could place them over Charlotte's grave, but Dinah wasn't even sure she had one.

David interrupted her thoughts. "You discovered

Emily called Tristan Teddy, is that what brought on this concern?"

She nodded as she crossed to the door. "Now I have to find her and apologize. I wasn't able to concentrate on anything she said after that."

Twenty minutes later, after searching every room in the house, the attic, the cellar, all of the outbuildings, and even the shady places Emily often liked to paint, Dinah tried valiantly to fight her fears. She couldn't find Emily anywhere. Something Emily had said to her one day came back to haunt her: Whenever she was truly upset, she would walk to Hatter's Horn.

Dinah didn't want to alarm anyone. This was her problem, and her fault. If she hadn't been so preoccupied with stupid notions of Tristan and Charlotte, she wouldn't have ignored Emily and the woman wouldn't have disappeared. Dinah didn't want to involve anyone else in the search. She would try doing it her way first. If she was lucky, she'd overtake Emily on the road.

Donning her shirt, trousers, and boots, Dinah went to the stable and hitched the horse to the rig, grateful she'd watched Miguel do it the day the children had planted corn. As she rode out of the yard, Little Hawk stepped from the barn.

"Where ya goin'?"

She waved and smiled, hoping she appeared casual. "I'll be right back."

She'd gone a half mile and hadn't found Emily. She'd called her name and had gotten no answer. Discouraged, she didn't notice the peddler's wagon approaching her until the peddler shouted a greeting.

Dinah pulled the rig to a stop beside him. "Have you come from Hatter's Horn?"

"Indeed I have, ma'am. Going in to shop? I'll bet I have what you need right here." His smile was wide; he sported a gold tooth. She remembered him from the day he'd been visiting with Lucas near the road.

"Oh, thank you. But I'm actually looking for someone. Did you meet anyone on your way from the village? A woman?"

The man frowned and scratched his grizzled jaw. "Didn't meet anyone. Sorry I can't help you, but I'd like to show you some of my wares." He reached around and pulled out a box in which there were a variety thimbles, baby whistles, pudding sticks, and playing cards.

Dinah tried to be polite, but was anxious to move on. "I'm so sorry. Why not stop at the house sometime? I really must get go—"

He came off his wagon seat like a shot and grabbed the reins. "You aren't going anywhere just yet."

From behind a bushy juniper, Emily had watched Dinah stop and talk to the peddler man. Dinah was looking for her, Emily knew that, but she couldn't let herself be found. Somehow, she'd upset Dinah. It was the picture. The picture of Tristan had made Dinah act funny. Dinah hadn't liked it. Emily had worked on it so hard, and Dinah didn't like it.

When the man took the reins, Dinah seemed afraid. Puzzled, Emily was preparing to see what was wrong when another man rode up. Dinah knew him. Emily knew who he was, too, but she couldn't remember his name. He had come to the house and had been nice to her.

They were visiting in the road. The man who had ridden up on a horse took Dinah's arm. At first, Dinah jerked it away, then the man said something to her and she dropped her arms to her sides and went with him, leaving the rig in the road.

Emily huddled beside the juniper, wondering why Dinah left the rig in the road. Then she understood. The peddler man left his wagon and drove the rig up a path and into the trees.

She was sleepy. The trip to Hatter's Horn had been

been easier when she was a little girl. She yawned and curled into a ball on the grass.

Dinah had no choice but to go with Charles. He claimed to have Emily. They rode through the brush and bramble, deeper into the woods. On the fringes of Dinah's consciousness, she heard the wail of a mourning dove. The air was pine scented and pungent. The sun spattered through the flickering leaves, creating curious, shadowy patterns on the grass.

"Taking Emily was dirty and uncalled for, Charles. She's no threat to anyone."

"All's fair, Dinah."

"Why are you doing this?" She didn't understand. Even when she'd seen him appear beside her and the peddler, she hadn't been willing to believe it.

"Money, of course." His grip was firm at her waist.

She shook her head. "All those years you struggled for money to care for your mother. What happened to your values?"

He chuckled a laugh behind her. "I discovered values have no place in my life, especially if they keep me from getting what I truly deserve from society."

"In other words, the world owes Charles Avery a living."

"Something like that. After Mother died, I discovered I was in debt clear to my chin. Your uncle offered me a way to get back on my feet."

"At my expense," Dinah answered, almost to herself. "What would your mother think of this?"

His laugh was caustic. "Don't try to bombard me with guilt, Dinah. Mother's dead. Dead, don't you understand? She's not looking down at me from some lofty heavenly cloud, watching my every movement, disappointed at how I turned out."

Dinah sighed. "Charles, Charles. When did you become such a cynic?"

"When I discovered that my entire life I'd been a first-class fool, following the rules like a good son."

"You were a nice person then."

He didn't respond.

Dinah heard the creek close by. She also recognized her surroundings. "The cabin," she murmured, her heart sinking.

Charles's chuckle was almost evil. "Ah, yes. You had quite a swim yesterday, didn't you?"

She felt a jolt of fear, remembering Tristan's silence as they'd ridden home. He'd seen something. Closing her eyes, she prayed he would remember when she and Emily didn't return home. Her heart pounded and her stomach rebelled. She observed, "I wouldn't have thought you the voyeur type, Charles."

"I'm not." He sounded indignant. "I didn't sneak down and watch you screw your husband in the water, Dinah."

She flushed, embarrassed at his tone and his words. "If you've hurt Emily in any way, Charles Avery, I'll see that you burn in hell."

He snickered. "I don't believe in heaven and hell, remember?"

She saw the cabin in the distance. Although Charles had not said it, she knew Uncle Martin was there, waiting for her. Of that she had no doubt.

Lunchtime came and went, and when neither Emily nor Dinah arrived, David began to understand Alice's concern. He had a few worries of his own. Tristan wouldn't be back until tomorrow morning, so he had bade David farewell, making him promise to return after he'd delivered his paper in San Francisco.

David tried to console Alice. "Maybe Emily and Dinah went somewhere together."

Alice uttered a shaky sigh. "They would tell me where they were going if they did. And they'd never miss lunch. Well, that tiny Dinah might, but Emily wouldn't."

"How can you be so sure?"

"Because I told her last night that I was making rice pudding for lunch. It's her favorite. In any case, she wouldn't just not show up."

A nervous knot twisted in David's stomach, but he said nothing.

"Uff dah. They're in danger. I can feel it in my bones. Besides that, Dinah is a responsible girl. She wouldn't keep Emily out so long. Emily needs her rest. And I haven't seen either one of them since early this morning."

"I saw Dinah just after Tristan left. She told me she was going up to talk to Emily then." He'd also sensed that although Dinah wouldn't take foolish chances, she was angry enough with her uncle and upset enough about Charlotte to do something she normally wouldn't.

Alice's face was a mass of worry lines. "Well, maybe they are together then. But where? And why haven't they returned?"

Just then, Little Hawk barged through the door, breathing hard. "Me'n Henry found the rig!"

"What? What're you talking about?"

He caught his breath. "This morning I saw Miss Dinah leave in the rig. She—"

"Was Emily with her?"

He shook his head. "She was alone, ma'am."

"Did she say where she was going?"

"Nope, but she said she'd be right back. Then, me'n Henry decided to follow her, but we lost her. We took a short cut back and found the rig. The horse was standin' there, eatin' grass."

Alice caught the edge of the table and gripped it hard. "What's happening around here? Lord, this is a fine time for Tristan to be off chasing calves in the high country."

The door opened and Emily entered. Her skirt was torn and streaked with grass stains.

Alice stumbled to her and took her in her arms,

praising the Lord Almighty for keeping her safe. Drawing away, she touched Emily's face.

"Uff dah, my girl, you had us scared to death." She clucked her tongue as her gaze wandered over Emily's disheveled appearance. "What have you been doing?"

Emily lowered her head and studied her shoes. "I fell asleep."

Alice craned her neck, searching the space behind her. "Is Dinah with you?"

Emily appeared surprised. "No. Dinah went with the man."

David rose slowly from his chair. "What man, Emily?"

"You know," she said to Alice. "The one who was here before. He was a nice man."

Alice gasped into the handkerchief she'd been using to clean Emily's face. "You mean that Charles Avery?"

Emily nodded. "The man who was here before."

With her arm around Emily, Alice led her to the table and made her sit. "Well, if she went with him, I guess I shouldn't worry too much, but why did she leave the rig?"

David didn't dare voice his concern. He was afraid he knew why Dinah went off with Avery, and he was certain it wasn't by choice.

19

DINAH STEPPED INTO THE CABIN, NOTING THE DANK SMELL. IT was sparsely furnished with a table, two chairs, and a crate on which stood a pail, the dipper handle hanging from the lip. There was no stove, and the ashes in the fireplace looked cold. Off to the right was a door leading to another room. Uncle Martin stood at the window. How strange it was to see him again. She felt no tugging emotion. No familial ties.

"Well, well. If it isn't my favorite uncle," she managed, her voice laced with sarcasm.

He turned, giving her a grim smile. "Even when your life is threatened, you make jokes."

"It's either that or tell you what I really think of you, you slimy pile of maggot-infested cow dung." Though her hands were tied behind her, she clenched her fists, itching to get her fingers around his neck.

"Please," he said, holding up one hand. "Don't hold

back. Tell me what you really think of me, then ask me if I care."

Dinah studied him from across the room. He'd fattened up some, like a lazy, grunting hog. Blood vessels had broken in his bulbous nose, making her wonder how much of her father's fine brandy he had swilled.

They continued to study one another.

"I can see how much you hate me, Dinah."

She gave him a dry laugh. "Hate requires too much energy, Martin. I prefer to save my strength."

He smiled, a sinister movement of his mouth. "For what?"

She ignored his question. "Where's Emily?"

He tossed Charles a questioning look. "Emily?"

Charles stepped forward. "She was out looking for Emily Fletcher. I told her we had the woman. It was the perfect ploy to get her to come without kicking up a fuss."

Dinah sagged with relief. Thank God. Emily would be safe anywhere but here.

"Untie her," Martin ordered. "Then chain her to the bed in the other room."

Charles pulled her into the other room. It was small and dark, and Dinah fought her recurring fears. Her heart began to pound and breathing became an effort, but she forced herself to stay calm. She wasn't entirely successful, because Charles noticed the change.

He pushed her onto the bed and untied her wrists. "What's the matter with you?"

Dinah didn't want to give them any ammunition to use against her. "N-nothing. I'm cold, that's all." The only light came from the other room, and that would be gone once they closed the door. She glared at Charles as he chained her wrist to the iron bedstead. "How can you work for that . . . that lickfinger, Charles?"

Charles raised his eyebrows as he tested the tension of the chain around the bedstead. "Your vocabulary has taken quite a turn for the worse."

She forced a laugh. "Having to live with the dregs of society will do that to a person. And I don't mean the patients, Charles, I mean the so-called sane help."

He finished his chore, then stood and simply looked at her.

"Well? Was there something else?" He was a silhouette in the doorway; she couldn't see his face.

"I'm sorry things didn't work out for you, Dinah."

She curled her feet under her, tucked her free hand between her knees to keep it from shaking, and returned his gaze. "Don't take pity on me yet."

Martin ambled into the room, appearing pleased. "You know, Dinah, insanity runs in your mother's family. It's only a matter of time before you succumb to it, just as your sister did."

Her anger was overcoming her fear of the room. "If anyone's insane in the family, it's you, Martin. Charlotte would have been fine if you hadn't tossed her into Trenway as if she were some worthless criminal. You are responsible for her death. I don't blame anyone else."

"I didn't want her to die, Dinah. I just wanted her out of the way. How was I to know she was such a weakling?"

She could barely stand the sight of him. "You knew."

Charles hovered nearby like a servant.

Martin glowered at him. "Get outside and keep watch." Like a servant, Charles obeyed.

"You talk so tough," Martin mused, then laughed, a snorty, wet sound that rose up from his lungs. "I used to admire that in you. It gave you spunk." He shook his head and sighed. "What a precocious child you were, Dinah-mite."

Her father's endearment on her rapacious uncle's tongue made her want to vomit. "Don't call me that. You have no right to call me that."

He leaned close enough for her to smell the liquor on his breath, and though it was dark, she imagined she could see the pores in his splotchy nose oozing brandy. She resisted the urge to spit in his face.

"Yes, you are a spirited little filly. I find it a disgusting quality in a woman." He made an impatient gesture, then crossed to the door.

"I have some papers for you to sign, Dinah. That's all I want from you. If you sign your money over to me, I'll let you go. Now, isn't that fair?"

Dinah swallowed a laugh of disbelief. Even though Martin was her blood uncle, she had no doubt that her life was in danger whether she signed the papers or not.

"You can't break Papa's will, Martin."

"Perhaps not. But I've retained a lawyer who says that with your signature, we have a good chance of tying the trust up in legal mumbo jumbo for years. By then, even if they deny my request, I'll have made good use of the money, and there won't be a cent left for those pompous asses at the university."

"What if they freeze the funds, Martin?" She could have bitten her tongue for badgering him.

Martin stood at the door, appearing agitated. The thought had obviously occurred to him as well.

"You could be hanged for murdering that nurse, you know."

She had wondered when he'd bring that up. "I didn't kill her."

"So you say. What other scenario is there? That she crawled into that black box and locked herself in? Amazing feat, considering it locked only from the outside."

Dinah refused to be baited. Pleading with him to listen to her story was a foolish waste of energy.

"So this is all about the money. It's been about the money from the start, hasn't it? Papa would feel so bad if he knew what you'd done."

"My brother was a tightfisted fool."

She closed her eyes, blocking out the image of this

despicable man. "Papa was good to you, Martin. He was generous. He gave—"

"He gave me handouts. He had all the luck; I had none. Believe me," he snarled, "it wasn't easy playing the kindly uncle all those years."

A grizzly thought made Dinah swallow a lump of fear. "It wouldn't surprise me if you were responsible for Mama and Papa's deaths, too."

He laughed, truly amused. "That's the wonderful part of this whole thing. I didn't have to kill them. I wanted to, I even worked out a plan, but"—he lifted his shoulders—"in the end, I didn't have to. Isn't that priceless?"

She remembered a time when his laugh made her giggle. Now, it made her want to gag. "Papa didn't leave you out of his will, Martin."

He cursed. "No, the skinflint left me with just enough money to pay my debts. No more."

"Then maybe you should have gone out and gotten a job."

He lunged and grabbed her ankle, squeezing so hard Dinah nearly cried out.

"You are pushing me too far, Dinah Odell."

Her ankle throbbed. "Why Papa left you as our guardian I'll never understand."

He released her and returned to the doorway. "Who else was there, Dinah?" His voice held a hint of irony. "I'll leave you to ponder your fate, dear niece. Although I don't see what there is to think about. Your money or your life. It's as simple as that."

Giving the chain around her wrist an angry yank, Dinah watched him go. It was probably simpler than that. Her money *and* her life. No choice at all.

He closed the door, enveloping her in darkness. She heard her ragged breathing and her heart, clubbing her ribs. Curling into a tight ball on the bed, she squeezed her eyes shut and pressed her free hand over her mouth.

In the back of her mind she knew she couldn't let her fear get the best of her. It would make Martin the winner, and she refused to lose to him again.

Instead, she thought of Tristan. Tristan, who had married her to keep her safe, yet didn't know she was in peril now. Even if they hadn't argued before he left, he would have gone. She would not blame him. Could not.

She had to shoulder all the blame. She'd been distracted by the words under Emily's picture. Her distraction made Emily feel rejected. Because she was responsible for that, she had to undo it. That's where she'd gone wrong. She shouldn't have tried to find Emily on her own. She'd promised both Tristan and David she wouldn't leave the ranch, and she had. She was to blame for the predicament she was in. No one else.

Now, she had to do something. She couldn't simply roll over and let Martin have his way. She had too much to live for.

She said a quick prayer for Emily's safety. At least she wasn't here, sharing her fate.

By now, someone would have missed her. But with Tristan gone, would anyone do anything about it?

It was barely dawn when Tristan and the boys rode into the yard. His last conversation with Dinah had gnawed at him all night, and he itched to get home.

David met him at the door.

Tristan smiled and grabbed his hand. "I'm glad you're still here. Sorry I had to rush off like that. I want to sit down and have a good visit. Can you swing by here on your way home?"

"Tristan," David began, his face serious, "did Lucas find you?"

"Lucas? No, why?"

David frowned and rubbed his neck. "He went to look for you. There's been . . . Something has happened."

"What? What is it?" He felt as though his heart was being squeezed.

David expelled a heavy breath. "There's no easy way to say this."

"What, damn it?"

"Dinah's gone."

Tristan's stomach plummeted. "Gone? What do you mean, gone?"

"Little Hawk saw her leave here yesterday morning in the rig. From what we've pieced together, she was probably going to look for Emily, but Emily came back alone."

Tristan swore, but his stomach continued to twist. "I leave for one day, and all hell breaks loose. She knew better than to leave the ranch. She *knew.*"

David explained what he thought had happened, starting with his conversation with Dinah earlier in the morning. "And, since Emily says she saw Dinah leave with a man she knew, we figured it had to be Avery. There was a peddler there, as well."

The peddler. How had he allowed himself to forget the peddler? Tristan rubbed his hands over his face, his stubble rough against his palms. He should have taken the time to talk with Dinah about her fears yesterday before he left. Reassure her that he understood them and understood why she was feeling the way she was.

His instinct told him she was distraught and anxious because of her uncle, therefore her judgment was questionable. He didn't believe for a moment that she thought he'd molested her sister, but he'd been insensitive to her. He should have known better.

He'd married her to keep her safe. Now, he loved her. She was part of his heart. His soul. And he couldn't keep her safe from anyone. Anything. What an arrogant bastard he was to think that he could. He should have sent Lucas into the high country. This was his fault. He should have stayed.

"So Odell has her by now."

David was quiet beside him as they entered the kitchen. "That would be my guess."

Tristan swore again. "They could be anywhere. On their way to New York, for that matter."

"I rode to Hatter's Horn yesterday and wired the train station in Sacramento, hoping they could give us some information."

Tristan poured himself a cup of coffee, noting that his hands shook. "And?"

David refilled his cup. "Nothing."

"Emily saw her go off through the woods with Avery. Not down the road. Is that right?"

"That's the way she remembered it."

Tristan studied the steam that rose from his cup. "Wouldn't that indicate to you that they weren't going to the village? I mean, they can't take her straight into Hatter's Horn. Someone might recognize her."

"Couldn't they bypass the village?"

"Possibly. But I have another idea." He rose from the table.

"Where are you going?"

"First I have to talk to Little Hawk and have him take me to where he found the rig. I have a feeling I know where they are. Then," he added, tossing David a wry grin, "we're going to do a little play acting."

He left the house, surprised when he met Little Hawk at the bottom of the porch steps.

Little Hawk was carrying a tattered travel bag that Tristan recognized as Dinah's.

"What are you doing with that?"

Little Hawk appeared agitated. "Miss Dinah didn't want it anymore. She told me to throw it away, but I kept it instead. I was looking through it, Tristan. It's got lots of pockets and secret compartments. Inside one of them, I found this." He handed Tristan a letter.

Curious, Tristan slid the paper from the envelope, opened it, and read:

> On this day, the thirteenth of February, eighteen seventy-five, I, Daisy Jenkins, exonerate Dinah

Odell from any wrongdoing regarding the circumstances of my death. I planned it, I executed it. It is my life, I am entitled to do with it as I wish. I am dying. I don't expect to live until morning. Miss Odell reluctantly did my bidding.

Daisy Jenkins

Tristan hadn't realized he was crying until a tear plopped onto the paper, slightly smearing the ink. Grinning at Little Hawk, he wiped the moisture from his eyes, grabbed the boy, and hugged him hard. "You're a hero, my man."

Little Hawk was plainly puzzled at Tristan's show of emotion. "Huh?"

"If you hadn't found this letter, Dinah might have had to go to jail." Although he'd never expressed his fears, Tristan had been afraid that Dinah's story wouldn't stand up in court by itself.

Little Hawk's dark eyes were as big as dinner plates.

"Now," Tristan continued, "take me to the place where you found the rig."

Dinah was stiff and sore and her head ached. She'd been awake most of the night, or at least what she thought was night. She'd kept her gaze on the thin band of light that shone under the door, trying to gauge time.

She'd slept in the dark only two nights since she'd come to the ranch, and both nights had been in Tristan's arms. Now, her only companions were a chain clasped to her wrist and memories of black, metal punishment boxes and dark, damp rooms that reeked of filth.

Somehow, she had overcome most of her fears. Once that happened, she discovered that the darkness was a good place to think. It was up to her to get herself out of the trouble she was in. Everyone at the ranch might worry, but with both Tristan and David gone, it would be left to Lucas to do something. Dinah wasn't sure what he knew.

Pleading with Martin wouldn't work. He hated weakness. Telling him to go to the devil wouldn't work either, because he hated her strength.

She grabbed the chain, yanking it repeatedly, hoping to make enough noise to bring Martin in. The door opened, and she curled into a tight ball, dredging up the memories she'd recently overcome. She stared straight ahead and prayed.

Martin stepped close. A lamp tossed light over the bed. Dinah forced herself not to react, although having been cloaked in darkness for many hours, she discovered the light brought tears to her eyes. She withstood the sting, allowing her eyes to water, but made no other response.

He scrutinized her, drawing the light over body. "Dinah? No theatrics, please."

She felt lifeless. Boneless. She was amazed at what her mind enabled her to do.

"Why aren't you calling for your husband, Dinah?"

She didn't react. *When he comes, he'll kick your butt twelve ways from Sunday.*

"We didn't get around to talking about that, did we?" He sat on the edge of the bed, speaking in a conversational tone. "What possessed you to marry? You know I won't tolerate that. But the idea that you might do that very thing had crossed my mind. You're a resourceful girl."

More than you'll ever know.

He continued to study her. His thumb lifted her eyelid. Her eyes fluttered, but she allowed no other reflex.

"I suppose you thought you could convince Avery to release you. Sorry, dear. I'm paying him too well."

With my money, you frog-spitting swine.

He sighed and touched her neck. She held her breath

until she could hold it no longer, then expelled it covertly. Her pulse pounded rapidly.

Cursing, he put the lamp on the floor and leaned over her. "Dinah." He took her shoulders and shook her, trying to get a response. "Dinah!"

He muttered another vile oath, then slapped her. "Snap out of it!"

She was amazed at how she was able to control her body. Why hadn't she learned this before? It would have saved her hours of misery at Trenway if she'd been able to escape into herself like this.

Charles stepped into the room. "What's wrong?"

Martin rose from the bed. "Oh, she's in some sort of trance or something. Can't get her to respond. Hell, I slapped her and she didn't even blink."

"Don't hit her!"

Martin swore again. "Go into that village and buy some smelling salts or something. I've got to bring her around long enough for her to sign that paper."

Charles didn't move. Dinah felt his gaze on her.

"Well, get out of here!" Martin ordered.

Again, Charles obeyed. *Oh, Charles. I feel sorry for you.*

After Charles was gone, Martin leaned over her once again and touched her hair. She fought to stay calm, but she wanted to shrink from his touch.

"You have hair like your mother's. I always loved your mother. In my perfect world, I would have killed your father. Then, like the dutiful brother I am, I would have stepped in and filled his shoes."

Dinah swallowed a revulsive shudder.

He patted her arm and rose to leave. "You're beginning to worry me, Dinah. Unless you snap out of it, I'll have to go to my other plan." He stopped at the door, still studying her. "I suppose transporting you to New York under these conditions wouldn't be so bad. I'd have to drug you to make sure you stayed like this, but at least you wouldn't give me any trouble," he added, laughing his disgusting laugh.

He finally closed the door, shutting her in darkness again. She took a deep breath and sagged on the bed. She couldn't let them take her back to New York. Surely there was another way.

20

MARTIN CROSSED TO THE TABLE TO RETRIEVE THE PAPERS. How in the hell would he get her to sign them if he couldn't bring her around? He didn't want to drag her east with him. Perhaps he couldn't break the will with her signature, but it was worth a try. Better than hauling her carcass back to Trenway, where she might find the means to escape again.

Of course, if she were convicted of the nurse's murder, she would be put away forever. The evidence pointed to it, and the police had no reason to believe she wasn't guilty. There was no way to explain how the nurse had gotten into the box unless Dinah had put her there.

He heard the chain rattle again. Curious, he stuffed the paper into his pocket and returned to the bedroom with the lamp. He opened the door. She was sitting up! He hurried to her side.

"Dinah?"

She rubbed her hand over her face and squinted at

him. "Uncle Martin?" She weaved on the bed, her head lolling to the side. "I'm so . . . so weak."

"Are you strong enough to sign the paper, dear?" He held his breath. Perhaps things would work out after all.

She looked at him, puzzled. "Paper?"

He paused. "You don't remember me mentioning the signature I needed?"

She looked at the chain attached to her wrist, appearing surprised to find it there. "What's this for?"

"Oh," he answered, sounding disgusted. "Well, we don't need that anymore, do we?" He stroked her hair. "You were thrashing around on the bed so severely, I was afraid you'd hurt yourself."

Still squinting and appearing weak, she peered around the room. "Where am I?"

She seemed genuinely confused. He hid a smile. "Why, we're in my cabin. We went fishing."

She tugged on the chain. "Fishing? We did? Where's Charlotte?"

Oh, this was getting better and better. "She's at the river. With . . . with your papa." He waited for a response.

"I want to fish again, Uncle Martin. Please, can't I go fishing again?"

"Of course you can, dear. After you sign the paper your Papa wants you to sign."

She lolled onto the bed again, appearing to have difficulty staying awake. "All right, Uncle Martin. I'll sign it." She swayed forward.

Martin unfolded the paper on the bed. Dinah hovered over it, then fell to the side. He dragged her upright again and put the pen in her hand. She jabbed at the paper, but dropped the pen and slumped to the pillow.

"I'm so sleepy."

Martin deliberated. He didn't know what was wrong with her. As far as he knew, she was healthy. Of course, after a year in Trenway, that could have changed. She could be faking, too, but he didn't think she was. She was a clever girl, but not that clever. Still, he'd keep an eye on her just in case.

"I'll unlock the chain and we can go out into the other room. Maybe a little walk will wake you up. You can sign the paper at the table." If he had to prop her up to do it, damn it.

He released her, prepared to wrestle her to the bed if necessary.

She frowned at her clothing. "Where did I get these trousers, Uncle Martin? Did you buy them for me? And the boots?"

He hauled her off the bed, holding her around the waist. "Yes. Do you like them?"

She gave him a vacuous smile as she leaned heavily against him. Her knees buckled, and he had to drag her to the door.

"I can run in these, Uncle Martin. And play."

"Of course, dear." He all but carried her to the table and lowered her into a chair. She leaned sideways, and he had to catch her or she'd have fallen to the floor.

"Come on now," he urged, losing patience. He put the paper in front of her and stuck a pen in her hand. It dropped onto the table.

Biting back his impatience, he pressed the pen into her hand again, this time holding it.

"I can do it, Uncle Martin. Really, I can." She shook her head, as if trying to stay awake. "Could I have a glass of water, please?"

He stood behind her. "Of course, dear." When he was certain she was signing her name, he crossed to the crate and filled a cup with water from the pail.

On his return to the table, she slumped to the side again. He grabbed the paper and shoved it into his pocket and put the cup in front of her. With lightening speed, she rose from the chair and drove her fist into his fleshy abdomen.

"I can run in these, Uncle Martin," she repeated. The words sounded completely different from how they had before.

Martin gasped and doubled over, unable to catch his breath.

She was gone when he finally staggered to the door. He spied McCafferty and his peddler's cart on the path near the creek.

"Stop her!" He waved his arms frantically and continued shouting until McCafferty motioned that he understood.

Dinah ran through the brush like a deer. McCafferty tackled her. She kicked and screamed, then suddenly was quiet.

Wiping the sweat from his face, Martin hurried toward them, wincing at the pain in his gut. "Damned hooligan doubled her fist and rammed it into my stomach," he groused as he neared them.

McCafferty rose. "I've experienced her punch a few times myself. Hurts like hell, doesn't it?"

Martin froze. "Who in the devil are you?"

Dinah stood and wrapped her arms around the man. "He's my husband, Uncle Martin."

Uncle Martin took a frantic look around, as if searching for a means of escape.

"I don't think I'd try it, Odell. There's no place for you to go, really."

"Where's McCafferty?" He had the appearance of an indignant crook, backed into a corner. Which he was.

"He and Avery are already in jail."

"But . . . but . . . but," he sputtered, "she signed her money over to me. Now it's mine! It's mine!"

Dinah gave him a merry smile. "I don't think so. Did you check my signature?"

Martin fished out the paper and studied the name at the bottom of the page. His face became red and his eyes nearly bulged from his head. "What is this? Who in the hell is the lady with the sausage nose?"

Tristan threw his head back and laughed. His glee was infectious. Dinah joined him.

"She's a murderer," Martin roared. "She killed that nurse in New York. She did!"

For a moment, Dinah's stomach pitched downward.

"'Fraid not, old man." Tristan pulled a letter from his pocket. "This was found in Daisy Jenkins's travel bag. It exonerates Dinah from any wrongdoing."

Dinah gasped, grabbed the letter and read it. Oh, Daisy, she thought, relief rushing through her. "She didn't tell me about this."

"I think she probably meant to, but from what you've said about her, she was probably too sick to remember everything. Fortunately, Little Hawk decided to keep the travel bag instead of throwing it away as you'd asked him to. He found the letter while he was examining the bag."

The sheriff and his men appeared on the path and took Martin into custody.

Dinah watched them cart her uncle away with a relieved sense of finality. "So, it's really over? I won't have to explain myself?"

"I think everything is settled, my love." Tristan tucked her close and rested his chin on top of her head.

"Then we can go home?"

"Immediately."

She inhaled sharply. "Emily—"

"Emily's fine. She saw your abduction, but didn't understand it. She thought you'd left with Avery willingly."

"I did. He and the peddler had heard me calling Emily's name. Charles convinced me he had her, so I had no choice but to go with him."

They stood together, enjoying their victory.

"Has David left?"

"He's put off his trip until tomorrow. He helped me with this charade by approaching the peddler and keeping him occupied while I went around behind and smacked him on the head. He also went for the sheriff."

Dinah felt a great sense of peace although there was much on her mind. "I've been thinking."

"Oh, oh. Not again," Tristan teased.

She gave him a love pinch and he winced. "I'd like to offer David an endowment for his work. I want to help all of those women who weren't as lucky as I. We don't need all my money, do we?"

Tristan's eyes were warm and filled with admiration as he gazed at her. "I'm sure David would be honored, love."

"And Tristan? There's something else. There's a chance that Charlotte's baby is alive."

He turned her toward him, his gaze intense. "You're sure?"

She nodded. "David said as much, but he told me not to get my hopes up. But darling, I have to at least try to find the child." She gave him a beseeching gaze.

Tristan's fingers brushed hair from her temple. "Of course you do. We'll do everything we can."

She hugged him, grateful for his love and understanding. "I knew you'd agree."

"I'd be hard pressed to deny you anything, my sweet."

She sniffed at his clothes, wrinkling her nose. "You smell a little ripe, sweetheart."

"I don't think McCafferty believed in bathing."

Dinah kept one arm around her husband as they walked to the road. "You know what I'd like?"

He growled in her ear. "I think so."

She gave him a playful swat. "Besides that."

"What?"

She'd conquered one of her fears, it was time to conquer another. "I want a bath. In the tub."

"That's my girl. Care for company?"

She felt warm and coddled and loved. "Is there room?"

"Someone has to wash those very special places you can't reach."

She laughed, sensing the stirrings of desire. "I can reach every place except the middle of my back."

"Ummm." He nuzzled her ear. "But not as well as I can. Now, let's go home."

Home. Yes, it was a home. One soon to be filled with more love and laughter than any of them had thought was possible. She would see to it. If it took her the rest of her life, she would make certain that everyone knew they were loved. Especially her husband and all of their current children, to say nothing of the ones she planned to give him. And they would name their first daughter Daisy.

Epilogue

Fletcher Ranch, 1885

"PAPA!"

Grinning, Tristan squatted and stretched his arms toward his three-year-old daughter. She flung herself at him and he raised her high in the air. "How's my Daisy-girl this morning?"

She giggled, her dark russet curls flopping in the wind. "Good, Papa. Mama and Sarafina taked Daisy with them to the dress place. Ficker Fedder came, too."

"Ficker Fedder did, did she?" He planted a wet kiss on her neck. "That's nice. Is Sarafina's wedding dress pretty?"

"Oh, it's bee-oo-tiful," she exclaimed, clasping her chubby hands together in an ultrafeminine way that charmed him.

Tristan was in awe of his daughter. He loved all of his children and tried not to be partial. The eight older ones would always have a special place in his heart.

Beau was born a year after the day Tristan had

discovered Dinah in his tree. He was the bookworm. He was the one who also looked the most like his father. Each time Tristan studied the portrait Emily had painted of him as a man and as a boy, he marveled at how much of himself had turned up in Beau.

The twins, Adam and Gabriel, arrived three years later. They thrived on adventure. Tristan had almost given up having a daughter of his own. He'd decided the only chance he'd have at spoiling a baby girl would be when one of the older children had children of their own. He wasn't ready to be a grandpa, but if it happened, he knew he'd be as obnoxious as any grandfather on earth.

Dinah approached, and they exchanged smiles. Nearly ten years, and his love for her had not diminished but had grown. His brother had been right about him all those years ago.

She had been exonerated by the police regarding the incident with Daisy. The one thing that marred their happiness was that they hadn't discovered anything about Charlotte's baby. If it was alive, it would be older than his own children. Tristan was no longer sure there had ever been a child at all, but he continued the search. He desperately wanted to extinguish the final hint of sadness in his wife's beautiful eyes.

She stood on her tiptoes and kissed his jaw. Hugging his daughter to his chest with one arm, he drew his wife close with the other and nuzzled her vibrant hair. "I have trouble believing you're mine, Dinah-mite. You're the most beautiful creature on earth."

"I've always thought you were, my darling," she responded.

He bent and kissed her; she had the sweetest mouth in the world. He often thought of the softness of her, those special places he'd come to adore. He loved every inch of her, but was constantly delighted and amazed at the tender insides of her upper arms and the tiny blue veins that threaded across her breasts. He especially revered the slight, silvery lines on her abdomen that were evidences of her deliveries. Of the blessed children she'd given him.

She broke the kiss and tugged on Daisy's dress. "Don't you fall asleep up there, sweetheart. The girls have your lunch ready, I'm sure."

Daisy jammed her thumb into her mouth and played languidly with Tristan's hair.

Dinah lifted something from her purse. "I stopped at the telegraph office before I came home. Two wires, dear. David is returning to San Francisco to do a seminar on mental health."

"He couldn't continue his work without your support, Dinah."

"You know it's the least I can do. I wish I could do more."

She continued to fund David Richards. Tristan knew it gave her pleasure.

"Oh, and this came, too." She handed Tristan a wire. There was a twinkle in her eyes.

He read it, unable to stop his smile. "Little Hawk's on his way home." His grin widened. Henry and Flicker Feather had arrived from school the week before. Tristan hadn't been sure Little Hawk would be able to get away.

"He doesn't want us to call him that anymore, darling."

"I know, I know. Hawk. Just plain Hawk."

Tristan had offered all of the children the chance to attend the same college he had, in the east. Henry and Flicker Feather had been enthusiastic. Rose and Sarafina took teacher's training in San Francisco. They both taught at the reservation school. Dawn had stayed on the ranch. She'd been doing many of Alice's chores for years.

Swift Elk and Jose lived nearby and helped Miguel work the stock. Then there was Little Hawk.

Tristan's smile turned grim. He'd had to blackmail the boy to go east with the others and attend college. "But I want to work with the horses, Pa. Why do I need college?"

Tristan had left it up to each of them to decide what to call him and Dinah. He'd felt intense pleasure and accomplishment when they finally chose to call them mother and father.

Tristan had told Little Hawk that when he finished his schooling, after he learned how to handle money and property and the law, he could return home and work with the horses. Tristan wanted at least one of his children to be capable of taking over every aspect of the ranch when he no longer wanted to work it himself.

Little Hawk would be a spectacular lawyer. Whether he decided to work as one was his choice. Tristan simply wanted the boy to have the knowledge because he was bright. Exceptionally so.

Henry and Flicker Feather loved it in the east; Little Hawk couldn't wait to get home to the mountains. Tristan had heard from the Harvard staff on numerous occasions, for Little Hawk had more of a penchant for mischief than for learning. Even so, his marks were remarkably high. But he was always pushing the boundaries. Testing the system.

"I wonder how his foot is," Dinah speculated.

Tristan chuckled beside her. "Will you ever stop worrying about his health?"

"I'm his mother. It's my job." Her chin was set at a stubborn angle.

"It's been five years, sweetheart. It's as healed as it's going to get."

"I know," she answered on a sigh, "I don't want him to limp, that's all."

Tristan squeezed his wife's dainty shoulders as they walked toward the house. "He'll always have a limp. At least it's not as pronounced as it was, and he can wear shoes."

They had been terrified to subject the boy to a surgery that might not work. When Little Hawk turned sixteen, they had sat him down and explained the procedure to him, allowing him to help make the decision. It had been a bigger success than even the surgeon had expected.

"From the look of things, everyone will make it home to celebrate Alice's seventieth birthday," Dinah observed, smiling with pleasure.

"I can't believe she doesn't know what's going on."

Dinah smoothed Daisy's curls as the baby cuddled with her father. "She's far too busy to be concerned about her age, much less her own birthday."

Dawn and Rose appeared on the porch, announcing Daisy's lunch.

"Mother?"

"Yes, Dawn?"

"We're going to bake bread this afternoon. Want to help?"

Tristan laughed. Since the day he'd told everyone at the dinner table about Dinah's confrontation with bread dough, and his poor rooster's attachment to it, no one had let her forget.

"I'll learn to bake bread one of these days, then you'll be sorry you've made such fun of me." She shook a playful finger at Dawn.

Daisy kissed her father soundly on the cheek, then squirmed from his arms and ran to the door. The girls hustled her inside.

Tristan brought his wife close to his chest and nuzzled her hair. "Are you sorry we didn't adopt any more children?"

"That decision was up to you, darling."

He sighed. "I think a dozen is enough, don't you?"

"Whatever you say."

Tristan raised a skeptical eyebrow. His wife was not usually so amenable.

"By the way, where are the boys?"

"The twins are with Miguel. He's teaching them how to rope. I think Beau is in the library, reading."

"Naturally," Tristan responded with a wry smile.

Between Little Hawk and Beau, Tristan knew his ranch and all of his holdings would be in good hands. He would need both of them in the future.

He tilted Dinah's face to his and kissed her again. She returned his kisses. She was still the sweetest tasting women on earth.

She pulled away. "And Emily?"

"She's in her studio working on that special project for Alice. Did I hear her tell you she has another show in San Francisco next summer?"

Dinah nodded. "But I think it will be her last. For a while, anyway. She tires so easily these days, and her work is in such demand. Oh, darling," she added, gazing at him, "did she tell you that President Cleveland had seen one of her paintings in the senator's home and has commissioned her to do one for him?"

"That's great. Terrific. I still recall the time you discovered she was painting in the attic," he answered, the painful memory softening. "She's come a long way, and all because of you."

"Without your love and understanding, none of it would have happened, Tristan."

He smiled privately. Over the years, he and Dinah had had their disagreements, but all in all, they had mutual admiration as well as love.

They strolled to the steps. Lucas exited the barn and waved, the ranch's two new pups romping at his heels. Amy and Wolf had passed on, and Tristan had taken it hard. He had discovered that the breed was not known for its longevity, and he knew he couldn't go through it again. Not with the same kind of hound. Their decline had come so swiftly. One day they had been lively, the next they were near death.

The new youngsters were mutts. Tough as nails. Tireless. Excellent horse and cattle dogs. There was a twinge in Tristan's chest each time he thought about his precious wolfhounds, buried behind the stable.

"Darling?"

Tristan noticed the hesitation in her voice. "What is it?"

"Would you be very disappointed if . . . if we had a baker's dozen?"

Elation surged through him and he effortlessly lifted her into the air. She braced herself on his shoulders and studied him, her face serious.

"Are you sure?"

At her cautious nod, he lowered her to eye level and kissed her again. "Hell," he murmured, rubbing his nose to hers, "maybe we'll get lucky and have two more."

He held her in his arms and entered their home, thinking about his own father. A man who had saved him from abandonment. A man who had taught him to love and care for others. Tristan hoped the spirit of Cecil Fletcher was close by and that he was resting peacefully in the knowledge that his troubled son was happy at last.

Dear Readers:

If you read the two excerpts at the front of the book, you might get the impression that I'm writing a story on male bashing. I'm not. The book that prompted me to write *Winter Heart,* and whose quotes I used, is *Women of the Asylum, Voices from Behind the Walls, 1840–1945,* by Jeffrey L. Geller and Maxine Harris, Anchor Books, Doubleday. We are aware that in the previous centuries and early into this one, men dominated the field of medicine, including mental health. What shocked me was how women were treated by families who simply wanted to get rid of them, and by doctors who could be bribed into incarcerating them.

I was touched by the strength of these women who bravely related their tales of horror. Certainly they didn't come out totally unscathed, but many of them did get out, and a few wrote their stories in journals and letters, perhaps hoping that one day someone might understand the helplessness of their gender at that time in history.

Had I used more of the material, *Winter Heart* would not have been a romance. Had I used less, I would have devalued the despicable conditions that existed well into this century. I hope I've struck a balance, and that you enjoy the story.

Jane Bonander

The following is a preview of
Warrior Heart. . . .

Riverside boarding house,
Thief River, California—1891

"Hold still, dear. I can't get a straight hem when you wiggle."

Dawn's movements quieted, and she expelled an exasperated sigh. "I'm sorry, Mama. It's just that I promised Mahalia I'd go into the woods near the river and pick her some berries for dessert tonight."

Libby took the last pin from her mouth and fastened it to the yellow, flower-sprigged calico. She caught her daughter's glance and smiled, noting how well the bright color suited her dusky complexion.

"Walk to the door so I can see if the hem is even."

Dawn pirouetted away, her thick, dark braid swinging.

Libby scrutinized her work, satisfied. "It's nice

of you to want to help, dear, but you don't have to take orders from Mahalia."

Dawn giggled and studied her reflection in the mirror. "Why not, Mama? You do."

Libby caught her daughter's eye and winked. "I do, don't I?"

"It's almost like she's the boss and you're working for *her* instead of the other way around." Laughter lingered in Dawn's voice as she twirled.

"She does have that effect on people, doesn't she?" Libby put the pincushion in the sewing basket and set the basket beside the rocking chair. She had mending to do tonight.

"I like her, though," Dawn mused as she swayed to some internal music. "She'll make anything I want, and bakes the most delicious apple pie in the whole world."

"That she does." Libby's hands automatically went to her own hips, which had rounded significantly since she'd hired Mahalia as her cook and assistant three years before. She couldn't call Mahalia a whirlwind, for her larger-than-life appearance and presence likened her more to a tornado.

"Have you finished your lessons?"

Dawn stopped dancing and wrinkled her nose. "I have sums to do."

Libby swallowed a sigh. Sums were Dawn's nemesis; this wasn't the first time she'd finished all of her other lessons, leaving the sums, hoping they'd somehow miraculously do themselves.

"You can take off the dress, dear."

Dawn stepped out of her new dress, and Libby noticed that the knee of one of her cotton stockings was torn. Dawn attempted to move away, but Libby caught her arm.

"What happened to your knee?"

"It's nothing, Mama. Really."

Again she attempted to leave, but Libby drew her close and examined the rip, noting that blood had soaked through the fabric. Gently pushing the cloth aside, she saw the ugly scrape on her daughter's knee.

"How did this happen?"

Dawn wouldn't look at her. "It was nothing, Mama. I . . . I tripped, that's all."

An angry ache settled in Libby's chest. "You were pushed, weren't you?"

Dawn finally pulled away and picked up her school dress. "I told you, I tripped."

Libby clenched her fist and pressed it against her mouth. This was the third time in a week that Dawn had "tripped" on her way home from school, ripping her stockings. But the stockings be damned. Libby refused to believe her daughter was that awkward and clumsy.

"It's those other children, isn't it? They're teasing you again, aren't they?"

Dawn stood before her in her muslin chemilette. The lace edging the hem of one leg was torn. "It happens all the time, Mama."

How could she be so calm? Libby raised up, a sense of maternal possession causing her blood to boil in her veins. "I'll get to the bottom of this—"

"Mama, please," Dawn pleaded. "If you interfere, you'll only make things worse." She hugged Libby's waist. "It's not so bad, really. I can usually outrun them. I don't mind so much."

Libby returned the embrace, pressing her nose against Dawn's shiny black hair. "But *I* mind."

Dawn patted her shoulders, as if Libby were the one who needed the encouragement. "I can take care of myself, Mama."

Leaning away from her daughter, Libby swallowed the lump in her throat and gave Dawn's braid a playful tug. "What will I do when you no longer need me?"

"That won't be for a long, long time," Dawn assured her.

Libby forced a smile. "I guess you need me to tell you to get out of those stockings and have Mahalia bathe your knee." She lifted an old brown cotton dress off the table. "Put this on before you go cavorting in the woods, please."

Dawn shrugged into the dress while Libby folded the new one and hung it over the sewing chair.

"Perhaps you should do your sums before you go off picking berries. I know you. Once you're in the woods, you'll have no concept of time, and I'll have to come looking for you."

"But if I do my sums first, it'll be dark before I can get to the berry patch."

"Sums come before berry picking, Dawn."

Dawn's beseeching look was a well-practiced one. Although it confirmed her youth, there were times when Libby swore her daughter was twelve, going on eighteen. The realization filled her with bittersweet emotions.

"But, Mama, I—"

Laughter erupted on the porch below, and they both turned toward the open window.

Dawn skipped across the room, ignoring the cat

that slept on the cushioned window seat, and peered outside. "Oh, look! How darling!" She sped past her mother, scrambling to button the last few buttons of her dress before she disappeared out the door. Her footsteps clamored on the stairs.

Libby frowned and stepped to the window just as a horse's rump disappeared beneath the porch roof.

Raising its battered head, the cat on the window seat made a raspy sound and glared at Libby with its one good eye.

Libby stroked its scarred ears, lingering on its neck. "I'm sorry, Cyclops. I didn't mean to disturb your nap."

The roof hid the Bellamy brothers from view, but Libby heard them chortling. She wondered how many decades Burl and Bert had been living at the boarding house; they'd been here when she arrived twelve years before.

Now, as every day, they rocked on the porch, snorting with laughter at something or someone Libby couldn't see. They spent most days that way, making running commentary on every passing stranger.

"What the hell do ya call *that?"* Burl Bellamy's cackle turned into a fit of coughing.

"It's a dog."

The voice—rich and deep, tinged with a hint of justification—reminded Libby of bronze and polished mahogany.

"A *dog?* That ain't no dog," Burl argued. "Hell, a real dog'd eat that'n fer lunch and cough up a hair ball bigger'n a stallion's balls."

Bert Bellamy howled at his brother's wit.

Her interest piqued, Libby hurried down the stairs and went to the front door, pulling aside the short curtain that covered the window. She peeked outside, squinting at the stranger.

"Oh, my." The words came out on a rush of breath, and she put her hand to her chest, feeling an odd fluttering there.

He stood by his mount, big and luxuriously muscled with a chest as wide as a door and arms as big around as porch pillars. His face was deeply tanned and as leathery as the saddle cinched around his horse's belly. Deep brackets were etched on either side of his mouth, and his jaw was square and hard. Unrelenting, Libby decided.

"Oh, what kind is it?" Dawn stood on tiptoe by the stranger's horse and peered at his saddlebag.

Libby's gaze was riveted at the man's face, which had softened slightly when he smiled at her daughter. He removed his hat, revealing sun-bleached streaks in hair that was as brown as strong coffee.

"It's called coyote bait, little gal," Burl suggested, obviously still having a good time at the stranger's expense.

"He's a Shih Tzu." The stranger's smile vanished, and his voice was gruff and defensive.

Burl guffawed again. "Hear that, Bert? It's a shit-soo!"

"A shit-sioux? What's that?" Bert asked, clearly amused with himself. "Some kinda Injun dog?"

"Can't be, Bert. Ain't enough of him there to feed a whole tribe."

The brothers chortled again, always tickled with each other's humor.

Dawn turned and glared at the old men. "Shame

on both of you. You know how I feel when you make fun of the Indians."

"I'm sorry, little gal," Burl said, still laughing, "but ya gotta admit it ain't much of a dog."

Dawn turned toward the saddlebag again. "I think he's adorable, especially with that leather thong holding his hair on the top of his head. Is that to keep it out of his eyes?"

The stranger continued to study Dawn, a look on his face that Libby couldn't identify. She sensed he hadn't had much experience with girls Dawn's age. "That's right, young lady."

Dawn gazed up at him. "Can I hold your dog? Maybe play with him?"

He lifted the dog from the saddlebag and handed it to her. "I think Mumser could use some exercise."

"Oooh, Mumser. What a cute name," Dawn said with a giggle as the pup licked her face. "You're much more fun than our cranky old cat."

Libby watched Dawn carry the wiggly pup to the grass, where she ran her fingers over its long, silky coat before it scampered away from her, obviously anxious to play. Her gaze lingered on her daughter as the child romped with the pup. Libby was grateful for Dawn's resilience. Somehow she had to keep her innocent and sweet, but with the world the way it was, she knew that wasn't possible. Prejudice against half-bloods was rampant, even in bucolic Thief River, California.

Dawn's laughter tinkled through the air. With such a playmate, she would certainly forget her sums, and perhaps even her promise to pick berries.

"Is this the boarding house?"

Libby was drawn back by the rich timbre of his voice.

"Shore is. Riverside. Built in eighteen-seventy on the banks of Thief River by the late Sean O'Malley," Burl recited. "May God Almighty bless his Irish soul." He spat a stream of tobacco over the side of the porch, hitting one of Libby's prize chrysanthemums.

With an angry gasp, she flung open the door. "Burl Bellamy! How many times have I told you not to spit your disgusting tobacco onto my flowers?"

He turned and grinned, exposing his toothless mouth. "Well, afternoon, Miss Liberty, how long you been standin' there?"

"Long enough to see you do it." She put her fists on her hips and glared at him. "If you can't use the spittoon, then quit chawing tobacco."

Lifting her skirt with one hand, she grabbed with the other the sprinkling can she kept on the porch and hurried down the steps to the grass. With her fingertips, she gingerly held the stem of her beautiful pink mum, then doused it with water.

"There, there," she soothed, almost feeling the mum's anxiety.

"Who knows, Miz Liberty, mebbe tobaccy juice is just what them posies need," Bert offered.

Libby rolled her eyes and swung around. "That stuff is poison. To my flowers *and* to you." The last three words lost their punch as she met the stranger's gaze. She swallowed hard, having momentarily forgotten he was there in the flurry over her flowers.

His hat was still in his hand. His eyes were such a brilliant blue, they appeared painted.

"He's wantin' a room, Miz Liberty."

"She don't rent to folks with dogs," Burl announced.

"Heck, Burl, that ain't no *real* dog."

Libby continued to stare at the stranger, her mouth working yet nothing coming out. For anyone to render her speechless was quite an accomplishment, she thought, bemused.

"Mumser!"

Hearing her daughter's cry of alarm, Libby pulled her gaze to the other side of the path that led to the house, where more of her chrysanthemums grew.

"Oh, no!" The damned dog was digging in her precious flower bed!

Flinging away the sprinkling can, she flew at the dog, making threatening motions with her hands. "Get away! Shoo! Shoo!"

With its rump in the air and its tail wagging, the pup clearly thought Libby wanted to play. She disregarded the mutt and fell to her knees next to the flowers. Ignoring the playful growling and the tugging at her skirt, she returned the dirt the little beast had dug up around the stems, pressing it over the roots.

"I'm sorry, Mama. He just sort of got away from me." Dawn was contrite as she bent to help her mother put the flowers to right.

"I don't think he did any real damage." Libby held a tight rein on her temper, which could be volatile. Although she never displayed it in front of her daughter, it often made her feel as if she were going to explode. Like now. It was unreasonable to get emotional over flowers, but she'd worked so hard on them and they were truly the most beautiful mums in Northern California. Everyone told her so. Why, perfect strangers would stop and compliment her on their beauty.

She took a deep breath and continued to pack the dirt when she heard the keening rip of fabric, followed by Dawn's gasp and cry.

"Cyclops! Mumser! No!"

Libby turned in time to see her battered, one-eyed cat giving chase to what appeared to be, for all intents and purposes, a small shaggy mop racing over the grass. A length of her own lacy petticoat fluttered along behind.

Jackson cringed as he surveyed the chaos and covertly studied the girl. When he'd ridden up, his emotions had been exposed like raw nerves, but he'd quickly shoved them into the corners of his mind, where they belonged. His first glimpse of the girl had nearly done him in. It was hard for him to keep from staring at her. She was a beauty. More than that, she appeared sweet-tempered and compassionate. He felt a rush of pride, followed by a surge of guilt that washed every other feeling away.

Mumser raced past, the cat not far behind. Mumser was trained to know the "come" and "heel" commands, but at this point, under these circumstances, Jackson wasn't sure it made any difference. Still, he had to try. He whistled a command, then called his dog. Mumser ignored him, as Jackson knew he would.

With his hat in his hand, he crossed to where the

woman continued to fuss with the dirt around her posies.

When she'd first stepped onto the porch, he'd noticed her fire. White women were always full of fire. Always had their backs up about one thing or another. They never left a man in peace. But if Jackson thought she showed her temper when the old coot spat tobacco on her flowers, wait until she discovered why he was there. *Then* he'd see a damned inferno, he had no doubt about that.

He hadn't been drawn to a white woman in over ten years, for all the reasons that had just run through his head. Give him a geisha any day. Or, he thought, remembering painful years passed yet not forgotten, an Indian maiden. There was something soothing about women who knew how to please a man, and white women hadn't quite gotten the hang of it.

And he was tired. Damned tired of getting paid to fight someone else's battles in dirty corners of the world. He was ready to retire and settle down. More than ready.

"You should really have a fence of some kind around those flowers, ma'am."

The woman stood, her hands on her hips, and gave him an icy stare, although her eyes were the color of hot coals not yet turned to cinder. "Until today, I didn't have need for one."

He cleared his throat. "The name's Wolfe, ma'am. Jackson Wolfe." He bit back another groan as the animals raced past.

"Cyclops!" The young girl continued to chase them, her braid, as thick as his fist, swinging from side to side.

"After all this," Jackson began somewhat hesitantly, "I . . . er . . . don't suppose you have a spare room, do you?"

Her mouth opened, then snapped shut. "After all this," she countered, throwing her arms wide with a flourish, "you actually think I'll rent you and . . . and your *dog* a room?"

As soon as folks in this town learned he'd just signed on as acting sheriff until Sheriff Thomas was back on his feet, he'd have his pick of rooms. But this was where he wanted to stay. No other place would do. He'd camp outside if he had to.

"I'd rather hoped you would, ma'am."

She turned away, but not before he saw her jaw clench. "As Burl said, I don't rent to people with pets."

"I noticed you have a shed out back. That'll do."

She swung to face him, her expression incredulous. "You want to sleep in my shed?"

Nodding, he added, "I'll pay you five dollars a week."

Her jaw dropped. "You'll pay me five dollars a week to sleep in my *shed?* My regular rooms aren't even that much."

The young girl nearly skidded to a stop beside them. "Mama, we have two empty rooms, and you said we needed—"

"Never mind what I said, Dawn. Has Mahalia looked after your skinned knee yet? And what about your sums?" Her voice was stern but not scolding.

"But, Mama, you said we needed the money for—"

"Ma'am," Jackson interrupted. "I'll be gone

most days, all day. I'll take Mumser with me. Why, you won't even know we're here."

"Yes, Mama, we won't even know they're here."

The girl's eyes held a familiar twinkle in their depths, and the excitement he saw there weakened him. His gut clenched like a fist.

With her arms crossed over her chest, the woman continued to study him. During the fracas, wispy threads of hair had come loose from her neat hairdo, and now blew gently over her forehead and cheeks. There was a lushness about her that reminded him of sultry Spanish nights. Warm wine. Willing women. His thoughts surprised him, for this one, with her snapping dark eyes, was anything but willing. Though her face was expressionless, those eyes told him that anyone who would spend five dollars a week to sleep in a shed had ulterior motives.

If that's what she thought, she'd be right. He'd come for his daughter, Dawn Twilight, and he wasn't leaving without her.